RESURRECTION
Impure

J. R. BAILEY

iUniverse, Inc.
Bloomington

Impure
Resurrection

iUniverse books may be ordered through booksellers or by contacting:

iUniverse
1663 Liberty Drive
Bloomington, IN 47403
www.iuniverse.com
1-800-Authors (1-800-288-4677)

*Because of the dynamic nature of the Internet, any web addresses or links contained in
this book may have changed since publication and may no longer be valid. The views
expressed in this work are solely those of the author and do not necessarily reflect the
views of the publisher, and the publisher hereby disclaims any responsibility for them.*

*Any people depicted in stock imagery provided by Thinkstock are models,
and such images are being used for illustrative purposes only.*

Certain stock imagery © Thinkstock.

ISBN: 978-1-4620-2032-4 (sc)
ISBN: 978-1-4620-2033-1 (hc)
ISBN: 978-1-4620-2034-8 (e)

Library of Congress Control Number: 2011908883

Printed in the United States of America

iUniverse rev. date: 07/07/2011

For those I've lost along the way

Chapter One

Some say the eyes are a window to the soul.
Then I guess one might think of the eyelids as shutters.
I would rather liken them to inward facing mirrors; when we close our eyes, we
don't find ourselves lost in the darkness.
We stare back into our own soul and, when we dream, we can't look away.
What do you see when you close your eyes?

1

BLOODCURDLING CRIES. THE DEATH wails of something that didn't seem human crept across the darkened fields like an icy, groping hand. It could reach into your heart and squeeze it tight, choking the life out of you like your blackest fears. Worse still was the rattling. Chains. There could be no doubt; such a sound has a certain quality, a texture that can be felt down to the bones. Sometimes the sound was frenzied, like a terrified animal trying to tear its mutilated leg out of a trap. But other times, when the screams would grow silent, it was as if the chains were being dragged against each other; heavy, black links ground together by a terrible strength.

The source of this chilling cacophony stood alone in a wide and shallow gulley. It was an old, ruined prison tower built from dark blocks of stone. Though there was a pair of heavy wooden doors at its base that had once sealed the

1

structure from the outside, the tower's east wall had crumbled years ago, revealing its guts to the open air. A clearly exposed stairway led to an iron door, laden with rust and age. But what was beyond that door, the top floor of the tower, was hidden from sight. This room had been built with more care, with the diligence of a craftsman who wanted whatever was inside to never find its way out.

Living things had always shied away from this ground. Birds wouldn't land here. The structure wasn't choked by vines or the roots of nearby flora, nor was it touched by moss or fungi. Not even grass would grow. Only gray, decrepit trees, the sap of life having long since fled, were in attendance. They stood motionless, their cracked and withered branches drooping near the ground, like mourners weeping at a never ending funeral. It had always seemed such a dead place—until that night.

It wasn't until daybreak, as the gentle sunlight poured over the horizon, that a lone figure approached the tower. The sounds of the night had been unsettling, and though he may have been too wary to approach before dawn, what terrifies us in the dead of night becomes more pale when touched by the sun.

A gray cloak was draped across his broad shoulders, stitched with an image of the sun, licks of flame spiraling out in every direction. His dark hair hadn't a single fleck of white, but his strong features had been weathered with age. The heyday of his youth had passed, but his limbs still retained their strength, and his eyes shined with awareness.

The man shook his head in disgust, both with himself and with the heavy doors, one hanging by a single joint. The wood had decomposed very little, but everything that had once been metal had turned to rust. The hinges had broken, and with a stout shove it became clear the lock had as well.

The entryway was strewn with dust and rubble from the collapsed wall, and the stairs weren't as sound as they had appeared from the outside. The rough footing made progress slow, and the lighting was dim. Not dark—sunlight could stream in from the gaping wall—but diffusely lit enough to remind the trespasser of what he'd felt hearing those sounds in the dead of night. But there was more to it than that; the closer he came to the top of the tower, the more a sense of deep dread crept into his bones. It was this sensation that kept all other living things away. Animals are born with sense enough to pay heed to such intuitive dread, but the man only shuddered and continued his ascent.

The upper door was more imposing than it had seemed from a distance. Though it had suffered the advances of rust as well, by virtue of its sheer mass it had been little damaged. Even the lock was in operable condition. The man carried with him a skeleton key; he'd been told it could open any lock on the sanctuary grounds.

With a sharp twist of the key and a harsh snap, the door popped open a hair, never to close again. It was a portal of uncommon size, the likes of which the trespasser had never seen before. It took all his strength to nudge the bulwark open just wide enough for him to slip through, stumbling into the interior with a groan of exertion. Inside, his heart leapt into his throat, and he wished he'd entered with more caution.

The chamber was nearly as black as pitch. Shadows flitted across the walls, cast by the light that passed through where the door stood ajar; it was the first light that had touched these walls in a very, very long time.

The first thing he saw was a stand wrought of marbled stone, crafted to resemble a pair of angelic wings. This was a style that had been favored by the lightwielders in decades past, though it wasn't seen much anymore. Nestled in the wings was a weapon of unusual and unique design; one could call it neither sword nor axe nor spear. It had a long handle, longer than any sword, and no guard at all, with a measure nearly the height of a man. It was topped with a wide, single blade with a flat back, but angled like the edge of a guillotine. The blade seemed to gather up all the light and reflect it like a mirror, gleaming even in the gloom. This was a sanctified blade, a holy weapon of the lightwielders, pure enough to rip through the flesh of even the darkest monster. The man snatched up the weapon without a thought, the dread he'd felt growing in him during his approach nearly overwhelming, now. It had more heft than he'd expected, too much to carry in a single hand. It was an unwieldy thing; its balance was akin to the axe of an executioner—an instrument designed for an instant, savage deathblow.

That was when he saw it. It was black stone banded with steel, and though it wasn't shaped like a coffin, he knew that's what it was. A heavy, steel chain wrapped around it thirteen times, criss-crossing in every direction and at every angle, and it was all bound together by a single, enormous lock. This chamber hadn't been exposed to the elements, and the restraints appeared to be in functional condition, if not ideal.

The man stood there, frozen. It seemed like days before he could bring himself to move his feet from that spot, and then only to grope around the walls in search of a lantern or torch, anything for more light. But there was nothing; had there been, it would have been rendered useless with age.

As the man's eyes adjusted to the darkness, he glanced uneasily back at the coffin. He was surprised to see an unusual depression in the stone's surface. Gathering his nerve, he warily approached, holding the sanctified weapon in front of him. It was not only a defensive gesture; he found he could use the shining blade to gather up and reflect what little ambient light there was.

The abnormality he'd spotted wasn't merely a depression, but a cut through the stone, a shaft piercing through to whatever was inside. He ran his finger along the finely chiseled edge, trying to determine just how thick the stone was. But such a gesture wasn't without reaction.

It was subtle at first, a stirring that could have been a squirrel on the roof if the trespasser didn't know better. It was coming from inside the coffin and growing louder. At first he couldn't move, he wanted to believe the sound of links of metal being scraped together was just his imagination. But when he began to feel the stone tremble beneath his fingers, he leapt back with a gasp, nearly tripping over his weapon in fear.

In a moment of lucidity, he realized the slot in the stone was precisely the same width as the weapon's blade. They were made to work in concert; the instrument could be driven into the breach, piercing the ribs and heart of whatever was locked within. There was hardly a moment of hesitation before the weapon was drawn up to strike, poised to rid the world of evils better left not unleashed upon the world.

"Stay your hand, Jonathan Vade," a voice boomed as the light from the entryway darkened. "I'll not ask you twice."

A man with a thick, brown and gray beard pushed the door open wide using only his right hand, making the massive iron barrier look like a toy. He was forced to use only the one hand; this was all he had, and an empty sleeve dangled on his other side. A shining chain hung around his neck, suspending a medallion wrought in the shape of the blazing sun, the contemporary symbol of the lightwielders, the children of Aura. The garments he wore were distinctive, but not gaudy, an attire that signified his rank among his order.

"Executor Mourne!" Jonathan blurted out, startled.

He was able to recompose himself in an instant, placing the weapon on the ground before him and dropping to one knee. The older man approached with a powerful stride that belied his age, casting wise and commanding eyes down on the younger man.

"Don't do that," the executor grumbled. "I get enough of that in the sanctuary;

it's rare that I can sneak off and be away from those twitchy old men who call themselves my council."

His tone was even and his words slow, as if he wasn't aware of the increasingly feverish sounds issuing from the coffin between them.

"Executor," Jonathan spat out, quickly rising to his feet, "There's something inside this coffin! Something still alive!"

"Yes, I know," he said in a low voice, laying his hand upon the edge of the stone. "I had hoped you wouldn't enter this place. Curse your Vade name; your great-grandfather was every bit as over eager as you, even when he had no idea what he was getting himself in to. But I suppose it can't be helped, now."

"I'm sorry, executor," Jonathan said, bowing his head, though he wasn't exactly sure what he was apologizing for. "I sent my oldest to notify the lightwielders in the sanctuary. I didn't expect you to come here yourself...especially not alone."

"Your key," the executor said, acting as if he hadn't heard a word. "It will open this lock as well."

He gestured at the mechanism that held the chains fastened tight around the coffin. Jonathan reached into his pocket with a shaking hand and produced the object in question.

"You're white as a sheet," Mourne sighed heavily. "Lightwielders can feel the flow of tainted blood all around them. You'll be in no danger with me here."

Jonathan nodded and approached the lock with the key in hand, his apprehensions little eased. It opened with a heavy click and the chains parted, unraveling themselves and falling to the ground in seconds. Whatever was inside the coffin went silent.

"Now, assist me in removing the lid," the executor ordered, grabbing an end of the stone slab with his one hand.

Jonathan didn't dare hesitate, even though his gut told him he should. Executor Gregan Mourne was the highest ranking lightwielder at the sanctuary, one of only seven executors in the empire. They answered only to the high executor who resided in the capital, and the high executor didn't even answer to the emperor himself. He was a man to be respected and revered, but, lightwielder or not, Jonathan was beginning to doubt his judgment.

It took both men all of their strength, but the heavy stone lid slipped off with a groan and crashed to the floor. The impact reverberated throughout the tower.

Jonathan's eyes went wide and his heart went still in his chest at what he saw. Smaller chains, stained black with age, wrapped around a still figure, binding it like a mummy. They twisted tightly around the arms and legs, the neck, everywhere. There were even individual chains running between the fingers, all rigged to keep the captive's hands crossed at its chest. These chains were then anchored to the stone with iron plates and spikes, forbidding even the slightest movement.

The entombed figure wore a mask, or perhaps it would be better called a muzzle. It was a brown, leather strip that covered the mouth and hooked under the chin. A pair of buckles behind the head made it impossible to remove without free hands, though one side of the device had been torn or fallen apart with age. The prisoner's hair was unnaturally long, as if it had kept growing for as long as this confinement had lasted. With the mask and hair both obscuring its face, Jonathan could make out only one feature—a mark underneath the right eye.

It was the mark of the necromancer. A dark design too complex and perfect to be natural, yet it hadn't been placed there by human hands. Jonathan had only seen it in person once before, but even then he'd known it well. The Vade family carried the blood of Aura, the divine gift that granted power to the lightwielders. Though his family hadn't been blessed with a lightwielder in four generations, since Jonathan's great grandfather's time, they were well acquainted with the marks borne by those of tainted blood. Most necromancers sought refuge far to the north, where their combined threat was just enough to keep them hated and feared, but alive. However, the further they strayed from those lands, the more likely they were to encounter people who thought they were too much of a threat to be left alive.

"Mr. Vade," the executor warned, "Keep your weapon at the ready."

"What? I thought you said we were in no danger!" he said, scrambling to pick up the halberd, which he'd let drop to the floor.

The executor didn't get another chance to speak. The coffin erupted with the clamor of snapping metal and a feral growl as the chains were torn asunder by an inhuman strength. The entombed creature leapt from its confinement, the shattered chains streaming behind it like the tattered wings of a devil. It landed hard on the stone floor, staggering to one knee. Its hands were still bound at its chest and its back was turned toward the two intruders, and Jonathan thought to take advantage of the opportunity and strike the creature down while he had a chance. Executor Mourne stopped him with his only hand.

"Executor, I saw the mark on its face! It's a vampire!" Jonathan protested.

"Jonathan Vade!" he bellowed, nearly knocking the younger man off his feet. "Don't assume you know what stands before you better than I!"

Jonathan was stunned, and for half a second he couldn't even speak.

"I-I'm sorry, sir," he said, taking a step back. He felt like he'd made a fool of himself.

The creature rose to its feet and turned toward them, its black, over long hair dragging across the stone floor. It stared down the two men with the fiercest eyes Jonathan had ever seen. They bore both the intensity of a predatory beast and the cunning of a man, a disconcerting combination.

"What is this thing, executor? What's going on?"

Gregan sighed deeply and said, "I suppose I have no choice."

2

(Sixteen years before present)

BY THE TIME THE lightwielders reached the town of Ravensweald, there was no sign of anyone who had been left alive. The Great Citadel to the north had fallen and along with it, its protector, Arach Altessor, the Black Guardian. Now the barbarian hordes spilled southward, like a torrent of water from a broken dam, taking whatever they wanted and destroying everything else.

Gregan had never seen such berserk ferocity from man or beast in all his years; everywhere he looked there was murder. The scene was a regular feast for the carrion birds; they seemed to populate the land in limitless numbers. Not only had the barbarians slain the men who had tried to fight against them, but the women and the children as well. And those who left their lifeless, mangled corpses behind may have been considered lucky; at least they hadn't been taken as slaves or toys or concubines. But the barbarians took surprisingly few prisoners, seeming to enjoy the thrill of bloodshed more than plunder.

Many of the buildings had been reduced to smoldering skeletons, barely able to support their own weight. Merchants' carts had been overturned, leaving their wares strewn across the narrow streets. The place was the very face of war, the embodiment of all the horrors men would so willingly inflict upon one another. There seemed to be only one building left intact: a large, stone structure near the center of the community. Gregan had only visited Ravensweald once before, but he recognized it as the town hall.

He led his beleaguered party through the carnage and toward the building. They were a tattered group of six lightwielders and eleven guardsmen, and were all that remained after the trial of the days before. They'd lost all of their horses, and so were forced to make their way across the realm on foot. After everything he'd seen, Gregan felt lucky to have this many still with him. The guardsmen had been hit the worst and, were it not for the lightwielders' protection, he doubted any of them would be left at all.

Amidst so many bodies of slaughtered villagers, they found the corpse of a single barbarian. Among the civilized people of the south, Gregan was considered a man of imposing stature, but even he was dwarfed in comparison to these giants of the north, barely standing at mid chest. The deceased raider was dressed in heavy leathers and furs, garments meant to keep the biting cold of the northlands at bay more than blade or spear. Even without armor the giants were as hard to bring down as a brown bear, and they seemed to revel in the pain of their wounds. They attacked like dervishes wielding weapons of tremendous mass, some with one in each hand, crashing through shield formations and cavalry with reckless abandon.

But this barbarian hadn't been brought down by sword, or arrow, or any other weapon wielded by men. He laid face down, his limbs twisted in agony, a look of perpetual terror carved into his dirt-caked features. His back was ripped open, skin flayed from his shoulder blades down, exposing his vital organs to the open air. The crows had already picked at the corpse, making it difficult to judge just how severe the wound may have been. But it was clear the barbarian had been brought down while running from something, and Gregan had never known their kind to flee, even in the face of death.

"Paladin Mourne," one of the lightwielders said respectfully, "This place has an evil air. There is nothing we can do for these people anymore, and we are far from being out of danger. We should keep moving. It is our duty to report what's happened to the high executor personally."

Gregan slowly shook his head. They'd all seen more than their share of blood and pain over the last few days, and he certainly didn't want to put them through more traumas. But he couldn't leave this place just yet.

"Do you know what this village is?" Gregan asked the lightwielder.

"I'm not sure I follow you, paladin," he replied uneasily.

"This is the home of Arach Altessor," Gregan explained. "Though he may have lived in the citadel, his family has always lived here."

"Arach the Deathbringer," the lightwielder whispered in a low voice, distaste clear in his tone.

Gregan shook his head, "Arach tried to leave that name behind him, though it seems to have stained him permanently, much like the blood on the hands of a murderer. As you know, he and I were good friends; we both served the emperor during the western rebellion."

"With all due respect, I don't understand what you're trying to say."

"I've already lost a dear friend," Gregan answered, no hint of emotion in his voice in spite of his words. "I'll not let his family die while there is anything that can be done. After all that's happened, I owe him that much."

The lightwielder shook his head, but offered no further protests.

"When the village was attacked, anyone with the ability to do so would have fled to the town hall. It's the only building large and sturdy enough to withstand an assault, and the most easily defended."

With those simple words, Gregan directed his subordinates to the community's center.

As the troupe drew near, it became clear that many who had tried to flee to this last haven had never reached their destination. Men and women alike had been pierced or cleaved and left to die on the blood-soaked ground. There were more barbarians, as well, all exhibiting the same sort of grievous wounds they'd witnessed on the first. The party tried to ignore these brutalized corpses; their wounds meant there was something even more deadly at play here than the barbarians, a notion they didn't dare contemplate.

A set of wide stone stairs led to the face of the building. The steps were broad and shallow, and the masonry had begun to crack with age. Once they had ended in a set of enormous wooden doors, but these had both been ripped from the walls and hurled into the courtyard below. The closer they came to this threshold the more bodies they found, both of the villagers and the raiders. The stairs were still sticky with their blood, and the acrid, copper smell overwhelmed the senses. Gregan approached the entryway, straining his eyes to pierce the darkness within.

A scream ripped through the air, nearly sending the paladin tumbling backwards down the stairs. For a moment, no one moved. They didn't even breathe.

"There's no way anyone could still be alive in there," one of the guardsman said in disbelief.

"This is no time for doubts," Gregan barked, hurdling over the bloodied bodies and rushing inside. "Three of you stay here and watch the door; the rest with me."

Gregan nearly retched from the stink of blood. Outside in the open air had been one thing, but this many dead bodies in a confined space was almost too much for him to bear. Still, he pushed on into the gray halls, trying to find the source of the scream. The clamor was earsplitting and continuous, and it bounced off the walls and high ceilings, creating an indistinguishable echo. Gregan couldn't pinpoint where it was coming from until one of the guardsman announced that he'd found something.

Gregan discovered the man in a small, dark room. The guardsman was trying to find a light. He'd found a lantern, but it had been knocked over and the glass had shattered across the floor. The room appeared as if it had once been used for storage, but it had been torn apart, crates broken open and their contents thrown to the ground. It even seemed the floor had been damaged in the barbarian's fervor, but it quickly became clear this wrecked area was more than it seemed. Gregan drew his sword from its sheath with his left hand, his dominant arm, and held it upright before him.

"Cast thy glow across the darkness of this earth, light my path and accept my prayers, blessed goddess, Aura." The sanctified blade began to shine, faintly at first, almost as if it were only reflecting light that was already there. But the glow spread quickly across the dim chamber, a pale and pure light, soft and clean like a beacon draped with fog. Gregan could plainly see a concealed portal that had been built into the floor. However, it had been demolished by the invaders, leaving only scraps of timber still dangling from its hinges, and revealing stairs that lead to the floor below. The women and children had surely fled here to hide from the barbarians, though some unfortunate twist of fate must have given them away. But the screams were coming from the darkness below, which meant there had to be at least one survivor.

Gregan bounded down the stairs, the wood creaking under the weight of his heavy armor, and the rest of his troupe followed close behind. Once he'd reached the bottom, he found that he could hardly find a solid piece of ground to stand on. The corpses of barbarians were everywhere, some of them torn to pieces, leaving an arm laying here or a leg there. There were also the bodies of women and children; Gregan couldn't bear to look at them. But in the midst of the chamber was a zone bereft of human remains, as if there were an invisible screen there that had kept anything from entering. In the center of this open area was a young man laying on the dirty floor, his back arched nearly to the point of breaking, his arms and hands contorted like the claws of some beast, and his mouth open wide in a spine chilling scream.

Gregan rushed to the boy, trying not to think about what he was stepping on in his haste. He drove his sword into the bare earth and dropped to one knee before this sole survivor.

He couldn't have been more than sixteen or seventeen years old. His eyes seemed inhumanly fierce and feral, and they stared past the old paladin as if he wasn't even there. His short, black hair was covered in dirt, dust and blood from flailing about on the filthy ground, and under his right eye he bore the mark of the necromancer. Gregan hadn't seen the son of Arach Altessor since he was a baby, long before the mark had appeared on him. But the location, as his friend had described to him, was unmistakable. This was Koristad, the only son of Arach the Black Guardian.

Gregan heard the sound of steel on leather all around him, the unmistakable music of swords being drawn. His troupe had gathered around the two of them, forming a circle of men and blades.

"I've given no order to draw your weapons," Gregan growled at them. "You will put them away at once."

"Paladin Mourne, this boy is turning into a vampire," one of the lightwielders replied, exhibiting no signs of yielding. "We are all far too familiar with the signs. Look at his fangs; the turning is nearly complete."

It was true enough that the boy's canines had elongated and ended in wicked points. His eyes were growing blacker by the second, a sign that the dark power within him had nearly overwhelmed his soul. Still, he was fighting with every ounce of will he possessed, struggling in vain to impede the unbearable process of becoming a monster.

In Gregan's mind, it was now quite clear what had transpired in this wide scene of carnage: to defend the townsfolk, Koristad had used his fledgling powers to call up something horrible to defend them. No, that wasn't quite right; the people in the north may have tolerated the presence of the children of darkness, but they certainly didn't accept them. With the mark so clear on his face, the boy had certainly suffered the hatred and distrust of his peers, and been ostracized for it. He may not have cared at all what happened to the villagers, but his mother, Charisse Altessor, had been hiding in this cellar with him. Gregan could see her body lying limp among the others, her once striking beauty marred by death. When he and Arach had first met the girl, the necromancer had insisted to his friend that she was the most beautiful woman he'd ever laid eyes on. Or perhaps he'd said it himself; Gregan couldn't seem to remember. Memory is funny that way.

To try to save her, and to save himself, Koristad must have used necromantic magic that was far beyond his control. He was too young to understand his limits. Now he'd exceeded them and was forced to pay the ultimate price, the price that must be paid by all children of darkness who delve too deeply into their own hell-stained souls. The boy would become a vampire for his transgression, and the lightwielders would have no choice but to end his cursed unlife. Gregan couldn't imagine what sort of phantoms this young necromancer had pulled over from the other side, what sort of dark power could have delivered such grievous wounds to not only the barbarians, but also to any villagers who had still been alive when he lost control. He shouldn't have known an invocation of that potential. Certainly his father would have done everything in his power to prevent such a tragedy.

But now, he would die. This was the end of the Altessor line; Gregan had seen enough suffering in the last few days to fill an entire lifetime, and now he would watch as the son of his friend was slaughtered. The soldiers began to close around the two of them, swords in hand, ready to face the monster that could turn upon them at any moment. But Gregan remained close to the boy, his sword planted in the ground, defenseless.

"Stay back!" Gregan snarled.

The men, shocked at the ferocity of his order, hesitated in their advance. The paladin removed the steel gauntlet from his left hand and let it fall to the ground with a thud. He reached out with his bare hand, placing his palm on the frantic boy's chest.

"What are you doing, Gregan!?" one of the lightwielders shouted, panicked. "You know this boy is beyond the reprieve of the healing powers of Aura!"

Another said, "You're only putting yourself in danger! Please, take up your sword and let us do our duty and rid the world of this monster! That's the only compassion we can offer him now!"

Gregan closed his eyes, shutting their protests from his mind. There was no healing invocation for what he was about to try, and so he remained silent. He could feel the dark blood coursing through the boy's body, growing stronger with every beat of his heart. It was like a plague of black, ravenous locusts descending upon Koristad's very soul, ripping it apart and consuming it. Soon, his heart would sound its last beat, and all that would remain would be that terrible swarm, ever hungry for more. If only there was something he could do to make them stop. He could almost see them, their powerful mandibles ripping and tearing, multifaceted eyes gleaming red with ardor. They rose and descended again and again, moving with a single intelligence, like a lone entity.

But something was changing about their pattern. At first, Gregan couldn't tell what it was. . .had they finished with the boy? Was he too late? Then followed a grim realization; they were becoming aware of the intruder in their midst, of the lightwielder trying to spirit away their prey. Gregan couldn't even react; their descent upon him seemed instantaneous. The horrible, biting insects turned their hunger on him now; the pain of their attack was intense, beyond anything he'd ever felt before. His eyes popped open as he cried out in pain and terror, stumbling away from the boy.

He fell hard onto the bloody ground and his companions rushed to his aid. Gregan could still feel the biting pain in his left arm. He was almost too frightened to do so, but when he looked at his hand, he found it was turning black and refused to move. He desperately ripped at his spaulders, snapping their leather straps with his turbulent strength. The blackness was clearly moving up his limb, carrying with it a horrible, cold sort of agony. An agony like death.

"Take it!" Gregan shouted through clenched teeth.

"Sir!?" his men questioned, appearing every bit as panicked as their commanding officer.

"My arm! You have to take it!" Gregan screamed, his vision growing dark. He wasn't sure how much longer he would be able to keep his consciousness through the pain. "Now! Do it now, damn you!"

One of the guardsman gestured for the others to step back, their faces grim. He lifted his sword high over his head, preparing to swing in a powerful, downward stroke.

"Aura forgive me," he said, and let the blade fall.

3

"AT FIRST, WE THOUGHT I'd given my arm for nothing. Koristad hadn't turned into a vampire, but he didn't appear to be alive, either," Gregan finished in a low voice, bringing his tale to a close. "But he had a pulse; it was so slow, so faint, it was almost imperceptible. But he *was* still alive."

"So you brought him back here?" Jonathan asked apprehensively.

"Yes. The executor was reluctant to let him stay; no one could even say what he was," Gregan explained with a shake of his head. "That was when I became a sage. I'd lost my sword arm; I couldn't be a paladin anymore. But I could use my new influence to ensure Koristad would be kept, rather than simply disposed of as a threat."

Jonathan wanted to question if that was wise, but he couldn't bring himself to speak the words before the monster's unwavering stare.

"That was some sixteen years ago. For a time, I journeyed to this tower nearly every day, to see if he'd awoken from his prolonged slumber. Years passed, and I came to check less often and, eventually, not at all. I suppose I lost hope," Gregan said with a sigh, approaching the chained apparition. "Do you remember any of this Koristad?"

He reached his hand toward the boy, preparing to remove the damaged, leather muzzle from his face.

"Executor, I don't think that's wise," the panic was clear in Jonathan's voice. "If he's been locked in that coffin for so many years, there's no way a human could still be alive. He must have become a vampire."

Gregan looked over his shoulder at the younger man with a raised eyebrow, "When a necromancer turns, the frenzy for blood is unstoppable. If he's not tried to attack us yet, then I don't believe he will."

Jonathan took little comfort in that reasoning, but he didn't dare question the executor any further.

The leather straps of the muzzle came undone with a snap and fell to the ground. The face underneath was pale, but Jonathan couldn't see if the mouth bore any fangs, which was the only aspect of Koristad's appearance that concerned him. Gregan, however, noted the remarkable fact that he appeared no older than when he'd been entombed, somewhere between a boy and a man.

"Tell me, Koristad, do you remember any of this?" Gregan asked again.

Koristad tried to speak, but the only sounds that issued from him were unintelligible rasps. His voice had been ripped and tattered by his screams, desperate to escape his black confinement. He swallowed hard and cleared his throat, then attempted to communicate again.

"Vaguely," he whispered, his voice harsh and barely audible. "As if it were a dream. I can see my life as though I were looking through a glass. None of it seems quite real."

"I see," Gregan said with a sad expression. "I suppose it's to be expected after…"

"Get these chains off of me," Koristad interrupted, plainly not interested in what the old man had to say.

Gregan seemed unperturbed by the boy's rudeness, and he turned his gaze back to Jonathan.

"Mister Vade, the key, please."

Jonathan still couldn't trust this young necromancer before him. There was something primal in the pit of his stomach that told him something wasn't right about him. He regretted having ever set foot in this tower; if he could have had his way, they would have put Koristad back into his coffin and shut it tight forever. But he knew well he had no authority and so, with a shaking hand, he passed the key to the executor.

Gregan followed the lines of the dark chains, searching for the lock that held them in place. He'd been present when Koristad was bound, but it had been so many years ago, he could hardly remember how it had been done.

"Tell me what happened to my father. How were the barbarians able to attack our settlements?" Koristad asked, his voice growing stronger and more clear.

"Your father…," Gregan paused for a long moment, seeming to be choked up. "I'm sorry, but he was slain and usurped by a vampire. I'm sure you know that vampires hunt living necromancers. By drinking their tainted blood, they're able to steal their dark power. That vampire consumed your father's blood and unleashed a terrible evil."

"A vampire?" Koristad asked, unable to believe what he was hearing.

"That's right, I'm afraid," Gregan replied sadly. "That monster took control of the citadel and allowed the barbarians to cut their bloody path into civilized lands. No one knows this vampire's name; he has come to be known only as the Vampire King." With that, Gregan found the lock he'd been searching for and it came undone with a metallic click. The chains loosened around Koristad's body, and he began to brush them away like the tangled web of a spider.

"He *is* known?" Koristad growled angrily. "You're saying this monster has been allowed to live?"

"Yes," Gregan answered. "He still resides in the citadel. He…"

"Why hasn't he been destroyed?" Koristad demanded, the rage clear in his fierce eyes. "Aren't lightwielders the slayers of vampires and other monsters? Or are you only able to harass innocent mages?"

"Koristad!" Gregan bellowed as his tolerance reached its end; he rose up to his full height, towering over the young necromancer. "The empire has fought hard over these years to reclaim the lands in the north. There have been dozens of campaigns, and the barbarian hordes have been decimated. But the power the Vampire King wields is beyond our measure, and the Great Citadel has remained beyond our grasp."

Koristad snorted, seemingly unfazed by the executor's intimidation, though his next words didn't carry the same impudent tone.

"I'm glad he's still there."

Gregan was silent for only a moment before he replied, "You're thinking of revenge."

"My father was a great man who gave his life to protect others," Koristad answered. "He deserves to be avenged, at the very least. I'm glad I'll be able to carry it out myself."

"Koristad…," Gregan said with a sad shake of his head. "I can feel the turbulence of the blood within you. You may not have become a vampire yet, but you sit on the very brink of oblivion. I'm sure you can feel it as well. The use of the magic within your blood, no matter how slight, will send you tumbling over that brink."

Koristad let the last of the chains that had bound him fall to the floor with a clang. He stared down at them for a long time; it was as if the multitude of black links was the blood he'd inherited from his father, infused with dark power, now useless and impotent at his feet.

"I will have my vengeance," he insisted, the hate clear in his voice.

"The Vampire King has stood against all the armies of the empire," Gregan said, placing his hand on Koristad's shoulder. "All who have ever attempted to destroy him have failed. What do you think a lone, disempowered necromancer can do against a monster like that?"

Koristad lifted his head, looking up at the executor through his long, unkempt hair. There was no fear in his eyes, only a determination Gregan had seen only once before.

"I swear to you on my life, I will see that monster dead at my feet."

Gregan sighed heavily and put his arm behind his back. He paced back and forth before the young man, seemingly lost in thought.

"Perhaps I can offer you a better alternative," he said at last. "Better than suicide, at least."

After a long pause, Koristad answered in a low voice, "I'm listening."

"A long time has passed since you were sealed away," Gregan spoke frankly, still pacing. "The world has changed. Fighting the barbarians on open ground took a terrible toll on the empire; as I've already told you, there were many campaigns devised to end their incursions. Many loyal soldiers lost their lives, and resources were spread thin. This led to poverty for many citizens, and poverty turned into crime. With so many soldiers in the north, faith began to wane in the emperor, and this lead to chaos."

"I'm sure this is a lovely story," Koristad interjected rudely, "But I don't see what it has to do with me."

Gregan continued, unperturbed, "When there is chaos, violence and lawlessness spread like a disease. Through the common people, through the mages, and even monsters who had once stayed hidden have grown more bold. Not only were many soldiers slain by the barbarian hordes, but many lightwielders have fallen under their blades, as well. Our numbers dwindle, but there are more devils and rogues in the land than ever."

Jonathan, who had remained dutifully silent in the shadows, couldn't help but think, looking at the ragged necromancer, that they had released another devil upon the world.

"I would like to extend an offer to you," Gregan finished at last. "I want you to work for us, to carry out duties as a...shall we say, *proxy* lightwielder."

The silence in the dark chamber was almost palpable and seemed to drag on for an eternity. But all at once it was filled with the roar of Koristad's laughter, made even more piercing by its echo off the adjoining walls.

"You want me to do the work of a lightwielder?" Koristad could barely bring himself to speak. "You must either be joking, or you've lost your mind to senility, old man."

Gregan narrowed his eyes at him and frowned.

"I think it would have made your father happy," the executor said.

At that, Koristad grew quiet.

"It may have," he answered sternly.

"Certainly more so than having his only son rush off to his senseless demise," Gregan added.

Koristad stared at the ground for a long time, remaining silent, but at last he said, "I admired my father, executor. But the path I walk will be one of my choosing. Not his, and certainly not yours."

"I see," Gregan replied solemnly.

"However," Koristad added strongly, "I'm not some parasite who only cares about himself. You risked your life and you gave your arm to save me. I owe you a great debt, one that will not be easy to repay. But I do intend to repay you before I hunt down the creature that killed my father, since I know well I may not return. If it is your wish that I repay that debt by playing "proxy lightwielder", as you put it, then I can hardly refuse."

Gregan smiled broadly. The boy was much like his father, after all.

"Executor," Jonathan said quietly, unable to hold his tongue any longer, "The Council of Sages, not to mention the other executors. . .won't they oppose the idea of allowing a child of darkness to perform such holy work? He's already shown great strength, and I don't doubt his ability," he added quickly with a hand raised at Koristad, hoping not to anger him, "But the mark upon his face. The people will fear him. . ."

"I can deal with the bureaucracy," Gregan answered. "And, for the rest of it. . .I'm sure it's nothing that can't be resolved through a little ingenuity. And I've always known the Altessors to be remarkably clever."

Jonathan nodded, a sign of defeat rather than agreement.

"I've no doubt that this is the beginning of something beneficial for us both, Koristad," the executor beamed. "Now, Jonathan and I must return to the sanctuary. I'd invite you for dinner but, sadly, you'd be unable to attend."

Koristad scowled and waved them off, hardly amused by the humor.

Gregan added, "You may use the tower as a domicile for the time being; I'll send a servant shortly to attend to any of your needs; food, a bed. . .a barber, perhaps. Please, try your best not to frighten her."

Gregan gestured Jonathan out the door and the man was quick to comply, eager to leave the dreadful place. He let the halberd fall to the ground with a clang and hurried toward the exit, Gregan only a few paces behind.

"Executor Mourne," Koristad called out suddenly. "I need to know something."

Gregan turned toward the young man and raised his eyebrows.

"Certainly, Koristad."

The question was hard for him to pose, and he stood there in silence for a moment, trying to find his nerve.

At length he let out a deep breath and asked, "My mother. . .what happened to her? I...I can't remember. Was she killed by the barbarians or...by what I called up?"

Gregan balked at the question, but only for an instant.

"It was the barbarians, Koristad," he lied. "Don't let what happened to her hang over your head. Goodbye, my friend."

Chapter Two

KNOW WHAT I KNOW

What a strange notion it is to teach.
Students almost invariably resent those who try to share their wisdom.
Is it pride? Sloth?
There could be no more common human characteristics: vanity and lethargy.
It isn't until after those who tried so hard to instruct us are gone that we can finally
reflect and treasure those lessons they imparted.
Only when it is too late, for both our respect and our gratitude.
The only thanks we can give is to carry on with those gifts of wisdom, using them to
better ourselves and our world.
And maybe even pass them on to someone else.

1

THE SPARSE ENCAMPMENT WAS filled with unease and a pervasive sense of dread. Situated far to the north in the foothills of the Bittereach Mountains, the high peaks on the horizon jutted into the sky like a row of jagged teeth. Entering these lands was prohibited by the emperor; it was a narrow corridor between the reclaimed realms to the south and the deadly territory of the barbarians to the north.

Coming to such a place was like an invitation to death.

That's what Leorra was thinking as the elegant, black coach she travelled in drove down the muddy road and into the expedition. The carriage was large, almost twice as long as was typical. It was divided into two sections. Only the front half bore any windows or an exit; this was the passenger's area which Leorra occupied. The second half could only be accessed from inside, through a heavy, wooden door. It had steel bindings and a heavy lock, and could be further sealed by situating a nearby plank across its width. It was a cell intended for prisoners who were too dangerous to be casually restrained.

She gazed out the narrow window at the residents. They were mostly large men clad in wet, dirty clothes from working through the drizzle that had persisted through the morning and into the afternoon. The sun had finally begun to show through the clouds, but they seemed little encouraged by it; instead, they stopped in their tracks and warily observed the carriage's passage.

Leorra leaned toward the other passenger of the carriage and asked in a quiet, testing voice, "Can you sense anything unusual, Peril?"

The young girl was sitting upright with her hands in her lap, gazing out the opposite window with an eager look in her eyes. She turned quickly toward her mentor with an expression of surprise and uncertainty. It was her typical reaction when she was addressed while lost in thought, which was the case more often than not.

"Um…I don't think so," Peril answered, a look of doubt in her large, blue eyes.

She had delicate features and a fair complexion, with soft skin that made her seem very young. This impression was deepened by her small stature, no taller than a child. The only quality that corrected this notion, indicating she was a woman rather than a child, was a surprisingly buxom chest for a girl of her size. She wore a long, white gown that laced up to her neck, wrapping neatly around her slim figure. Her hair was straight and long, a very pale blonde that was very nearly as white as her dress.

She was certainly an idol of youthful beauty, but Leorra often found her protégé to be overtly carefree and naïve, displaying little perception of the subtleties occurring around her. Much as she was doing now.

"You're not trying," Leorra scolded her with a frown.

"Yes I am," Peril pouted in response, turning her face toward the window once again.

She tried to make it clear that her feelings had been hurt and she didn't wish to discuss the matter further, but her mentor couldn't be so easily deterred.

Leorra placed her hand softly on the small woman's shoulder and instructed, "Try to close your eyes. Breathe slowly, reach out with your senses and feel what's around you."

Peril did as she was instructed and remained quiet for a long time. Leorra half-expected the next words out of her mouth to be about what the clouds outside were shaped like, or how she'd heard that the high executor had taken ill, or about the time she'd ridden the steam train to the capital.

Finally, Peril answered, "It's like there's something twisted here...I'm not sure how to say it. Like there's something so wretched and corrupted it's polluting the very air."

"See? That wasn't so hard," Leorra encouraged with a pat on the girl's head, mussing her hair. "There's certainly something not right here. We've finally found him, and it looks like he's flaunting the laws of the empire once again. I'm afraid the executor's leniency is wearing thin with this one."

Peril frowned and looked down at the wooden floor of the carriage. She knew that, as a lightwielder, it was her duty to keep the peace and uphold the laws of the empire. But she hated being involved with the capture or punishment of outlaws. Which wasn't to say that she felt Leorra to be overly harsh; quite the contrary, she had always known her mentor to be both merciful and compassionate, and she hoped she would never have to see her reach a point where mercy could no longer be afforded.

"This must be it," Leorra announced. She poked her head out the window and called out, "Driver, you can stop here!"

The moment the horses came to a halt, she popped open the carriage door with a click. Peril could see they'd stopped in front of a tent that was much more extravagant than any of the others, and larger than a small house. It was black and gray, still glistening from the morning precipitation, and the roof had many peaks which denoted a complex frame.

The two women cautiously descended the short wooden stairs, Leorra taking a wide step away from the muddy road onto wet grass. Peril, who had much shorter legs, couldn't take the same stride and stopped on the last step, appearing concerned that she might dirty her elegant, white gown. Leorra crossed her arms impatiently and tapped her foot, appraising her protégé and finding her delicacy bizarre.

"Please, let me help you, my little dove," came the soothing voice of a man.

He had pushed aside the flap of the tent and stepped out into the sunlight, greeting them with a charming smile that animated his entire face. He was lean and tall, towering over Peril even as she was perched on the carriage steps. He had a handsome, clean shaven face; his dark hair was short and well-kempt. He was adorned in fine, black garments that sported a white poet collar and a shirt that was open in the front.

He walked to the carriage, showing no concern at stepping in the soft mud, and lifted Peril by the waist, effortlessly setting her on the firm ground next to Leorra. He took a step back and gazed at the two of them, the friendly smile never leaving his face.

"It's good to see you again, Leorra," he said warmly, sounding quite sincere. "It's been too long."

"Leer," she replied in a hushed voice, put off by the man's over-friendly greeting. "Don't play dumb. You know the emperor has declared these lands off limits. What are you thinking coming to a place like this?" The tall man's expression remained unchanged. He crossed his arms, waiting politely for the lightwielder to finish. "I can't imagine what you had to pay these laborers to come with you, but bringing them here is only going to make things worse."

Leer seemed nonplussed by her comments.

"The two of you have travelled a long way," was his only response. "Please, come inside and have some tea."

He didn't wait for their reply, but quickly disappeared into his pavilion.

"So, this is the necromancer we've come to find?" Peril asked merrily. "He seems nice."

She started toward the entrance that Leer had used, but was stopped by Leorra's hand on her shoulder. Looking back at her mentor, Peril noted that she wore a severe expression and her left hand was resting firmly on the pommel of the broadsword at her waist.

"Leer Valcroix is a snake," Leorra warned in a stern voice. "Mind yourself around him."

With that, she stepped cautiously through the opening in the tent wall, her hand never leaving her blade. Peril crossed her arms and stuck out her bottom lip as she watched her mentor disappear into the dark confines.

"I'm not a little kid, you know," she sulked, but only after she was certain Leorra was too far away to hear the comment and scold her for her attitude. Then, suddenly remembering she actually wanted to go inside, she hurriedly slipped through the entryway.

The interior was dimly lit, only illuminated by a few small openings in the walls and a lantern that Leer had set on a table in the center of the room. The table was ovular and wrought of dark wood; several matching chairs with deep lavender cushions were spaced around it.

"You'll have to forgive me," Leer apologized as he took a seat. "There's little to offer in the way of simple comforts in an inhospitable land like this, but I brought what I could."

The two women sat down opposite their host and Leorra immediately began to appraise the room. It was surprisingly cramped, and judging from the size of the pavilion from outside, she guessed this was less than a third of the tent's total size. There was a high, cloth partition that nearly reached the framework ceiling, forming the room into a triangular shape. A narrow portal was cut into the makeshift wall but, even as she strained to see, Leorra could make out nothing of what lay beyond. But even without the aid of her eyes, her intuition told her the source of the corruption she'd felt earlier was emanating from somewhere nearby.

She turned her attention back to her host, catching him engaged in small talk with her protégé. Peril would look down at the table, and then up at Leer. It was quite clear to Leorra from the way she batted her eyes and twirled her hair while he was talking that she was quite taken with him. Leorra knew personally how enamoring Leer could be.

"You still haven't given us an explanation of why you're here," she interrupted, eager to put a quick end to the flirtation. "I ordered you to inform me if you were going to be away."

"I suppose I must have forgotten," Leer explained simply, brushing the question off with an easygoing shrug of his shoulders. He added with a wry smile, "It would be a terrible tragedy if I managed to slip my leash."

"You know we keep a close eye on you for a reason," Leorra snapped. "You've forced us..."

"Tea!" Leer interjected suddenly. "Where are my manners? I'd forgotten why I'd brought you inside in the first place." He leaned his head toward a nearby partition, and called out, "Maria, please bring my guests some refreshments."

There was a sound of shuffling behind the wall and, after a few moments, the fabric parted and a young girl stepped into the room. She was carrying a large, black tray with a white teapot and three cups. She set the tableware before the guests and her master, then began to pour the hot drink with shaking hands.

She was young, not much older than Peril, with a dark complexion and chestnut hair. She could have been described as pretty, but that wasn't what Leorra saw. She seemed tired, as if she hadn't slept in days, and her bones moved with a sense of age unbefitting such a youthful woman. When Leorra looked in her eyes, she saw dullness and lack of life. It was as if there was nothing behind them.

As Maria finished pouring the tea, both Leer and Peril reached for their glasses, smiling at one another. Leorra, however, made no move toward her cup, instead casting a harsh stare upon the necromancer.

"Don't look like that," Leer said. "I promise I haven't poisoned it; we're old friends, aren't we? Besides, I'm drinking from the same pot, see?"

He took a sip from his cup and set it back down on the table.

"Peril," Leorra said in a severe tone, "Go and wait in the carriage."

"What?" she sulked. "But I…"

"Do as I say," she snapped in a tone that made it clear she would tolerate no more back talk.

Peril, looking hurt and slighted, sprang to her feet, knocking down the chair she'd been sitting in. She made no move to pick it up before storming out of the tent.

"Well, that was rather rude, don't you think?" Leer said as his servant righted the fallen seat.

"I won't play this game of yours any further," Leorra hissed at him. "What do you think you're doing to this girl?"

She gestured at Maria insistently.

Leer's eyes grimaced and he covered his mouth with his hand, though Leorra believed it was only to conceal the fact that he was still smiling.

"Uh-oh," he chimed like a child whose mother had caught him with his hand in the cookie jar. "It looks like I'm in trouble."

"I thought you had more talent than this," she scolded. "I could feel the corruption you placed upon her before I even reached this camp of yours."

"Well, I suppose my skills must be getting rusty," he explained, plainly not as concerned as he probably should have been. "You children of aura have forbidden me from using my magic, you know."

"I was wondering if you remembered," she snapped back at him, frustrated that he didn't seem to grasp the severity of his situation. "It's bad enough you're using your black magic to dominate her mind, but do you understand how much you're hurting her by using such a vicious and twisted enchantment? How long have you kept her this way?"

"It's simply too much for me to keep track of little details like that, I'm afraid."

"You will release her at once," Leorra demanded, rising to her feet and wrapping her right hand around the hilt of her sword.

Leer put his hands up defensively.

"Please, old friend, there's no need for anything like that," he pleaded. "Of course I'll let her go, as you say."

Maria had been standing at the edge of the table motionless for some time, seeming by all accounts to be oblivious to what was being said. Leer reached out and held the palm of his left hand before her eyes for a moment; when he removed it, the girl collapsed to the ground as if she'd fainted.

Leer was unarmed, and his mind control powers would have no effect on a lightwielder or anyone bearing tainted blood. Still, Leorra kept a cautious eye on him as she knelt down next to the girl. She brushed the hair away from Maria's face and saw she was sweating profusely. Her eyes were shut tight as if she was in pain. She moaned slightly at Leorra's touch, but made no sign that she could move. The lightwielder rose to her feet and glowered at the necromancer.

"Do you see what your dirty magic has done to this poor girl?" she said. "She'll probably be ill for weeks after this. How long was she like this, Leer!?"

Leer's expression bore no glimmer of remorse. Unbelievably, he was still wearing his charming smile.

"You children of aura have no sense of humor at all," he complained. "My magical inclinations are rather specific. It seems unfair that I shouldn't be allowed at least one toy."

The brazen comment was enough to push Leorra into a rage, but she restrained herself as best she could.

"Give me your hands," she said furiously, her jaw clenched tight.

"That hardly seems necessary..."

"Now!" she roared, unsheathing half of her sword as a threat.

Leer, with a startled look on his face, held both of his hands in front of him, wrists together. He knew from experience where this was heading. Leorra produced a set of silk bindings from her belt and fastened them tightly around his outstretched limbs. So tightly, in fact, that Leer winced in pain, but she hadn't a shred of pity left for him.

"Now move," she ordered. "I'm locking you up before you can cause any more harm to these people."

2

AS LEORRA EXITED THE tent with Leer in tow, she found the residents of the camp had gathered around both the pavilion and her carriage. It wasn't much of a surprise; the children of Aura were a rare sight and, if the residents knew their employer was a necromancer, they certainly expected something significant to happen. Her driver, a slender man in his later years, was sitting atop the coach and watched the people warily. The horses seemed restless as well, snorting and stamping in the soft earth.

She led the prisoner toward the carriage, giving the men a look of warning to make it clear she would tolerate no interference. She didn't expect they would impede her work; they were common laborers, not mercenaries. And though some of them were large and well-muscled from a lifetime of toil, they carried no weapons aside from shovels and hammers. Beyond that, under the law of the emperor, harming a lightwielder or interfering with their holy work was a transgression worthy of execution.

Still, they seemed reluctant to move away from the carriage, and Leorra decided to offer them an explanation before loading Leer into his mobile prison. This way, she hoped, there would be less chance of an unpleasant incident. She loosened her grip on the silk bindings and turned to face her prisoner, as well as the throng of men who had filed in behind him with bewildered expressions.

"This child of darkness stands accused of using his black magic to dominate the mind of an innocent woman and leading an expedition into territory decreed off limits by the emperor," she announced in a thunderous but formal tone. "He will be taken to the Snowdove Sanctuary to face judgment. I see no reason to punish anyone else. Take whatever this man has paid you and leave this land at once; do this, and I guarantee you will not be reprimanded."

Leorra was about to turn toward the carriage when she felt large, powerful hands grab both of her arms and pin them behind her back.

"What do you think you're doing?!" she demanded in surprise, seeing that two of the men had crept up behind her. "Do you know what they'll do to you for this?"

The realization struck her suddenly; she'd been such a fool. The magic on the young girl, Maria, had been nothing but a subterfuge. Of course, Leer was too talented a necromancer to allow his domination to become so twisted and corrupted, unless he had made it so intentionally. Such a vile spell had spilled out everywhere, making it impossible for her to sense that everyone in the camp had been trapped in a more subtle web of mind control. Leer hadn't paid the expedition to come to these dangerous lands with him; he'd simply forced them.

"Miss Leorra!" the driver called out. His lithe hands moved swiftly to the crossbow that was mounted next to him and slid an iron bolt onto the table.

"Go!" she yelled frantically. "Get Peril out of here!"

"The wearied left eye obscured in moonlit shadows," Leer began to chant as the driver feverishly cranked back the weapon's lever. "The exhausted right eye buried in sand. Now, sleep."

The driver instantly closed his eyes and slumped forward, the crossbow slipping from his hands and plummeting into the mud below. The incantation had thrust him into a dreamless haze from which he couldn't wake.

Leorra struggled violently against her captors; though she was much smaller than they were, the blood of Aura that coursed through her veins could give her immense strength when she called upon it. The two men fought to keep their footing, threatened with being thrown to the ground.

Leer raised his hands at the three of them, spreading his fingers wide and exposing his bare palms. Veins bulged out of the men's flesh, and one of their eyes washed over red from a ruptured blood vessel. Leorra could feel them growing unnaturally strong, fueled by the necromancer's dark power.

"You know, pouring this much of my energy into the living will quickly snuff out their lives," Leer said, showing her an overly pleasant smile. "If you continue to struggle like that, they'll die."

Leorra grew still and her subjugators moved in to place a firmer grip upon her. She didn't want the blood of these innocent men on her conscience, even if Leer was truly to blame; there had to be something she could do without sacrificing them. Leer blithely lifted his bound hands toward one of his thralls; the man quickly untied the necromancer and let the silken cords fall to the earth.

"Those are terribly uncomfortable," Leer complained, slowly rubbing his wrists. "Not very friendly, Leorra. Not at all."

"What are you doing, Leer?" she demanded bitterly. "Or do you even have a plan?"

"Are you trying to play mind games with me? You think maybe you can talk your way out of this? Or perhaps you're stalling for time?" Leer sneered at her. "You forget; *I'm* the master of mind games."

"For what you did to the girl, you would have merely been imprisoned," Leorra spoke in a low voice. "But if you lay a hand on me, every lightwielder in the empire will be after your head."

For the first time, Leer's expression grew truly severe.

"Do you know what it's like for someone like me to be imprisoned?" he hissed, stepping toward his captive, his face just inches from hers. "They can't keep me in a cage with the other prisoners; they don't dare expose guards or wardens to my power, or I might use my influence against them."

He took a step away from her and began to pace back and forth with his arms behind his back.

"The last time you took me to your sages for judgment, they threw me in a hole: a narrow shaft, so deep that the light of the sun could never reach me. Down in that low place I had only enough room to lie down on a straw mat. Twice a day they would lower a tray that bore tasteless meals and a pair of candles. But I had no use for the light; there was nothing to see in that place but the rough stone walls and my own filthy body.

"The candles piled up and I lived in darkness. I don't know who brought me my daily meals; they didn't dare speak to me. I would have loved to converse with them, with anyone; I didn't even want to use my magic.

"I was so painfully alone in that place; it was enough to drive a man mad.

"You look at me as if I really did lose my mind," he laughed softly at Leorra's pitying expression. "And maybe I did. When they finally freed me from that dark hell, I had no idea how long I'd been trapped there. Had it been months? Years? You know the answer, don't you, my friend?"

Leorra cleared her throat and answered in a sad voice, "You were imprisoned for twenty five days."

"How long do you think they would lock me up this time?" he whispered in her ear, leaning in close with an absurd smile on his face. "The laws of your empire mean nothing to me. And I will not return to that darkness ever again. I will sooner die."

He reached out and grabbed the hilt of Leorra's broadsword, unsheathing it with the satisfying ring of steel against leather. He took a step back and put the blade to her throat.

"Please, don't do this, Leer," she whispered desperately.

"Are you begging me for your life?" Leer asked with a grin and a curious cock of his head.

Leorra frowned and hissed back, "I'll beg nothing from you."

"Ah, that's much better," Leer said with a snort. "Fitting last words for a child of Aura."

When he cut her throat, he did it with a smile. Blood ran down her chest in a torrent. She tried to say something, or maybe just cry out, but instead of words leaving her mouth there was only more dark, red fluid. In an instant she was gone, and the two men who had been holding her released their grip, letting her lifeless body slump to the ground.

"No!" came a shrill cry from behind.

Startled, Leer spun around to see Peril standing next to the pavilion, her head peeking around the corner while her body stayed hidden. She wasn't in the carriage as he'd expected; instead, she had simply crept around to the other side of the tent to listen in on the conversation between her mentor and the charming necromancer.

Leer mused that she must have used every ounce of will to keep herself silent and hidden during his exchange with Leorra, only to let her emotions get the better of her now. Peril was thinking the same thing. She regretted crying out; she didn't even feel as if she'd taken any action. It was like she'd lost control of her voice as she witnessed the grisly scene. Now she stood there deathly still, utterly terrified, feeling as if all the blood had rushed to her head and threatened her with fainting.

"Please, don't look like that, my little dove," Leer tried to soothe her with his pleasant voice. "You're much prettier when you smile."

Peril took a step back, but couldn't look away from him.

He continued in a more remorseful tone, "I'm sorry. I didn't want this to happen, but she didn't leave me any choice. But I could never hurt you, Peril. I promise. Please, come here so we can talk."

She couldn't believe he was still able to smile. As frightened as she was, though, she couldn't help but feel sorry for him. The dichotomy of his actions and expressions proved he had to be completely dead on the inside, full of ice and stone.

But that didn't stop her from turning and running as fast as she could. She didn't know where she was going or how she could escape; her only thought was of getting away from that bloody scene as quickly as she could. Leer laughed as his thralls chased after her, thinking she wasn't quite as naïve as he'd thought.

The encampment wasn't large and it didn't offer Peril many places to hide. Even if she tried to duck inside one of the tents, with the men so close behind her, she would have only been trapping herself. So she just kept running into the open countryside toward a nearby copse of trees. There was no reason for it in her mind; it was simply the only feature she could make out in the barren land, and her terrified mind sent her running toward something. But she wasn't fast; she had shorter legs than her pursuers and her long dress only slowed her further. They were gaining quickly, and she was already huffing and out of breath, tears streaming down her face. She looked back once and saw they were almost upon her; she shut her eyes tight and ran with everything she had.

There was a whoosh like a heavy curtain blowing in the open wind, and she was certain they'd caught her. Her eyes snapped open. She saw she was in the trees now, and when she turned to look back at her pursuers she realized the chase had ended.

A young man, appearing only a few steps out of his boyhood, had intervened between Peril and her pursuers. His body was covered by a long, sackcloth cloak that ended in a high collar, rather than the hood typical of such a garment. The collar covered his face up to his eyes: eyes that were fiercer than any Peril had ever seen, like something that belonged to a monster. His hair was long and black, streaming down to his shoulders in wild tousles. He carried an enormous weapon slung across his back; it looked like a sword with a hilt as long as its blade. Around his neck he wore a large, copper emblem; the symbol of the lightwielders, the blazing sun.

Peril wasn't aware of any other children of Aura who had come to this off-limits area, but as her pursuers came to a halt, so did she. The man stood there, still as the trees around him. Leer, who had followed the party at a more leisurely pace, arrived a few moments later.

"Well, I wasn't expecting any more company today," he called out with a grin. "Might I know your name, stranger?"

The man shook his head and replied, "I'd heard a rumor someone was up here trying to dig up my father's old research. I guess I should have known it would be you, Leer."

The smile left Leer's face instantly and was replaced by a look of confusion and surprise.

"You can't be," he asserted.

The cloaked man reached up with his right hand and pulled down his high collar, revealing his face and the mark of the necromancer plainly under his right eye.

"This is *not* why I came here," he groaned with dismay.

"Koristad!?" Leer cried out in surprise.

3

(Twenty-two years before present)

A YOUNG KORISTAD, HAVING ONLY recently celebrated his tenth birthday, leaned over the stone ramparts of the Great Citadel and looked out at the snow covered mountains with wonder. From his home, these mountains were just a feature on the distant horizon, something that had always seemed so impossibly far away he could never reach them. It was hard to believe a five-day ride could bring him so close that he could almost reach out and touch their snowy cliffs.

The fortress had been constructed to seal off a pass through the mountains, the only safe traverse for a hundred miles. It stood tall and forbidding, like an unbreachable wall, or a dam meant to keep the wild barbarians from spilling out. Koristad didn't realize the snowline he was so wondrously admiring would have taken another day and a half to reach. Still, the scene was breathtaking looking out from atop the high walls, the mountains to the north stretching so high up into the sky they could have been the edge of the world.

"You know, I think your father told you he didn't want you to come out here by yourself."

Koristad was startled by the voice that came from behind him. He turned and saw a young man with dark hair, just a few years older than he was, looking at him with a friendly smile. Koristad must have had a concerned expression on his face, because the older boy added quickly, "Don't look at me like that; I'm not going to tell on you."

"Your name is Leer, isn't it?" Koristad asked nervously. "You're one of my father's students."

"That's right," he answered with a nod. "Leer Valcroix."

He stepped up to the battlements and stood next to Koristad. Gazing out at the vista, he looked like a man without a worry in the world.

"So, you're a necromancer?" Koristad asked, feeling a little intimidated by the older boy.

"I am," Leer replied with a grin, pulling his collar down and exposing the mark that was on his chest.

It was cold up in the mountains, cold enough that they could see their breath as they spoke. Leer quickly returned his collar with a shiver.

"I hope my mark appears soon," Koristad replied with a sigh.

"Well, it usually doesn't show up until you're a little older," Leer explained. "If it appears at all. Even though your father is a necromancer, there's no telling when it will manifest in a bloodline. In my family, I'm the only child of darkness I know of. I don't even know where my tainted blood came from."

Koristad frowned and said, "I want to be a necromancer more than I want anything."

Leer cocked his head at the younger boy, that perpetual smile imprinted across his face, and said, "I think your father would say the same thing. It seems strange...when the mark appeared on me, my family was heartbroken. My mother wouldn't even look at me. She wouldn't let me be in the same room with my younger brothers and sisters unless my father was there."

The younger boy cringed and offered his consolation, "I'm sorry. That sounds terrible."

A genuine look of surprise crossed Leer's face and he quickly added, "No, I didn't mean to sound like that. It doesn't bother me at all, so don't feel sorry for me. I think my father started looking for a way to get rid of me the day he found out, and that's how I ended up a student of Arach the Black Guardian. Honestly, I'm happier now than I ever could have been with them."

Koristad wasn't sure what to think; the thought of being taken away from his family and everything he'd known was terrifying and tragic. But for Leer the situation had been much different; looking up at the older boy and his cheery expression, Koristad guessed for him it must have felt liberating.

Leer leaned onto the battlements, cradling his head in his hands and looking out into the mountains. The sun was low in the sky to the west; soon night would fall and they would be able to see the innumerable flickering campfires of the barbarians on the mountain slopes. Leer had always found the sight reassuring and homey in a strange sort of way, as if they were all gathered around those campfires as families, singing and eating and laughing. But when they came down from their mountains, clad in bloody furs and with a murderous look in their eyes, it was hard to think of them as anything but monsters.

As if he was reading Leer's mind, Koristad asked, "Do the barbarians come down from there?"

"They do," Leer said with an unconcerned shrug. "They pour down from the wilds in hordes." He noticed a nervous expression cross his young companion's face, and he remembered this was Koristad's first time visiting the citadel, so he quickly added, "But you don't need to be worried. They won't attack while you're here, and even if they did, your father would deal with them. He always does."

"But it doesn't seem like there's anything to stop them," Koristad replied with a scowl, peering down over the ramparts.

Indeed, there were no impediments to slow the barbarians as they advanced through the pass; they could walk unhindered to the very wall on which the two boys stood.

Directly below was an enormous gate, more than sixty feet high, made of interlocking iron and stone. It was tremendously heavy and could only be operated by enormous clockwork mechanisms underneath the structure. Too demanding for any man, it was constructed to be pulled by beasts of burden. No one was certain if the mechanisms would still work; the gate hadn't been opened in over thirty years. Not since an expedition of soldiers and explorers had ventured north to chart the unexplored lands, and never returned. If one wanted to exit to the north side of the citadel, the only way was through smaller iron doors on either side of the gate, so deftly camouflaged that even the keenest eyes couldn't spot them until they were almost within arm's reach. And, even if one did discover them, they were so thick and heavy that they were nearly unbreachable; breaking through the stone walls would have been easier.

The citadel itself was built around this gate, the broad, stone walls stretching in either direction until they came in contact with the rocky walls of the mountains themselves. There were only two watchtowers along the entire length, but they soared high into the mountains, allowing anyone inside to see for miles in every direction.

Koristad's mother had told him stories about his father, of how he'd become a hero during the western rebellion, and how he was the most powerful child of darkness who had ever lived. But he still found it hard to imagine him standing alone against a horde of vicious barbarians.

"There's plenty to stop them," Leer reassured. "Take a look at the field below us."

Koristad peered down, but the ground was nearly one hundred feet below and it was hard to make out any clear details.

"It looks like a paved courtyard. There's a lot of litter. White stones, I think."

"They're not stones," Leer explained. "We call that the Field of Bones. You can't see it, but on the floor there's an ensorcelled diagram your father inscribed. It prevents the souls of the dead from finding peace and passing on, trapping them in the world of the living. Your father can command those souls to return to their remains and fight once again."

Leer turned away from the field and pointed to the tower on his left, "Both of the towers employ a similar mechanism; though they each hold only a single wraith, a ghost of a watchman who died long ago. They look out upon the mountains, waiting for any sign that the barbarians are advancing. They never sleep, they never eat, and they never look away. And the instant they spy anything, your father is aware."

Koristad looked up at the towers with a puzzled expression; he'd wondered why there were no watchers set in them. The windows were dark, but as he looked on he thought he could see movement inside.

"Did you see something?" Leer asked, reading his young friend's expression.

"I'm not sure," Koristad answered, perplexed. "I thought I saw something move."

Leer nodded in approval, "I'm impressed; if you can see that much, I'm certain the mark will appear on you soon. The children of darkness can see the dead just as clearly as we see the living. Sometimes it's hard to tell the difference; a spirit appears as it did in life, so long as it can remember. The watchmen, however, they've been dead for so long, they can't even remember what it *was* to be alive."

"It's amazing," Koristad said in awe. "I can't believe my father could do something like this."

Leer nodded in agreement, "This citadel was once garrisoned by several hundred soldiers, and they could barely hold the line. Your father does so almost singlehandedly; he is truly deserving of the title 'The Black Guardian'."

A sudden, chill wind blew in from the mountains and both of the young men shivered.

"It'll be night soon," Leer announced. "It gets bitterly cold here after the sun sets, even more so than in the foothills. We should head inside."

As the two of them walked along the parapet, Leer leaned in close and said in a low voice, "You know, there are no other children of darkness who can perform feats of magic like your father. Some say he has all of the secrets of necromancy hidden away someplace where no one else can find them."

"That's not true," Koristad protested, but then he reflected on the fact that he'd hardly seen his father over these last few years. Arach's time was spent at the citadel, but he preferred to keep his family hidden away from harm; Leer probably knew Koristad's father better than he did. "Is it?"

Leer shrugged, "I don't know about all the secrets of necromancy but, shortly after I began my apprenticeship, he took me to a hidden vault somewhere near Ravensweald. He picked out a few volumes to help me with my studies. But there were stacks of books, diagrams, and research everywhere; complex formulae I still can't understand."

"I didn't realize there was such a place," Koristad said with a frown. "I wish I could see it."

"Your father told me you were a regular prodigy with arcane script. He said you could digest and recite the incantations faster than any student he'd ever taught, though you don't yet have the blood to give them form. I wonder...," Leer trailed off and appeared to be contemplating something.

Growing impatient, Koristad said, "You wonder what?"

"You live in Ravensweald, don't you?" Leer asked at last.

Koristad answered with a nod.

"I wonder if we could find that vault between the two of us. I don't know the area very well, but I do know what the entrance looked like."

"I don't know…," Koristad said uneasily. "We could just ask my father to take us there."

"That's true," Leer said. "If you asked for both of us, I'm certain he'd agree. But I'm not really sure if I should have told you about it in the first place. He might be angry with me if he finds out."

Koristad nodded in agreement; he certainly didn't want to cause his new friend any trouble.

Leer added, "Besides, if he was there, he'd supervise what we could and couldn't look at. Wouldn't you want to look through whatever you wanted, without reservations?"

"Of course!" Koristad declared.

Most children grew up playing with toys and always wanted to have a new doll or wooden soldier to entertain them. But for Koristad, who dreamt every night and fantasized every day about how he might one day be a powerful necromancer like his father, nothing was more enjoyable than perusing the esoteric scripts written by the children of darkness. Arach had only allowed his son small tastes of the art, bits and pieces here and there to appease the eager child. But he'd never allowed Koristad to explore at his own discretion.

"Then why don't we help each other?" Leer proposed with a smirk. "We'll have a lot of fun together and, if we keep it a secret, no one will ever know."

Deep down, Koristad knew it was a bad idea, but he hadn't the wisdom to obey his own intuition.

"Okay!" he exclaimed in vehement agreement.

4

"I WAS TOLD YOU WERE killed when the Great Citadel fell!" Leer exclaimed with excitement. "But here you are, and you look like you haven't grown up nearly as much as you should have. I have many things I want to ask you about, but we'll have to catch up later. First, the business at hand; I have to do something about this annoying lightwielder."

"I won't let you do that," Koristad growled in reply.

Leer shrank back a step, but managed to keep his smile, "I see; that emblem you wear is the sun symbol of the children of Aura. It's more than just an ornament."

"That's right, Leer," Koristad said slowly, emphasizing every word. "It is."

"I never thought I'd see the day that the son of Arach Altessor would allow himself to be made a dog of the lightwielders," was Leer's retort. "I wonder what your father would think."

"I could say the same about you."

"I'd prefer if this didn't come to violence between us, Koristad. Why don't we look for your father's vault again, like old times?"

"I'm not here for my father's old notes," Koristad threw his cloak over his shoulder with a sweep of his arm and placed his hand on the haft of his weapon. "But I didn't come here for you, either. Just walk away and I'll try to forget I ever saw you."

"That is not a request I can honor."

Peril, who had remained silent all this time, cried out, "He killed my mentor! The lightwielder Leorra Natarra!"

Koristad looked at her in surprise, as if he'd forgotten she was behind him. "He wants to get rid of me so I won't tell anyone!"

He let out a long, heavy sigh.

"I won't ask if that's true or not," he addressed Leer. "I would take her word over yours, anyway."

"That hurts, my friend," Leer mocked, placing his hand over his heart and chuckling.

"You'll be through laughing soon enough."

Koristad drew the halberd from his back, the shine of the sanctified steel flashing across the faces of Leer's nearby thralls.

"That's an impressive weapon," Leer commented, taking another step back. "Are you sure a child like you can wield something of that size?"

"You'll know in an instant."

"Or maybe I should ask if you *want* to wield it against us," Leer added with a smirk. "These are innocent people under my power. Would you cut them down just to get to me?"

Koristad slowly looked over the faces of the men who stood before him, a wall of flesh between their master and his blade. Their expressions betrayed no emotion, but he thought he could see a hint of fear and pain in their eyes. They were fully aware they were being controlled, but were like passengers in their own bodies, despising Leer for his enslavement but unable to disobey his commands.

They didn't carry any real weapons; though a shovel or pickaxe could inflict a fatal wound, they were like toys next to Koristad's halberd. Even outnumbering him seven to one, they would have fled the better armed opponent if they had the will to do so.

"I hate to do this, my friend," Leer sneered at him. "If you change your mind, you're welcome to help me search for your father's vault. As a ghost, of course."

One of the men lunged at Koristad, as if he'd been prodded with a hot poker, trying to drive the wide blade of a shovel into his gut. But the worker lost his footing and stumbled to the ground as Koristad effortlessly dodged to one side, raising his weapon defensively as the other men approached. They fanned out around him, blocking any route of escape.

Peril had recoiled deeper into the copse as the enemies approached, but continued to watch the melee unfold while peering around a tree. Her rescuer stood against every advance and pushed back in exchange, but it was clear he was fighting a defensive battle. The thralls had a few bruises on them from being thrown to the ground, but were otherwise unharmed. Peril knew what he was doing; trying to think of a way to end their offensive without killing them, just as Leorra had.

"You can't fight them like that," she pleaded. "Holding back is what cost my mentor her life!"

She didn't think he would hear her over the clamor of the battle, but he shouted out his reply, "Then she died with no regrets. Isn't that the way of a child of Aura?"

His words were heavy and forced; it seemed he was already growing weary trying to fight so many foes with such a massive instrument.

"Yes, he's quite right."

Peril gasped in fright as Leer placed the broad side of his stolen weapon across her chest. She'd been so focused on the clash between her rescuer and the laborers she'd disregarded the errant necromancer. Now he was standing to her left, having picked his way around the skirmish, facing Koristad and his attackers with that unsettling smile. Peril couldn't help but question if she was really as empty-headed as Leorra had always alleged.

Leer gave no sign that he intended to harm her, but he gibed at Koristad, "You're proving to be quite a disappointment. I assumed you would try to wrestle for control of their minds…have you forgotten all of those incantations we learned? Or do you simply realize you could never beat me at my own game?"

The laborers took a few steps back from their adversary as their master spoke, but continued circling him, ensuring he couldn't escape.

"I don't need magic to deal with someone like you," Koristad said. "You're just a second rate necromancer. Dominating the minds of the weak is your only trick; you don't even have the talent to call out the feeblest of ghosts, or to animate a corpse larger than a housecat."

Peril was surprised her captor didn't take offense at the insult; instead he sniggered at his enemy and said, "What can I say? I've no interest in pursuing a school of arcana I've no capacity for. But you'll find my other skills will more than compensate…I think maybe I've been making this too easy for you."

He lifted his left hand, spreading his fingers and showing his palm much as he had when Leorra had tried to struggle against her subjugators. Koristad heard a deep, gurgling growl coming from the men around him as the dark magic poured into their bodies. One of the men, who looked a bit older than the others, almost instantly collapsed to the ground and began retching and shaking. But even with their numbers reduced to six, Koristad knew they were much more dangerous than before.

One of them swung a pickaxe at Koristad in a powerful, overhead arc. The proxy lightwielder was barely able to stop the attack with the haft of his weapon, his feet sliding backward half a foot in the soft, slippery earth. He could see the veins bulging in the man's forehead as he tried to overwhelm him with his imbued strength, and the others were rushing in to finish off their enemy while he was engaged. Koristad brought the haft of his weapon around faster than his attacker was prepared for, and he stumbled forward into two of the others. A broad, whistling swing struck one more with the blunted back side of the halberd's blade, sending him sprawling into the dirt and knocking two of his teeth into the air.

The air vibrated with the hum of the enormous weapon as Koristad spun it over his head in a wide circle, trying to keep the men at bay. He was surprised to see the man he'd struck was able to struggle to his feet and rejoin his comrades, and even the man who had been overwhelmed by the force of the evil magic was now up again and ready to fight.

"Still trying to buy time, Koristad?" Leer said with a disapproving shake of his head. "Go ahead and kill them, if you can. Prolonging this battle will only lead to their demise, anyway. Unlike you, I have no qualms about killing, and I'll pour my power into them until you, or they, are dead."

Without warning, three of the men lunged in unison; the force of the blow was so great that the crash of the weapons echoed across the countryside. Koristad stumbled back, toward Leer and Peril, and fell to one knee. They didn't hesitate to take advantage of his vulnerability. One of them swung a shovel at his face, forcing him to fall back and roll away to avoid being stuck.

Leer could see Koristad was drawing closer to his position but, at this range, he wasn't any sort of threat. Still, he put his sword to Peril's throat as a sign of warning.

The girl cried out in fear, pushing the necromancer's arm away as she stumbled to the ground. It was a bold move, and not a reaction Leer had expected, but he needed to keep her as a hostage to ensure his safety. He turned toward her and pointed the blade at her face menacingly, but the sword unexpectedly fell from his hand.

No, that wasn't quite right. His hand fell with the blade, along with half of his arm. Leer's eyes grew wide as he perceived Koristad standing next to him, the bloodied blade of his halberd buried in the ground at his feet by the power of his swing.

"But, you couldn't do anything to me from that far away...," he protested feebly, not yet able to feel the pain of his wound, but knowing it was on its way.

"I knew if I held back you'd leave me an opening," Koristad whispered, so quiet only the two of them could hear. "Now see if you can keep your concentration through the agony."

Leer put a death grip on the stump of his right arm and fell to his knees with a sharp intake of breath. That smile of his was finally gone, replaced by an expression of anguish and panic. He bit down on his bottom lip so hard that blood trickled down his chin, but he wouldn't allow himself to cry out. Not in front of his enemies.

The necromancer could no longer maintain control over his thralls, and once they were released they staggered to the ground almost instantly. The toll on their bodies had been immense, like a two-day forced march with neither food nor water. They panted and groaned, their muscles throbbing.

Peril scrambled to her feet, her white dress now spattered with red blood. She looked up at Koristad like a child who had just been woken from a dream. He ripped the blade of his weapon from the soft earth and took a step back as Leer, overcome by the loss of blood, fell to the ground face-first. He made no attempt to stop himself. Peril looked down on him with pity; without aid, he would bleed out in a matter of minutes.

She dropped down to one knee before him, not exactly sure what she was doing, but obeying an undeniable instinct. She rolled him onto his back with a grunt and saw his eyes were still half open, but there was no awareness behind them. Cringing, she took the stump of his right arm into her hands and closed her eyes. There was no way to reattach his limb, but she thought the powers granted to her by Aura, as meager as they were, might be enough to save him before his life faded away.

She began to whisper a prayer, anticipating that the young man with the halberd would interrupt her before she could do anything. But Koristad looked down at the two of them with a blank expression and said nothing. Soon the grievous wound began to seal, and the bleeding slowed.

One of the laborers, lurching unsteadily to his feet, pleaded, "What are you doing? Let that monster die, it's all he deserves!"

Another one added, "He can't be allowed to live! What if he tries to influence us again?"

Those two, who appeared to be the only ones in fit enough condition to move, began to hobble toward the young lightwielder, intent on interrupting her work. But Koristad intervened, stepping between Peril and the men. They stopped in their tracks and looked at him with puzzled expressions.

"Why don't you stop her?" one asked desperately. "You know how dangerous he is!"

"A necromancer can't dominate anyone unless that person can either hear his voice or see his eyes," Koristad asserted with a grimace. "He will be gagged and blindfolded, and then taken to a sanctuary for judgment." Then he added, for good measure, "You should know it's a crime to interfere with the work of a lightwielder."

The men looked at one another, then down at the ground and grumbled, but ceased their attempt at intervention.

After a few minutes the bleeding had stopped entirely and, though Leer looked as pale as death, he was still alive. His breathing was heavy and labored and his eyes were shut tight; he gave no indication he would be waking anytime soon.

"I trust you have materials to bind him with?" Koristad asked Peril. "I assume you came here for him." Peril looked weary from her effort; never before had she attempted to repair such severe damage.

"Y-yes," she stammered out. "There should be something in the carriage, back at the camp."

Koristad threw Leer over his shoulder with an implausibly strong motion and ordered, "Lead the way."

Peril dutifully turned toward the camp and took a few steps, but then stopped, suddenly thinking of something.

"What is it?" Koristad demanded.

"Will you bring the sword he had?" she asked. "It was my mentor's, and she should be buried with it."

"What?" Koristad questioned incredulously. "Why are you asking me? If you want it, go get it. I'm already carrying *your* captive."

"But...," she whimpered and began to sulk.

"But what?" he insisted.

She couldn't look him in the eyes, so she turned her face to the side and whimpered, "His *hand* is still on it!"

Koristad looked down at the small girl for a moment, absolutely stunned. Then, with a groan and a shake of his head, he marched over to the severed arm, pried open its fingers, and took the weapon. The limb itself was left for the scavengers.

"Now go," he ordered. "And the rest of you had better come with us."

The men did their best to hobble after them as they made their way back. Peril was surprised; when she was running away it seemed as though she wasn't covering any ground at all, but in reality she'd gone quite a long way.

She was relieved upon their return to see that Leorra's corpse had been covered with a wide sheet of cloth, now discolored with blood. The young girl who Leer had domineered, Maria, was sitting on the ground nearby, her arms wrapped around her knees. She was rocking back and forth, shaking and sobbing like a baby. Certainly her experience had damaged her both physically and emotionally.

Peril tried not to look at the covered body as she climbed into the carriage, the driver still slumped over in the coach box. The horses were restless, frightened by the smell of blood, and they likely would have fled if they hadn't been wearing blinders. Koristad ducked into the dark confines behind Peril, and the men who followed plopped down on the ground outside, some of them trying to comfort the crying young girl.

Koristad glanced around his surroundings of soft, cushioned benches and artistically carved woodwork and snorted. The two lightwielders certainly hadn't been roughing it during their journey.

"I thought lightwielders took vows of poverty," he grumbled.

"We do!" Peril said. "This carriage doesn't belong to us; it belongs to the Snowdove Sanctuary."

She opened the door that lead to the rear compartment of the coach. Inside it was pitch black. There were no windows that opened to the outside, only the slim, barred opening in the front.

Koristad unceremoniously dropped Leer to the ground while Peril sorted through the carriage's supplies. Finally finding what she'd sought, she produced a peculiar looking black mask with thick patches over the eyes and leather buckles in the back. It had been designed by the lightwielders specifically to thwart the magic of a necromancer. They forced it over the unconscious man's face and strapped it on tight, and also decided to take the precaution of binding his arms to his sides. They had to be cautious not to disturb the severed stump of his arm. Though it had been tended to with Aura's blessing, the wound was grievously severe, and they knew it could easily begin bleeding again. They then placed him in his cell and, as they stepped out, Koristad slammed the door behind them.

"Good riddance," he spat as he fixed the nearby wooden plank across the door. "It's better than he deserves."

Peril nodded slowly in agreement, though she didn't feel the spite toward the necromancer that Koristad plainly expressed. She certainly had every reason to hate him after what he'd done, but after listening to his story of how he'd been locked away, she felt sorry for him more than anything.

"I didn't think you would let me save him."

Koristad looked surprised as he turned toward her.

"Of course I did," he replied. "I've known Leer since I was just a kid. Maybe he is a monster now, and maybe he will have to die, but I wouldn't want his death on my hands. I'm glad you did what you did."

"He'll certainly be executed when he's taken for judgment," she said sadly, staring at the locked door. There was a heavy silence between them.

"I don't care," Koristad said at last, anger clear in his tone.

He immediately turned and left the dim confines.

As he stepped out, the gathered mass looked at him with fear and distrust clear in their eyes. Even the horses were plainly upset by his presence, whinnying and stamping their hooves. He stepped down to the wet grass and pulled his cloak around him, lifting up the high collar to hide the mark on his face.

"Rest here and regain your strength," he ordered in a harsh voice. "I'm traveling with a lightwielder who should be arriving before the day's end. He will guide you back to safety."

That was all he had to say before he began walking down the old road to the north. He didn't feel welcome among these people; even after what he'd done for them, they still hated and feared him for what he was.

As he made his way down the road, he saw the clouds above were beginning to part, sending streams of bright sunlight down to the earth. He then heard hurried footsteps coming from behind.

"Wait!" Peril cried, running to catch up with him. "Where are you going?"

"You changed your clothes," he said, appearing only mildly interested.

She had placed a tan hood over her blonde hair, and wore a lacey bodice with a loose fitting skirt; high, black boots; and a light pack strapped to her back. She was no longer wearing the medallion that showed she was a lightwielder, having left it in the carriage in her haste. Koristad thought these may have been her "traveling clothes;" certainly more modest than the gown she had been wearing, but he still didn't think it looked like the kind of garment that should be worn outside in the elements.

"Of course I did," she answered with a frown. "There was blood on my dress. But you left so suddenly…where are you going?"

"I already said I didn't come this far north for Leer or any of this," he dismissively waved his hand at the camp and continued walking at a fast pace.

Peril hurried to keep up.

"You know…you were so brave when you jumped in front of those men to save me," she gushed. "You were like an angel."

Koristad continued moving and gave no sign that he intended to reply.

Unperturbed, Peril went on, "I really didn't think I was going to make it. I'm grateful you showed up when you did."

Still, Koristad said nothing. Peril struggled to keep up with his long stride with her shorter legs.

"Why are you following me?" he demanded at last.

"Well, I…," she mumbled, unsure of herself.

"Go back to the camp and wait with the others," he ordered callously.

Peril stopped in her tracks and watched him walk away with eyes that grew wet with tears, but Koristad continued without a backwards glance.

Chapter Three

THE ABLE AND THE UNCLEAN

The only conceivable end of human violence is the end of human nature.

1

THE ROAD THAT LED from the encampment wound across the bleak countryside until it reached a wide ravine. It had once been circumvented by a picturesque bridge built of gray stone, but years of disrepair had taken its toll on the masonry; the barbarians bore only animosity for the craftwork of the men of the south, and it had been a victim of cruel vandalism. Now all that remained were abutments at either end, their magnificence and grandeur having long since cascaded into the murky waters far below.

The only crossing that remained was a narrow bridge of wooden planks and rope, shoddily constructed by the barbarians. It wasn't sturdy enough to support a horse, nor was it wide enough to accommodate a carriage. If one were to travel this far north with either, they would be forced to circumnavigate the obstruction, a detour that would require several days and a fording of the river.

Beyond the ravine, the remains of Ravensweald could be seen, though the only structure that still stood after so many years was the town hall. Koristad avoided that place, trying not to even look at it. On the other side of town, in a shallow valley, he found what he'd come for. Executor Mourne's directions had been surprisingly accurate after all these years.

He gazed across a field of wooden markers, the graves of all the people who Gregan and his troupe had lain to rest. There were no names, no remembrances, nothing to tell one from another. There had been many bodies to inter, and the company stayed no longer than it took for their commander to recover after his unfortunate dismemberment. Koristad stood at the head of the mass, his head bowed in a sad silence.

He wished the sky was still as dreary and overcast as it had been at the encampment. The sun was bright in the sky now, and he loathed how it contrasted with his mood. He wanted to cry, but there were no tears. He knew one of these graves belonged to his mother, Charisse Altessor, but all he could offer her was silence.

"Thinking of bringing her back?"

The words issued from the thin air in a hollow, disembodied voice that carried with it the chill of death. The question was dry and emotionless. The source faded into view not far from Koristad, an ever-shifting patch of darkness that could sometimes appear almost human, but at other times was nothing more than a wisp of smoke. The only constant about it were its eyes: large, glowing orbs that stared out into the world unblinkingly. It was a creature trapped between the world of the living and the dead, and as such could only be seen by the children of darkness.

"Of course not, Wraith," Koristad whispered, displeasure at the interruption clear in his voice. "Even if I granted her undeath with my magic, it wouldn't be my mother. And I'm not a necromancer anymore, besides."

"But you were thinking something like that," the empty voice insisted. "I can tell."

Koristad sighed, thinking that Wraith only showed up when it wasn't wanted.

"I guess I was hoping she might still be here. I should be happy; her spirit is gone, and that means she was able to find peace after death. But I would have liked to have seen her one more time."

"The living make no sense at all."

"You may be right," Koristad sighed. "I'd like to be left alone for awhile."

In an instant Wraith faded from sight, into the nether from whence it came. Koristad bowed his head in silence once again, not wanting to move from that spot. He'd traveled so far to find this place. He'd thought if he came here to mourn her passing it would bring him some kind of peace. It hadn't. It had only dredged up painfully vivid memories of that day, and of his life before, like salt on an open wound.

"Mother..." he whispered in a voice so quiet only he and the dead could hear, "I hope you've found father on the other side. I hope you're happy. I miss you both so much. I'm sorry I wasn't strong enough to save you...I'm certain if father would have been there, he could have protected us both. I promise you that I *will* become stronger. I'll become strong so you and father can both be proud of me. And I give you my word that, when I have the strength, I'll put an end to the monster that cost both of you your lives."

That was all he could think to say, but still there were no tears. His mind wandered north, to the Great Citadel, the stolen abode of the Vampire King. He knew he could be at the foot of the structure in just a few short days, though he wondered what sort of attention he might draw approaching so near. He sighed and told himself this wasn't the time; when his debt to Executor Mourne was repaid, he would walk this road again, perhaps for the last time.

"Someone has followed you," the disembodied voice materialized again. "The girl who you met at the camp."

"I know," Koristad answered. "Why do you think I moved so slowly coming here?"

"You wanted her to follow you?"

Koristad snorted and spat out defensively, "Of course not. But I couldn't just leave her behind. This territory is treacherous; she would never survive out here alone."

"I don't understand," Wraith said. "You owe her nothing."

Koristad shook his head at the apparition and said, "I guess it's just a consequence of being alive."

"I'm inclined to disagree."

Koristad turned from the graves and faced the edge of the valley, where a handful of untamed shrubs were cradled in a patch of tall wildflowers.

"Skulking about like this isn't very becoming of a child of Aura," he called. "Now come out."

For a moment nothing happened; Peril hoped if she was quiet and still enough then he might decide he was mistaken. But, when it became clear he wasn't going to be deceived, she stood up from behind one of the bushes.

"How did you know I was there?" she asked, feeling embarrassed and averting her eyes.

"You're bad at shadowing," Koristad said bluntly. "Now come down here."

He pointed to the ground at his feet with a stern expression. Blushing and feeling very foolish, Peril picked her way down the uneven terrain until she was standing before the necromancer. She looked down at the ground, not wanting to meet his gaze, and looked much like a child who had been caught misbehaving by her parents and was about to be scolded.

"I hope you know how dangerous it is here," Koristad said, and Peril was surprised to sense what she thought was concern in his voice. "If you're going to be out here, you'll have to stay close to me."

Peril nodded cautiously and asked, "Where are we going?"

Koristad began walking at a fast pace; she rushed to catch up.

"I'm taking you back to the camp, where you should have stayed in the first place," Koristad replied. He added in an exasperated tone, "That moronic lightwielder will probably be there by now. That's great. Utterly fantastic."

"The traveling companion you mentioned?" she asked in a soft voice. "You don't seem to have a very high opinion of him."

Koristad's pace didn't slow and he continued traveling in silence.

When Peril decided he wasn't going to reply, he grumbled, "I don't need a self righteous, paladin wannabe looking over my shoulder."

"The executor appointed him to be your mentor?"

"Of course not," Koristad snapped at her. "I don't need a mentor. You know I'm not a lightwielder. Or have you already forgotten about the mark on my face?"

"No, I haven't!" she fired back at him. "You don't always have to be so mean to me, you know! I only wanted to know who your companion was, and why he didn't come to the encampment with you."

Koristad gave no hint of an apology for his rudeness, which came as no surprise to the young girl.

"My companion was ordered to stay with me by Executor Mourne of the Sunrise Sanctuary, to lend me credibility as one of his agents and, I presume, to prevent me from going rogue. He didn't want the job, and I didn't want him with me. It was as simple as that."

"So you didn't get along?"

"You might say," Koristad said with a chuckle. "All he wanted to do was preach to me about his faith. Aura did this and Aura said that, it was enough to make me puke. So, when I got sick of it, I left him behind."

"He could get in trouble for that, you know," Peril cautioned.

"That doesn't bother me," Koristad stated heartlessly. "I hope they forbid him from speaking. Anything would be better than hearing him sermonize."

"Don't you believe in Aura?" Peril asked, a puzzled and almost disbelieving look on her face.

Koristad only shrugged, not even looking in her direction.

"But what about the magic of the lightwielders that came from Aura sharing her blood with our ancestors? Even the mages received their powers from the archangels who tried to imitate her gift."

"You know," Koristad spoke slowly, making sure his point would get across, "The last person who said that to me, I left behind in the wilderness."

Peril took his hint and grew silent. The two of them had already covered quite a bit of ground and were coming upon the ravine, but as they drew close to the shoddy rope bridge, Peril's gait slowed to a stop.

"What's the matter?" Koristad demanded. Peril looked self-conscious, as if she didn't want to answer the question.

"That bridge isn't safe," she answered timidly. "I'm scared to cross it."

"What do you mean? You came across this bridge on your way here."

"That's how I know it isn't safe!" she blurted out. "I didn't think I was going to make it before. Half way across I looked down; I got dizzy and almost fell over the edge!"

She flinched when Koristad raised his arm; she wasn't expecting any kind gestures from him. But he merely held his hand in front of her, palm up.

"Take my hand," he said in what may have passed for a compassionate tone. "I promise I won't let you fall."

She was shaking as she reached out to him, but she was surprised at how much safer she felt when she placed her small hand into his. His grip was firm and unwavering, like a mountain caught in the gale of her turbulent emotions. After what had happened to Leorra, Peril had felt lost and alone in the world; her heart ached at the loss of her friend and mentor. But Koristad's resolute strength seemed to pour into her, giving her the courage to move forward. Her heart was pounding in her chest, but she wasn't certain if it was because of the terrifying drop below or from the young man's touch. She didn't even notice when he began to lead her forward.

Before she knew it, they were almost halfway across the bridge, but once again, she made the mistake of looking down. Her eyes grew wide; it seemed as if the ground was rushing up at her. She reached out and gripped Koristad's fingers with her other hand, holding on tight, but he hardly seemed to notice. The bridge swayed back and forth as they crossed, creaking under their weight and threatening that it could give out at any moment.

They were nearing the far end when Koristad came to a sudden halt. At first Peril, who had been too overwhelmed by the swaying bridge and the river below to notice much of anything, didn't know why. When she looked to the other side of the ravine the cause became instantly clear. There were three figures on the far side; tall, hulking men clad in furs and holding bare weapons at their sides.

"Barbarians," she whimpered. "What do we do?"

"If we go to the other side it's bound to end in violence," Koristad thought out loud. "But if we turn back the way we came, they might just decide to cut the bridge and let us fall."

"Maybe if we just give them whatever they want, they'll let us pass," she said hopefully.

"They're not bandits," he said. "If they want something, they'll just take it off our bodies." Peril looked up at him, desperately hoping for some hint of reassurance. "When we get to the other side, I want you to stay behind me. I won't let any of them get to you."

"O-okay...," she stammered.

Koristad drew himself up as tall as he could, but as they drew closer to their obstructers he realized he would have to stand on Peril's shoulders to not be dwarfed by the massive brutes. Two of them stood close to the bridge, ready to intercept them. They were both young, with sparse facial hair that hadn't yet filled out their faces. They wore their hair long and unkempt, and their clothes were poorly put together and unmaintained. They were thickly built, bristling with heavy muscle, the same as every barbarian Koristad had ever seen. The mountains were a cold and rocky wasteland; he couldn't imagine what they ate to grow so big.

One of them hefted a large, single bladed axe over his shoulder and spoke in a voice that was thick with the barbaric accent; a rough growling that sounded almost animal, "It's foolish to travel here with only two. We don't expect to see the southmen in our lands with fewer than ten."

"They are foolish," the other agreed, wielding a pair of short clubs, each wrapped with two iron rings. "Or maybe they wish for death? I will gladly grant *that* wish."

He took a step toward them and Koristad's hand shot to the haft of his weapon, but before the barbarian could act on his aggression, the other grabbed him by the shoulder.

"You killed the last ones," he snarled. "These are mine."

"That was days ago," the other argued. "It doesn't count."

The first barbarian pulled hard on the other's shoulder, spinning him around, and raged, "I said these are mine!"

"The two of you can feel free to kill each other," Koristad interjected glibly. "Then I'll be on my way."

They both turned to face him with wrath in their eyes. Koristad knew his mouth had a way of getting him into trouble, and this would have been an excellent time to practice keeping it shut. The furious looks from the two brutes were intimidating, but it was even more frightening a moment later when one of them began to smile; a wicked, murderous smile.

"We know how to settle this," the barbarian with the clubs said. "We both try to kill him, and let our strength decide who takes the glory."

With no more warning, he lunged forward, swinging both clubs in a powerful, inward arc. Koristad, who hadn't yet drawn his weapon, leapt out of striking distance, holding up his left arm to protect Peril. The clubs came together where he'd been standing, slamming into each other with a force that would have turned his bones into powder.

The second barbarian was quick to continue the offensive, swinging his axe in a broad, powerful arc at Koristad's chest. With inhuman ease, like a flick of his wrist, Koristad's halberd was drawn, and it stopped the mighty swing like a stone wall. Peril backed as far away from the three of them as she could, scooting out along the edge of the ravine. She was too frightened, however, to wander too far. The third barbarian, who had yet to take part in the melee, was still out there.

Her eyes darted back and forth, and she spotted him lounging on a small boulder a short distance off the path. His expression was calm, showing no concern at all for the safety of the two who were fighting. He leaned back, watching the unfolding violence with a jaded sort of disinterest.

He was big, even for a barbarian. The first thing Peril noticed about him wasn't his face, but a line of three terrible scars that ran from his shoulder, down his chest, and continued to his waistline. Like most of his kind, his body was covered in scars from constant fighting, but these were so severe and grievous she couldn't believe the wound hadn't killed him on the spot. He was older than the other two, with a long, shaggy beard and thick body hair. He was also better clothed and groomed, dressed in fine wolf hides and with clean hair, though it was still long and messy.

Peril's attention turned back to the fighting when she heard a loud grunt, followed by the sound of someone retching. The club wielding barbarian was doubled over on the ground, having taken a severe blow to the gut that had cost him his lunch. The one with the axe howled with rage and charged at Koristad, but the necromancer batted away the incoming strikes with his own. Finally catching the barbarian's axe just under the blade, with a hard upward swing, he pulled the weapon out of the barbarian's hands and sent it spinning into the air.

Peril could hardly believe how fast her protector could move with such an enormous weapon. He certainly hadn't been lying when he told Leer he'd been holding back. She realized that, if it wasn't for her, he could have easily evaded the three attackers and darted into the wilderness. Luckily, it appeared he had defeated his opponents anyway.

The now unarmed barbarian glared at him uncertainly, his arms spread wide, unsure if his opponent would cut him down before he could retrieve his axe. The other still hadn't risen to his feet and was clutching his chest and coughing like he couldn't breathe. The blow may have even broken his ribs.

Koristad held his weapon high, his breathing rough and sweat on his brow, ready to strike. But he couldn't let the blade fall. He knew with all certainty that, given the chance, either of these two men would take his life without a thought. But he couldn't bring himself to use his weapon like an executioner against an unarmed foe.

The barbarian and Koristad both opened their eyes wide in shock as a long blade erupted through the defeated man's chest, hot blood running in a torrent from the gaping wound. The sight had faded from his eyes before the blade was withdrawn. He fell to the ground in a heap, revealing the killer standing behind him. It was the third barbarian, an enormous sword in his right hand and a long punching weapon in his left. He looked down at the bloodied corpse in disgust.

"What are you trying to...," Koristad began to ask, but the ruthless man ignored him and stormed toward the other injured warrior.

"Stop!" Koristad shouted, too stunned by this strange development to move.

The man with the clubs tried hard to rise to his feet, but he staggered and fell to all fours. The older barbarian planted a fierce kick in the man's side and, if his ribs hadn't been broken before, the sharp crack made it clear they were now. He tumbled across the ground toward the ravine. As he spilled over the edge he reached out with his right arm, but there was nothing he could hold on to, and he fell with a cry.

"Why...," Koristad barely finished that one word before the barbarian came at him with an underhanded swing so powerful that parrying it made his hands throb.

"They were nothing," he snarled. "Just pieces of trash that didn't even have names."

"That's cruel," Koristad protested through clenched teeth as the barbarian pushed him back, his feet digging tracks into the earth. "Maybe you didn't bother to learn them, but they had names. They were people, just like you or I."

With a mighty shove the barbarian sent Koristad to the ground, landing on his back with a grunt.

"No, southman," the barbarian said with a shake of his head as Koristad sprung to his feet. "Our people aren't like yours. You give names to children when they're born. For us, a name is much more; it's something you must earn through the glory of battle. Those without names are like animals; if I want to kill them, then I do so. No one complains when a hunter slaughters a deer, do they?"

"So, you killed them because they were weak?" Koristad asked, breathing heavily and holding his weapon defensively as he inched away from his enemy. "You're the animal."

"Yes they were weak," he said with a rough, growling laugh. "And they were in my way. So I removed them. *They* may have been trash, but you, southman, you fight like a demon. I'm eager to take your measure. Tell me your name before you die."

"I'm Koristad Altessor, son of Arach the Black Guardian."

"I know that name," he said with surprise. "Though I haven't heard it in a long time."

"He killed legions of your kind," Koristad growled. "I guess I'll have to continue that legacy."

"That look in your eye!" the barbarian howled with glee. "It's absolutely perfect! It tells me it's time to start cutting you up!"

The barbarian moved toward Koristad with both weapons at the ready. There wasn't a hint of fear in his eyes; there was only exhilaration.

The instant before his attack he issued a frenzied cry, "As you fade from this life, know the name of your killer! Azoman!"

The sound of steel striking steel rang out across the countryside, a crack of thunder as the berserk assault came down like a flash of lightning.

Koristad couldn't help but think: it was an unusual name for a barbarian.

2

(Thirteen years before present)

A YOUNG BARBARIAN PUSHED HIS way through the deep snow that covered the high mountaintop, grimacing from the effort and sometimes stumbling over the concealed rock outcroppings. He would try to catch himself as he fell forward, but his hands sank into the soft, wet slush, burying his face in the snow.

He was inadequately clad for such extreme cold; snow covered his face and body from his many falls. His leather moccasins were coated with ice and stuck to his feet, but he hadn't been able to feel them for hours. A large sword was strapped to his back, the iron weapon frozen into its sheath. A lesser man would have given up, even laid down in the cold and waited for the sleep of death. But this barbarian pushed on with a persistent fervor, oblivious to the elements.

He was a man with no name. It was a fact that shamed him; ate away at him with his every waking moment. He could have no possessions, no women, and no glory. He was like a pet to those who had already earned their place, a tool or slave fit only to serve.

Among his people, there were two methods to earn a name. If one was glorious in combat, cutting down many powerful enemies, they could gain the respect of their fellows. With enough respect, a barbarian who had a name could choose to bestow one upon the aspirant warrior. This was rare, however. The rivalries between great warriors were fierce, and were more likely to end with one or both parties dead in a pool of blood.

The other (more common) method was to face a named warrior in open combat before the clan. If the challenger was victorious, then he would adopt the moniker of the slain. Those with names were endlessly tested by usurpers, forging their already powerful will to fight into a finely honed weapon.

The young barbarian was stronger and more aggressive than most. He'd already trounced most of his brothers and any barbarian with the nerve to fight him. He enjoyed fighting. It was all he knew. He liked to punch and grapple his enemies until they went limp, but he loved even more when he could use his blade and hack his opponents to bits. The thrill of battle and that intoxicating, metallic smell of blood—these were the things he loved most in life.

Still, no one had seen fit to grant him a name. They looked down on him as a child. An upstart. He didn't realize they feared his potential, as well. He was young; still green and weak, but when he grew older he would be strong—perhaps strong enough to challenge them for *their* names.

He wasn't willing to wait until he was older. The lack of a name hounded him like a hungry pack of wolves, biting at him more deeply than the cold of the snow he waded through. He swore he would not enter his manhood without one.

The young man's father was named Thundercry. He was nearly fifty years old, an ancient among the barbarians who tended to live short, brutal lives followed by bloody, violent deaths. He had seen more battles in his time than perhaps any barbarian still alive, and had even fought against Arach the Black Guardian in the dark days when his people had been trapped in the mountains. He was a survivor; many had lost their lives facing the necromancer, and only those with great strength or luck lived to tell the tale.

Despite his years, few would dare challenge him; those who did found his aging body still had the strength of the mountain flowing through it.

The barbarians had no formal leaders; the only power that could be derived among them was the power of brute force and the fear of being on the receiving end of it. But if there had been a leader among his people, it would have been him. He was a figure of great reverence even among the named.

He had many sons. The barbarians didn't marry; among those who respected nothing but brute strength, women were merely possessions. Thundercry had seventeen women, and dozens more over his many years, and they had bore him many children. His people believed their women should always be with child, always bringing life into their clan to replace the countless who were killed in the never-ending story of violence.

But even to Thundercry, who had more children than he could hope to keep track of, this young man was special. He could see the bloodlust in the boy's eyes, the frenzy and the desire for battle. It was befitting of his offspring. It was Thundercry who had sent this barbarian to the snowy peaks of his ancestral mountain home.

"There is an ancient monster that lives atop the peak, my son," he had explained one night in secret. "None who have tried to slay it have ever returned to the clan. The glory of defeating such a mighty opponent would be worthy of a name. Bring me the monster's head, and you will have one."

It was a simple offer, one the young man hadn't questioned for an instant. He left his home at dawn the next morning, carrying only his blade and a few scraps of food, and bid farewell to no one. He was like a beast who knew no fear.

He was nearing the summit. His body tingled with excitement for the battle that was to come.

He crested a high drift, and what he saw on the other side sent a chill down his spine. The snow was awash with dark red blood, a long swath like a glacial pool. There were bits of short, curly fur everywhere; the fleece of a mountain goat, perhaps even a family by the scale of the massacre. As he looked back and forth, the scene grew even more gruesome as he spotted bloody bits of the animals scattered on the ground. There was a severed hoof, the tendon still hanging from its end, and half of a head, its gooey center exposed to the snow.

He drew his blade from its sheath, the ice cracking and falling to the ground as the sharp metal slid into the frozen air. He smiled. The kill was fresh; he knew he was drawing close to his adversary. He was able to follow the trail of blood to the summit of the mountain. He moved recklessly, making no attempt to assess what was before him.

At last he came upon a level plain of snow. Red-white bones were scattered everywhere, sticking out of the drifts. Many were animal bones, but not all. Opposite the plain he could see the mouth of a cave; icicles hung from the entrance like the long, sharp teeth of the mountain itself, water droplets slowly dribbling from their sharpened tips like voracious saliva. Huddled in the entrance was a figure that made even this stalwart warrior nearly lose his nerve.

The creature was enormous, out-sizing the barbarians at least as much as the barbarians out sized the men of the south. It held a bloodied goat carcass in its tremendous hands; the left appeared to be covered in a steel gauntlet. However, it wasn't armor; the plates of steel were part of the creature's body, scales of metal that grew from its thick flesh. It tore at the raw meat with a wickedly fanged mouth, blood running down its chin as it gorged itself on its meal. The monster's skin was white as the snow, and its eyes were as black as the fear it instilled in those who looked upon it. Its head was covered in sharp protrusions, and its ears were pointed and long enough to rise above the creature's scalp.

The creature eyed the approaching barbarian with disdain and continued eating. It wasn't until the enemy was only a few feet away that it tossed the bloody meat to the ground. It reached into the cave behind, drawing a mammoth sword wrought of a dark metal the barbarian had never seen before.

"Another offering, I see," the creature hissed, drawing itself up to its full height. "Let us see how long you can entertain me."

The barbarian didn't wait for the monster to attack. He lunged at it, swinging his sword in a broad arc that could have slashed a man in half.

The blade stopped dead in the creature's open left hand. The metal plates rang against the iron blade; the barbarian pushed forward with all his might, trying to overpower his larger opponent. Using brute force was his only means of fighting, and it had always served him well in the past.

But he had never fought an enemy like this. The beast's metal fingers changed shape, sprouting into elongated points with the speed of flying arrows. The barbarian, stunned by the unnatural attack, stumbled away from the engagement, nearly losing his footing in the snow. A gash opened under his left eye, a stream of blood gushing down his cheek.

The monster's hand remained in its new form, a three bladed claw. Still, the barbarian was eager to continue; the pain of his wound was the first badge of glory of what would be a terrific battle. His only concern was returning the favor to his enemy.

Metal rang against metal as he delivered a frenzied series of blows, but he couldn't produce an opening through the monster's sword and claw. He felt the warm wetness of blood running down his left arm. He hadn't even perceived the attack that had opened the wound.

A mighty swing from the creature sent the young man flying into the air. He rolled across the snow, leaving spots of red blood behind him. He had hardly regained his senses in time to duck away from the next swing and answer with his own. He fought hard to make his way back to his feet, but he still couldn't seem to penetrate the monster's adamantine defenses. Its left hand seemed an impenetrable shield, but the barbarian was certain the rest of the creature's flesh would part under a sharp blade, if only he could reach it.

Finally, the opening he'd been waiting for presented itself. The monster thrust at him with his sword, and the barbarian dodged it almost entirely. What was intended to be an impaling strike had only slashed his side. It was the worst wound he'd suffered in the battle thus far, and perhaps even more grievous than anything he'd received in his whole life. But the pain didn't slow his movements; he reached down with his left arm, grabbing the sharp blade with his naked hand.

The metal bit deeply into his flesh, cutting into his bones. The agony meant nothing; it only added to his bloodlust and his will to see his foe slashed to pieces.

The monster looked at him with surprise, caught off guard by its opponent's willingness to mutilate his own body. The young man brought his blade down in a potent crosscut against the monster's right shoulder, pouring every ounce of strength into the crucial blow.

Iron bit flesh, shooting out a spray of blood. But the monster's hide was tougher than the barbarian had expected; the attack would have cleaved through a man's shoulder blade and collapsed his lung but, against this thing, the wound was deep, but not mortal. The creature bellowed in pain and rage. The scream was like an earthquake, shaking the snow all around them and causing slides in the slopes below. The cry could even be heard by the barbarian's clan, far away, beyond the tree line.

The monster snarled and drew up its left hand, bringing the blades down on the barbarian like an eagle diving into water. The attack cut him from his shoulder down to his calf, a deep wound that sent out showers of blood and drove the mighty warrior to his knees. Suddenly, he felt cold. It was as if the frozen air that clung to his skin had driven in through the wound and turned his blood to ice. He tried to climb to his feet, to raise his sword, but his limbs refused to obey him. He was defeated. He looked up at the monster that towered over him, only desiring to see that look in his eye; the look of victory over the enemy.

But he couldn't see the creature's face. He couldn't see anything. He was in darkness, cold and alone. His heartbeat slowed and his breathing shallowed. He couldn't have been happier. He had faced a worthy adversary, fought a valorous battle, and for his efforts he'd been granted a glorious death. The ice of the mountain sunk into his heart, freezing it to the core.

3

(Thirteen years before present)

THEN, THERE WAS FIRE. A fire like molten lead running through his veins, scalding his organs and melting his bones.

"The blood of a demon spells agonizing death to a human," the harrowing voice of the monster echoed in the darkness. "But you are my kin. If you have the strength to endure, then you will be granted fortitude to recover from your wounds.

"You impress me, mortal; most of your kind are cowards at heart, but you understand what it truly means to be a warrior. If you survive, it would bring me great pleasure to fight with you again."

And there were nightmares. The young barbarian could see eyes in the darkness; blood red eyes of tiny, ravenous animals. They gathered at the edge of his vision, piling on top of one another until their gleaming occuli shone like the embers of a dying fire. All at once they swarmed over him, attacking while he was too wounded to defend himself. Their grimy fangs tore at his flesh, devouring his tattered body. The gashes they left festered and began to crawl, instantly leaking pus and erupting with long, black maggots.

But the fire continued to burn on in the dark. It erupted from his mouth, eyes, and the terrific wounds that scored his body; red flames spread out and enveloped everything. It scorched away his verminous parasites, but it could not burn his body. The feeling of the demonic blood in his veins was both agonizing and intoxicating. He could see faces in the blinding fires, twisted into a mockery of mortal expressions; screaming and laughing, crying and grimacing. There were more than he could count. They were everywhere, crowding in and pressing against him.

But they weren't there to torture him. They'd come to seek out his strength, to bow down and admire him. They lifted him from the ground, pushing up like the gust of a scalding, volcanic vent. He rose higher and higher until he was above the flames, above the darkness, and in a world of pure white mist. The blistering heat began to fade from his body. He wondered if he was finally going to die.

He heard a woman's scream. His eyes slowly opened and, for a moment, he wasn't sure if he was still trapped in that world of nightmares or if he'd at last escaped into the waking world. The ground underneath him was cold and wet, and the crisp air smelled of the mountains. His wounds ached, and he knew he was once again in the world of the living.

The scream rang out again and he tried to rise to his feet, but he was too hurt to stand. The woman cried out a third time, but the sound was cut off by the sound of wet choking. He didn't hear it again.

Glancing about, he saw he was in an underground chamber. The dim sunlight and his crude logic lead him to believe he was in the inner recesses of the cave he'd seen upon the mountain summit. He wasn't able to move freely enough to fully assess his surroundings, but he could see there were bones on the floor around him. Some were human, some were animal, and many of them still had bits of rotting flesh or hair clinging to them. The stench of death was powerful. It would have been enough to make a normal person sick, but the young barbarian was accustomed to the odor. He'd even grown to like it.

He didn't know how long he'd been lying on the stone floor, fighting off the phantoms of his own nightmares, but he saw his wounds had already begun to close. The healing seemed rough and unnatural, as if his flesh was reaching out and trying to bind itself back together. His body was sticky with his own blood, and he was terribly thirsty and hungry.

He was able to lap up water from the floor where it had collected in small pools, melted snow that trickled in through the rocks from outside. It was cold and tasted foul, tainted from the offal that was strewn about him. A few hours later a slab of meat landed near him with a thud, though he couldn't see who or what had thrown it. It was bloody and raw, and he didn't even know what sort of beast it had been cut from, but his hunger didn't allow him to hesitate before tearing into it with his teeth. The barbarian cuisine he was accustomed to was only slightly more refined.

He laid there for days or weeks, slowly regaining his strength. Eventually he was able to lift his body into a sitting position, and he found his sword lying nearby. When he was finally able to stand, he took the weapon and hobbled toward the source of the dim light which, he assumed, was the exit to the cave.

The monster was waiting for him at the cave's mouth. It sat on the wet earth with its back against a rough stone wall, its tremendous frame blocking much of the light from the outside. When the beast first spotted the young man, it began to grin, but its look of appreciation was quickly replaced by a grimace and a shake of its massive head.

"You're not well enough to fight me, yet," it said.

The barbarian lifted his sword as if he might try to attack, but he could barely keep his feet. He stumbled forward and caught himself by planting the sword blade in the ground and leaning upon it, like an old man upon a walking stick.

"Why haven't you killed me?" he demanded. "You defeated me. I should be dead."

The monster groaned and answered, "I explained this already. I wish to fight you again, though not until you've regained enough strength to give me proper entertainment."

"You love fighting that much?"

"I do," it replied with a sinister grin. "You and I are kindred spirits."

"Are you...," the barbarian hesitated, unsure if he should say it, "A clanfather?"

The ancients who had founded the thirteen clans were often described as monstrous and beastlike, but his people had no written language, and it was difficult to tell what was true and what was legend in an oral tradition. The young man had always thought of them as great men, not monsters, but the words of this creature echoed the philosophy they had been imparted upon his people in ages past.

"I am a demon," it growled, bringing a huge, balled up fist to its chest. "I came through to your world during the second incursion. It was a glorious time, filled with bloodshed and war, and I was a mighty general who commanded a vast legion. But our armies were ultimately routed and scattered by the children of Aura and their allies. Thirteen of us fled north, and here in these mountains we found a weak and primitive people who lived off the land in peace.

"Peace!" it howled with rage. "We decided we would make them our toys. We forced them to kill each other; we took their women and used them for our pleasure. Our blood mixed with theirs, and the mountains screamed with the sounds of battle and ran red with blood.

"But our toys grew strong, and became resentful of our enslavement. Our infernal heritage had given them strength beyond that of common mortals. Some of them began to rise against us, attacking in numbers, and many of my demon brethren were killed. I fled into the mountains, up to this peak. From here my demon eyes can see for a hundred miles, and I watch with glee as my toys lash out against the civilized men of the south who exiled me from their lands.

"Does it sound to you like I'm a...what was it?" the demon tried to recall the name. "A clanfather?"

"That isn't the story I was told by Thundercry," the young barbarian said, scarcely able to believe what he'd heard.

"Ah, Thundercry, your traitorous kinsman," the demon laughed to himself.

"Traitorous?" the barbarian questioned warily.

"You haven't figured it out yet?" the demon sniggered. "You were sent here to die. Thundercry knows very well what I am, and he knew there was no chance you could defeat me."

"I don't believe you," the young man protested in a harsh voice.

"Believe whatever you wish, mortal," the demon hissed at him. "It doesn't change what is and what is not. I came upon Thundercry many years ago, not long after he'd been named. I meant to kill him as I had so many others, but he was a coward and he shrunk away from me and begged for his life."

"No, he would never...," the man didn't finish his sentence.

"I show no mercy to my enemies. But he said something that intrigued me," the demon said, gazing at the ceiling as if he were recalling a fond memory. "He said he was a man of great respect within his clan, and he promised he would send me women from his own people as often as he could spare them. That piqued my interest, but I also demanded, as further terms of his release, that he send warriors for me to test myself against, as well."

"You're a liar!" the barbarian fumed, his hands shaking with rage.

"Am I?" the demon mocked. "You're a great warrior. The first who has wounded me in years beyond what I can remember. If you were not so young, I'm certain you would be preeminent among your people. But, in order to be a true warrior, one must have a keen mind as well as a strong arm; you've figured it out by now, haven't you?"

The cave filled with silence. The barbarian didn't want to believe what this monster was telling him, but something in his gut told him it was the truth. He couldn't believe he'd let himself fall prey to such simple machinations, but he was blinded by ambition and trust in his father. It was trust unbefitting one of his kind, and he felt ashamed of it.

"He feared if I grew older I would be a threat to him," the young man said with a deep scowl, his expression slowly turning to one of crimson rage. "I'll kill him."

The words were barely a whisper in his mind, but they echoed off the cave walls over and over again, until a chorus of hate filled the air around him.

"That bastard! I'll kill him!"

"You won't leave this cave with your life, mortal," the demon growled, "Unless you're able to defeat me, first. Disappear from my sight until you've recovered enough to give me proper sport. If you show your face again while you're in such sorry condition, I'll acquaint you with the true meaning of suffering before I end your life."

4

(Thirteen years before present)

THE YOUNG BARBARIAN DID as he was told. His wounds closed with unnatural haste, and it wasn't long before his desire for revenge against his treacherous father brought him blade to blade with the demon once again. He fought with every ounce of fervor that was in his tortured soul, but the monster he faced was too great an adversary to be felled with mere resolve or passion. The man was quickly overwhelmed, beaten and slashed, and he stained the white snow of the mountain scarlet with his blood. All sensation fled from his ragged body, and his vision grew dim; his last memory before being swallowed up by the blackness was falling face-first into the cold snow.

He expected to never open his eyes again. But the demon had checked its blows, and while the wounds it inflicted bled profusely, they weren't as deep as those it had caused on the first day. The gashes bound themselves together quickly, as they had done before, and soon the barbarian was ready to make a third bid for freedom against his devilish captor.

This became his life. A brutal routine of combat, being slashed by razor sharp weapons and claws, and subsisting on melted mountain snow and rotten meat until he was well enough to try again. He lost all sense of time, and instead marked his progression by his mounting strength. Not only was his body growing larger and stronger as he became a man, but his fighting prowess sharpened as he was molded in the blood and ferocity of combat.

But no matter how strong he became, his foe was always stronger. He realized the demon had only been toying with him in the beginning. Just as he began to think he was becoming faster or stronger than his captor, he would find the monster had untapped reserves waiting to be unleashed. Just how deep those reserves ran, he had no idea.

He knew eventually his luck would run out and he would suffer a truly mortal wound, or the demon would grow weary of him and simply slay him outright. But, even if his days were numbered, and even if the foe he stood against was beyond his abilities, he continued to fight. At first he told himself it was the rage he felt for Thundercry that drove him; then it also became the consuming desire to vanquish his foe, to feel the glory of defeating such a truly powerful rival. But the truth was even simpler than that: he lived for the thrill of battle. If there had been anyone to ask him, he would have said he'd never been happier in his life.

But everything must ultimately come to its end.

The demon pushed him back with its heavy blade and the barbarian fell to his knees, bloodied and gasping for air. His heavily muscled body was glistening with sweat; his clothes were little more than tattered rags, and a long, unkempt beard hung from his chin. He tried to lift his sword to continue the fight, but the demon's foot came down on the flat of the blade, snatching it from his hand as it clattered against the stone floor.

"You've stopped improving," the demon scorned. "Has your mortal body reached its limit?"

"I'm nowhere near my limit yet, demon," the man hissed, panting from his exertion. "I'll be at my limit after you're dead."

The demon shook his head, "Those are brave words, and there's fervor behind your eyes, but there is nothing that can change what we are. This is it for you; you've done much better than I expected. You should be commended but, in the end, you are only human. I think...yes, I think it's time I finally bring this entertainment to a close."

The barbarian looked up at the demon's black eyes in shock. It lifted its sword high into the air, cutting through the frozen mountain wind as it blew into the dank cave. Was this the end? He wasn't ready. It wasn't a fear of death that gripped him; it was the desire to fight. The blade hung there in midair, as if time had stopped. The man waited for the fatal blow to fall upon him, his eyes open and unafraid, but it never came. The demon sighed and let the blade drop harmlessly to the ground, clattering against the rocks.

"How amusing," it said with a disgusted snort. "I find I don't want to end your life, after all. Perhaps this is what it's like to have a pet."

The man looked up at the demon in disbelief, but the monster turned away from him and strode toward the light of the cave's mouth. He picked his sword from the rocky ground and followed.

Their skirmishes had sometimes taken the barbarian out of the cave, but this time it was different. It was the first time since he'd been captured that he'd been under the open sky, and been able to look at it, without the fear of a fatal blow coming down upon him. It seemed impossibly bright, and he squinted his eyes tight as he tried to adjust. He felt the cool mountain wind blow through his hair and across his skin. But he felt no sense of freedom even after his long confinement. His physical body had escaped its prison, but his psyche was still very much caged.

He found the demon sitting on a large boulder atop a nearby outcropping. From this overlook, he could see all across the wide mountain range, a truly breathtaking view. The man approached cautiously, uncertain of how the demon might react to him.

"What now?" he asked as he drew near, stopping as his feet neared the ledge.

"What do I care?" it hissed without a glance in his direction. "I grow weary of your presence. Be gone from my sight."

The barbarian frowned deeply and said, "I came here for a name. I still don't have one, and unless I bring back your head, I won't be getting one."

"Do you think I can remove my head as if it were a hat?" the demon sniggered at him.

"Even if you could, I would never accept such charity," he snapped. "Unless I can defeat you with my own hands, it would be meaningless."

"We both know that will never happen," it replied frankly. "You should return to your clan and take your vengeance upon Thundercry. That would entitle you to his name." The demon seemed to think for a moment, then shook its head in disgust. "But that would never do. You are too pure a warrior to use the name of that coward."

"Then fight me!" the barbarian cried out in desperation, lifting his sword into the air. "This time I'll cut you down and earn my title!"

The demon appeared unfazed by the threat of violence and waved his hand at the barbarian in a dismissive gesture.

"I already said I have no further interest in battling you," it protested sternly. "You are not my equal. You never will be."

The barbarian lowered his sword, defeated by the monster's words.

"But I would be pleased if you would take my name and return to your people. I can imagine the havoc and the massacres that would come in your wake, and it would be a great pleasure to hear my name on the wind once again, whispered with respect and fear."

"But how can I? I haven't earned any name in the eyes of my people."

"The clans respect only strength; if you announce your name and they voice doubt, then you will strike down those who question you," the demon explained with an evil grin. "The next time, there will be fewer who question. And, soon, none at all."

"The name of a clanfather," the barbarian pondered. "It would be a great honor. But I don't know your name."

"My name," the demon grumbled in a voice that sounded like the mountain was coming apart, "Is *Azoman.*"

5

KORISTAD GRITTED HIS TEETH as he struggled to parry the vicious blows Azoman rained down upon him. The ferocity of the barbarian's attack was so great he couldn't find an opening to take the offensive, or even to put some distance between them.

"You're faster than me, southman!" Azoman howled, still striking with his blade and steel claw. "You may even be stronger than me! But you're far too green to win this battle!"

As Koristad struggled to keep his footing, he had no choice but to accept his opponent was right. The darkness that had been unleashed in his body when he had nearly turned had given him speed beyond what human physiology would allow, but every move he tried to make Azoman could see through instantly. A subtle change in his footwork, a nearly imperceptible drop in his shoulders; to the more experienced barbarian these signs were as plain as the sun in the sky.

Koristad had never been a warrior in his youth; he'd always dreamed of being a necromancer like his father, and had devoted his childhood to study. After he learned he could no longer call upon the darkness, he'd trained hard with his halberd, the weapon that had originally been designed to end his life, imagining that he might one day plunge the sanctified weapon into the heart of the Vampire King. He was a quick learner, but he had only recently been released from his tomb, and he certainly didn't have any experience against skilled combatants.

Koristad grunted in pain as sharp steel licked across his leg, drawing blood just above his knee. For a fraction of a second, he let his guard down. It was a nearly fatal mistake as Azoman swung hard at his chest, expecting to land a fatal strike. Koristad perceived the attack at the last instant and attempted to leap away; the

blow connected, piercing his flesh near his collar bone and sending a spray of blood
across his face, but the wound wasn't nearly as deep as it might have been.

Peril cried out and took a step toward him, but he held up his hand as if to
stop her.

"This is nothing!" he insisted, his words dipped in rage. "Just stay back!"

Once again, his lack of focus was putting him at risk. He should have known
better than to remove his grip from his weapon; Azoman was upon him in an
instant, and Koristad barely had enough time to return his hand to the halberd.
It took all his might to hold back both of the barbarian's weapons. For a moment,
the brute was so close that Koristad could smell the sweat on his skin, but the
barbarian feinted his attack, causing Koristad to stumble forward. Azoman took
decisive advantage of Koristad's loss of footing, assaulting him with a frenzy of
strikes the young necromancer barely had a chance to parry. He was forced to
backpedal away from his enemy as quickly as he could only to avoid his deadly
attacks.

Before Koristad realized how much ground he'd covered, he saw the rope
abutments of the ravine crossing come up on either side of him. The bridge was
just a few steps behind, and he was moving toward it.

"What are you doing!?" he exclaimed as his foot came in contact with the
wooden planks. "You're going to get us both killed!"

One of the flashing blades glanced across a rope, causing the outermost braid
to spin rapidly as it frayed.

"This is life, southman!" Azoman shouted with glee. "Enjoy the thrill! Savor
the rush before you die!"

Koristad's heart pounded like a hammer striking his ribs as the barbarian
pushed him farther and farther across the bridge. It certainly was a thrill, but not
one he took any pleasure in. Dark blood spurted from his wounds, and his chest
ached terribly. He wasn't sure how much longer he would be able to hold off his
opponent's ferocious onslaught.

The bridge swayed wildly under the brutal melee, and its support ropes were
cut and frayed in numerous places. The bands were extremely thick; nearly the
width of a child's arm, but Koristad was surprised none of them had been severed
completely. He knew it was only a matter of time before the crossing's structure
was too badly damaged to withstand such vigorous motion.

Peril watched helplessly from the ravine's edge, her knuckles white as she
nervously clenched her hands into tiny fists. She prayed to Aura to help Koristad,

to let him live, even if he didn't believe in her. She didn't dare think about what might happen to *her* if Koristad was defeated.

There was a pop like the sound of a cracking whip as the support to Koristad's left tore itself apart, causing the wooden planks to drop out from under him on that side. He grabbed the other rope with his right hand and tried to brace his foot against the hanging timbers. Azoman did the same, grabbing the rope with the hand that carried his punching blade, leaving his sword arm free.

Koristad was unprepared for the attack that came an instant later. To him, it was incomprehensible to continue an offensive after being thrust into such a precarious, lethally dangerous position. But to Azoman, whose lungs breathed combat and heart pumped violence, there was no cessation of battle. This clash could only be ended by his death or his opponent's. Or, as events were beginning to auspice, for them both.

Azoman's blade bit deep into his side, slicing through flesh and meat. Koristad cried out in pain as a crimson torrent of blood rushed from the grievous wound. He couldn't believe how much of it there was; he didn't think he had that much in his entire body. His flesh grew chill and his vision darkened. He could feel his right hand losing its grip on the rope, but he couldn't seem to do anything about it.

"Done already, southman?" Azoman demanded, his voice filled with disappointment, the point of his blade still imbedded in his enemy's body.

Koristad couldn't manage a reply, not a cynical or snide comment, as his vision continued to fade. Time seemed to stand still as he hung there, dangling high above the sweeping current and sharp rocks far below.

"Is this where you're going to die, Koristad?" the hollow voice of Wraith seemed to echo all around him, or maybe only within his own head.

"I can't move," he whispered. "He's too powerful; I was no match for him."

"When I came to you, I didn't realize you could give up so easily. You haven't even used your power yet."

"I can't use my magic anymore," Koristad protested desperately. "That's all behind me now. If I call upon the darkness then it will pull me into the world of the dead. I'm too close to the precipice."

Wraith answered cryptically, "Magic. Spells. Necromancy. These are manipulations of energy, a priming and design that use the human body as a vessel for the darkness. The soul must be opened so that the power can come through, exposing the fragile spirit to a force beyond its comprehension. Opening the soul in this way can cause it to lose its stability and be pulled through to the other side."

"Those words..." Koristad couldn't believe what he was hearing. "Those were words I read from my father's hidden research notes. How can you...?"

"But you are closer to that source of power than any child of darkness. Opening your soul to it would be like jumping into a whirlpool, and you might be pulled through instantly. Whether or not you take that risk is your decision, not mine. However..."

Koristad wasn't sure how, but he knew instantly what Wraith was going to say next, a quote from another of Arach's passages, and he spoke the words before the ghost had the chance.

"...when a child of darkness becomes a vampire, the mortal life force is overwhelmed by the darkness. The body contains no vitality of its own, and therefore must consume blood in order to sustain its immortality. But this is also the source of the vampire's power; the darkness imbues the body with power and speed, and the more the monster calls on that darkness, the greater it becomes."

Wraith's glowing eyes came into view behind Azoman who, like the rest of the world, seemed frozen in time.

"Your body has retained its life force. But it has also welcomed the darkness. If you won't open your soul to that power, perhaps you could cultivate what's already there."

"But what happens if I go too far?" Koristad asked. "That power might eclipse my life force. Even if it doesn't, what will happen to me?"

"You tread through unknown lands. There has never been another like you," Wraith answered coldly. "But the means of your death are yours to choose. One way, or the other, it makes little difference to me."

With that, the spirit vanished and the world instantly came back into focus.

"Done already, southman?"

Koristad twisted his left hand around the haft of his halberd as it hung at his side. The means of his death were his to choose?

He swung the weapon in an underhand arc at Azoman, who caught it with his blade and stopped it dead. Koristad could feel the darkness in his soul shift and spread like a spider casting its web in every direction. He swore to himself he wouldn't lose control. But he was losing blood fast and, if he didn't act now, he wouldn't get another chance.

Azoman could no more stop the fury of his opponent's mounting strength than he could have held back the river below. His powerful arm gave way, and the sanctified steel slashed across his body, leaving a deep, bloody wound that stretched from his sternum to his shoulder blade. His eyes went wide in shock. He'd thought his opponent had already been defeated...where had this sudden strength come from?

The blade passed through the barbarian's body and bit into the remaining support rope, severing it instantly. The bridge, no longer able to support the weight of its occupants, came apart, throwing old, wooden planks in every direction. The two warriors, both covered in their own blood, plunged into the ravine below, vanishing from Peril's sight.

Chapter Four

THE BALEFUL MASQUERADE

We attract and repel each other.
Like magnets, or the moon and the tides.
It's an ugly thing to hate, like a gaping wound on the soul.
Or to be hated for what we are, or what we're not.
If we were all alike, would the world be filled with peace and kindness?
Or would we simply hate each other for our sameness?

1

PERIL'S HEART WENT COLD as the two men disappeared, plummeting into the chasm below. She stood there, wide-eyed, wringing her hands and uncertain of what she should do. She moved toward the gaping ravine to peer over the edge but, without the bridge to stand on, it was too treacherous to approach near enough to glimpse over the precipice.

She'd had a perfect view of the bone shattering drop into the rushing current of fetid water so far below. Koristad had been critically wounded before the fall; even if he'd miraculously survived the plunge, his injuries would certainly prove fatal.

"I don't believe it!" she declared loudly to no one but herself. "He's alright. He has to be."

Koristad was a necromancer, but there was more to him than that; she'd already seen him accomplish feats of speed and strength that went far beyond the means of any ordinary child of darkness. She didn't understand just what it was, but there was something special about him.

She paced up and down the edge of the ravine, seeking a route shallow enough for her to pick her way down. The search went on for what felt like hours, but there was no easy path to the water below. She could only find one spot where she was able to get close to the ledge, and the descent was steep—more of a climb than a hike. With no other options, however, she decided to make the attempt.

She moved slowly, expending at least as much effort trying not to look down as she did making her descent. The river had eroded the ravine slowly over many centuries, giving vegetation ample time to adapt and creep down its walls. Peril was able to find roots and rough undergrowth to wrap her fingers around, without which she was almost certain she wouldn't have been able to force herself downward. Still, the delicate foliage wasn't substantial enough to support her weight; more than once she felt it give, threatening to let her fall.

Soon she was weary and out of breath, unaccustomed to such strenuous physical exertion. There was no ledge on which she could rest. She ventured a look down, certain she had to be nearing the base, but she was only a little over halfway. She wanted to quit or cry, but there was nothing to do but carry on.

When she finally reached the bottom, her feet sank deep into the soft, muddy ground. She was relieved to finally have the earth beneath her, even such as it was. There was only a narrow corridor of earth that descended sharply into the rushing water. With every step the land would give out, tumbling into the current. She made her way carefully down the bank, leaning all of her weight against the dirt wall while holding herself upright with both hands.

Her eyes stung with sweat and her legs ached from the strain. She followed the river downstream. She thought with dread that, in the time it had taken her to get down the cliff, Koristad must have been washed miles away by the powerful current. As she picked her way down the bank, she came across a handful of natural alcoves that had been eroded away over the years. Here the ground was marginally drier and more firm, and she stopped in one to sit down and try to catch her breath.

She didn't inspect her surroundings before she plopped down on the ground. As she glanced about, she was shocked to see small bones lying here and there, half buried in the earth. She wasn't well versed enough in such things to know what sort of creature they came from, but they were clearly too small to be human.

This prompted her to inspect the ground more closely, and she was able to make out tracks moving to and fro, following the bank of the river. Clearly there were some animals that made their homes near the source of the water, creating their own ecosystem in this slender world.

Peril didn't allow herself to rest long; as soon as her lungs stopped burning and her legs stopped throbbing, she was back on her feet. But it was starting to get dark, and she was beginning to lose hope she would find Koristad. The thought made her stomach tie up in knots; she'd barely made her way down the side of the ravine—there was no possibility she could climb back up. Her only way out would be to follow the river until the walls gave way. She had no idea how long that would take and, even then, she would be hopelessly lost.

"Koristad, where are you?" she cried, feeling tears of hopelessness well up in her eyes. She kicked a pile of dirt into the river and told herself it was all her fault; if she'd only listened to him and stayed in the camp then none of this would have happened. Now he was gone and she was lost in dangerous territory.

That was when she spotted something caught in the undergrowth near the riverbank. She wiped away her tears and saw it was a heavy, sackcloth cloak. She ran toward it, her hopes high, but found Koristad wasn't inside. She removed the fabric from its entanglement and wrung it out as best she could, then bunched it up and carried it under her arm. She'd only moved a few paces further when she spied Koristad's weapon buried in the ground, its haft sticking straight up and its blade plunged deep into the earth.

She tried to pluck it from the ground, but the wet suction of the sticky mud held it tight. She dropped Koristad's cloak and wrapped both hands around the wooden hilt, spreading her feet far apart, and pulled as hard as she could. With a repulsive, slurping sound, the weapon slid free. She lost her balance and stumbled backwards into the mud, dropping the weapon as she fell.

She struggled to her feet and tried to wipe off her clothes, but they had been utterly soiled during her adventure. She wearily picked up the sanctified halberd. It was astonishingly heavy. Koristad had used the weapon with such grace and ease—she hadn't imagined it could carry so much mass.

She moved on with her two trophies, at last feeling some sense of accomplishment and hope. Koristad had fallen near here, and if his cloak had been caught so early in the current, perhaps he would be nearby, as well. But deep shadows stretched across the ravine, and she knew soon it would be too dark to continue her search.

It wasn't until the sun had completely vanished, when the light was so dim she could hardly distinguish color in the shady chasm, that she spotted someone lying sprawled out, halfway on the shore. His legs were waving in the current as if he were kicking, though the rest of his body was completely still. Her hope mixed with apprehension as she approached; the barbarian, Azoman, had also fallen into the ravine. What would she do if it was him she found rather than her protector?

She was relieved that she didn't have to answer that question; as she approached, she found the form she saw was Koristad. He was soaked and muddy, but it was him. Somehow he'd managed to crawl far enough onto the bank to escape the rushing water, but now he was still and his eyes were closed.

Peril reached out as far as she could, barely able to get her hands around Koristad's wrist without falling into the water herself. She leaned back and pulled with all the strength that was left in her tiny frame, dragging his drenched and lifeless body onto the muddy bank.

She rolled him onto his back and checked him for a pulse. It was slow and shallow, but still there. His complexion was white as a sheet, and his lips and the skin around his eyes were dark, almost blue. He'd lost so much blood Peril couldn't understand what was keeping him alive, but she knew he wouldn't last much longer unless she did something to help him.

She was merely an initiate among the lightwielders and, though she carried the blood of Aura, she'd developed little skill in utilizing its power. The older and more talented children of Aura could perform truly incredible miracles of faith, things she couldn't even understand. She wasn't sure if she had enough power to save someone who was so terribly injured; so close to death's door.

She laid her hands on Koristad's bloody chest and began to pray. She wasn't any good at learning the proper litanies to call on Aura's blood, but her faith was strong. Even if she didn't know the words, her tears and purity were enough to call on the power of the light. When she'd run out of words to say, when no more prayers could reach her lips, she merely begged, "Please...please, Koristad, don't die."

As if he were responding to her words, his breathing began to grow stronger and more regular, and she could feel the warmth return to his skin. She laughed with delight and cried at the same time, hurriedly removing her pack and rummaging through it. She'd brought bandages and ointments she could use to bind his wounds, though she hadn't expected she would need to use them.

By the time she was finished, the sun had fled from the sky and left her in darkness. Her stomach rumbled, and it was starting to get cold, but there was neither food to eat nor wood for a fire. She wasn't certain if the water from the river was safe to drink, but she was dehydrated from her long exertion, and decided to take the risk. It tasted muddy and foul.

She shivered and gathered up the sackcloth cloak, wrapping it around her body like a blanket. Then she looked over at Koristad, lying motionless in the dark. Feeling guilty, she surrendered the garment and covered his body with it instead. She sat down and leaned against the dirt wall of the ravine, huddling up in her arms for warmth.

She closed her eyes. Even though she was exhausted, it was impossible for her to sleep. She was frightened and her muscles ached, and the muddy earth wasn't a comfortable place to rest. She couldn't remember ever sleeping under the stars before.

She heard movement to her right and her eyes fluttered open. The night had grown nearly pitch black now. Even though there was a bright moon in the sky, its light could hardly penetrate into the deep ravine. It was only by virtue of the eyeshine effect she was able to make out a pair of animalistic oculi in the gloom. They bobbed back and forth but didn't approach, and she froze in fear. She wasn't able to judge how far away the animal was, or its size. Her imagination began to get the better of her, and she concluded it was a large animal, like a wolf or a mountain lion, that was still some distance away.

She and the shining eyes stared at each other in the darkness for what felt like an eternity, but at length the animal began to take a few tentative steps forward. Peril cried out and leapt to her feet, searching frantically for Koristad's halberd which she'd left somewhere on the ground. When she found it she spun around to face the creature, though it had retreated some distance after she'd made such a commotion.

Still, it stared at her with those shining eyes, and she imagined it was licking its chops, waiting for her to let her guard down or fall asleep. She wasn't sure what she could do with the tremendous weapon if the animal came after her; it was so heavy she would lose her balance if she tried to swing it. She fought back tears as she wished she had something to start a fire. *That* would keep any animals at bay.

She felt pathetic. She was a lightwielder…wasn't she supposed to be a protector of the people, willing to face even the most terrible monster without fear? A lightwielder. . .hadn't Leorra told her something about her blood having the power to create light? She strained to remember. Why hadn't she paid more attention?

"Cast thy glow across the darkness of this earth," she intoned uncertainly. "Light my path and accept my prayers, blessed goddess, Aura."

But no light appeared.

She'd been taught with all magic the prayer or incantation itself had no power. In fact, it wasn't even necessary. But the mental pattern created by the words could help the speaker weave the sorcery into the proper design, making the process simpler and more powerful. She tried again, focusing her mind on the blade of Koristad's halberd, visualizing it erupting in a light as brilliant as the sun.

As light filled the ravine, the nearby coyote scurried into the darkness. It wasn't nearly as bright as she'd imagined, only as luminous as a lantern or a small campfire, but she was glad to have it. She planted the haft into the ground, the blade sticking up like a torch, and hoped the magic wouldn't fade during the night.

She was still too frightened to sleep and, unlike a fire, the magic light gave off no heat. The night was growing colder still, and her body was unaccustomed to the frigid northlands. She looked at Koristad, who was still as motionless as stone, and she recalled how much safer she'd felt when he'd held her hand as they crossed the rickety bridge. Moving tentatively, as if she thought he might suddenly wake from his slumber to yell at her, she inched her way toward him.

She reached over and took his hand, wrapping his larger fingers around hers. She smiled. Even though he was still unconscious, the touch of his skin reassured her that everything was going to be alright. She lay down on the soft earth next to him, and had already begun to dream before her head fell upon his shoulder.

2

KORISTAD AWOKE TO FIND Peril cuddled up against him, using his cloak as a blanket. Her face and arms were streaked with mud and her hair was dirty and disheveled. She was snoring softly, her mouth wide open and drooling on his arm. He opened his mouth to yell at her, but snapped it shut before a growl escaped his lips.

The last thing he could remember was plummeting into the chasm, seeing the water rush up at him, certain it was the end. If he was alive, it had to be because Peril had saved him. Another person might have been very grateful.

Koristad shoved her away, making no attempt at gentleness. She rolled onto her back, rousing with surprising sluggishness considering her unkind awakening. She yawned and stretched her arms over her head, then sat up, blinking and looking at her surroundings, disoriented. When she saw Koristad was alive and well, her eyes lit up and she smiled brightly.

"You're awake!" she cried excitedly. "Good morning!"

Koristad struggled to sit up, his movements shaky and uncertain. Every inch of his body hurt; his bones ached, every muscle was sore. The wounds in his chest and his gut were throbbing, piercing deep into his core. But none of this took center stage in his mind. He was feeling something else, an obscure sensation that existed not in his body, but in his mind. It was a kind of pollution and intoxication, ferocity and hunger, darkness and vague desire. He'd only felt it once before, but it was something he couldn't forget.

It was the same feeling he'd had when he'd been released from his entombment. He didn't have to ask Wraith to know it was the dark power he'd called upon affecting him. What was the power doing to him? Could it taint his soul and cause him to turn?

"We should get moving," he grumbled. "Before that barbarian, Azoman, finds us."

"What are you talking about?" Peril asked. "It's a miracle you managed to survive. He has to be dead."

"No," Koristad shook his head, gazing at the swift river, "He's alive. If I survived that fall, then I'm sure he did, as well. Now let's go."

Koristad hobbled to his feet, gritting his teeth against the pain.

"You can't travel yet!" Peril insisted, hopping in front of him and motioning for him to lie back down. "I couldn't heal your wounds completely; if you move too much, they'll reopen!"

"I'm fine," Koristad growled at her.

She took a step away and looked down at the ground.

He sighed and added in a gentler tone, "You did an impressive job caring for my injuries. I may not be in perfect health but, if it weren't for your skill, I wouldn't be alive. But we have to keep moving or things are just going to get worse out here; I promise, I won't push myself too hard. Now, come on."

Koristad turned away from her and snatched up his cloak with a groan, wrapping the dirty rag around his body and fastening the collar to hide his face. He retrieved his weapon from the mud, wiping the blade on his trousers and hefting it over his shoulder. Without a glance back at his companion he began walking southwest, downstream, at a slow rate. After a moment, Peril hurried to his side, matching his pace.

"I've been wondering something, Koristad...," she said.

"Do I want to know?" he sighed with annoyance.

"Well, when you were fighting Azoman, why didn't you use your magic against him?" she asked. "You only used your weapon."

"I don't have any magic."

"That doesn't make any sense; I know you're a necromancer...you have the mark," she looked at him with a puzzled expression. "How can you say you don't have any magic?"

"I said I don't have any magic," he snapped, glaring at her with those inhumanly fierce eyes. "Don't ask me about it again."

Peril looked away and grew silent. She didn't understand why he seemed to dislike her so much. Other men had always been kind to her, smiling and trying to win her affection. Koristad hadn't smiled at her even once. In fact, she couldn't remember him smiling at all in the time they'd been together. Was it because of her? Did he really hate her?

They walked in silence for a long time, until the walls of the ravine began to grow short and the sun grew bright overhead. Peril was beginning to get woozy from hunger, but she didn't dare complain to her companion. She felt he'd made it very clear he wasn't interested in what she had to say. But her body didn't want to cooperate with her; she stumbled in the soft earth, though she wasn't sure if it was from weakness or sheer clumsiness. She fell forward, but a strong arm caught her and helped her steady her footing. She blushed and looked over at Koristad, embarrassed.

"What's the matter?" he asked sternly.

"I'm starving!" Peril cried, unable to contain her emotions any longer. "I haven't eaten anything since yesterday morning!"

Her stomach rumbled angrily as she thought of the sweetbreads and jam she'd left behind in the carriage. Since she'd been taken in by the lightwielders, she'd lived a coddled life, sleeping in a soft bed and never missing a meal. They saw a beautiful and delicate young girl, and so she'd been pampered as much as one could be at the Snowdove Sanctuary. Koristad could see the recent trials had taken their toll, but he had no intention of pitying her.

"There's nothing we can do about that while we're down here," he said. "Just keep moving and we'll see what we can find once we're out of the ravine. You can lean on me, if you have to."

"How is it you have so much energy, still?" she thought aloud. "You lost so much blood in the battle yesterday. You should be even weaker than I am."

That wasn't a question Koristad wanted to think about. He remembered how Wraith had told him his body was utilizing dark magic, the same power that gave vampires their strength. Perhaps it was that dark power that kept him going, even as his mortal strength faded. He felt off center, as if the world wasn't quite real; like that dark power he'd used was obscuring his view of the living world and trying to turn his attention to the land of the dead. Maybe his body was wasting away, and he wasn't even aware. It wasn't a pleasant thought. He tried to put it from his mind, ignoring Peril's question.

"Where are we going?" she asked disconsolately. "It seems like we've been walking forever!"

"Don't worry," Koristad said, "I used to live in this area; I know my way around."

"How could you have lived here?" she looked puzzled. "This land has been overrun with barbarians since I was born. You don't look much older than me."

Koristad had to disagree; Peril looked quite young. Even if they were the same age, she would have still looked much younger than he did.

"I'm older than you think," he said simply. "If we follow the river for a bit longer, the walls will be low enough for us to climb out, and the river will be shallow enough for us to cross. Once we're out of here, we should be able to find some gooseberries, or something, to eat. They're common in this area. It might not be the most filling meal, but it'll keep us going."

"I don't think it's very safe to be travelling through the wilds like this," Peril said doubtfully. "We need to get to a road, to the civilized part of the empire."

"If we hurry, I can get us to the town of Banock by tomorrow," Koristad said. "Then we can rest and resupply, and from there we can get wherever we need to. Do you think you can hold on that long?"

Peril frowned and replied, "I'll try."

3

T HE TOWN OF BANOCK was one of the last vestiges of civilization before the empire gave way to the wild, dangerous north. The barbarian hordes had been beaten back many times by the soldiers of the empire, and a nearby garrison deterred them from returning. The town had stood long before the fall of the Great Citadel, and the efforts of imperial knights and a diligent civilian military had prevented it from being razed during the violent onslaught. Though the town itself escaped undamaged, the price of protection was paid with many lives. A bitter battle in the nearby fields had left the ground stained red with blood.

The citizens had only a hint of how lucky they had been. They knew well that, if the barbarians had been victorious in the battle, Banock would have been burned to the ground and not a single citizen would have been left alive. They only had to look at their neighboring villages, or what charred remains were left of them, to know that much. But what few realized was that the battle should have, by all rights, been hopeless; the forces stationed there, as bold and determined as those young men were, were no match for the full fury of the barbarian hordes.

The northern savages were wild and disorganized; as they pushed south their army fractured and fragmented. Spreading across the land with uncontained glee, they dispersed into the wide open lands they had yearned to conquer for so long. Soon, what had been a massive army was dozens of smaller bands, and eventually, hundreds of even smaller groups. It was due to this fact alone that the garrison at Banock had been able to hold off the tide of bloodshed. When the soldiers of the empire arrived, they had been able to recapture much of the land that was lost.

Now it was a simple town which milled about with its common business, expressing little concern for those dangers that lurked not far away. Peril and Koristad approached, looking worn and exhausted after their perilous journey. The townsfolk cast suspicious looks their way, wary of these apparently ill-fated newcomers, but none were so bold as to interrogate them.

Koristad had only vague memories of Banock. He'd been so young the last time he'd come here, he wasn't sure why he'd been brought in the first place. The people were all different now, and the town had grown and changed. It all seemed unfamiliar. It was a cold reminder of how long he'd been gone from the world, and he was surprised he'd been able to locate the town at all.

"We need to find an inn," Peril suggested. "I'm really hungry. And I'm tired. And I want to take a bath."

Koristad sighed and shook his head at her. He'd been thinking the same thing, but he wasn't about to say that to her.

"I think the last time I was in Banock there was an inn not far from here," he said flatly. "Let's hope it's still there."

He moved down the busy street, grimacing and holding his side, Peril not far behind.

"Are your wounds bothering you?" she asked softly.

"I think the one in my side has reopened," he said through clenched teeth. "The bandages feel wet." Peril looked up at him with concern on her face, and he added gruffly, "Don't look at me like that."

"Like what?" she demanded crossly. "I'm only worried about you."

"I'll be fine, I just need a little more time to recover," he said. "So stop worrying."

Peril frowned and looked down at the ground.

"When we find the inn, you should let me change your bandages and try to use my magic to heal you. It's more difficult with wounds that aren't fresh, but I might still be able to help."

Koristad didn't answer. He didn't even look in her direction.

They were grateful when they spotted the inn not far down the road, looking just as Koristad had remembered it. Of all the things in town, it had changed very little over the years, a weathered old building with a simple sign over the door that read "Banock Inn." The title wasn't particularly creative or extravagant. It bore a resemblance to the inn itself, which was a large building constructed simply, with little concern for artistic trappings.

The front door opened into a large dining hall where the inn's clients could purchase their meals or drink away their troubles. Koristad was surprised to see the patrons all seemed to be normal folk, with no unsavory characters, like the rag tag bands of rowdy mercenaries that had grown so common in the north. Peril didn't say a word before she hurried to the nearby counter where a large, friendly looking man was serving food. Koristad stayed one step behind, telling himself he had to keep the naïve young girl out of trouble but, in truth, his mouth was watering from the aroma of proper food, just like hers.

She pulled up a stool, struggling against her small stature to sit in the tall seat, and the man behind the bar asked with a smile, "Is there anything I can get for you, miss?"

He had a thick, brown beard and cheery eyes, the kind of person who, in spite of his intimidating size, seemed kind and gentle.

"It all smells so good!" Peril said. "Anything would be fine!"

"You flatter me, young lady," the man laughed, a deep and hearty bellow. "I'll bring you something special right away."

He turned toward Koristad, his eyes squinting over his broad smile. "And you, sir?"

"I'm not hungry," he lied as his stomach grumbled at him angrily. "But we need a place to stay. Do you manage the inn here, as well?"

"Oh, yes sir, I'm the proud owner of the Banock Inn, Jaras Pichgrove," he explained as he busily prepared Peril's meal. "My father purchased this property when I was just a tyke, and left it to me as an inheritance."

Koristad bit his tongue, trying hard not to tell the man he wasn't interested in his life story. He supposed being extra-friendly came with the business, and it wasn't a good idea to get on the bad side of someone who could force you to spend the night outdoors.

Jaras placed the plate of food in front of Peril, who had been eyeing the fare eagerly, and he asked, "Will that be one room for the two of you?"

The very thought made Koristad's head ache.

"Two, if you have them," he explained sternly and clearly, and thought to himself it would be best if they were on different floors, or even different buildings, if it could be arranged.

Jaras nodded and picked two keys from their pegs on a nearby wall.

"Rooms twenty eight and twenty nine," he said, handing both keys to Koristad. "Up the stairs and to the right. That's six silver crowns."

Koristad paid the innkeeper with a sinking feeling in his gut; Gregan had provided him with some coin to fund his expedition, but it wouldn't go very far at this rate. He cast a sidelong glance at Peril, who was stuffing her face with food, and he supposed he would be paying for her meal, as well. Peril noticed him looking at her as Jaras moved on to help other customers, and she quickly swallowed the mass of bread that was in her mouth.

"This is really tasty!" she beamed.

"You're in a terribly good mood," Koristad said cynically.

"Well...it feels great to be under a roof and sitting in a real chair," she seemed to be thinking awfully hard on how to explain herself. "And I feel a lot better now that I've eaten. You should have some!"

She pushed her plate closer to Koristad, who eyed the victuals hungrily.

"No thanks," he grumbled and half turned his back on Peril and her offering.

"What? Why not?" she cried as if Koristad had insulted her own cooking and refused to eat it.

The eyes of the patrons were beginning to turn their way, but she was either oblivious or wanted the attention.

"You have to be just as hungry as I am. I know you are!"

Koristad glared at her and shook his head very slowly, then said in a firm, clear voice, "I said I don't want any."

But Peril wasn't having it.

"You have to eat something, Koristad!" she scolded him. "If you don't eat then you won't have enough strength to start our journey tomorrow!"

"Will you stop this?" he tried to keep his voice down. "Everyone is looking at us."

For a few seconds the two of them stared each other down with fierce expressions, neither one of them wanting to back down. Koristad turned away, as if the matter had been settled. This prompted Peril to do something very, very childish.

She grabbed a piece of toasted bread from her plate and jumped at him, catching Koristad entirely off guard. She giggled as she moved, prompting a roar of laughter from the nearby witnesses of the strange scene. She intended to stuff the bread in Koristad's mouth and force him to eat it, so she pulled down the high collar of his cloak to access his face. The laughter of the patrons died almost instantly, though Peril was far too naïve to understand why.

When Koristad looked at her, it wasn't a look of anger, but of sheer disbelief. There were murmurs floating around the dining hall; they didn't sound friendly.

A man's voice rose loud above the others, crying out, "You're not welcome here, you dirty taint!"

Taint. It was a term of derision for necromancers and other mages, referring to their tainted blood. The word circulated around the room, over and over, filling Koristad's ears.

The reception was even worse than what he might have expected. He was in necromancer territory, after all. But that only meant these people likely had more reason to hate his kind than anyone; it would only be fear of retribution from other children of darkness that would keep them in line. At the moment, it appeared that fear was nearly absent.

"Your kind doesn't belong in Banock!" someone else yelled at him. "Why don't you leave now and never come back?!"

The crowd was drawing in close, and though they were telling him to leave, it didn't look like they were about to let him actually do it. Peril was surprised that Koristad hadn't berated her for what she'd done, but he was doing something even worse. He wasn't even looking at her; it was like she wasn't even there.

She stepped in front of him, opening her arms wide, trying to make herself a wall between the necromancer and the angry mob. She yelled for them to stop, but her words went unheeded, swallowed up by the clamor; she was too small and weak to make them halt. It was looking as if the scene could turn violent, and Koristad's hand crept slowly to the haft of his halberd. He had no intention of using it against the unarmed aggressors, but he thought the threat of the weapon might at least give them pause.

"Stop right there!" a voice boomed over all others, a deep and powerful bellow that instantly forced the mob to grow silent.

It was Jaras, the innkeeper.

"This man has already paid me for his room, and I won't allow anyone to harass one of my guests!"

"Y-You can't be serious, Jaras...," a man in the crowd stammered, caught entirely off guard, but another grabbed him by the shoulder and motioned for him to be silent.

Koristad guessed Jaras was a figure of great importance and respect in Banock; it appeared no one was willing to stand against him.

The crowd began to disperse almost immediately, and many of the patrons must have suddenly lost their appetite. They promptly departed the inn, leaving plates of half finished food and mugs of half drank mead. They weren't about to eat in the same room as a necromancer.

"I'm sorry about the trouble," Koristad said to Jaras in a low voice.

The innkeeper only grunted at him and turned away. Koristad excused himself from the bar and walked toward the stairs that lead to his room.

"Koristad, I'm sorry!" Peril chased after him, grabbing his cloak.

He turned toward her, but she still saw no sign of anger in his eyes. They were dead and emotionless. He took her hand by the wrist and firmly placed one of the keys in her palm, then walked away.

She stood there for a moment, stunned. She glanced around the dining hall, and those few patrons who had stayed gave her unwelcoming looks. She followed Koristad up the stairs but, before she could catch up to him again, he slammed the door to his room behind him. The walls shook with the force of the blow.

Peril slumped to the ground outside, cradling her head across her arms. She couldn't believe how stupid she'd been; everything was going so well, until she'd ruined everything. She didn't understand how those people could hate Koristad just because of a mark on his face. Maybe he was a necromancer, but did that make him a bad person? They were called the children of darkness, but Peril had never thought of him like that.

She couldn't imagine what it was like to be treated like that; to be hated for something he didn't even choose.

On the other side of the door, Koristad was thinking back to his childhood. When the mark had appeared on him, it had faded in slowly, growing slowly darker over a matter of weeks. He remembered looking in the mirror every day, like a boy waiting for his first moustache to grow in, feeling so proud that he had become a necromancer like his father.

He also remembered how his classmates had called him a taint and beaten him with rocks, sending him running home covered in bruises and blood; how his teachers had told his mother that he wasn't welcome at the school anymore. And that sad look in his mother's eyes when she knew her son would never have a normal life.

4

IT WAS LONG AFTER the embers in the hearth of the Banock Inn had grown cold that two masked men crept down the hall that led to Koristad and Peril's rooms. The masks were made of indistinct, white cloth; articles intended only to obfuscate the identities of the wearers, rather than gaudy coverings painted to look like demons and fierce animals to intimidate one's enemies.

Of the two of them, one was of average size while the other was much larger.

The big man carried a thick, short club in his hand and a small sword at his hip. The smaller man carried a length of rope and followed his companion at a timid pace.

When they came to the door to Koristad's room, the larger man put his finger to his lips, then reached into his pocket and produced a key. It slid into the lock with silent ease, emitting only the slightest click as the mechanism shifted and the door slid open. They slipped into the dark room as stealthily as they could, and the large man approached the bed with the club raised high over his head. He didn't attack immediately; he needed to give his eyes time to adjust so he could make one swift strike to the necromancer's skull, knocking him cold or even killing him before he had a chance to act.

The blackness gave way to gray, and the man felt the time to make his move had come. But when he looked into the bed, he found it empty. The blankets and pillows were mussed as if someone had been there recently, but their target was absent.

"I really would have liked to have gotten a good night's sleep," Koristad spoke from the darkness. "But I'm actually glad you're here."

The two men spun around to find the necromancer crouched in the corner adjacent to the door, his halberd unsheathed and cradled across his knees. He was dressed only in his underclothes, displaying the dark bandages that covered his leg and most of his torso. He was grateful that Wraith had given him warning of their approach; it was the first time Koristad had seen the apparition since his long plunge into the ravine.

The men stared at him, dumbstruck, and he went on, "After the scene today, I've been in a perfectly dreadful mood, but taking the two of you apart might make me feel just a little better."

The large man stood firm and remained silent, but the smaller man looked at Koristad, then to his companion, and then back again.

"To hell with this!" he cried, making a mad dash for the door.

Koristad didn't move to stop him. As he ran down the hallway, he was nearly bowled over as the door to the next room popped open, sending him crashing into the wall before he regained his footing and continued his retreat.

It was the door to Peril's room; she'd been so certain that Koristad would leave her during the night, she'd awoken to every sound in the creaky, old inn.

As she rounded the corner, the scene she encountered wasn't at all what she'd expected; the fleeing man had left the door fully ajar, flooding Koristad's room with light. The large man drew his sword from its sheathe, wielding both weapons at once, and leapt at Koristad without speaking a word. He was strong and surprisingly fast for a man of his size, and the ferocity of the attack caught Koristad off guard. It was all he could do to catch both weapons across the haft and blade of his halberd and push up from his crouching position.

The man stumbled backward, shocked. He couldn't believe how strong his opponent was; he looked like a young boy, less than twenty, and was little more than half his size. But he was helpless against such a powerful retort. Before he could regain his footing, he felt something blunt strike him under the ribs, knocking the wind out of him and forcing him to drop to his knees. He tried to hold it back, but he retched on the wooden floor.

There was a flash of light, and the next thing he knew he was laying on his back. His head throbbed painfully with every heartbeat. When his vision cleared, he saw the young necromancer standing over him, the razor sharp blade of his weapon at the larger man's throat.

"Any last words?" Koristad growled at him, thinking it was more than the animal deserved.

The man's eyes darted back and forth, trying to find a way out, but there was nowhere for him to run. His weapons had rolled out of his hands. He closed his eyes and waited for the end.

"Koristad, don't you do it!" Peril cried.

Koristad didn't respond, but he didn't make a move to attack, either.

She went on, "You said you were working for the lightwielders! So you have to follow our rules, and we don't kill unless we absolutely must, and we show mercy to our enemies!"

Still, Koristad didn't move; his eyes remained fixed on the shining blade that rested across the throat of the man who had tried to murder him. He hadn't even glanced at Peril, and she wondered if he was in such a blood rage that he didn't even hear what she said.

Then he laughed. A soft, gentle sort of laugh, and he took a step away from the masked man.

"You don't have to tell me," he said with a shake of his head. "I wasn't really going to kill him."

The large man scrambled to his feet and dashed toward the door, not daring to make even the slightest motion toward the sword or club that lay on the ground. They heard him clamor down the stairs, and he was gone.

"Are you alright?" Peril asked.

As soon as the danger had passed, Koristad's hand had gone to his side. When he pulled it away, his palm was stained with dark blood. He hadn't given his injuries the time and peace they needed to heal, and this action had only made things worse. She gasped and took a step toward him.

"This isn't going to kill me," he said. "But we can't stay here. Go get dressed so we can leave."

The comment made Peril suddenly aware that she was wearing only a thin, short gown that left little of her body to the imagination. Further, were it not for his proliferation of bandages, Koristad was wearing even less than she was. Her face instantly turned bright red and she darted into her room, not allowing Koristad to look her in the eyes.

She dressed quickly, and soon there was a knock on her door and Koristad asked if she was ready. She let him in, and he looked at her with surprise.

"You had a change of clothes?"

"Of course I did," she said. "I kept them in my pack."

"But you never changed when we were traveling here," he said, confused, "You just kept wearing the old clothes, even though they were dirty and covered in mud."

Peril's face had only returned to its natural fair color moment's ago, but now it turned red again.

"Well, I wasn't going to change in front of you!" she blurted out.

Koristad laughed, which only made her blush more. He looked behind her and noticed there was a large bag that they hadn't brought with them.

"What's that?"

Peril swelled up with pride, feeling uncharacteristically useful.

"When you shut yourself in your room, I decided to go into town and get the supplies we needed for our trip, so we'd be ready in the morning. It looks like it turned out to be a good idea."

"Wow, I'm really impressed," Koristad said with a nod.

Peril nearly fainted at the compliment.

He added, "I wouldn't have thought you were capable of planning that far ahead."

In an instant, everything had returned to normal.

"Now let's go."

It was a little known fact that the Banock Inn had a basement. It was a secret room with a small table and more than a dozen chairs, a makeshift meeting place. This was where the large, masked man fled after his confrontation with the necromancer. He staggered forward, holding his side. He ripped off the mask that had been stained by blood and vomit, revealing his face and thick beard.

"I won't let you do this to me, necromancer!" Jaras Pichrove snarled, the fire of hell in his eyes. "I won't allow your kind to hurt anyone again!"

5

(Twenty-three years before present)

WHEN JARAS WAS A boy, he'd been small for his age—a runt amidst his classmates. It did little to improve his standing with his peers that he cried easily and was always hanging on his mother's hand.

He remembered his mother as the most beautiful woman in the world, with deep brown eyes and long, blonde hair. She was never unkind to him; when they were in the same room her face would light up with a smile, which he joyfully returned.

Her name was Vandra, and on this day Jaras found himself hiding behind her skirt, peeking his head out just far enough to catch a glimpse of the newest patron of their inn. The man sat alone at the end of the bar, as far from everyone else as he could get, dining silently as if not to attract undue attention to himself. He was finely dressed in dark clothing; the most distinctive article being a long, black cape that was trimmed with crimson thread. He was a handsome young man, with dark eyes and hair. But his disposition seemed cold and distant; those few times he did look up from his meal, he eyed his surroundings cautiously, as if he couldn't trust those around him.

At the moment, Vandra was pondering the same man.

Noticing that her son was trying to hide, she asked softly, "Oh, Jaras, what are you doing?"

"He's scary, mama!" Jaras whispered, afraid that the man might hear. "Father said that man was a necromanster!"

She smiled and ran her fingers through his thick hair, "A necromancer, huh? Is that so scary?"

"Uh huh," came Jaras's fragile reply. He seemed to think for a moment. "They can summon ghosts that kill people while they sleep, and they can control people's minds like they were puppets. And they drink blood!"

"Oh, Jaras, only vampires drink blood, not necromancers," she corrected him sweetly. "And do you know how necromancers became what they are?"

Jaras shook his head slowly, looking up at his mother with eyes filled with innocence.

"When the archangels were sent down to the world from the heavens, they knew they wouldn't be able to stay in the world of mortals long before they would ascend. After they were gone, the people of this world would still need protection. The lightwielders were scattered and few, so the archangels decided to pass their blood to the mortals who they felt were most good, just as Aura had done ages before them. So, the mages, including the necromancers, were born to protect this world."

"But necromansters aren't like lightwielders," Jaras insisted with a frown.

Vandra considered this for a moment, trying to think of a way to help her son understand.

"Just think of this, Jaras—the city of Banock is safe right now because it's protected by a necromancer who lives in the Great Citadel; Arach the Black Guardian."

"Arach the Deathbringer, you mean," came a gruff voice from nearby. "That's the name they gave that butcher after he returned from the west."

The two of them looked behind, surprised to see Jaras's father, Brogan. He'd only recently purchased the inn and had been busy the last few days seeing to odds and ends that needed fixing and attending to. He was a large man, and when Jaras grew up many people who knew his father would say he looked like him. This wasn't entirely true; they were both men of great stature, with the same color hair and thick beards, but Brogan's eyes were unlike his son's. They were hard and stern, and the man always seemed to be in a sour mood. He was strict with discipline, and had on more than one occasion taken the lash to Jaras's backside. To the young boy, Brogan was a man of equal parts fear and respect, and he'd learned to never question him.

"I was just telling our son he doesn't need to be afraid of our new guest," she explained.

"Stop coddling the boy," he groaned. "He's nearly ten years old."

Vandra only looked sad and nodded; over the years, she'd learned it was better not to question him, as well.

"Don't you have work to do?"

"Of course," she said quickly, patting Jaras on the head and showing him a soft smile before she departed.

Vandra was in charge of the girls who cleaned the rooms and did the laundering for the guests of the inn, but the family didn't have enough money to hire all the workers they needed, so they were always shorthanded.

Brogan kneeled down next to his son and said in a low, harsh voice, "You're right to be afraid, boy. All mages, and necromancers especially, are no good lowlifes. They're a danger to anyone who's near them and, if you ask me, the emperor should enforce a law to put them all down, just like was done to the artificers."

Jaras was afraid to ask the question, but he mustered up his courage and said, "But why are you letting him stay here? I don't like it."

Brogan smiled, but it wasn't a kind smile. It was a cold smile; the kind of smile that flashes across a conman's face as his mark hands over everything he owns.

"Because he has money, and he's paid for his room and a little more just to be left alone," he explained. "It would be foolish for me to turn him away."

Jaras still didn't understand, but he nodded as if he did.

His father put his hand on his back, giving him an unsubtle push, and said, "Now go outside and play. You're in the way."

6

(Twenty-three years before present)

THAT WAS THE LAST clear memory Jaras had of his family while they were still alive. He was the one who found them; a small boy stumbling onto the scene of a bloodbath. For years he couldn't remember it clearly. All he could recall was the blood, that distinct shade of red, but even more than that was the smell. That strange mix of organic and metallic scents, it was like that of a slaughterhouse. He was a grown man by the time the memories started to invade his mind, striking him in the dead of night. He would cry out and wake in a cold sweat, then he would be wracked by tears and sobbing and be unable to sleep. It all came back to him in fragmented scenes, each lasting only a moment, and those dreams were the only recollections he could ever muster.

He saw his father lying on the wood floor of his parent's bedroom, wearing the same leather cooking apron he always had on when he was running the dining hall. Both of his hands were wrapped around the handle of a long cutting knife, and the blade was thrust through his throat, jutting out the back of his neck. He was covered in blood, too much to be just his own, and his apron looked like the attire of a butcher.

He remembered blood splattered across the walls and even the ceiling. The floor was sticky with it.

He remembered the sheets of his parent's bed, which had always been white, had been stained red. He didn't want to look, but the carnage poured into his open eyes no matter how hard he wished it away.

It was his mother. She'd been too savagely attacked, slashed and hacked, for Jaras to recognize her face. But he was able to recognize her beautiful, blonde hair. Now, it was matted with blood. But she wasn't alone. A body leaned back across the mattress, the head hanging off the end, a pair of blank, dead eyes staring at the traumatized young boy. It dangled unnaturally, bending farther than it should have; his throat had been deeply slashed. Jaras didn't recognize him at first; it was only later that he learned the man was the young necromancer who had recently taken residence in the Banock inn. The two of them, Vandra and the mage, both lay naked in the blood soaked bed.

Jaras didn't remember leaving the room. He didn't recall running for help or being incapable of putting words to what he'd seen. It seemed only a moment later the massacre had been wiped away and he was sitting in the empty dining hall with his uncle Osmond, his father's younger brother. The room seemed vast without the usual bustle of guests and barmaids, and was dimly lit with only a few candles on the table at which they were sitting. The light didn't even reach the far walls; it seemed as if that darkness could have stretched on forever.

"Are you listening to me, boy?" Osmond didn't look much like Jaras's father, but the voice and those stern eyes were the same. "I said I'll be taking care of you from now on."

"I don't want you to take care of me!" Jaras bawled, more a crybaby now than ever. "I want my mom!"

Osmond sighed; a deep, heavy sigh, and put a broad hand on Jaras's tiny shoulder.

"I know you do, Jaras. But that isn't possible anymore. I'm sorry."

Jaras's face turned red and he batted his uncle's hand away, then turned in his seat, showing Osmond his back.

"Just leave me alone," he pouted.

Osmond leaned back in his chair, seeming little perturbed.

"My wife and I will be moving to Banock," he said. "We have a little girl, Carmilla. She's only a few years younger than you. I hope the two of you will be friends."

Jaras frowned, but remained silent.

"I'll be running the inn, for now. But when you come of age, all of this will be yours. I think Brogan would have wanted it that way."

At the mention of his father, Jaras's bottom lip began to quiver as he tried to hold back the tears. Osmond put his arm around the young boy's shoulder, and Jaras began to shake and sob. He wrapped his scrawny arms around his uncle's neck and held on like he was the only thing left in the world.

There were no witnesses to what had happened on that bloody day; whatever had transpired was buried with the three who had lost their lives. Of course, no one was forthcoming with Jaras; no one wanted to talk to him about what everyone thought had happened. But it wasn't hard for him to piece it together, hearing whispers on the streets and eavesdropping on bits of conversations.

The people of Banock had looked at Vandra and Brogan and seen a troubled marriage. Brogan was gruff and unkind to his wife, and she was nearly ten years his junior. They claimed she had fallen for the striking young necromancer and the two of them had given into lust, forsaking her marriage vows. When Brogan found the two of them together, he'd killed them both in a fit of rage. When that was done, unwilling to face the shame of what had happened or the punishment for his actions, he'd taken his own life. It was a simple little package, a story they could tell to pacify themselves and forget it had ever happened.

But Jaras had a story of his own, one he'd put together as he'd grown older and more wise to the ways of the world. The young necromancer had used his magic to take control of Vandra to satisfy his own perverse desires. When Brogan had found the two of them together, he knew nothing could free her from the wicked magic, and the only way to give her peace was to end her life. So, he'd done what had to be done; he used his cutting knife to end the lives of both the mage and his wife. But before that foul necromancer had breathed his last, he had one final cruel spell to weave: he took control of Brogan's mind, plunging the blade that had ended his own life into the throat of his just executioner.

Jaras knew his mother was good and pure, and she would have never betrayed his father in such a horrible way. And his father had been a strict and rough man, but he could have never slain his wife in an act of jealousy. The rest of Banock could believe whatever they wanted, but Jaras knew the truth.

It was the necromancer's fault his world had been torn asunder; he'd lost everything on that day. It was *all* the necromancer's fault. But nothing could be done for it now; all he could do was try to protect others from the same twisted fate.

7

"WHO WERE THOSE MEN, Koristad? Why were they wearing those strange masks?" Peril demanded suddenly as the two of them hurried along the road leading south from Banock.

The city's lights had faded away in the distance behind them, leaving them in relative darkness, but the moon was nearly full and the sky was awash with stars. The sun would rise in just a few short hours.

"You don't know?" Koristad said, surprised.

Peril shook her head.

"They call themselves the Order of Purity, or sometimes just the Order. From the name you wouldn't think they ruthlessly hunted down mages and persecuted them, but you'd be wrong."

"So, those weird masks are a symbol of their group?"

Koristad shrugged, "I suppose so. But I think the real reason they wear them is so they can't be recognized; there may be many people who agree with their views on how to deal with mages, but the laws of the empire protect us just like they protect anyone else. For now, at least."

"But you didn't do anything to them!" Peril cried.

"I'm surprised you don't already know all of this," Koristad gave her a quizzical look. "Haven't they taught you anything at the sanctuary?"

"Of course they have!" she protested. "But no one ever told me there were people like that. Maybe the lightwielders don't even know about them."

Koristad laughed.

"Then they would be the only ones. The Order is commonplace this far from the capital, though I've never heard of them settling this far north. The foothills are a haven for necromancers, or at least they used to be. They should be careful, or they might wind up crossing a child of darkness who won't tolerate such insolent behavior."

"When I get back to the sanctuary, I'm telling the executor about this!" she exclaimed angrily. "They can't treat people like that!"

"Go ahead, if you think it will make any difference," Koristad said without a glance in her direction. "Most of us with tainted blood are used to being treated this way."

The two of them had managed to cover quite a bit of ground. They were glad to be leaving Banock behind them, even if it meant they would be traveling through the night. Peril yawned and wondered how much longer it would be before sunrise.

Wraith faded into sight near Koristad, his glowing eyes hovering along the road.

"There are more of them coming this way," it said without passion. "More of the masked men, moving swiftly on horseback."

Peril didn't react to the apparition, though it was only a few feet from her. She was unaware of its presence and couldn't hear its voice.

Koristad's eyes darted back and forth. He could already hear the sound of galloping hooves approaching from behind, and he knew it would be only moments before they arrived. He couldn't see clearly in the darkness, but he thought he spied a stand of high bushes not far off the road.

He grabbed Peril by the wrist and ordered, "Come this way!"

"What? Where are we going?" Peril asked in surprise; she hadn't noticed the sound of horses drawing near.

Koristad didn't have a chance to answer; he felt a sudden pain in his side and for a moment everything went dark. When he could see again, he was down on one knee, his arms wrapped around his torso.

"Damn, not now!" he gasped.

The wounds Azoman had inflicted would have killed most men, and Koristad knew if he didn't give them time to heal, they might prove fatal to him, as well.

"Koristad, are you alright!?" Peril cried, kneeling down next to him.

It was only an instant before masked riders were upon them. There were nine of them in all. Jaras had roused every member of the Order of Purity in Bancok from their beds for what he believed to be the most holy of causes. Many of them carried torches, blazing bright in the night air, both for light and as weapons. Two of them carried crossbows, including Jaras. His was a special weapon of considerable size, with a draw so powerful there were few in Banock with the strength to load the monstrosity. It held a heavy bolt of solid iron, a weapon that was intended to protect the town in the event of a barbarian raid. He supposed it could kill a mage just as easily.

The horsemen fanned out and surrounded their prey, their torches casting an eerie light across the scene. Koristad drew his weapon, though he was still clenching his jaw against the pain and couldn't seem to fight his way to his feet.

"Let the girl go, taint," one of the men growled. "We're not after her."

Peril narrowed her eyes at the man, then jumped to her feet and put her hands on her hips angrily.

"Why don't you just leave us alone!?" she screamed at them. "We already left your town! What more do you want from us!?"

The masked men looked back and forth at each other, then one of them growled, "She's probably a taint, too. Why else would she be travelling with a necromancer?"

"She's a real looker, though," another chimed in. "Maybe we should strip her down and see if we can find a mark on her, just to make sure."

A few of the men laughed.

Koristad found his way to his feet, though he was shaking badly. He felt weak and lightheaded; he wondered how much blood he'd lost. Peril looked at him with surprise, but he put a hand on her shoulder and pulled her behind him, away from the threatening men.

"You said I'm the one you want," he insisted, his words soaked in his own blood. "Leave her out of this."

The men of the Order were plainly threatened by his words, and even the horses stamped their hooves and threw their heads, unnerved by his presence. Jaras kept his crossbow trained on Koristad's chest, ready to let the bolt loose at any moment.

Peril stepped around the necromancer, an indignant expression on her face and her hands still on her hips.

"What do you think you're doing?" she demanded. "You're in no condition to be protecting me!"

Koristad, annoyed by his assailant's persistence and suffering badly from his wounds, was in no mood to be questioned.

"Just shut up and stay behind me," he snapped at her. "I'm not too hurt to deal with trash like them."

"Not feeling well, eh, taint?" one of the men mocked, but his words fell on deaf ears.

"Just this once, I wish you would listen to me!" Peril yelled, her face turning red with anger.

Jaras glanced at the other man who was armed with a crossbow and saw his hands were shaking badly. He imagined sweat was pouring from the man's brow, but couldn't see anything behind the white mask.

"This doesn't concern you," Koristad said in a low voice. "They're looking for a mage, and they've found one."

"What do you mean it doesn't concern me?!" Peril's tone was growing more and more shrill. "I'm surrounded by masked horsemen wielding torches!"

The horses, already agitated, started to panic at the girl's shouting. They were beasts bred and trained for work, not for war, and were ill-accustomed to violent confrontation. Jaras saw the mount of the other crossbowman rear back in surprise. The man, unprepared for such sudden movement, let his finger hook the tickler of his weapon. With a twang, the bolt flew toward its target. Jaras didn't have an instant to think; as if by its own accord, his own iron bolt followed the first.

There was a whoosh of air as Koristad lashed out with his halberd, then the sound of wood snapping and a noise like two swords clashing between mighty adversaries. The men couldn't even follow the movements of the young necromancer; one moment he'd been arguing with the girl, and the next he was standing in front of her, the blade of his weapon buried in the earth after his two savage swings. The bolts were gone, and the two were unscathed.

The horsemen, feeling suddenly disarmed, began to back away from this clearly dangerous child of darkness. But Jaras didn't budge. The others may have been ready to give up the hunt at that point, to flee back to Banock with their tails between their legs. After all, who would know what had happened besides themselves? But Jaras had no intention of backing down. He looked at Koristad's face, into those fierce eyes, and what he saw was the necromancer who had killed his parents. He didn't care about anything else; he just wanted to rid the world of these dark monsters once and for all. It didn't matter if it cost him his life, or even his soul.

He let his mighty crossbow fall to the ground and reached to his belt, drawing a long, double edged sword. It was an old weapon, a blade his uncle Osmond had fought with when the barbarians had struck into the south. Now it was his; a gift for when he became a man. He fought to regain control of his frightened horse, preparing for a violent charge.

"If you do this," Koristad warned in a bleak voice, "It will end in death."

No one had a chance to object or intervene. Peril's skin had grown pale, and her eyes were wide as she looked up at the enormous masked man, his blade held high and his horse's nostrils flared with excitement. He looked like a monster; a shadow out of a dark fairy tale.

The steed took off at a dead gallop, in a desperate charge toward Koristad. Jaras cocked back his arm, preparing for a swing he imagined would cut the necromancer clean in half. Peril closed her eyes and covered her head with her hands, and the other masked men looked on with dismay, wishing they were back at home in their warm beds.

Koristad watched the furious man and frightened horse approach with a still demeanor; there was a calm in his eyes even the most battle hardened war veteran would be hard pressed to match moments before being ridden down by a mounted adversary.

Jaras felt certain the necromancer's defeat was imminent. He wasn't moving; perhaps he was too injured to act, or maybe he'd just given up. He readied his blade for the final strike that would end this monster's life. It wasn't until the very last moment that Koristad made his move, his weapon screaming through the air like a flash of silver lightning.

The blade didn't strike Jaras, or even clash with his sword. Instead, the sharp edge cut into the flesh of the horse, slashing into its chest and carving its way through the ribs and organs. The animal contorted in pain, throwing Jaras from its back, and made a sickening, choking sound. It couldn't stop its forward movement; there was too much momentum behind the massive animal. The blade cut through to its belly before exiting, nearly stripping the weapon from Koristad's hands. Blood, guts, and organs washed onto the road from the gaping wound, turning the hard dirt into mud. One of the men stripped off his mask and leaned over the side of his horse, vomiting.

The animal died almost instantly. Koristad looked down at the steed with a scowl. He would have preferred to strike the rider. It seemed paradoxical; the horse was a strong and noble creature, but its master was the true beast.

At the sight of the carnage, the masked men could no longer control their horse's fright. They fled in every direction, fighting against their steeds and trying to make their way back to Banock.

Jaras lay on his back by the side of the road, stunned and only barely conscious. He felt as if he were dreaming.

In his mind, he could see the child of darkness stepping in front of his companion, raising his arms in her defense. And he recalled Koristad standing over him, the blade of the mighty halberd at his throat; and then he remembered the necromancer letting him live.

And, as his last few moments of consciousness faded away, he recalled his mother's words.

"...the mages were born to protect this world...the city of Banock is safe right now because it's protected by a necromancer..."

And he felt it was strange; he hadn't thought about those words since her death.

Chapter Five

*Shut your eyes tight, still your beating heart—listen close—and perhaps you, too,
will hear the unrelenting howls of my personal demons.*

1

IT WAS ONLY MOMENTS after the necromancer and the young lightwielder
had departed that the company of erstwhile thralls began to grow restless. First,
it was low grumbles about being abandoned by those who were supposed to be
looking after them. Soon, their complaints took a more sinister turn.

They realized that, with the outsiders gone, they had been left alone with
the object of their pain and frustrations: the necromancer, Leer Valcroix. Bound
and masked within the carriage, he was helpless to defend himself against their
retribution. Even the driver, who may have tried to uphold some sort of civility
and lawfulness, was still sound asleep. Leer was exceedingly gifted at commanding
the living, and he'd used an incantation when he'd induced the man's unnatural
slumber. He wouldn't wake for many more hours.

"I say we drag him out here and string him up!" one of the men barked. "I'd
feel a lot better if I saw that bastard dangling on the end of a noose!"

The young girl who Leer had subjected to such vile domination, Maria,
flinched at the loud commotion.

"Hell, why let the rope have all the fun?" another man chimed in. "We should just grab some shovels and beat him to death!"

The party grumbled their hoarse agreement and continued with their imaginative plans of execution. Before long, they'd worked themselves into a mob.

Maria sprung suddenly to her feet and let out a loud sob, tears streaming down her face. The men were too surprised to react; before they knew what was happening, she'd dashed into the carriage and slammed the door. They looked at each other with sighs and grimaces on their faces.

One of them said, "What does she think she's doing?"

The answer came from a man whose face was wrapped in bandages, like a mummy. It was the man who Koristad had struck with the blunt side of his weapon during the conflict with Leer. In addition to losing several teeth, his jaw had been fractured. He'd tried to care for the injury as best as he could, but he knew little of medicine, and the resultant binding had left little of his face exposed. When he spoke, it sent sharp pains down his fractured nose; this in addition to his missing teeth made it difficult to understand what he was trying to communicate.

"Just leave her alone," he mumbled. "She's had it worse than any of us."

One of the men glanced over at him and cocked an eyebrow.

"Aw, Kent, you're just sayin' that 'cause you're sweet on her."

It was difficult to know for certain, but Kent may have looked irritated at the comment.

"I ain't sweet on nobody," he said, storming away from the party to sit by himself.

One of the men, annoyed by the girl's actions, approached the carriage and attempted to open the door. It didn't budge. Frowning, he rocked the handle back and forth, rattling the wooden frame, but the portal was locked tight. He groaned in defeat.

"I guess it doesn't make any difference. If she wants to stay locked up in there by herself, then let her."

He plopped down next to the others and struck up a new conversation, their dreams of revenge dashed, at least for the time being.

Soon the clouds began to part and bright sunlight washed across the camp. The warm rays did little to lighten their spirits, however. They still waited in dangerous country for their protectors to return, or for the arrival of the other lightwielder who'd been mentioned.

The door of the carriage popped open with a click and Maria poked out her head, looking left and right across the company. Finally, she spotted Kent in the distance, rummaging through a tent and throwing together supplies, his poor disposition clear in his handling of the goods.

"Kent, will you please come sit with me?" she said in a shaky voice. "I need to talk to someone."

Kent looked surprised; he wasn't close to the girl. The company hadn't known one another before they'd been brought together under Leer's power, and what interactions they'd had were superficial, considering their nearly absent faculties. Maybe she'd heard what had been said after she'd retreated into the coach, and believed he would be more sympathetic to her woes than the others. Or perhaps, since his injuries made it difficult for him to speak, she thought he would make a better listener.

"Of course," he mumbled incoherently, tossing the gathered equipment into a pile at his feet. "I'll be right there!"

He hurried into the carriage and the door latched shut behind him. The rest of the company grumbled at this new development and turned angry eyes toward the filling coach.

"What, does she think that's her *house* now?" one of the men said with a shake of his head.

"She must've been a noble, before Leer nabbed her, to act so self important."

"Or a nobleman's whore."

The men shook their heads. They were on edge and tempers were running high; this certainly wasn't the time to be causing dissent.

One of the men said with a disapproving look, "You don't suppose they're…"

Another put up his hands, shaking his head, "I'm sure she got her fill of that, and then some, from the necromancer. Besides, with Kent's injuries…it just wouldn't be pretty."

As if in response to his name, Kent's voice suddenly issued from the dark coach, erupting in a bloodcurdling scream of agony. The men jumped in surprise, almost too flabbergasted to know what to do. One of them dashed to the carriage door, but it was still locked. He banged on it and yelled, but to no avail. He was preparing to break it down, or at least give it his best try, when the door creaked open at last.

Kent stumbled out of the carriage, leaning on Maria for support. He held his hand as if it had been injured—there was blood running down his sleeve. He seemed weak and unstable, as if he might collapse at any moment, and Maria was white as a ghost, her eyes wide.

"What's going on!?" the men demanded. "What happened!?"

When the two didn't answer right away, one of the men darted into the carriage to see for himself. The first thing that struck him was the overwhelming and sickening reek of blood. He found the inner door which sealed prisoner's compartment was wide open. It was dark inside, almost too dark to see clearly, but as his eyes adjusted he saw the prisoner was lying on the ground, his remaining hand twisted into a painful claw.

His throat had been slashed, spilling blood everywhere; it was incredible how much there was, as if every drop had been squeezed from his body. The floor was sticky with it, and the man took an involuntary step back, unable to look away. He was grateful the mask still covered the man's face; the sight of those dead, glassy eyes staring at him would have given him nightmares.

He emerged from the carriage and doubled over, certain he was going to be sick. He braced himself against a large, iron bound wheel, looking up at the semicircle of laborers who'd gathered around, demanding answers.

"What happened in there?!" one of them said.

"Th-they killed him!" stammered the sick man. "They cut his throat!"

Livid eyes fell upon Kent and Maria; of course, the rest of the party had been ready to kill Leer just moments before. This new development had merely robbed them of that satisfaction, though that didn't stop them from calling the two murderers.

"It's not like that!" Maria pleaded, raising her hands defensively. "We only opened the door to talk to him. But his severed arm was free and he tried to attack us!"

"You're a liar," one of the men accused bitterly.

"It's true!" she maintained. "If Kent hadn't protected me, I might have been killed! But the exposed bone cut his hand when he stepped in front of me…please, let us through, we need to get bandages to care for his wound."

The two tried to push their way through the crowd, but no one was giving an inch.

"That still doesn't explain why you had to cut his throat," one of them said with a sour look.

Maria looked terribly distressed, near the point of tears.

"We were only defending ourselves," she cried in desperation. "He was like a rabid animal!"

The men grumbled in frustration, but finally allowed them to pass. Kent wasn't looking well, as if he might collapse if forced to stand any longer without treatment for his injury. The two of them retreated to a nearby pavilion. Maria cast an apprehensive glance over her shoulder before she closed the flap behind them.

"What do you think?" one of the men asked of no one in particular. "Are they lying?"

Another man spat on the ground and shrugged, "Does it make any difference? The necromancer's dead now. There's no changing that. I guess we'll let the lightwielders decide what to do about it."

2

MARCELLUS KRISTIAN LET OUT a heavy sigh of relief as the Snowdove Sanctuary came into view on the horizon. It had been a dismal journey through dreary and treacherous lands, leading a handful of soggy and down spirited porters. It seemed more a funeral procession than a traveling company; the body of the fallen lightwielder, Leorra Natarra, lay atop the carriage, covered with white linens. Inside, the corpse of the necromancer was laid out flat and draped in a thin shroud, still covered in the flaking dust of his own blood. Marcellus imagined the carriage would have to be burned; never would that overwhelming reek of ichor be removed.

When Koristad had abandoned him on the road, Marcellus had almost decided to turn back and return home. He was prepared to offer a formal complaint concerning the necromancer's behavior but, as he went over the protocol in his head, he began to realize how foolish he would appear. Even a hint of disgrace worked the lightwielder into a red faced fervor, and he decided instead to proceed to Koristad's destination, where he would teach him a lesson in manners. He was prepared to return the child of darkness to the sanctuary in chains, if that was what it came to.

But he was utterly unprepared for the scene at the encampment. He hadn't expected to find anyone in the prohibited northern steppes, much less an entire company looking after a slain child of Aura. When they related the recent events, his bitterness toward Koristad was quickly replaced by concern for these wayward souls, and a desire to see them safely back to civilized lands.

By the time he'd arrived it was nearly dusk. It was decided the company would wait for Koristad and Peril to return until dawn. After that, they would be forced to depart. To remain in these lands for too long would risk an attack by the crazed barbarians, and Marcellus knew it would be impossible to defend the entire party by himself.

Early the next morning, the driver awoke from his unnatural slumber, desperate for water and understandably distraught to find his ally had been slain. Still, he was well enough to drive the coach and was able to give Marcellus details about the task Leorra and Peril had undertaken. It was clear to the lightwielder that his duty required him to return both of the bodies to the Snowdove Sanctuary, along with the possibly murderous conspirators, which brought him to the present end of his expedition.

The fact was, he didn't blame the prior thralls for executing the necromancer. He would have felt justified doing the same thing, were it not for the responsibility leveled upon him by his position.

The survivors had claimed the sole conspirators in the slaying, a pair named Kent and Maria, had fled in secret shortly after the crime. Marcellus had no way of knowing if they spoke the truth or if they had merely created these fictional murderers to assuage their own guilt. Even if the pair had genuinely gone into hiding, things being what they were, he was in no position to conduct a search for them. If the sages and executor decided they had to be punished for what they'd done, he would let them send their own agents to hunt them down.

Snowdove was encircled by a high, stone wall. The fortifications had been constructed during the first incursion, when the original lightwielders had taken up arms and used the holy ground as a stronghold against the legions of invading demons. Those ancient battlements should have long since crumbled, but the children of Aura maintained the lofty stone barriers as a matter of façade and symbolism.

Marcellus rode to the front of the procession, seated upon a powerful brown mare and clad in heavy armor. The gate was a high portcullis of riveted iron, more than twenty feet wide and just as tall. At present it was raised, though it was clear that, were it brought down, it would make an imposing barrier. Two guards stood watch, clad in light ringmail and holding polearms at their sides. They drew themselves up as the company approached, holding their weapons upright, but not displaying them in any menacing way.

"Good afternoon, travelers," one of the guards said. "What brings you to the sanctuary?"

He may have been suspicious of the beleaguered crew, were it not for the blazing sun medallion Marcellus wore around his neck.

The lightwielder called the company to a halt and replied, "My name is Marcellus Kristian, a lightwielder of the Sunrise Sanctuary. I bring dire news; one of your own has fallen in her duty, the lightwielder Leorra Natarra. I've come to return her remains to you, as well as the remains of the necromancer she was hunting."

The two men exchanged quick glances, understandably surprised.

"I'll fetch the executor at once!" one exclaimed, dashing through the gate.

"Please, lead your company inside," the other said, stepping out of the road. "I'm certain the executor will see to this business immediately."

On the other side of the wall, Marcellus found himself in an enormous courtyard. The main walk was paved with white marble and lined with tall statues on either side. They were icons of legendary paladins who had made this sanctuary their home, stretching back to time immemorial, exaggerated in stone to be more than ten feet tall. Behind the statues there were grassy flats and evergreen trees, common foliage in the wintry climate, evenly spaced and meticulously manicured.

Several side paths jutted off from the first, leading to small stone buildings, but it was the structure straight ahead that drew every eye, consuming every particle of wonderment and causing all peripheral distractions to melt away entirely. It was a domed structure of smooth gray stone, fifty feet high at the apex, and ringed with mighty columns so immense two grown men couldn't reach all the way around a single one.

Even Marcellus stared at the sight with wonder, though he'd visited this sanctuary in the past. The Sunrise Sanctuary was an artistic and architectural masterpiece in its own right, but was no more like Snowdove than the sun is like the moon. The refugees who were seeing the sight for the first time looked about wide-eyed and murmured amongst themselves.

Between a gap in the pillars stood an enormous set of double doors, so large it would have taken four men to push open either side. However, embedded in the large pair was a smaller set of doors, built more to a scale of functionality.

It was through these that a man with pepper-colored hair exited, surrounded by several attendants. He was clothed in the garb of the executor. Marcellus had met the man only once before, during a formal sort of greeting, but all lightwielders were familiar with the names and reputations of the executors.

"Executor Kailas, it's an honor to make your acquaintance once again," he said, hopping down from his horse and bowing respectfully. "I wish it were not under such unhappy circumstances."

The executor wasn't a large man, a head shorter than Marcellus and rather thin. His face was clean-shaven and his hair cut short, a fact that made him look younger than his sixty years. He gazed at Marcellus with dark eyes filled with troubles, seeming uncertain.

"Marcellus Kristian, lightwielder of the Sunrise Sanctuary," he introduced himself quickly, thinking the executor didn't remember him.

"I'm told you've returned with a fallen child of Aura," Kailas said in a hoarse voice.

"Yes, Executor," Marcellus said, hustling to the coach and directing the men of his traveling party to help him move the body to the ground. Leorra was transported with as much delicacy and care as possible, lowered to the stone walkway by many hands.

The executor approached with a downcast gaze, lowering himself to one knee beside the still body. He gently pushed aside the linens that hid her face and, when he saw the unblinking eyes of Leorra, Marcellus thought the old man looked choked up. He pulled the shroud back over her face, as softly as he'd removed it. He then rose to his feet, slowly dusting himself off, as if he were giving himself time to let the tragedy sink in.

"And the necromancer?" he said with a grimace. "I wish to see Leer Valcroix. I want to see with my own eyes that he's paid for his sin."

"Of course, Executor," Marcellus said as he opened the carriage door. "Though it isn't a pleasant sight."

He locked his arms under the dead man's armpits and dragged him into the light, his feet knocking against the steps as he was brought to the ground. The lightwielder laid him on his back, the arm with the severed hand sprawled out across the white paving stones, blood issuing from the wound no more. The executor looked on without emotion as Marcellus unbuckled the mask's bindings, pulling it off and exposing the man's face.

It was an ugly sight. His jaw rolled open the instant the hood was removed, revealing a mass of broken and missing teeth. It hung open in such a way that it was clear the bones had been fractured, though Marcellus didn't recall the men of the camp mentioning he'd been assaulted in such a way. Kailas turned pale and his eyes grew wide; he dove upon the corpse, tearing open its dark surcoat and staring at the bare chest in disbelief. It was an action unbefitting the dignity of an executor but, in that moment, Kailas had lost all sense of etiquette.

"Executor?" Marcellus said in surprise. "What's the matter?"

"This man isn't Leer Valcoix!" he growled lividly, gesturing emphatically at the dismembered body. "Leer's mark is on his chest!"

One of the men from the camp took an uneasy step forward, swaying back and forth as if he might fall over from the shock. The others looked on in wide eyed disbelief, shaking their heads as if it might wake them from this nightmare.

"How could this have happened?" the man said in a hushed voice. His whisper suddenly exploded into a scream of bewilderment. "How!? This man... it's Kent!"

3

(Several days before present)

LEER AWOKE IN UTTER darkness. His last memory was seeing his right hand, still clutching Leorra's broadsword, slashed from his body and falling to the ground. He tried to reach out with his left arm to see if it was really gone, but discovered it wouldn't budge from his side. Both of his limbs were bound tight to his body. His struggles triggered pain that confirmed, without question, his hand had truly been severed.

He wanted to curse Koristad's name, but he couldn't speak. Something was in his mouth, gagging him; he rocked his head back and forth and moved every muscle in his face, trying to liberate his faculty of speech, but to no avail. He realized he had been bound in a mask the lightwielders kept especially for captured necromancers; it wasn't his first time being trapped in one.

He wasn't sure where he was. Had he already been taken to the prison grounds, just outside the sanctuary's walls? The darkness permitted him no clues. Regardless, there was no doubt his execution was inevitable. The children of

Aura weren't merciful to those who had killed one of their own, in spite of their preaching about such charitable virtues.

Leer wasn't about to lay back and wait to die; he had important business to attend to, and an early death would severely hamper his ability to carry it out. He knew the weak point of his bindings was his missing hand. Though the cuffs were pulled excessively tight, almost like a tourniquet, there was nothing to stop them from sliding off. He gritted his teeth and pulled, trying to push the pain from his mind. But it was hopeless; the agony was overwhelming, and after only a few seconds of effort he surrendered to the pain, shaking and feeling lightheaded. His arm felt sticky and wet, and he feared he may have reopened his wound.

He heard the click of a door opening and then slamming shut, but it was muffled, as if behind a screen. He became silent and still, curious of this new development. He listened intently, and soon he heard a sound like a door rattling, and some banging, but it died off quickly. Then he heard light footsteps coming in his direction. They stopped suddenly and, for several moments, there was silence.

At last, he heard a clattering and a sound like a block of wood being dragged against the wall and hefted to the ground. There was the creak of another door opening, this one right next to him, exposing him to the unseen visitor. He tried not to move or even breathe. He didn't have a plan; it was a simple defensive instinct, playing dead and hoping he'd be left alone. He waited for a kick to the side or to be violently drug to his feet by some self-righteous prison warden, but no sort of assault came upon him.

Instead, he felt a pair of hands slide gently across his face to the buckles behind his head, slowly and deliberately unfastening him. The hood was pulled away from his eyes and, for an instant, he was blinded by the light. The chamber was poorly lit, but it was a sea of shining luminosity next to the utter darkness he'd escaped.

A form began to fade into view, hovering above him. He blinked rapidly, his eyes in pain from the sudden bombardment of light. He thought he could recognize the face looking down at him, but he was surely mistaken. Was it Maria? But why would she remove his mask? Wasn't she afraid she might fall under his corrupt power once again? She stood there, looking down at him with expressionless eyes for so long that Leer felt he had to say something.

"What are you doing?" he demanded.

Her eyes grew suddenly pitiful and she whimpered, "Please, let me go."

Leer narrowed his eyes at her suspiciously.

"What are you talking about?"

"It's not the same as before," she whined, casting her eyes downward as if it was an affront to meet his gaze. "But I can still feel you in my head. Please, just let me go. I'll do anything."

That playful and cunning smile grew on Leer's face once again. He knew he had no control over this girl; the bonds with all of his thralls had been severed the instant he'd faded from the waking world. But the domination Maria had been subjected to was particularly foul and dangerous, like the work of a sadistic amateur. He'd actually worried the corruption might have taken her life before he had a chance to make use of his clever scheme, but she'd managed to cling to existence with surprising tenacity. It now appeared her mind may have suffered more severely than her body.

Though his magic no longer made her a thrall, she'd lost her sense of free will, her ability to think for herself, perhaps even her self-awareness. Maybe she genuinely believed Leer had control of her mind. It was possible she simply couldn't function without his direction and chose to deceive herself. It made little difference to him.

"Where are we?" he demanded.

Maria delivered an emotionless briefing of the events that had transpired since he'd blacked out, as well as their present situation. Leer listened intently, pondering all she had to say, and often stopping her in mid-sentence to demand more details.

When she was finished, he announced, "I have to get away from this wagon before Koristad or this other lightwielder gets here. But the men outside won't let me simply walk away."

"But you can command them to let you pass," Maria said in confusion, believing him like a god.

"I'm too injured. I don't have any strength left to utilize my magic," he explained. Maria looked even more perplexed. He quickly corrected himself, "All the power I have left I'm using to keep you under my control. But I'm too drained, now; that's why it feels so different."

Maria nodded and offered, "What can I do for you?"

Leer sighed. He supposed it was too much to hope for that this damaged young girl could help him piece together a scheme. But he hadn't survived as long as he had without being clever. It took him only a few moments to come up with a plan, and only a few more to work out the details.

"Unbind my hands," he ordered, and Maria quickly obeyed.

He struggled to his feet, noticing that the girl made no move to aid him without him directing her specifically to do so. He was hardly able to stand and wobbled back and forth uneasily, bracing himself on the nearby carriage walls. He saw his stump of a hand had begun to bleed again, oozing out dark red liquid through his bandages, but he was in no danger of bleeding out.

He stumbled from the prison chamber into the main compartment, pushing Maria unapologetically out of his way. He rummaged around with his good hand, taking stock of the tools available to him. Eventually he came across a light hatchet stowed away in a box under the seats, intended for breaking down firewood. It would do nicely.

He turned to Maria and asked, "I trust you still have the dagger I gave you?"

He'd felt it was prudent to keep her armed, since she had always been by his side. Potential threats may have been wary of the necromancer, but they would pay little heed to the pretty young girl standing behind him. Maria produced the weapon, which had been tucked away in her right boot, and held it up to display its presence. The look in her eyes was apprehensive, but she pushed the feeling deep into her mind, drowning it.

"Good," Leer said with his charming smile. "I want you to bring the man with the broken jaw in here, and then I want you to cut his throat."

Maria grew pale.

"I-I can't do that," she said, mortified.

Leer continued to wear his smile despite her resistance, staring her in the eyes to break down her fragile will.

"If you do this," he said gracefully, "Then I'll set you free."

Maria looked down at the ground. Her hands were shaking.

"You want to be free, don't you? To go back to the way things were before?"

She nodded.

"Good. Then you'll do as I say."

"You promise you'll set me free?"

"Of course. I promise."

She nodded again and walked to the door of the carriage. She took a deep breath as she undid the lock, then pushed open the door and called the man inside. Leer hobbled into the prisoner's compartment, though he didn't shut the door. As Kent drew closer, Maria took a step away from the door, both to allow him entry and so she was out of sight. She turned to face Leer, tears in her eyes.

"Please, I can't do this," she whimpered desperately.

"I'm too injured to do this myself!" Leer hissed at her in a low voice. "Do as I say, or I'll keep you as my slave forever!"

Leer shrank into the darkness as Kent entered the carriage, pulling the door shut behind him. Kent took one step into the compartment and realized something wasn't right. His eyes went wide when he saw the prisoner's door was standing open, and Maria glided silently behind him and locked the carriage door.

Leer took a step out of the shadows, allowing the man to see his unmasked face and his sinister grin. Kent didn't understand what was happening, but fear and hatred seized control of his body. He took a step toward Leer, preparing to lunge at the necromancer and lock him in the sealed chamber before he had a chance to sew his corrupt magic. He felt an arm wrap around his neck from behind.

"I'm sorry," Maria sniveled as she put her dagger to his throat.

She wasn't much of an assassin; Kent screamed in pain before the blade silenced him.

Leer glared at her and snarled, "Stupid girl! The men outside certainly heard that!"

"I-I'm sorry," she whispered, barely audible, staring at the blood on her hands.

"Quickly, help me exchange clothes with him!"

For a moment she didn't react, staring down in shock. Leer grabbed her by the arm, digging his fingers into her flesh, leaving a line of bruises. "Now!"

The exchange occurred faster than Leer would have thought possible. Fear and desperation can push a person to do incredible things, even one so injured as he. Still, it was only a matter of moments before someone was banging on the door, demanding to be let in. Maria had finished fixing the hood to Kent's face, and Leer was fumbling with the bandages around his own, when he handed the girl the hatchet he'd found.

"His hand," he said in a harsh whisper.

Maria shrank away, looking at him as if she couldn't take any more. But one severe glare from the necromancer set her in motion, striking off the limb with a single blow. Leer tossed the dead hunk of flesh behind the door in the prisoner's compartment, where it wouldn't be seen. Finally, he was ready.

He stumbled out of the carriage, leaning on Maria for support. He seemed weak and unstable, as if he might collapse at any moment, and Maria was white as a ghost, her eyes wide.

"What's going on!?" the men demanded. "What happened!?"

4

L EER PULLED THE BLOODSTAINED bandages from his face, tossing them to the side of the road with disdain. Maria followed, just a few steps behind, staring at the ground. They were traveling an old path not far from the expedition, running south and east. Leer didn't know exactly where the road was taking them, but they were moving toward the civilized lands. Surely it would lead to a village, and there he would be able to replenish his company of thralls, and eventually return to the north to resume his search for Arach Altessor's hidden research.

The day grew overcast and breezy, and there was a chill bite to the wind. The path they traveled had vaulted high into the air, with a sheer wall of rock on their right and, just a few feet away, a steep drop onto jagged rocks some forty feet below. The path was unmaintained and narrow; if two carriages were to meet along the corridor, there would be no way for them to get around each other without one of them being pushed to a deadly plunge. But, traveling on foot, it seemed safe enough.

"Sir?" Maria said quietly, not daring to speak his name.

"What is it?" Leer said with a smile, though his tone dripped with annoyance.

"You said you would set me free if I helped you escape," she said, cringing.

When Leer didn't voice any sort of response, she added, "You promised."

Still, the necromancer remained silent.

She desperately grabbed hold of his sleeve, dropping to her knees on the dirty road, and cried, "Please! I don't want to be like this anymore!"

Leer came to a halt and roughly batted the girl's hands away. Still, the smile didn't leave his lips.

"You're a fool!" he declared callously.

Unable to suffer her imprisonment any longer, Maria collapsed to the ground and began to sob.

"Please, please, please…," her cries faded into unintelligibility.

"Stupid girl, I don't have any power over you," he said. "I haven't since Koristad took my hand."

Maria quickly grew silent and pale. She looked up at the necromancer, her face streaked with tears.

"No," she said. "That isn't true."

Leer shook his head at her in disgust.

"Do you really think I would let you question me if I had power over you?"

"But it's different now," she said in disbelief. "You said so yourself…because you're weak from your injuries."

"I'm not so weak *now*, am I?" Leer drew himself up. "I can walk on my own without any aid, and I'm not shaking like before. Do you really think I'm too weak to use my magic if I wanted to?"

"But if I'm not being controlled…"

Leer finished the thought for her, "Then everything you've done has been your choice."

"But Kent…," she whimpered.

"You took his life, with only the slightest push from me," he laughed. "For a moment, I wasn't certain you could really pull it off. But you did. Good show."

As Leer gave her mocking applause, Maria stopped crying. Perhaps, over the last few days, she'd managed to cry away every tear in her little body.

Leer snapped at her, "Now get off the ground and keep walking. Or stay here and rot; it makes little difference to me."

With that, he turned away and continued moving down the narrow path.

He'd only taken a dozen steps when he heard Maria rise to her feet, pushing the dirt out of her way with miserable, dragging paces. He didn't look back; she still carried the little dagger he'd given her, but she didn't have the will to use it against him.

A mere instant of silence passed as the young girl hesitated, peering over the ledge with terror and longing. He heard her feet slip off the road; there was a sickening crunch as her bones shattered on the jagged rocks below, killing her instantly.

Still, that clever smile never left his lips.

Chapter Six

BLACK AND WHITE

When we're children, it all seems simple.
There's good and bad, virtue and vice, as plain as black and white.
But, as we grow older, we realize reality is never so plain as good and evil.
I wish we could all live in that simple world again.
But making that world is more difficult than it seems.
I still can't do it.

1

KORISTAD RELAXED ON HIS back, arms behind his head, and gazed up at the clouds that scattered lazily across the bright blue sky. The birds sang in the distance and a warm breeze, heavy with the aroma of pollen and flowers, drifted across his skin. He basked in the cool shade of the prison tower where he had once been entombed, glad to finally be back home, such as it was. His halberd rested on the deep green grass near his feet, and he had sweat on his brow; his muscles burned from his morning exercises, but in a pleasant, invigorating way. His wounds had closed with remarkable speed; a normal man would have been ailing for another month after all he'd been through, but Koristad's lesions had turned into little more than scratches, and weren't even leaving any scars. He sighed contentedly and closed his eyes.

"What are you doing out here?" Peril demanded.

Koristad cringed at the sound of her high pitched voice. After all of the commotion at Banock, he'd taken her back to the Snowdove Sanctuary, where she'd resided before striking out to find Leer Valcroix. She had told him goodbye and looked at him with sad eyes; in her mind, the parting was made even more bitter by the fact that Koristad, with his tainted blood, couldn't even set foot in the sanctuary to which he'd delivered her.

Koristad had felt relieved. He was, in fact, quite vocal about his relief, though there was something more to it. He supposed some small part of him was sad to see her go; maybe it was simply the fact that in the time they'd spent together she'd always talked to him and treated him like an ordinary man. Since he was a boy, when the mark had appeared on his face, others had looked at him and seen only a necromancer, a dangerous child of darkness to be watched with suspicion and avoided. Things had only gotten worse after his entombment.

He had tried to put the thought out of his head, instead focusing on the long journey back to the Sunrise Sanctuary. The trip had seemed much less daunting on his way north. His injuries made it impossible to travel with the expeditiousness he desired.

When he arrived, forbidden by his blood to enter the sanctuary grounds and announce his return to the executor, he'd returned to the dilapidated prison tower that was now his home. He told himself he needed to rest and let his wounds heal for a few days, but the truth was that he dreaded being reprimanded by Gregan for leaving his pompous overseer behind in the wild north. When he finally did see Executor Mourne, the old man wasn't in nearly the sour spirits he'd augured.

As it turned out, Peril had decided the moment Koristad left her sight that she was going to relocate to the Sunrise Sanctuary. She was used to getting her way. The younger lightwielders coveted her; the men, at least. The old sages treated her like their long-lost granddaughter. With Leorra gone, there was little holding her at the Snowdove Sanctuary, in any case. So, she'd batted her eyes and asked nicely. When that didn't work, she stuck out her lip and begged. Then she pouted and cried and, before long and to no great surprise, she was finally given what she wanted.

Executor Mourne was fond of Peril right away, finding her naivety refreshing. Her arrival was the first indication he'd received that Koristad had returned from his expedition, though more than two weeks had passed, and he'd taken it upon himself to show her the way to the necromancer's place of residence.

It was then that Gregan related to the proxy lightwielder what had become of

Leer. Koristad appeared unconcerned about what had transpired after the criminal had been apprehended, expressing no interest in what, if anything, was being done to find him. Peril, on the other hand, only appeared to be worried that Leer might be able to find her, seeking retribution. She'd been informed of his escape by Executor Kailas before departing the Snowdove Sanctuary, and it was a matter that had caused her to miss several nights of sleep. After seeing the wicked man slay her mentor, he'd haunted her nightmares as a terrifying apparition. Executor Mourne reassured her that the necromancer would have his hands full merely trying to avoid being recognized and captured, and wouldn't have the means to consider reprisal.

"Leer isn't like that, anyway," Koristad had added in a knowing voice. "You're no threat to him now; he wouldn't even think to seek you out. Though it would probably be for the best if you didn't cross his path, by some odd chance, again."

The matter apparently settled, Gregan announced he had duties that needed attending to and took Peril back to the sanctuary.

Like all lightwielders, Peril resided upon the sanctified grounds, but every day Koristad would find her at his tower. So, it was no great surprise that she was there now, though Koristad tried hard to forget.

"What are you doing?" she repeated when Koristad didn't answer, hands on her hips and stomping on the grass to make her point.

He opened his mouth as if to respond, but wasn't sure what to say aside from the obvious. He snapped it back shut and simply shrugged.

"I asked you to carry in the supplies from the wagon," she went on with a frown.

Koristad didn't recall being asked anything; rather, he'd been told, ordered, and commanded. He hadn't realized someone so small could be so bossy. He glanced back at the girl with his eyes only half open, a look of blissful lethargy on his face. Peril was standing at the foot of the tower's worn, exposed staircase, her hands gray with dust and a straw broom propped up on the nearby wall.

"I'm doing all of this work for you, Koristad! I thought you would want to help! I had no idea you could be so lazy."

Koristad gave no sign that he disagreed with her assessment; he simply nodded, though it was difficult to tell whether it was in agreement or if he was merely nodding off. Peril went on frowning and glaring at him and, after a few moments, he could feel her eyes boring a hole into his perfectly relaxing afternoon.

His eyes snapped open, and he calmly said, "I never asked you to do any of this. I was perfectly happy with how the tower was before."

Peril had been appalled when she saw what Koristad called his home. The structure was exactly as it had been when the executor released him from his bindings; stones were strewn across the staircase, there was a thick layer of dust on everything, and there was hardly a hint of light in the upper level.

Koristad didn't seem to have any interest in cleaning or redecoration, so Peril thought she would do something nice for him and help make the old tower a livable habitat. Though her intentions were explicitly altruistic, she was surreptitiously motivated by the fact that she intended to spend time at the tower as well, and her fair skin and posh demeanor didn't encourage her to spend that time outdoors.

Peril was silent for a moment, trying to devise a new tactic.

In a much sweeter voice, she purred, "Koristad, will you please help me?"

"No." The response was instantaneous, and he didn't even bother to look at her.

"Please?" she insisted stubbornly. "Please, please, please, please..."

Peril might have gone on like that for some time, hours if that's what it took for his compliance, but she was suddenly distracted. At first, all she heard was the sound of a horse's hooves walking at a slow pace, and she thought the horse she'd brought from the sanctuary had gotten loose. Then she spotted someone moving down the path toward the tower; squinting her eyes, she could make out a powerful chestnut horse and its rider, armed and armored.

"There's someone coming," she warned Koristad.

For a moment, he wondered if this was some new ploy to force him to do her bidding; he'd been so intent on blocking out the sound of her whining that he hadn't even heard the stranger's approach. He decided it couldn't hurt to take a look, and when he turned his head he found the visitor was already drawing close.

The horse was absolutely magnificent. That was the first thing he noticed. Koristad wasn't familiar with the equine species. Since he'd emerged from his long imprisonment, animals had found him disconcerting; not even the bravest warhorse would willingly allow him near. But even he could see the animal was healthy and strong, with a broad chest and layered with powerful muscles. Its eyes shone with vigor and intelligence, and its gait spoke of some deep nobility; a true prince among horses.

The rider seemed no less noble. He was tall and clad in heavy armor from his feet to his neck. The mail was rich and ornately designed, finely polished and maintained, though it was also scarred from battle. No doubt these displays of valor had been left intentionally; a smith could have easily beaten them out. The thick breastplate was emblazoned with the sun symbol of the lightwielders; the ornament shined so brightly it may have been pure silver. There was a bastard sword strapped to his back, as well as a large, metal shield. He'd forgone his helmet, displaying strong and handsome features. His face was smoothly shaven, and his blonde hair was trimmed short.

Koristad disliked the man instantly. Everything about him seemed too clean and perfect, like a prince on holiday pretending to be a knight. The man dismounted from his steed with surprising ease, considering the clear heft of his armor, and approached the two of them with a placid expression, as if nothing in the world could disturb him.

"I'd heard the Sunrise Sanctuary had been keeping a child of darkness as a pet," he said with no ire in his voice, as if he was simply stating a fact. "I had to see it for myself to believe it. High Executor Kanan may be preoccupied with illness, but I wonder what he would have to say on this matter, were he aware."

Koristad didn't bother to rise to his feet, trying to acknowledge this intruder as little as possible.

"If I'd realized I was a local attraction, I would have been charging for tickets."

He mimicked the man's tone, as if he, too, was simply stating a fact.

2

"HELLO!" PERIL SAID IN an over-friendly tone. "My name's Peril! I'm a lightwielder, too."

The man looked at her as if he hadn't noticed her presence until that moment, and showed her only the slightest hint of a smile. It seemed forced and unnatural, as if the expression had no business with his countenance. He took Peril's hand in his cold, steel gauntlet and kissed it softly, a polite courtesy that caught Peril off guard after spending so much time with the ill mannered necromancer.

"It's a pleasure to meet you, Peril," he said in a soft voice. "I'm Paladin Vincent Night of the Silversword Sanctuary."

His words seemed sincere, but his tone belied no emotion.

"And to what do we owe the honor of your visit, Mister Paladin?" Koristad said with a snort. "I assume you didn't come all this way just to take a look and be on your way."

Vincent turned his way and said, "Executor Mourne should have known better than to allow your kind to do the work of a lightwielder."

Koristad rankled at the way he referred to "his kind", though Vincent's voice carried no more bile than if he were talking about the weather. Again, he was simply stating a fact.

Koristad sighed, swallowing his agitation, and announced, "I'll be sure to let the executor know of your opinion the next time I see him. Now, if there's nothing else, I was just about to take a nap."

He leaned back and closed his eyes.

"I'd also heard you fought with a blade," Vincent added, "And you fancied yourself a real fighter. Now that I've seen you, I have to say, I'm not very impressed. You look like nothing more than a scrawny boy, to me. If you're willing, I'd be happy to give you a lesson, and show you just how little our order needs one of your kind."

Koristad's face lit up with a broad smile. Now, that was more like it; that was just what he'd wanted to hear. He rose to his feet, dusted himself off, and picked up his halberd with one hand. Vincent appeared nonplussed.

"What do you think you're doing, Koristad?" Peril demanded, stepping between the two men. "You can't fight a lightwielder. That's just…just… stupid!"

She couldn't think of a more appropriate word.

"It's only a friendly sparring match," Vincent insisted with a wave of his hand, as if he were waving away a troublesome servant, which only made her more upset.

"I may not be an expert," she said, her face turning red, "But I don't think you spar with sharpened weapons!"

Koristad was still smiling, and was eager to show this pompous lightwielder a thing or two about combat. Vincent certainly spoke with confidence, but Koristad doubted he'd ever fought against an opponent with abilities like his.

"I can check my blows if you can," he suggested, as if it were nothing.

"Of course."

"Koristad Altessor!" she shouted at him, and would have added his third name if she'd known it. "Your wounds have barely healed! Do you enjoy being injured all the time?! I won't let you do this, I forbid it!"

Of course, this only encouraged him.

"Is this one your mother?" Vincent asked and, while it was clearly in jest, there was nothing in his tone or air to suggest that was the case.

Peril shot daggers at him.

Koristad put his hand lightly on Peril's shoulder and said in a deep, commanding voice, "I'm not going to get hurt."

Peril looked into his eyes and saw there was nothing she could do to convince him otherwise.

"Hmph!" she turned on her heel and stormed away from the two of them, stomping down the path by which Vincent had arrived. Koristad felt a little disappointed; he would have liked to have had a witness to the thrashing he was about to deliver.

Vincent drew his blade, a true hand-and-a-half sword, with a broad ricasso and a wide, sharply angled guard. Next he readied his shield, a tall oval of heavy wood covered in a layer of worked iron; it bore the same sun symbol as his breastplate. Koristad waited impatiently for the lightwielder to prepare, fidgeting back and forth in anticipation.

Vincent assumed a fighting posture, and barked, "Ready?"

Koristad had never been properly trained in combat techniques; he relied on his reflexes, instinct, and tenacity, as well as raw combat experience. But he knew no stances, no special techniques; he simply nodded at Vincent, his halberd held low and pointed toward the ground.

The two blades clashed with a ring of sharpened steel that echoed against the nearby tower. Vincent was clearly a talented fighter, trained by the most accomplished swordsmen; his motions were quick and agile, as difficult to read as his expressions, and carried with them the righteous strength of a holy warrior. But Koristad did well holding his own, matching him blow for blow, block for block, until Vincent finally forced some distance between them. Koristad thought perhaps his adversary was weary of their sport, but one look at his face dispelled this notion. There wasn't a drop of sweat on his brow, and his breathing was easy and regular.

"I see," Vincent said, narrowing his eyes, "You're not just an ordinary child of darkness, are you?"

"Is it hard for you to accept that a mere necromancer can give you a fair match?" Koristad said.

"No, there's certainly more to you than that," he continued. "I've fought against vampires; or their ghouls, at least. You move like they do, and you wield that same preternatural strength."

Koristad frowned at him, not enjoying Vincent's uncannily accurate assessment.

"What's your point?" he demanded crossly.

"It's clear you haven't turned," Vincent said. "You stand in the sunlight, and it doesn't seem to affect you. Just what are you, Koristad?"

"Does it matter?"

"Lightwielders destroy vampires because they are a danger to the innocent people of the empire," he stated simply. "If you, too, are a danger, then I will destroy you."

He said it without question or hesitation, as if it would be as easy as swatting a fly.

"You make it sound simple," Koristad growled at him, his face filled with anger, "But you haven't landed a single blow on me yet, lightwielder."

Vincent shook his head, disappointed.

"Do you know the difference between a lightwielder and a paladin?"

"It's a rank," Koristad answered, hardly giving the question a thought. "It means you lead other lightwielders if you go to battle."

"I suppose it is that," Vincent said, clearly not satisfied with the response. "But it's not a rank of hierarchy. A lightwielder can become a sage, or even an executor, without ever being named a paladin."

"What's your point?" Koristad was clearly growing impatient.

"The difference is power," Vincent spoke slowly, letting the statement sink in. "The blood of Aura gifts us all differently, just as all necromancers are gifted differently. But I wouldn't want you to make the mistake of thinking the strength of a paladin can be taken lightly."

"I'll keep that in mind."

"Good. Then let us continue."

As soon as he said the words, Vincent's eyes flashed brightly with an unnatural light. Koristad wouldn't have thought a man clad in so much armor could move so quickly, but he fell under a rain of powerful strikes almost instantly. He was stronger than before, but that was fine; Koristad could push a little bit harder, as well.

They exchanged rapid blows, their footwork pushing them back and forth across the gulley and around the tower. It was difficult to tell who was receiving the worse end of the exchange, but after some time Koristad leapt away from his enemy, and Vincent didn't pursue. A wide gash opened on the necromancer's arm, sending a warm stream of blood washing down to his fingers.

"You're not checking your blows, like you said," Koristad made the comment with a violent smile, gritting his teeth against the pain.

Vincent unfastened his shield and let it fall to the ground with a clank. His hand was twisted into a claw; his forearm was bleeding where he'd been cut by the shield's leather strap. It didn't appear to be broken, but he was clearly hurt, perhaps a sprain or a cracked bone.

"You're not checking yours, either," he said.

"I suppose I'm not as good at holding back as I thought," Koristad hissed at him, "Especially after being compared to a vampire and threatened."

"You're easily agitated, aren't you?" Vincent sighed. "You'll never be able to beat me if you're too frantic to focus on our battle."

"Talking down to me like that only makes you look weak. We're both men of action; if you think I'm a threat that needs to be dealt with, I'm right here," Koristad motioned him to attack. "Come at me with everything you've got."

"That's a foolish request," Vincent said, "But I suppose it would be disrespectful for me to refuse. Prepare yourself, Koristad; I will show you the *true* might of Aura."

Vincent buckled down, gripping his sword with both hands, like an animal preparing to pounce. Something didn't seem right to Koristad; Vincent's arm had been injured just moments before, but he no longer appeared to be pained by it.

Something began to change in the atmosphere. It was as if the air was vibrating, sealing off his ability to hear and clouding his vision. Was this some kind of energy emanating from the paladin? He readied his halberd; it didn't matter what kind of power this self-righteous pretty boy could muster, Koristad wasn't about to let himself be intimidated.

3

"THIS ALL SEEMS TERRIBLY serious," came a wizened voice from nearby. "I hope you don't mind if I intervene."

It was Executor Mourne, Peril in tow. Vincent instantly sheathed his weapon and dropped to one knee, bowing his head in respect. Koristad lowered his weapon, looking at the executor with an ill-concealed expression of annoyance.

"Executor, I apologize for not introducing myself at the sanctuary," Vincent proclaimed in a loud, clear voice. "I've not planned on lingering for long, and thought it would be rude to trouble a man of your stature over such a small matter."

Gregan scowled at him, not easily pacified by petty atonements.

"Then I think it would be wise if you didn't linger any longer," he said.

Vincent looked up in astonishment, caught off guard by his abruptness. The paladin was displaying more passion than he had even when engaged in combat.

Vincent rose quickly to his feet, making a slight, stiff bow toward Gregan and said, "Then I will take my leave, executor."

Without another word or a glance at Peril or Koristad, he picked up his shield and stormed to his horse, agitation clear in his gait. The proud horse whinnied as Vincent wheeled the beast around, and soon he had ridden out of sight. Gregan turned toward Koristad, a severe expression on his face, even more harsh than what he'd offered Vincent.

"What do you think you're doing, Koristad?" he seemed positively exasperated. "Do you know who that is?"

Koristad shrugged nonchalantly, "Paladin Vincent Night. That was what he said."

"That is his *name*, but that's not what I mean," Gregan said with a frown and a shake of his head. "Vincent is the cousin Gabrial Night. In case you don't recognize the name, I'll inform you: he's the executor of the Silversword Sanctuary."

"So? I should have let him win?"

"You shouldn't have been fighting with him in the first place."

Koristad raised his hands defensively, "He was the one who started a fight with me. I was perfectly happy enjoying my peaceful afternoon before that pompous ass showed his face."

"You didn't have to fight him, Koristad," Peril said.

Koristad glared at her.

"I can't believe you went and told the executor on me," he growled.

"I didn't!" she protested, waving her hands. "Well, at least, I didn't mean to…"

"I was already on my way here, Koristad," Gregan said in her defense. "We merely ran into each other on the road."

"I see," he replied suspiciously, not sure if he believed the alibi. "Then what is it you want?"

"Koristad!" Peril yelled at him with a frown. "Executor Mourne came all this way to address you in person. You're being rude when you should feel honored!"

Koristad laughed.

"Oh, it's no honor," he explained. "Gregan's only come himself because no one else at the sanctuary is willing to approach my tower. Scared or superstitious, I guess."

It was the truth; among the servants at the sanctuary Koristad had become something of a bogeyman. Gregan had never told him as much, but he didn't appear to be impressed with the young man's shrewdness.

"I'm here because I have a job for you," he explained, not wishing to explore that subject any further.

Koristad smiled and nodded, "That's good. I was getting bored with nothing to do."

Peril thought she'd given him plenty of tasks to hold his interest; he'd simply preferred to lie around doing nothing. But she didn't interject.

"Travelers and hunters have begun to go missing near the forest of Southsheaf Wold," Gregan explained. "Initially, bandits were assumed to be the cause, and a bounty was offered for the capture of any criminals. It turned out to be a deathtrap; many who went to that forest seeking fortune have never returned. One man did escape with his life, though he was the only survivor of his expedition. He claims his party was ambushed by a lycanthrope."

"A lycanthrope?" Koristad seemed surprised. "You mean a were-beast?"

Gregan nodded.

"A werewolf, actually. Such a monster falls under the purview of the lightwielders. It's unfortunate that anyone else became entangled in such a dangerous task. I want you to travel to the south; about ten days ride along the road will bring you to the town of Clemmensreve. Southsheaf Wold is nearby.

Find this monster and destroy it, using whatever means are necessary. It cannot be allowed to live."

Koristad was a little put out by the length of the journey, but hunting a werewolf seemed an excellent way to put his abilities to the test. He knew he would need to explore (and expand) his limits if he ever intended to face the Vampire King.

"That sounds simple enough, I suppose," he said with a nod, turning his attention toward Peril with a clever grin. "I guess you'll have to find someone else to bug for the next few days."

"Actually," Gregan interjected with a subtle chuckle, "She'll be going with you."

Peril stuck her tongue out at Koristad; the executor had clearly informed her of this fact during their walk to the tower.

"What? Why?" Koristad's brain was filled with questions, but those were the only two he managed to stammer out. "She won't be any help to me!"

"I will so, Koristad!" Peril cried.

"She's not even a lightwielder," Koristad continued, ignoring her utterly, "She's just an initiate!"

"There are no more lightwielders at the sanctuary who are willing to work with you," Gregan explained. "Not after what you did to Marcellus."

Koristad wasn't certain, but he thought that might have been the name of the lightwielder he'd abandoned before encountering Leer.

"That's perfect. I already told you I don't need anyone to look after me."

"Lightwielders don't work alone," Gregan said, refusing to budge. "You're no exception. With this, Peril will no longer be an initiate. You're ill suited to be her mentor, and I don't believe she would benefit further from having one. The two of you will be working as a team."

"Really!?" Peril exclaimed in excitement. "There's nothing I want more than to be a full-fledged lightwielder. You have to take me with you, Koristad!"

Gregan smiled pleasantly at the young girl as Koristad glanced back and forth between the two, feeling as if he'd been backed into a corner by the executor's clever machinations.

He could tell there was more going on in Gregan's head than what he was letting on, but he couldn't imagine what sort of schemes the old man had put together. Still, he could see there was no use in arguing.

"Fine," his shoulders slumped as he conceded defeat. "I'll do what you say. But if she gets in my way, I'll remember who made me bring her along."

"I won't be in your way!" Peril chimed in. "I'll be a help to you, Koristad, I promise!"

Somehow, he felt even less assured.

4

PRIOR TO THEIR DEPARTURE, Peril and Koristad had a small matter to attend to. They'd learned during their long walk from Banock to the Snowdove Sanctuary that, while Koristad could cover vast treks of land with inhuman swiftness and fortitude, Peril was not so able. The executor had given them a purse of silver crowns in addition to the ordinary mission expenses and recommended a local stable master who was accustomed to providing lightwielders with sturdy and reliable mounts.

Gregan had actually recommended she find a pony, to which she'd said nothing, clearly too respectful of the executor to disagree. However, when Koristad repeated the sentiment during the walk to the stable, she'd grown indignant.

"Why does everyone think I can't ride a regular horse?" she complained. "I'm not a child, you know!"

Koristad tried hard to ignore her. He wondered how it was possible for someone so small to be oblivious to her own stature.

When they reached their destination, they found a wide pasture surrounded by a wooden fence. It was composed of thick posts with two broad sets of boards nailed across them. There were many horses scattered about the enclosure, several coursers and destriers of high quality, with sleek coats and muscled bodies. Peril squealed and hurried toward them with delight, standing on the lowest board of the fence while leaning far over the other. She reached out with her hand, clicked and cooed, hoping they might come over and let her pet them.

As Koristad drew near, however, the horses pricked up their ears and sniffed the air. They whinnied frantically, rearing up and stumbling over each other in their haste to get away. Soon, they were all huddled on one side of the vast enclosure, stamping their hooves nervously, as far from the young necromancer as possible.

There was only one exception; a runt of a horse with a shaggy mane and a white coat. He was spattered with light brown spots on his chest and back, and especially on his rump. He pranced toward Peril as if he was oblivious to the sense of dread the rest of his kind felt so terrifically, brushing up against the fence and sniffing her hand.

Koristad was surprised, and even a bit confused. This was the first time he'd seen a horse, or any animal, come so close to him without being unnerved. With a sense of awe, he reached out his hand to allow the beast to catch his scent, as well.

The horse lifted his muzzle toward the necromancer's outstretched limb, allowing him to draw close, before chomping down on his hand with his wide, blunt teeth. Koristad cried out in surprise and leapt back, shouting every curse he knew at the animal, and trying hard to think up new ones just for the occasion.

Peril giggled hysterically and patted the horse on the head. By the time the stable master made his appearance, she'd already decided which horse she wanted to purchase. She found the entire incident so funny, in fact, she decided to name him "Jester".

"Are you sure about this one?" Koristad said. "I thought you said you didn't want a pony."

Peril huffed defensively, "Jester isn't a pony! He just didn't grow up as big as the others."

Of course, Koristad could understand how she might relate to that; he may have even found the statement humorous, if not for his aching hand. Instead, he made a comment about how he thought the animal was most likely part donkey and grudgingly handed the pouch of silvers to the stable master.

Chapter Seven

PAYING BY PENANCE

I've often questioned the difference between revenge and justice.
I think it comes down to this: revenge is decided and carried out by the person who's
been wronged, while justice is merely revenge carried out by people who weren't
involved.
Is that what we call being civilized?
Of all things in this life, it seems vengeance should be the most personal.

1

(One month before present)

A YOUNG MAN, TALL AND well built, marched purposefully toward a small cottage in the distance, smoke drifting lazily from its chimney. The expression on his face was of both determination and apprehension, severe and heavy, like a man facing an uneasy destiny. He was undeniably handsome, with long hair and skin darkened by a lifetime under the sun. Though he wore no beard, coarse hair grew upon his face, giving him a rugged, wild look. His manner of dress was unmistakably odd: leather moccasins and a hide jerkin that left much of his chest exposed. He looked like a man who had lived all his life in the wilderness, never setting foot in a city.

The cottage he approached sat isolated, miles from civilization. A narrow, winding path guided his steps, cutting through heavy underbrush on either side.

130

Looking to his left, he could see a forest springing up in the distance, thick with tall, leafy trees. He didn't know its name; never in his life had he traveled so far east. But his mind wandered to those titan trees, and he longed to run through them, to hunt the game and rest in the shade of the willowy branches. But his legs carried him ever forward.

As he drew near, he spotted a man dressed in dark clothes and wearing a wide brimmed hat. His head was tilted downward so the brim obscured his face, divulging nothing of his appearance. He sat alone on a wicker chair, his arms folded across his lap. The young man wasn't certain if he was asleep or if he was waiting for his unexpected guest to arrive.

He placed a foot upon the wooden steps leading to the deck and the old wood groaned under his weight. The man in black lifted his head at the noise, revealing a face with ancient looking eyes. He had deep crow's feet and his skin was rough and wrinkled. He frowned at his young visitor, a look of annoyance and loathing on his face, but he said nothing.

That look alone was enough to freeze the young man in place, and he stood there for a long time, taking a measure of the man in front of him before he spoke.

"Do you know who I am?" he said at last.

His voice was low and his tone stern. He'd thought about this meeting for years, played it over in his mind time and again, but in his imaginings the man in black hadn't appeared so old and frail. Now that the meeting was real, it carried a distinctively heavy and dreamlike quality, and he suddenly couldn't recall what had been said in his many eager rehearsals.

"I don't," the man in black answered, his voice sharp and cold like ice. "*Should* I know you?"

"My name is Evers Hayden."

The old man shook his head, looking even more annoyed than before, if that were possible.

"I think you've come to the wrong place."

"No, this is the right place," Evers insisted. "Perhaps the name Felice Hayden would mean more to you."

The man in black seemed to think for a time, mulling the name over in his head.

"Felice, Felice," he said softly. "It does sound familiar, but I can't seem to place it. When you get to be my age, you know all sorts of names."

Evers' face grew red and a severe expression marred his face.

"Then perhaps you remember the village of Greysham, and a trial that was held there."

The man's face lit up with recognition and, as he pondered times long passed, a subtle and sinister smile grew upon his lips.

"I haven't thought about that place in a very, very long time," he mused whimsically.

"I have," Evers spoke harshly. "I think about it every single day."

"Well?" the man in black demanded as he cocked an eyebrow, clearly growing impatient with his unwelcome guest. "Say what you've come to say, or leave me be."

"You murdered her," Evers snarled, the fire of rage lighting up his countenance. "My poor, sweet sister, Felice. She caught you disturbing our family crypt, and when she looked inside the remains of our parents were missing."

"Yes, well," the man in black said in a hoarse voice, awkwardly clearing his throat, "A child of darkness, such as myself, sometimes has need of human remains for research."

"Be silent, necromancer!" Evers snapped at him. "Your perversions with the dead are of no interest to me. But when my sister confronted you about what she'd seen, you chose to end her life rather than be reprimanded for what you'd done. Even worse, when you were brought to trial you bribed or cajoled the judge, and he spared you.

"You even claimed Felice had tried to attack you, and you'd only acted to protect yourself. But my dear sister was gentle and kind, and I know she would have never hurt anyone, no matter the cause. Everyone in town knew it; that was why you chose to flee Greysham, rather than face the people's justice. The laws of the empire may have set you free, but they would have seen you hang."

The necromancer's eyes sparked with a sudden recognition, and he exclaimed with delight, "You're that little rat, that bawling tyke from the trial!" He laughed cruelly and altered his tone to mimic a crying child. "He killed my sister, he *killed* her!"

At this, he cackled even more.

"This *little rat* has come to kill you," Evers announced with a growl.

The necromancer looked the young man up and down, confused and unimpressed. He didn't even bother to rise from his seat.

"You're alone and unarmed," he declared with a shake of his head. "What can you possibly hope to do?"

Evers' response was a mad lunge at the older man, arms extended to grab his frail body and squeeze the life out of him. As the two collided, one of the legs of the wicker chair snapped, sending them tumbling onto the wooden deck.

"How childish!" the necromancer grunted as he struggled to escape Evers' powerful grasp.

The younger man was clearly the stronger of the two, but strength alone wouldn't be enough. Evers felt a dozen bony hands, with fingers like icicles hanging from a crypt, wrap around his arms and body, pulling him away from his quarry. He couldn't see anything holding him, but he was drawn back just the same. The cold of the bitter restraints poured into his blood, turning it to slush and sapping away his strength. The necromancer rose to his feet and dusted himself off, looking at the young man indignantly.

"You see? Now what did that accomplish?"

Evers snarled and growled at him, foaming at the mouth like a wild animal, unable to form any coherent words.

"You're mad, are you?" he said with cruel pleasure. "Angry? Enraged? You know, you're right about what happened back in Greysham. I confess; I killed her, just like you said."

Evers closed his eyes as every muscle in his body seemed to tighten, veins bulging from his flesh as his face flushed red with fury. The necromancer, clearly amused by his attacker's predicament, leaned in close to whisper in Evers' ear.

"But there is one thing you don't know," he explained sadistically. "I'll be happy to let you in on it, since you won't be leaving here anyway. I didn't just kill her. I beat her, and I held her down, and I made sure she knew she was going to die. The terror in her eyes was absolutely...," he seemed to grasp for the proper word, "...rapturous."

He seemed quite pleased with himself at that. He turned from his captive, arms behind his back, and began pacing.

He continued, "There was also one thing you had wrong. I didn't have to bribe the judge; I didn't really have to do anything. It was simply a matter of fear. He feared me and, even more, he feared the retribution of my fellow children of darkness."

"You really enjoy the fear of others, don't you?" Evers growled.

The necromancer stopped in his tracks, turning to face the young man with a wicked grin.

"Being feared is an undeniable sign of power."

By now Evers' voice sounded more bestial than human, and the necromancer was certain he seemed larger than when he'd arrived. His breathing was heavy and hoarse, and the look in his eyes was unmistakably feral.

"I think it's time you felt that fear which you brought on so many others!" Evers snarled.

"What is it you think you can do, *little rat?*"

Evers' brawny arm flew forward, breaking free of the phantasmal hands that had restrained him. His open palm struck the child of darkness in the shoulder, where he firmly grabbed hold. Shocked, the old man stumbled backward and fought to escape the powerful grip. There was the sound of fabric and flesh shredding as he fell, and a bright spurt of scarlet ejected from his body.

He landed on his backside, looking up at Evers in disbelief. The hand that had grabbed him no longer looked human; the fingers were long and bent, ending in sharp, black claws. His entire arm was covered in coarse, brown fur, like that of a wolf. The necromancer put his hand over his wound, blood pouring from between his fingers.

"You're a primal!" the necromancer exclaimed in dismay. "A druid!"

He said this second term with loathing. Evers' other arm began to take the same shape as the first, and his posture became stooped and hunched over. Fur was springing up all over his body, and long fangs could be seen behind his lips.

"You'll die here!" Evers howled, though the words were almost too inhuman to be discernible.

He tried to leap upon the necromancer, to tear out his heart, but the ghostly hands that held him fought to maintain control.

The necromancer quickly cried out a chant, "Flesh and bone; in death, waste away! Rot!"

Evers cried out in pain as the flesh on his chest began to turn black and wither. The dead, dry remnants of skin scattered on the wind, revealing the ribs underneath. The agony was unbearable, unlike anything he'd ever felt before, as if every nerve around the wound was being plucked out and minced to bits. He staggered, darkness closing in all around him. He wasn't certain he would be able to keep his feet much longer.

The necromancer laughed as he saw Evers slump forward, supported only by his invisible captors. He made his way to his feet, struggling against his old bones.

"You may have caught me off guard, little rat, but you're no match for me. Your powers are weak and undeveloped. Perhaps if you'd trained for a few more years, you could have had your revenge."

"Maybe you're right," Evers gasped, trying to keep his focus through the pain. "When I was a boy, I watched you get away with murder. I wanted to kill you. Whenever I slept, my nightmares were haunted by your wicked face, the face of a murderer, the terrible Graham Balreigh. But I was too small and weak; I couldn't do anything. I swore I would do whatever it took to become strong enough to give you the justice you deserved.

"When the mark appeared on me, I knew it was a gift. A gift given for that very purpose. So I searched for you. I searched for years. When I finally found out where you'd hidden, I couldn't stay in the shadows anymore; my sister had waited long enough."

"Well?" Graham said expectantly. "Is that all? It must be a painful disappointment to know that, after all this time, you're going to die by my hands. What will you tell your sister on the other side, I wonder? I bet it hurts even more than your rotting flesh."

Evers slumped forward and hung down his head. The necromancer thought maybe he'd gone into shock, but he also realized it could be a trick. The young man was clearly still breathing; in fact, his breathing seemed heavy, but slow, with deep, deliberate breaths. Finally, the primal drew up his frame and lifted his head, fixing his eyes on his prey.

His eyes weren't human anymore. They were dark and terrifying, filled only with the rage and cunning of a savage beast. His face was like that of a wolf, with a wide muzzle, and fangs sprung from under his lips in a perpetual grimace. Fur continued to spread, quickly covering his entire body, leaving only bare patches of bone where his ribs had been exposed. There was almost nothing left of the man who had walked the road to this lonely cottage—both in his body, and in his mind. He was giving into his bestial nature, reveling in the ferocity and wrath. Even the most experienced druids were cautious to push their bodies and spirits so far, for once the beast was awakened, it was difficult to subdue it again.

Evers pounced on his target, the ghostly hands of his captors no longer able to restrain such indomitable power. Graham cried out and raised his hands, trying to push the monster away. It was like a child trying to hold back an avalanche. He tried to speak a frenzied chant but, before the first word escaped his lips, Evers bit down upon his throat. There was a crack as his spine was severed and warm blood washed into the beast's muzzle. The old man's limbs went limp, and he moved no more.

The wolf continued to rip and tear at his flesh, pulling it off in long, bloody strips. The meat tasted absolutely delicious; Evers couldn't remember anything ever tasting so good. He'd hunted many times as a wolf, less awakened than he was now, and the flesh of deer had always been satisfying, but nothing in comparison to this ecstasy.

As he devoured his human meal, blood running down his jaw and staining the ground red, he realized he couldn't become human again. It wasn't a true thought; his savage mind was an instrument of cunning now, not of abstractions. It was merely an echo in the farthest corners of his mind, where traces of humanity still lingered. A single tear, the last bit of his human soul, fell from his savage eye, and one last echo rung out over all others:

"I'm sorry, Yuka. I wasn't able to keep my promise."

2

CRYSTAL CLEAR WATER DECANTED down a shallow waterfall, splashing into a pristine pool with a soothing resonance. The reservoir was small, less than a hundred feet wide and half as long, and no more than ten feet deep. Its edge was littered with large white stones, smoothed and rounded by years of wear, as if nature herself had seen fit to pave the blissful scene.

Bright green plants and luminous flowers flourished all around the water. Long vines climbed the earth and stone wall from which the waterfall tumbled. Further out, massive trees stood tall and spread their leafy arms to block out the sun, leaving only the pond bathed in light, as if a shaft of pure illumination had fallen down from the heavens.

A splash echoed through the forest as a woman dove lithely into the pool, vanishing beneath the water. When she surfaced, she threw her head back, sending a spray of water from her long, black hair. Her naked skin was the color of cinnamon—smooth, and practically glowing with vibrant health. She was tall and slender, and she moved in a way that flaunted confidence and strength.

Her face was enticing and beautiful in an exotic sort of way, with large, dark eyes and thick, pouty lips. She leaned her head forward, submerging her hair in the clear water. She ran her fingers through the strands, cleaning it.

Not far away, at the perimeter of the pond and foliage, the earth sharply ascended, creating a natural wall on one side. The roots of a towering tree emerged from the rocky earth, reaching out into the open air as if they were searching for the water that had collected below. The trunk was covered in moss and surrounded by tall, dark green ferns. Koristad observed the scene transpiring below, hunkered down behind the leafy veil.

"What are you looking at?" Peril asked in a quiet voice, trying not to draw the attention of the forest to their presence.

He didn't offer any explanation, or so much as glance her way, so she crept forward as stealthily as she could and parted the tall, jagged leaves of the flora. Her face turned red and she immediately took a step back, crossed her arms huffily, and began glaring at him. She was certain that the intensity of her stare would burn a hole in him, but after a few moments it became clear he was ignoring her utterly.

Giving up on that approach, but still demanding his attention, she balled up her hand in a tiny fist and slugged him in the arm. He hardly reacted at all, brushing his limb as if an insect had landed there, then leaned toward her and pointed down at the water.

"Look," he said, his gaze never straying.

Peril narrowed her eyes at him. She wasn't quite sure what was down there that would be of any interest to her. She squinted and stood on her tiptoes, trying to get a better view of whatever Koristad thought she was supposed to see.

"What is it?" she demanded, having had her fill of him spying on the disrobed woman.

"There's a mark on her lower back," he said.

Peril leaned forward and squinted her eyes once again, but the woman was too far away for her to make out any clear detail. Still, she could see there was something there.

"A tattoo?" she asked, perplexed.

Koristad shook his head.

"It wasn't put there by human hands," he explained. "She bears the mark of the druid."

Peril looked again and said, "Your sight must be clearer than mine. Do you think she's the lycanthrope we're supposed to hunt down?"

"I don't think a druid who's become a were-beast can ever return to a human form," Koristad said thoughtfully. "But it is curious to find a primal in the very place this monster was last seen."

"Well, what do we do?" Peril asked. "Should we go down there and find out why she's here?"

"Well, I. . .," Koristad's face turned red as he struggled to find the words he was looking for. "Maybe we should give her time to finish bathing so she can get dressed."

Peril put her hands on her hips and cocked an eyebrow.

"You don't seem to mind looking at her when she doesn't know you're there," she accused.

"There's nothing wrong with admiring a beautiful woman," Koristad protested, raising his hands defensively. "Besides, I was only making observations that might help us with our mission."

Peril gave him a look that made it clear she'd never heard a more unconvincing lie in all her life. He shifted uncomfortably under her stare, wondering why she seemed so upset.

Finally, he cleared his throat and said, "Alright, let's go introduce ourselves."

They picked their way down the uneven terrain, dodging cleverly hidden roots and thorn covered bushes that seemed to block every advance. The forest was lush and heavy, with a canopy that seemed alive with the chatter of birds and small animals. Everywhere they looked some form of green life was struggling to take hold and grow, fighting against its leafy neighbors over the plentiful resources.

Peril had been forced to leave Jester stabled in Clemmensreve, though his contribution to reaching their destination as quickly as they had was undeniable. Koristad had insisted the horse would be more of a hindrance than anything under such thick tree cover. Peril had thought he simply didn't want the animal around. However, after experiencing it for herself, she had to admit she could cover ground just as fast on foot as she could have on horseback.

This far south, the climate seemed absolutely sweltering to Koristad, who'd spent most of his life in the comparatively frigid north. He'd even removed his high-collared cloak, fearing he'd be cooked alive inside.

When they finally reached the reservoir, the woman was nowhere to be seen. Koristad looked left and right, and even walked to the rim of the pool and looked in to see if she was underwater, but there was nothing.

"Are you looking for something?"

A woman's voice seemed to emanate from everywhere, echoing against the trees and fragmenting in every direction. The two of them scanned their surroundings but, without any direction, they were unable to spot her.

"I'm not really in the mood for a game of hide and seek," Koristad said with a scowl. "Now show yourself."

"My, aren't you demanding," she said with musical laughter. "I'd heard all necromancers were arrogant and self-important. And I guess I heard right."

He'd almost forgotten that, without his cloak, the mark on his face was as plain as day. Regardless of the common opinion of the children of darkness, he wasn't about to be insulted by anyone. He strained his eyes to find her, looking in every shadow.

"She's there, Koristad," Peril said in a whisper, pointing at a nearby tree. "Up in the branches."

With practice, she'd become more adept at detecting the tainted blood of mages. She could usually sniff it out, so long as she could quiet her mind and focus. Though, for her, that was a challenge in itself.

"I'm not here as a necromancer," Koristad announced with a loud call, his annoyance ill-concealed. "I've come as a proxy lightwielder. And if you don't get down here and talk to us face-to-face, I'll chop down that tree you're hiding in and make you."

He heard the sound of branches rustling above, and a moment later the woman came sliding down the woody trunk with a practiced and almost unnatural ease. Koristad was silently disappointed to see she'd dressed in the time it had taken them to make the short trip to her location, though her garb was notably sparse. She wore tall leather boots and a skirt that was cut short, allowing for freedom of movement rather than catering to proper decorum. Her midriff was exposed, with only a tight, hide strap wrapped around her chest. No civilized female dressed in such vulgar attire; she was truly a woman of the forest.

She took a few steps forward, standing between Koristad and the tree in which she'd hidden, as if she was protecting it.

"It would be a shame to allow anything to happen to such an ancient creature," she explained cautiously. "Here I am, proxy lightwielder."

"Why were you trying to hide from us?" he demanded.

"I think I should be asking you why you were spying on me," the woman answered with a crooked smile. "Were you satisfied with what you saw?"

Peril didn't appreciate her licentious tone or the seductive eyes she was casting on Koristad. It was more than simple jealousy; there was something very strange about the woman, something primordial and unsettling. Koristad, on the other hand, wasn't certain whether he should be embarrassed or enamored.

"You knew we were there?"

"Of course I did," she replied, gifting him once again with her musical laughter. "I could smell you from the top of the overlook. Even if I hadn't, the two of you make enough noise to disturb the entire forest."

"It's not really in my nature to skulk about," Koristad said with a grimace.

"I can see that," the woman replied and made a gesture to the halberd on Koristad's back. "I assume that enormous weapon is useful for activities other than felling defenseless trees."

"Like I said, I'm a proxy lightwielder," he said. "This weapon is used to protect those who can't protect themselves. The two of us are hunting a certain threat in this forest even now, which makes me wonder just what you're doing here."

The woman's playful smile vanished almost instantly, and she took a step away from the two of them.

"What's the matter?" Peril asked, disturbed by the woman's sudden apprehension.

"I know why you're here."

"Good," Koristad said with a scowl. "That saves us the trouble of explaining. But you still need to tell us why *you're* here."

"You should leave this forest at once," the woman wasn't suggesting or asking; she was clearly giving an order. "This doesn't concern you."

Koristad said with a deep sigh, "We aren't obliged to follow your commands. Now, tell me why you're here before my patience runs out..."

"You would never understand," she hissed at him.

Her face contorted with anger, but there was sadness in her eyes.

"No one can ever understand the fear and suffering of our curse! Leave this forest immediately. If you don't, then the next time we meet, we'll be enemies."

She took a step into the deep shadows of the forest and, as if she had melted into the darkness, was gone.

"That's no way to talk to people who haven't done anything to you!" Peril said, crossing her arms. "There's something wrong with that woman!"

"She didn't even tell us her name," was Koristad's only response.

"So, what do we do now?" she demanded, clearly in a bad mood.

"Well, we aren't leaving the forest," he answered with a shake of his head. "That goes without saying. But we'll have to be twice as cautious now; being a druid, she could prove to be very dangerous if she does turn aggressive. That on top of the werewolf that's supposed to be in these woods."

"I still think she might be the lycanthrope," Peril said with a frown. "Even if she did look human."

"You may be right," Koristad said with a shrug, gazing pensively in the direction she'd fled. "Her reaction was terribly strange."

3

YUKA STOLE ACROSS THE forest with the grace and stealth of a cat. She crept behind the trees and listened intently to the sounds all around her, sometimes coming to a halt and lifting her head as if she could perceive some slight far beyond the faculties of any normal human.

He was nearby. She was certain. She'd already found a fresh kill, a young doe that had been torn to pieces and almost entirely consumed. It was a victim of gluttony possessed by no natural creature, a desperate hunger embodied by the savage lycanthropes. Yuka had heard stories from her elders, tales of grave warning, but the ferocity of the scene she'd witnessed had left her stunned.

But there was nothing that could turn her from her course. She stalked her target with skill and precision, each step bringing her that much closer. Soon she heard the sound of tearing meat and cracking bone, and she knew her quarry had made another fresh kill. The scent of hot blood filled her nostrils as she drew closer, moving across the earth like a ghost. She put her back to a nearby tree, took a deep breath, and cautiously peered around the side.

An enormous, brown werewolf was huddled over its prey—a white tailed fawn, probably the baby of the doe it had already devoured. It held its meal down with its massive, clawed hands as it tore at the flesh with its wicked fangs, gulping down the meat greedily.

Yuka's heart froze in her chest when it halted in its feeding, taking a few sharp intakes of breath as if it had caught the scent of something out of place. It lifted its head, blood and sinew dripping from its ghastly maw, and its eyes darted back and forth across its surroundings.

The look in its eyes was frantic. It was tortured with fear—fear of being hunted, fear of being hungry. It was driven only by its desperation. There was no trace of the human mind that had once maintained control of the savage animal. That was what Yuka saw when she looked into those eyes. But, even as she saw it, she refused to believe it.

When the monster lifted its head the chest was exposed, displaying the dreadful wounds that had left its bone white ribs exposed to the open air. Involuntarily, Yuka gasped with shock and pity, and the monster's ears perked up at the sound. For a moment the beast was still, as if it had been frozen in place. She didn't dare move or make a sound, or even breathe. Slowly, it turned its enormous head in her direction, fixing those bloodthirsty eyes on her delicious looking body.

When their eyes met, Yuka was gripped by terror that seized her muscles and caused her to start trembling. But those eyes, savage as they appeared, were also familiar. She'd looked into those eyes a hundred times before and, even through her fear, it seemed clear what she had to do. She took a step away from the tree, pushing away from the trunk with her trembling hands, and stood exposed and unprotected before the vicious creature. She held her arms away from her body, showing that she had no weapons, no traps, nothing to harm the lycanthrope.

It snarled at her, lowering its body and taking a step back. Its posture was submissive, even intimidated, and Yuka thought maybe it recognized her scent.

"Evers," she said softly, so as not to startle the creature, "You know who I am?"

The werewolf bared its fangs at her and a low, rumbling growl filled the air.

"Do you know who you are?" she continued uncertainly. "Your name is Evers Hayden. And my name is Yuka Locke."

The bristly fur on the monster's back was standing on end, and its powerful muscles were growing tense, as if preparing to pounce.

"Please, remember me, Evers!" she pleaded, tears welling up in her eyes. "Come back to me!"

The monster's eyes were growing fierce and bold. It took half a step toward her. She thought maybe it hadn't recognized her scent, after all. If that were the case, then she knew she would look like nothing more than an easy meal for this ravenous wolf. But she stood her ground, refusing to give even an inch.

"Please, Evers, I need you!"

There was a snap of breaking wood as the werewolf lunged forward, swiping at her with its enormous, taloned hand. Yuka couldn't move in time; she stood there, frozen, unwilling to believe what was happening. The force of the blow came down on her side, striking her in the ribs. She grunted with pain as the wind was forced from her lungs. She tumbled across the detritus covered forest floor, rolling into a nearby tree. Her hands went to her injured side and sticky, red blood leaked from between her fingers. She was fortunate to escape with such a minor injury; an attack from such a powerful creature could have easily left her disemboweled.

However, it was clear that such fortune couldn't last. She fought her way to one knee, but found it too painful when she tried to stand. The wolf crept toward her, moving with heavy steps under its massive weight, hunger in its eyes and bloody drool seeping from between its sharp fangs.

Yuka's long hair was tousled and covered with dirt and leaves from her tumble, and she was crisscrossed with numerous scratches inflicted by sharp twigs and thorns. Her eyes were filled with sadness. She slowly closed them as death approached, stalking forward on its four, massive limbs.

It wasn't sadness for herself. What fear she did feel at the prospect of her own death was overshadowed. Wasn't there anything that could save Evers? Set him free from his own bestial rage? She could feel the hot panting of the monster wash across her skin, damp and foul. She held her breath and waited for the end.

Yuka's eyes popped open when she heard the sound of something rushing toward her from the side. For an instant, the werewolf's fangs were just inches from her face, but it leapt back as a pillar of shining steel came down from above, striking the soft earth. For a moment, it appeared the lycanthrope had escaped the attack unscathed, but blood began to slowly ooze from a cut across the side of its face.

Koristad stepped in front of the injured beauty, holding his enormous halberd in one hand. He said nothing; he had no words for a mindless animal. He only raised his weapon in preparation for the monster's counterattack, ready to finish it off with a single, lethal stroke.

However, the cut on its face burned like unnatural fire, the power of the sanctified weapon purifying the monstrous body. Hurt and faced with a dangerous adversary, the monster took flight almost instantly. Koristad might have chased after it under different circumstances, but he couldn't leave the injured woman in the forest to fend for herself. He turned to face her, momentarily pleased to see she'd managed to get to her feet, but that pleasure dissolved instantly when she slapped him remorselessly across his face.

"What do you think you're doing, necromancer!?" she demanded lividly. "I didn't ask you to interfere!"

It was clear the effort had taken its toll; her hands went back to her side almost immediately. She was shaky on her feet, as if she could fall at any time. Koristad's face turned red with anger.

"I just saved your life!" he barked at her. "If that isn't something you want, then I'll be happy to let that werewolf eat you next time, and I'll just clean up what's left!"

Peril pushed past him, giving him a dirty look, and rushed to Yuka's side.

"You're badly hurt," she said sympathetically. "Please, sit down, and I'll tend to your wounds."

Yuka pushed her away defiantly, nearly falling to the ground in the process.

"The two of you followed me here!" she accused through gritted teeth. "What do you want?"

"Well, Koristad thought we should keep an eye on you," Peril explained in a soft and doubtful voice, clearly uncertain of his motives.

"I don't need your help!" she hissed as she pushed herself away from the tree she'd tumbled into.

She began to walk away from them. Her first step was uneven, and her second was shaky, but the third one gave out entirely and she fell to the ground. She didn't even raise her arms to catch herself, her dark body collapsing full on into the leafy groundcover. Peril hurried to her side.

"Is she alright?" Koristad asked.

His voice was bereft of sympathy, stolen away by his stinging face.

"She will be," Peril said, checking to see if Yuka was still breathing. "She's only fainted."

4

EVERS SAT ALONE ON a slab of rust colored rock, his brow furrowed in heavy contemplation. Perched high atop a cliff, he gazed across the breadth of Valdoran Lake below as it sparkled and shimmered before the setting sun. From either bank, the savanna stretched on for what seemed like an eternity, far beyond the range of his unnaturally keen vision. The trees were sparse and short, and appeared as lazily gratified as trees might, their lowest branches drooping close to the ground. The grass, wild and as high as a man's waist, had wilted and turned an ochre shade of yellow, suffering under a burning hot sun and a long dry season.

The lake levels had dropped as well, revealing vast beaches of dark sand, littered with small stones and bits of driftwood that had once been submerged deep beneath the waves. But even as the rain grew infrequent, the fish and the animals thrived. It was a good place, free from the allegedly civilized hunters who considered the whole sale slaughter of every living thing their profession.

The wind blew softly through Evers' hair as he stared into the distance, lost in thought. He wondered if he would ever see another sunset like this one, so radiant and tranquil, bathing the still waters in deep reds and soft pinks. It was a stark beauty that reminded him painfully of how much he loved his home.

He turned as quick footsteps approached from behind, reacting just in time to catch Yuka in his arms as she leapt into his lap, planting a passionate kiss upon his lips. She gazed into his deep eyes and caressed his rough cheeks with her soft hands. She appeared happy, like a giddy child. But she always seemed that way—so full of life and joy.

"What's the matter?" she asked, seeing his eyes were dark and troubled.

She leaned to his side with her arms around his neck, resting her head upon his shoulder.

"I…," Evers seemed to be at a loss for words, thinking hard about what to say, or just how to say it. At last, he simply said, "I found him."

"Found him? Who?" Yuka seemed confused for a moment, but the realization suddenly set in. "You mean…"

"Graham Balreigh," he said with a nod, "The necromancer who killed my sister."

Her face flushed with sympathy and concern as she ran her fingers through his soft hair.

"Are you certain?" she asked in a gentle voice.

Evers nodded.

"Garou paid me a visit late last night," he explained. "He'd tracked the scent far to the east and found its owner. He had no doubts, and that makes me as certain as I can be."

Yuka seemed distressed, but she said, "He's a good dog, Garou."

"He's half wolf," Evers replied in a defensive tone, as if it were a fault to be a dog.

"What are you going to do?"

Evers response to the question was hesitant, though he and Yuka already knew the answer.

"I'm going to make him pay for what he's done."

"Killing him won't bring her back," Yuka wisely cautioned.

"I know that."

"It won't make you feel any better, either," she went on. "Revenge never does."

Evers huffed and shook his head, "It's not about that. It never was."

"Then what is it?"

"It's just. . .," for a moment, Evers couldn't find the words to express what he felt. He was a simple man of the wilds, not a poet, after all. "How can she rest in peace when the man who took her life lives on without consequence? No, this is something that has to be done."

Yuka looked away from him, out at the shining lake, and slowly nodded. She knew there was no hope of talking him out of it.

"Then I'll come with you," she said matter-of-factly.

"I'm going alone," he countered with a swift shake of his head.

"The children of darkness should never be taken lightly," she cautioned. "You're still young, Evers. You haven't had time enough to learn to control the beast inside you."

"I'm not that young," he protested indignantly. "Don't treat me like a child."

"I have many years more practice than you," she insisted, being almost ten years his senior. "You're truly gifted to have the control you do with your experience. But even I would be cautious approaching such a task."

"I'm sorry," Evers explained regretfully, "But this is something I have to do alone."

Yuka struggled to find the argument, those magic words that could make him change his mind—to forget about this dangerous, self-appointed duty and stay with her, in safety and bliss. But there was nothing she could say or do. Evers had chosen this path long before he'd met her, long before he'd learned he was a primal, and there wasn't anything under heaven that would deter him.

Instead, she looked up at him with sad eyes and pleaded, "At least promise you'll come back to me."

Evers appeared surprised by the request.

He smiled a soothing, handsome smile and said, "Of course I will. I promise."

Yuka wrapped her arms around him tight and buried her face in his chest, not wanting to let him go. He looked down at her, remorse plain in his eyes, and softly caressed her long hair. The sun melted behind the distant hills, casting one last twinkle of brilliance across the dusky sky before it vanished, its solitary radiance replaced by an endless sea of bright stars.

Yuka pulled his body against hers and whispered in his ear, "Will you at least stay with me tonight, before you leave?"

Evers smiled at her and replied in his deep voice, "There's nothing that could drag me away."

5

YUKA AWOKE SUDDENLY, JERKING into a sitting position, confused for a moment about where she was. She laughed at herself. She was dreaming about the past, as if remembering those moments in her waking hours wasn't painful enough.

There was a fire nearby, now burned down to little more than glowing embers, but it radiated some warmth and cast a pale glow upon the trees and undergrowth all around her. She could hear a low snoring. She found its source to be the little blonde girl who she'd met the day before, curled up in a sleeping bag near the fire. Yuka was wrapped in a soft blanket, too, though she'd brought nothing of the sort with her on her journey. She was a druid, a woman of the wilds. She could sleep on the bare earth as easily as a deer, or perched in the branches of a tree as easily as a cat. She often thought of such comforts as a weakness, but the soft fabric felt good against her skin, and she found its scent comforting.

She spotted a figure at the edge of the fire's light, sitting on the ground with his back to her. The halberd strapped to his back made it clear who it was, even in the shadows. She rose to her feet and walked toward him, bundling the sleeping bag under her arm.

"Bad dreams?" he asked.

She didn't answer, instead taking a seat next to him and wrapping the blanket snugly around her shoulders.

"Thank you for looking after me," she said in an apologetic tone, feeling rotten for the way she'd treated him.

"You should be thanking Peril," he answered, gesturing at the small girl. "She cared for your wounds while you were still asleep. To be honest, I was pretty useless."

Yuka looked at her torn clothes in surprise, finding there was no wound at all where she'd been so brutally clawed hours before.

"It's amazing. I don't even feel sore," she said with awe and admiration.

Koristad looked back at the sleeping Peril with a smile and said, "She's really a talented healer." Thinking better of that, he quickly turned to Yuka and added, "Don't tell her I said that, though."

She laughed softly. It felt good to laugh, a real laugh, and to hear friendly words. She'd been so melancholy lately she'd almost forgotten what it was like.

"It must be the middle of the night," she announced, looking skyward, though there was no hint of the moon or stars through the thick forest canopy. "Don't you ever sleep?"

Koristad shrugged.

"You'd be surprised. But I'm not going to let my guard down when there's a monster stalking these woods."

Yuka looked sad and asked, "You're going to kill him, aren't you?"

Koristad frowned and met her downhearted gaze.

"There's no way around it."

She looked at the ground, and the two of them sat in silence for a long time, the orange embers of the fire bathing them in ghostly light.

"What is he to you?"

The question was sudden and unexpected.

"Excuse me?"

"I heard some of what you said when you confronted the werewolf," Koristad explained. "I'm not so dense that I can't put together what's going on."

Yuka nodded and confessed heavily, "He was my lover."

"I see," Koristad leaned back and crossed his arms over his chest, searching his thoughts. "Once a primal loses control and becomes a lycanthrope, there's no way to come back, is there?"

Yuka was stunned by the bluntness of the question, and it took her a moment to put her thoughts in order on the subject.

"That's what I was always taught, by the older druids," she said stoically, but her voice began to crack as she continued. "But I really wanted to believe there was a way. I think all druids want to believe that."

"You sound like you *don't* believe it. Not anymore."

Yuka shook her head, "This was my first time actually seeing a lycanthrope. Evers and I used to spend time together in our awakened forms. But what I saw yesterday, that wasn't him. The wolf shape was familiar; there's no doubt it was his body, but they weren't his eyes. Nothing about those eyes reminded me of him."

Koristad nodded and she went on, "You're right. The only thing that can be done for him now is to put him down. I know that. But it breaks my heart to see him like that."

Koristad cleared his throat and said, "You shouldn't think about it like that. You should remember him as he was, as a human. I'm sure he would have wanted it that way."

Yuka smiled at him and said, "You're different from what I thought you would be."

"Is that so?"

"Very different," she glanced back at the sleeping young girl behind them. "I never asked you your names. I'm Yuka Locke."

"The little snore-machine back there is Peril," he said with a cock of his head in her direction. "My name is Koristad Altessor."

"Altessor?" she said with a perplexed expression. "Where have I heard that name before?"

"My father was Arach Altessor," he explained.

"The Deathbringer?" she said with surprise. "That's quite a shadow to live in. But aren't you a little too young to be his son? He died almost twenty years ago."

"That's a long story," he explained, "And not one I want to delve into. But I am his son."

"I thought it was odd that so few were sent on a hunt for a werewolf," she said with sudden understanding. "They're incredibly deadly creatures. Your executor must have great faith in your abilities, and now I understand why."

Koristad shrugged, and the two of them sat in silence, listening to the whispering wind and the low, crackling fire.

"I'm going to finish this tomorrow," Koristad said certainly, his voice low. "You won't try to stop me, will you?"

Yuka slowly shook her head.

"I think it's time I leave this forest," she answered sadly. "Evers will live on in my heart. That's all that's left for me to give."

Without warning, she reached over and grabbed Koristad's hand and looked him in the eyes with an intense and desperate expression. Her grip was powerful, her fingertips digging into his flesh.

"Please, don't let him suffer like this any longer."

6

*Y*UKA LEFT THE PARTY at dawn. She could linger in the forest no longer, and she told them she wanted nothing more than to return home. She expressed no concern of encountering the now murderous Evers again; she was at home in nature and could vanish into the forest if she needed to. Her mind was aflutter as she departed across the dewy earth, her eyes fixed forward, though she wanted nothing more than to look back.

After a short breakfast, Koristad and Peril resumed their hunt.

The forest was vast, but signs of the monster's presence were everywhere. They couldn't believe a single creature could feed with such a fierce and ravenous appetite, but the evidence was undeniable. Deer, rabbits, birds, squirrels—it didn't seem to matter to the monster what it consumed, only that it did so endlessly. The most astonishing scene was the corpse of a brown bear they found nestled in a narrow gulch, laying on its back with its eyes wide in terror. Its belly had been ripped open and all of the meat and organs consumed, leaving a deep cave of bone beneath its hollow ribcage.

Sometimes they would hear the sounds of feeding nearby, the crack of bone and the tearing of sinew. But when they stalked closer, they always found a half eaten kill with no sign of its devourer. Koristad wondered if the wound he'd given the monster had frightened it away; if it was fleeing at their scent to avoid facing the keen, sanctified weapon again. But, if the werewolf continued to consume with such voracity, soon the forest would be devoid of all life; every animal would have become food for the beast. The only food that would be left would be its hunters.

"I think it's this way!" Peril exclaimed, pointing to the northeast. "I can sense it."

Koristad groaned and said, "The last five times you said that, we ran half a mile into hard terrain and didn't find anything."

Peril frowned and crossed her arms.

"Well, you're not getting us anywhere," she accused. "So, just do what I say, and go that way!"

Koristad sighed. It was true. He wasn't a hunter; he couldn't follow even the plainest of tracks. He wished Wraith would make an appearance, announcing it had found their quarry, but the spirit only seemed to appear when it wasn't wanted. Reluctantly, he set out in the direction Peril had specified, the lightwielder following close behind.

He wasn't surprised that their path took them through a tall patch of nettles. Nor was he shocked when they reached a rocky slope that proved to be an exhausting and treacherous climb, though the traverse yielded an advance of only ten or twenty feet. On the other side of that, the undergrowth was tall and heavy. The trees were packed close together; he had to draw his halberd to cut them a path. Finally, they came upon a clearing, a circle of ground that had somehow resisted the encroachment of the arboreal armies.

Behind them was the forest, heavy and nearly impassable, with great sentinels of bark and leaf standing tall to impede any progress, shutting out even the sun. On the other side was a virtually sheer cliff of light shale, more than twenty feet high. It was a dead end.

"I should have known," Koristad said with a disgusted shake of his head.

"But I'm sure I could sense him!" Peril protested desperately. "I still can!"

As if set in motion by a queue, small stones began to tumble down the cliff face, loosened by a tremendous weight moving above. The source of the disturbance was hidden from view, obscured by both the cliff's edge and the thick foliage that lined the brim. Koristad strained to see. His eyes darted left and right, looking for some sort of passage up the escarpment. He spotted a tall beech tree at the edge of the clearing whose high branches overhung the cliff above.

"Where are you going!?" Peril's voice called out from behind as he raced ahead.

Guessing what he had in mind, she cried "I can't climb that thing!"

"You'll be safer down here, anyway," he said, leaping into the lowest branches. "I'll take care of the werewolf, and then we can get out of this sweltering country."

Peril huffed at him and complained, "I thought we were supposed to be working together!"

Koristad gave no answer; by now he was more than halfway to the top of the cliff. The branches swayed and cracked under his rough assault, but he hurried on with no sense of caution. The moment he placed his feet on the higher ground he could tell the monster was nearby. It was the smell; musk and blood, fear and rage, it all lingered around the savage monstrosity.

He found himself standing in the densest tree cover he'd yet seen in the forest. The trunks were packed tightly and the branches hung low; it was almost enough to make him feel claustrophobic.

He heard a sound like living bark being shredded from the body of a tree, and the great monster lumbered toward him through the heavy woods. There was a lethal violence behind its eyes, a far cry from the beast that had fled from him the day before. He reached to his back and drew his halberd, but the blade was ensnared by the low branches overhead, stopping it instantly.

"Well, aren't you clever...," Koristad said under his breath as the monster charged, all fangs and claws.

It all made sense. At first, the beast had feared the sanctified halberd, so it had tried to evade their pursuit. But no matter how far it ran, thanks to Peril's lightwielder senses, they would always find it again. In its primitive animal mind, it must have understood it couldn't escape its hunters, so it had lured them to a place where it would have the greatest advantage. Here, where the confined quarters limited the effectiveness of Koristad's weapon, with a cliff behind blocking the hunters' escape, but thick forest to cover its retreat.

Koristad struggled frantically to free the halberd from the web of branches as the monster closed the distance between them. In the nick of time there was a snap as the light wood gave way, and he brought the weapon down in front of him, holding the tip forward to stop the monster's charge, like a spear.

The wolf broke to one side, pushing against the trees with its powerful limbs and nearly tearing their roots from the ground, changing its direction almost instantly. It wheeled around the nearby trunks, moving in to attack from the side. Koristad tried to bring the weapon around, but the blade caught in the confined quarters; all he could do was hold the haft in front of his body in a defensive stance, and hope for the best.

The monster crashed into him like a charging bull, wrapping its mighty paws around the weapon's shaft and pushing Koristad onto his back. He struggled to keep the wolf at bay, pushing with all his strength even as the monster's jaws snapped just inches from his face. It snarled and drooled, ready for its next meal.

The monster's fear of the sanctified blade was apparent in its onslaught; Koristad found most of its weight was focused on that side. There was no chance he could bring the blade up against the beast, but he took advantage of its single mindedness by changing his grip to push forward with the blunt end of the weapon. It growled with anger as the halberd began to rise against it, propelled by inhuman power. Rather than redistribute its strength, it leapt away from its opponent, preferring to attempt another charge rather than risk losing control of the dangerous end of the weapon in such close quarters.

Koristad sprung to his feet and moved his hands closer to the halberd's blade, attempting to wield it like a small sword. He knew it would rob his strikes of much of their leverage and power, but he could see no more effective way to fight under the circumstances.

As the halberd appeared to shrink, the beast grew bolder. It approached in a low posture, moving on all fours, ready to pounce in a flash and tear into the soft flesh of its adversary. Koristad tensed his muscles for the attack, and when it came, he swung the weapon in a low arc.

The werewolf came at him claws first, and he intended to slash one of those hands clean in two and stop the other with the weapon's haft. But, when the blade bit into the monster's rough hide, it stopped dead. The beast wrapped its long, taloned fingers around the steel. It seemed to smile wickedly, if a wolf can smile. Koristad couldn't believe it. There was blood where the weapon had struck, but he couldn't push it through. . .how could the monster's hide be so tough? It was like a suit of mail; he realized he wouldn't be able to cause any real damage unless he could wield the halberd freely, in the open air.

The werewolf lashed out with its free hand as Koristad wrenched his weapon loose and jumped backwards, his heels hanging over the tall cliff behind. Three deep gashes appeared in his side and began pouring blood. The wounds were deep and bled terribly. He knew if he let this battle go on much longer, he wouldn't retain the strength to fight back.

Frenzied by the smell of blood, the werewolf charged at him, its wide open jaws frothing as it ran. Koristad hunkered down, as if preparing to absorb the charge, though they both knew it was an impossible venture. It wasn't a question of strength; the sheer mass and velocity of the monster, paired against his own meager size and weight, became the only variables of consideration. With the cliff just inches behind, they were doomed for a plummet to the ground below, but the werewolf, with its seemingly impossibly tough body, had little to fear from such a fall. Koristad wasn't entirely sure how well his own body would handle the impact. With the ferocious monster coming down on top of him, even if the force merely stunned him, he'd be torn to pieces before he had a chance to defend himself.

"Well, Gregan," he breathed, forcing a sly and nearly imperceptible smile, "Let's see if your faith in me is well-placed."

The monster drew near, reaching out with its long talons, and it was certain its victim couldn't evade. The necromancer was just inches away, and in an instant he would be dead. Then it could feed on his corpse, and hunt down the tasty little one that had accompanied him as dessert.

For the briefest moment, the werewolf lost sight of his prey. Koristad cut to the side with blinding speed, and the monster had no chance to stop itself before lunging headlong over the precipice. But escape wasn't Koristad's objective; after all, what would happen to Peril down there, alone with such a creature? He reached out with his left hand, wrapping his fingers around the werewolf's shaggy brown fur, lacing his digits snugly through the tangled mess, and held on tight as the two of them plunged toward the earth below.

His heart seized in his chest as he felt the emptiness of the air, the sheer pull of gravity dragging them toward the ground at a bone shattering velocity. The werewolf hunkered down, preparing to absorb the impact with all four of its limbs, while Koristad lifted up his halberd, pointing the blade straight down above the monster's neck. The guillotine shape of the steel was all too evident, and the sheer kinetic force of striking the ground would bring it down and lop off the creature's head. At least, that was what he hoped.

The plunge lasted only an instant; contact with the ground came harder than Koristad had anticipated, even with the beast absorbing most of the impact. For a split second, he lost control of the weapon, the blade instead plunging deep into the monster's left shoulder. His grip gave out, both on the monster's thick coat and on the haft of his weapon, and he tumbled across the ground with a grunt. The werewolf howled in agony, collapsing face first into the grass.

"Koristad, are you alright!?" Peril cried out in surprise.

She'd been trying to climb the tall beech tree to follow him to the top of the cliff but, try as she might, she was unable to reach even the lowest branches. Koristad tried to answer her, but the wind was knocked out of him, and all he could do was wheeze in affirmation. He struggled to his feet and limped toward the injured monster, shooting pain firing up his leg every time he put weight on his right ankle. The slashes in his side were bleeding even worse than before, aggravated by the impact. All in all, however, he thought he'd help up remarkably well after such a descent.

The werewolf, still whimpering in pain, tried to reach to its back and remove the weapon, the sanctified steel burning like holy fire. Koristad offered his vulgar assistance, placing his right knee on the monster's shoulder and drawing out the blade with a slurping sound. Blood gushed from the open wound, matting down the animal's fur and staining the ground dark red.

Koristad lifted the weapon high in the air, bright sunlight glinting off the steel, tinted crimson with blood. He prepared for one final stroke; then it would all be over.

"Please don't do it, Koristad!" a woman's voice came from behind him, but it didn't issue from Peril.

He glanced over his shoulder, weapon still at the ready, and saw Yuka emerging from the thick forest.

"I thought you weren't going to try to stop me," he grumbled.

The werewolf tried to rise, but it was too injured to offer much resistance, and Koristad was able to drive it back down with a hard thrust from his knee.

"It has to die," she agreed, sadness in her voice. "I know Evers would hate what he's become. But you shouldn't be the one to do it. You shouldn't have to live with that guilt."

"I can handle it," he answered without a moment's consideration, cocking back his arm for the deathblow.

"But I couldn't!" she cried.

Koristad froze in mid swing.

"I don't expect you to understand," she continued in a miserable voice, "But someone I love very much is suffering. If you kill him, he'll die as a hunted and frightened beast. But if I finish him, then he'll understand what's happened to him. He'll understand his death is an act of mercy, and he'll be able to rest in peace. That's what I believe."

Koristad was finding it harder to keep the struggling monster from breaking free; even with its grievous injury, its power and frenzy seemed boundless. He had to make his decision in an instant, or it would no longer be his to make.

"Like I already said, I'm not that dense," he said with a sigh. "I understand well enough."

"If I can't finish him...," Yuka spoke in a quavering voice.

"I know."

Koristad set the monster free and hobbled to where Peril was standing, not about to leave her unprotected with the deadly creature on the loose.

"Are you sure this is a good idea?" she asked.

"It seems almost cruel," he answered with a frown. "But I honestly think this way will be easier for her in the end than if I was the one to do it. Especially right in front of her."

"That's not what I mean!" Peril said emphatically. "That werewolf is going to rip her to pieces!"

"Don't forget, Yuka is a primal, too."

Yuka stripped off her skirt and top as the werewolf hobbled to its feet, the torrent of hot blood running down its legs. For an instant she stood there, naked, her eyes closed as she tried to pull together all the concentration and focus at her disposal. An ear shattering, utterly inhuman roar emitted from the lovely druid. A sleek, black coat sprouted from her flesh as her body began to transform; her hands and feet became paws, her ears rose on her head and sharpened into points as her face morphed into that of a cat. A tail sprouted from her back as she dropped onto all fours, appearing nearly identical to a black jaguar.

But no natural jaguar had ever been so massive and powerful. Her stature was nearly as great as that of the werewolf before her, snarling and baring its sharp fangs. The two enormous beasts circled one another, taking each other's measure.

Yuka had always been the stronger of the two but, with Evers losing control and becoming a lycanthrope, she understood the balance of power may have shifted. However, he was grievously injured, not only from Koristad's attack, but from the rib-exposing wound on its chest, the memento bestowed by Graham Balreigh.

Fur flew as the two animals tore into each other, emitting spine chilling growls and snarls as they tussled back and forth. Eyes wide at the brutal scene, Peril reached forward and grabbed Koristad's hand. He didn't seem to notice; even he was taken aback by the sheer ferocity that was unfolding before his eyes.

At first, the two combatants seemed evenly matched, but in an instant Yuka had turned the tables, leaping upon the werewolf and driving her long fangs deep into its neck. The beast struggled for a few seconds, but soon its eyes glossed over and its thrashing ceased. The mighty jaguar released her hold and slinked away, her ears back and her body low, as if she was sulking.

The fur retreated from her body as her face and limbs reverted to their natural form, the entire process lasting only a few seconds. She pushed up with her arms and stood on two legs, seeming a bit wobbly after the sudden transition. Eyes low, she turned toward Peril and Koristad, the dark blood of the enemy staining her face. Peril hurried to the nude primal, standing between her and Koristad, and pushed the bundle of discarded clothing into her arms.

"Hurry and get dressed before his eyes pop out of his head!" she demanded in a sour tone.

"Are you hurt?" Koristad asked as she put on her clothes, noticing that several bleeding scratches crisscrossed her dark body. They'd diminished as she returned to her natural form, now proportional to her smaller frame, but still looked rather painful.

"It's not so bad," she reassured. "I'm tougher than I look."

"That's good to know," he said with a nod, looking the other way and wiping his bloody halberd on the grass. "I suppose it's time the two of us return to the sanctuary and report the danger here has been dealt with. I expect you'll be departing, as well."

"Yes, I think it's time I return home," Yuka agreed, "I've been away too long."

"Will you be taking him back with you?" Peril asked, pointing at the bloody werewolf.

Yuka seemed surprised.

"Why would I?"

"Well...you know...," Peril seemed equally perplexed. "Aren't people supposed to be buried near their homes?"

Yuka shook her head, "That isn't our way. Evers' spirit is free to roam the earth now, carried on the wings of birds or the fins of fish, or even on the backs of wolves. If he wishes to return, then he will find his way."

"You'll bury him here, then?"

"I won't bury him at all," she explained. "It isn't necessary. His body will be consumed by the forest, and his flesh will return to the earth from which it came. That is the way of the druids."

It seemed strange to Peril; almost as if Yuka didn't care about the passing of her companion. But one look in her eyes dispelled that notion.

"We'll be traveling north," Koristad said. "You're welcome to travel with us as far as the Sunrise Sanctuary, if you wish."

Peril wanted to shoot him a dirty look for making such a proposition, but decided she should mind her manners. Yuka shook her head.

"Thank you for the offer, but I won't be making my journey by road," she said.

"Very well," Koristad said with a sigh, slinging his polearm across his back. "I wish you well on your journey. Let's go, Peril."

He turned on his heel and began walking in the direction of the nearest road, trying to look as sturdy as he could in spite of his injuries.

"Okay!" Peril peeped, surprised by the brevity of his farewell.

"Wait, Koristad!" Yuka called after him.

He stopped and looked over his shoulder.

"I owe you a great deal of gratitude for what you did here," she said.

Koristad shrugged and said, "It was nothing."

"Nothing...," she echoed back, hanging on the word. "Well, it was something to me. If you should ever need me, for anything, you can find me near the shores of Lake Valdoran. I won't forget what you did here."

Koristad smiled, pondering the idea of calling on the beautiful druid, and asked, "How will I find you?"

"You won't have to," she answered playfully. "If you come into my territory, I'll know you're there. I'll seek you out. You can count on it."

Koristad nodded a friendly goodbye and began his long journey back home, Peril in tow. Somehow, he knew he hadn't seen the last of Yuka Locke.

"I'm surprised you left so quickly," Peril said sourly when they were out of earshot.

"What do you mean?" Koristad sighed, already annoyed.

"Well...," Peril bit her lip, feeling suddenly uncomfortable with what she wanted to say. She simply retorted, "What do you think I mean?"

Koristad groaned and shook his head, "I don't really feel like playing a guessing game with you. I never know what you mean. I just thought we should leave her be. Some people deal with grief best when they're left alone. She seemed like that type of person."

Peril nodded in understanding, then mused with admiration, and a little envy, "She's very strong, isn't she?"

"The werewolf was a formidable adversary," Koristad said with a nod. "If I'd fought it with an unsanctified weapon, I'm not certain if I could have defeated it."

"That's not what I mean."

"Then what?"

"Even after she killed her own lover she didn't break down and cry," Peril said. "Most anyone would be sick with grief after something like that. She seemed completely composed."

Koristad shook his head.

"Didn't you notice?" he said in a soft, sympathetic tone. "After we started to walk away, and she didn't think we were looking...her hands. They were trembling."

Chapter Eight

THE DENOUEMENT OVERTURE

*Whenever two lives touch, they become connected, as if linked together by invisible
cords.
Some are links of love or hate, trust or betrayal, stretching off in every direction,
forming a tangled, disparate web.
I find the thought so aesthetically unpleasing, I might wish to cut those cords away,
leaving pristine simplicity.
But, without all those cords, what would hold us aloft?*

1

PERIL COLLAPSED ONTO A soft feather mattress, exhausted. Her arms
and legs were sore from working through the day, but she had finally turned
Koristad's tower into a livable habitat. In addition to the bed, she'd also
brought in a small armoire of dark wood where Koristad could keep his clothes,
and several rugs to cover the bare floor. She wondered what he'd been doing about
these amenities before she'd arrived; where did he sleep and keep his clothing? On
the cold ground, she guessed.

Her largest chore had simply been cleaning the ancient chamber. More than
a decade of dust and cobwebs had collected on the floor and walls. At times, she
wasn't sure if she would ever reach the end of it. But, at last, the room was spotless,
displaying the grand design and architecture that had been the original tower.

She'd brought in several mirrors as well, positioning them around the room so it would be filled with light so long as the sun was in the sky and the entryway remained open. The gaping hole in the tower's lower wall was pivotal to achieving this feat. For the dark hours, she'd also brought in several sconces and candles, from which the light was scattered by the mirrors with equal efficiency.

The stand that had once held Koristad's halberd, the weapon ironically designed to take his life, Peril had found to be a beautiful work of art after cleaned and polished. She'd pulled it against the far wall so Koristad might set his weapon in the angelic, stone wings as a display, though she'd never seen the halberd leave his side in all the time she'd known him.

As for the coffin in the center of the chamber, she found there was little she could do about it. Even if she'd been strong enough to lift its enormous weight, closer inspection revealed it had been mortared to the floor. Looking at it under a light, she'd found the surface of the stonework was inscribed with strange symbols. Though she wasn't familiar with them, looking upon them gave her an uneasy feeling in the pit of her stomach. Defeated, she'd decided to cover the eyesore with a light sheet and arranged a pair of chairs on either side. It was a little high set for a table, especially for one of her petite stature, but she certainly liked its look more than the stone tomb.

She'd even brought a glass vase to sit in the center of the makeshift table, and thought she might fill it with flowers when she had a chance. Or maybe Koristad would.

She gazed up at the vaulted ceiling, imagining how pleased the young necromancer would be with the improvements to his lodging. He would be so happy, she mused, he would leave at once to pick fresh flowers to fill the receptacle, because only then would it be absolutely perfect.

She'd be delighted and thank him for going through the trouble, and Koristad would say, "It's a shame these flowers seem far less lovely than they should, pale next to your beauty."

She would blush and Koristad would take her in his arms and...

"You're daydreaming again," Koristad said as he stepped into the bright chamber.

He was breathing heavily and there was sweat on his brow; his hands were red from swinging his halberd. Peril jumped off the bed, her face turning crimson, as if Koristad had been able to perceive what she was thinking.

"Did you come to see what I've been working on?" she asked hopefully. "You don't ever come up here unless I ask you to."

Koristad shrugged.

"I hadn't heard from you for so long, I thought I should make sure you were alright," he said, glancing around.

Peril smiled at him.

"What do you think?"

"About what?" Koristad asked without a thought.

Peril frowned.

"About what I've done with the tower," she said.

Koristad apathetically replied, "It looks different."

"Different?" she echoed in disbelief.

"Why are you looking at me like that?" he said, narrowing his eyes at her.

She supposed she did have a strange expression on her face; his reaction hadn't been quite what she'd hoped for. She wasn't sure whether she wanted to scream or cry.

Instead, she bounded to him and grabbed his wrist, tugging him about the room, showing him everything and telling him all she'd done. He tried hard not to fall asleep on his feet. He wasn't sure why he should care whether the armoire was made from oak or pine, and he couldn't fathom why an empty pot was sitting atop the stone sarcophagus.

When she was finished, Peril looked up at him, absolutely glowing with pride. Koristad stood there blinking at her, unsure of how to react to her plain excitement. She realized she'd never let go of his wrist and, looking down, she saw blood seeping from his hand where the skin had been rubbed raw.

"You're hurt!" she said.

Koristad looked at the injury with disinterest.

"This is nothing," he insisted. "I'm just sore from training."

"Sore?" she said with a frown. "You're bleeding. Let me bind it."

"That's not necessary," he said, snatching his hand roughly away from her.

Peril had learned well enough it was pointless to argue; he would never confess to feeling pain like everyone else. It was more worrisome that he'd brought the injury on himself.

"Why do you push yourself so hard?" she asked, concerned.

Koristad reflected for a moment. He could think of several reasons, though his revenge against the Vampire King stood out at the forefront of his mind.

No matter what it took, he would become strong enough to face the diabolical monster; he burned with hatred for an enemy whom he had never even seen.

The answer he gave was, "When I was a boy I studied the arcane until I thought my head would burst if I learned any more formulae, or I'd go blind if I read one more page. Now that I have no magic, I feel I should throw myself into martial training with equal fervor."

"No magic. . .," Peril said softly, barely a whisper.

"Are you going to ask me about that again?"

She shook her head, "I don't have to. Executor Mourne told me what happened to you."

Koristad looked a little taken aback; he wondered just how many people the executor had told about his unusual origins.

"So now you know. I'm surprised you're not too frightened to come here."

"I'm not afraid of you."

"No?"

"No. I don't care about any of that," her voice was firm but sweet, "Because I've seen for myself the kind of man you are."

Koristad's head perked up as a distraction assailed his ears.

"Do you hear that?" he asked quietly.

Peril listened intently but couldn't make out any unusual noises, and she told him so.

"It's horses, headed this way. A lot of them."

He bounded down the tower's stairway, curious to see what kind of amusing company had found its way to his tower. Peril sighed.

"Hmm. . .it was almost a sweet moment," she mused quietly, then hurried after.

Outside, they were quickly approached by several men on horseback, all bearing the blazing sun symbol of the lightwielders. Executor Mourne rode at the center of the mass with a wizened old man at his side, ancient even next to Gregan. Half a dozen armed men were also in attendance, clad in light armor and with long spears on their backs, though Koristad was unsure whether they were actual lightwielders or simple guardsmen.

"This is quite a party you've brought to my domicile, executor," Koristad called out good naturedly. "I apologize, but I'm not really prepared to entertain."

Gregan's expression was severe; he was clearly in no mood for the young man's inanity.

"This is only a small portion of our entourage," he answered solemnly. "The rest are waiting for our return, so I must make this visit brief. A few hours ago, a message arrived at the sanctuary. High Executor Alexander Kanan has passed from this life."

Peril collapsed to the ground, falling on her rear, as if she'd been knocked down by the blow of the news. Koristad was surprised; he'd never even known the high executor by name and, so far as he knew, Peril had never met the man. But, to her, the lightwielders were family, and Alexander Kanan had been her greatest patriarch.

"You're on your way to a funeral, then?" Koristad asked, uncertain of what to make of all the pageantry.

"There will be a time for mourning, but it isn't now," Gregan explained gravely. "Every executor and sage in the empire will be meeting at the capital to decide on a new high executor."

"You want us to accompany you?" Koristad asked, still baffled as to why the executor had made the unorthodox detour to inform him of the news.

"That won't be necessary," Gregan said. "I have another task for you. As an outsider, you may not be aware, but the high executor is bestowed with a sword as a sign of his position, an ancient weapon that has been passed down for over eight centuries: the Executor Blade. It is ceremony for this weapon to be delivered to the capital by fourteen lightwielders, two from each sanctuary. When it arrives, our deliberations will be brought to a close, and the new high executor will be named."

"It sounds like you want me to be one of the fourteen," Koristad said apprehensively, "Even though I'm not a lightwielder. That seems contrary to this ceremony of yours."

The old man next to Gregan scoffed, "Even the necromancer can see the folly in this, executor."

"High Executor Kanan was an elderly man who'd grown soft in his many years," Gregan declared, ignoring the sage next to him. "He was lenient with the executors under him, and allowed us to run our sanctuaries how we chose. But the new high executor may very well not be as understanding of certain...quirks. Such as having a necromancer play the role of a lightwielder. If you were to deliver the blade to him, he may be inclined to look favorably upon your service."

"Perhaps you'll be named high executor," Koristad said hopefully, "Then we wouldn't have to worry about this."

It seemed to Peril he was trying to weasel his way out of the assignment. She wondered whether he was simply being lazy, or if participation in the procession didn't seem exciting enough to pique his interest.

"The position is not one of prestige," Gregan explained, "But one of duty and sacrifice. If I am chosen, I will accept humbly and do all I can to fulfill the expectations of the title. But it is far more likely Executor Night will be the one chosen; he is both wise and powerful, and respected throughout the empire."

"Night...," Koristad cringed at the name. "You mean the cousin of the lightwielder I fought with."

"That's right," he replied grimly; "All the more reason to do what you can to fall under his good graces."

"Fine," Koristad groaned. "I'll do it."

"Executor...," Peril said uncertainly, climbing back to her feet and dusting herself off, "Will I be going as well?"

"Of course," Gregan replied with a soft smile, "Your partnership has proved advantageous thus far. I see no reason to interfere with it now."

Peril smiled, but it was artificial; a thin mask over the face of her grief. She was still quite shaken up over the news of the high executor's death.

"You'll need to be on your way immediately," Gregan said. "I apologize for the abruptness, but it is a long journey and if you don't hurry you'll keep the rest of the company waiting. In the town of Bainsreach there is an old church of Aura; this is where High Executor Kanan took ill, and where he lost his life. The company will be gathering there before beginning the trek to the capital."

"You'll need this," the old sage said, drawing his horse up next to Peril and presenting her with a rolled up parchment, sealed with Executor Mourne's mark. He turned dubious eyes on Koristad. "It will identify you as the chosen bearers of the Sunrise Sanctuary...please try not to make us regret it."

Koristad glared at the elderly man.

"I haven't let you down yet, have I?" he said.

Before he had a chance to argue any further, Peril grabbed him by the wrist and said, "You heard what Executor Mourne said. We should start making preparations to leave."

"There is one more thing you should know," Gregan announced, though it was clear sharing such surreptitious information with a relative outsider weighed heavily upon him. "No matter what happens, you must never touch the Executor Blade."

"I hadn't planned on it," Koristad replied with a shrug. He added cynically, "It must be too sacred to be handled by unclean hands."

"It's no ordinary weapon," Gregan said. "It is waiting for its new master. Anyone claiming the blade will be judged, and if they're found unworthy, it will kill them before it allows itself to be wielded by one with impure intentions. It is an artificer weapon."

Koristad looked shocked, and he absent-mindedly explained why, speaking as if he were talking only to himself.

"But I was told the first high executor ordered every artifact created by the artificers destroyed, at the same time she ordered them all put to death. They'd committed acts of unspeakable evil to forge powerful weapons, and were forced to pay the price in blood."

"That was many centuries ago," the executor said. "Of these ancient legends how much is truth and how much is fantasy is difficult to discern. But certainly one artifact did survive the reckoning, and it became a holy weapon that represented the lightwielder's during the second incursion, striking terror into the hearts of even the archdevils. And, now, that ancient weapon belongs to our high executor."

2

(More than eight centuries before present)

"WHERE ARE THEY?!" A young, blonde woman, her slim frame encased in a shell of steel armor, demanded impatiently. "I was told Lord Brian's men would be here yesterday!"

There were more than a dozen men and women huddled together under an enormous pavilion, gathered around a large wooden table covered with maps and notes. It was a war council, and every general present was plainly distressed.

Outside, a multitude of camps covered the terrain and swarms of soldiers milled about, or simply sat on the ground in a tense silence, awaiting the orders of their superiors. The grass was wet from two days of heavy rain, and the sky was overcast, as if a downpour could start again at any moment. Morale was low; many soldiers were injured, and others were frightened. Most of them would have packed up and gone home but, if this war wasn't fought and won, there would be no homes for them to return to.

"We intercepted a carrier pigeon this morning," a tall man with a thick, gray moustache explained. "Lord Brian is pinned down in the lowlands to the south east; he won't be able to reach our position."

"He knew very well he needed to move without being detected," she said with a frustrated shake of her head. "He was given that warning before he left his stronghold. He has nothing to blame but his own incompetence."

"Should we dispatch reinforcements to his position?" asked a brown skinned man with a large bandage that covered the left half of his face.

"If the enemy has discovered a weak force separated from the bulk of our army, it won't be long before the entire horde comes down upon their heads," she said coldly. "I won't hand any more of our soldiers over to the enemy. We will proceed without them."

"With all due respect, commander, the soldiers are weary and hurt," said the man with the moustache. "The demons seem to grow in number every day. I'm not certain this is a battle we can win."

"I've brought us this far, haven't I?" she asserted with a humbling confidence. "Your soldiers will do all they can; I do not doubt their resolve. My lightwielders will make up the difference. You're dismissed."

"Yes, Commander!" the generals saluted as they filed out of the conference, emboldened as they always were at the mention of the powerful troupe of lightwielders who fought under Commander Tricia Laurel.

Over the last centuries, the might of the children of Aura had been all but forgotten, but in only a few short campaigns it had been rekindled like a fire that warmed the spirits of the downtrodden fighters.

After all of the generals had made their exit, Tricia began to gather up her maps so she could return them to the coffer where she maintained all of her vital intelligence. She was beautiful and strong. Though she wore a mask of power and dominance when surrounded by her subordinates, when she was left alone her features would soften, revealing just how delicate and young she really was, barely out of her adolescence. There was sadness in her deep, blue eyes; a heavy burden that weighed down her every movement.

Empty chairs were scattered about the room, but as she continued with her toil, she realized one of them wasn't vacant. She glanced up to see that one member of the party had stayed behind. It was a young man, with wavy brown hair that was so long she mistook him for a woman at first glance. The dark locks hung down over his face as he stared off into oblivion, his strong jaw clenched in silent contemplation. Tricia knew every general, every soldier, and every laborer in her army, but this man seemed alien to her. However, a feeling of recognition lingered in her gut, and grew there, until she was struck with a sudden recollection.

"You're the artificer, aren't you?" she called out, startling the man nearly out of his seat.

"I-I'm an artificer, Commander Laurel," he stammered nervously. "My name is Ilaron Reede."

"There's no reason to be uneasy around me," she offered in a gentle voice. "I'm not as mean as everyone says."

"No one says that about you. . .," he began but, suddenly realizing she hadn't been serious, cut himself short.

He'd never been very good at reading people, a folly that had caused him many embarrassments in the past. He quickly decided to change the subject.

"You're not really what I expected," he confessed timidly. "I'd heard a brilliant lightwielder had taken command of the armies of Highcrest, winning one victory after another against the Black Legion. I had no idea you were a woman, or that you were so young."

Tricia cocked her mouth to one side and said, "I'm no younger than you."

"Oh! I apologize. . .," Ilaron exclaimed, realizing what he'd said may have been rude. "I didn't mean anything by it. I'm impressed, that's all. Actually, I'm more surprised you've chosen to fight on behalf of the ruler of Highcrest, Lord Arescin."

Tricia gave the young artificer a sidelong stare.

"What do you mean by that?" she asked.

Ilaron turned red and shifted uncomfortably in his seat; this conversation was going swimmingly so far. If he could have, he would have remained silent from that point forward.

"The stories I've heard about him, they. . .I'm not sure what to say," the artificer trailed off uncertainly.

"You can speak plainly with me," Tricia said. "I'm not going to reprimand you for your opinions."

"Well. . .I was told Lord Arescin was a tyrannical megalomaniac, determined to have every lord and king in the known world kneel before him," Ilaron explained hastily; "To have *everyone* kneel before him. I heard he's already taken to calling himself an emperor. I didn't expect the lightwielders would serve such a man."

Tricia sighed.

"Those stories may not be that far from the truth," she said. "Lord Arescin does indeed seek to unite all of the kingdoms under one rule. But right now, we need to be unified. The demons will rip this world apart one nation at a time, if that's what it takes. Separately, we don't stand a chance. But together, there's hope. It's only a faint glimmer, but it's there. And Lord Arescin is a powerful man who can trace his bloodline back to the original king of the seven tribes, named by Aura herself. If anyone can unite the kingdoms, it's him. At least, that's what I believe."

"I see," Ilaron nodded slowly. "I never thought I would see the day we would all be part of one great empire. Then again, I never thought I would see demons tear through the veil and invade this world, either. If this is what has to be done, then I'll see it done, if I can."

"I'm glad to have you aboard, Ilaron," she said with a nod. "We can use all the help we can get, and you're the only artificer who's joined us."

"That's what I'd been told," he said dejectedly, "But I'm afraid I may not be of much use to you."

Tricia gave the slightest nod, having some understanding of what he meant.

"I've heard rumors that the artificers aren't as powerful as the other mages," she stated bluntly, "Though you're the first I've ever had a chance to talk to. Do you think that's true?"

Ilaron pondered the question deeply.

"I think that...we're different from the other mages," he explained. "They all utilize a power that comes from within, so to speak, and I think it comes more naturally for them. We artificers have to turn our attention outward and try to understand powers and patterns that were invisible to us before we had this power, and make little sense even now. More so than any of the others, I feel we have much left to learn."

"I see," Tricia said, blinking and trying to absorb the information. "So you're familiar with other mages?"

"Oh no, I didn't mean to imply that," he said hurriedly. "Not at all. Are you?"

She shook her head.

"There aren't any summoners here; they're all huddled together in Highcrest, too terrified of the archdevils to show their faces. There are a handful of necromancers, but something about them makes me feel uneasy. I haven't tried to speak with one. The primals seem more animal than human; sometimes, I don't think they even realize they *are* human."

"Perhaps the mages won't prove to be as much help as the archangels had intended," he said sadly.

"The archangels..." Tricia pondered the divine emissaries with a pleasant smile, and then asked in a whimsical tone, "Did you meet them?"

"I did. One of them."

"What was he like?"

"It's embarrassing to say, but...before the incursion began, I wasn't sure if I even believed all the stories about Aura," Ilaron confessed, scratching the back of his head sheepishly. "I mean, a goddess living in the world of mortals for seven years before she ascended to the heavens, never able to return? Bestowing her creations with language, law, power over fire...all the things that make us human? It just seemed like stories old men would tell about times so long past no one really knew what happened."

Ilaron looked down at the ground and closed his eyes, as if overwhelmed by the memories, and continued, "But one look at the archangel, and there was no question he was one of the divine. He didn't look different from an ordinary man...or, perhaps I should say, he appeared a perfect specimen of a man. His mere presence was enough to overwhelm one's emotions. I don't know if all the archangels were the same, but this one never spoke. Not once. But one look from his eyes could convey more meaning than a hundred volumes of text, and there was never any doubt of what he wished."

"I envy you," Tricia said. "I wish I could have met an archangel. I never even saw one from a distance, though we've been fighting the same war."

"I thought they were supposed to *end* the war," Ilaron sighed. "Now they're gone, and it seems things are worse than ever."

"Unlike the goddess Aura who could stay in the world of mortals for seven years, the Archangels could only stay for seven days," she explained knowingly. "That's why, on their final day, they decided to mimic Aura's gift to the lightwielders by bestowing *their* blood upon the mortals who they most favored. They did what they could; my scouts report that, before their ascension, they were able to destroy eleven of the archdevils. We believe there are seven more out there among the

Black Legion; we must simply have faith and continue fighting until the world is safe once again."

"There's nothing more to do," Ilaron nodded in agreement. "That's why I'm here. For whatever reason, and I certainly can't understand what it was, the archangels chose me to protect this world from evil. Maybe I will be useless in the end. But that doesn't mean I'm not going to give everything I have."

Tricia smiled at him.

"That's well said. I only wish the other artificers thought the same way. It isn't those frail of body, or of power, who fail to protect what they care about. It's those who lack resolve, and deny their ability to do anything."

"Those are very kind words, commander," Ilaron said, turning red at her accolade. "I can see why you're so well respected."

"Please, there's no need to be so formal with me," she offered in a friendly tone. "We're going to be shedding blood together, after all. You can call me Tricia."

"Thank you, commander," he said. When the lightwielder gave him a disappointed look, he stammered out nervously, "I-I mean, Tricia."

"That's better," she said with a clever smile as she turned toward the tent's exit. "You'll have to excuse me. There are many preparations I must make before the battle."

"Wait!" he called out, perhaps a bit too loud.

"What is it?" Tricia said with a cocked eyebrow, surprised by his sudden candor.

Ilaron reached into the folds of his jacket and produced an iron medallion. It was shaped like an inverted pyramid suspended by a narrow chain. He held it at arm's length, as if he expected Tricia to take it.

"This is the only artifact I've been able to craft," he said. "It's meant to protect its wearer from harm. It may not be very powerful...," he cast his eyes at the ground in disgrace, "But it's the best I could do."

Tricia stared at him in silence, uncertain of what she should say or do. Ilaron continued.

"I'm not a fighter," his voice trembled with distress. "I don't know how to wield a sword. If I were on the front lines, I would only get in the way. But you're going to be out there, putting your life at risk, engaging the enemy toe to toe. I want you to take this with you."

"I couldn't do that," she protested. "This is your magic. You should keep it."

"Please!" the desperation was plain in his voice. "I know I'm not going to be any help. But if my magic can keep you safe, then I'll feel like I contributed in my own small way. Maybe it's self serving, but it would make me happy if you would take it."

Tricia eyed the artificer apprehensively for a moment, then slowly reached forward and took the pendant from his hand, inspecting it with curiosity. It was heavy, but no more so than one would expect from something made of solid iron. The work was plain but flawless, with perfect angles and polished smooth. She could neither see nor sense anything about it to hint that it was more than it appeared.

"Thank you, Ilaron," she said as she clasped it around her neck. "I feel safer already."

3

THE MOMENT VINCENT SPOTTED Koristad approaching the church of Bainsreach, he drew himself up as tall as he could and clenched his jaw tight. To an ordinary observer, the gesture may have been hardly noticed. To those lightwielders nearby, who knew Vincent and his stoic mannerisms, it was as if he'd begun shouting and pointing in that direction.

The gathered party, a dozen of them including Vincent, all turned to look upon the newcomers. That meant, to Koristad's chagrin, they were the last to arrive. He was even more put out when he realized Vincent was among the party. He grumbled to himself that he should have known, considering it was the paladin's own cousin at the forefront of the candidates to be named high executor.

The children of Aura were heavily armed and armored (surprisingly so, considering this was expected to be an uneventful journey), making Koristad something of an oddity, without a single plate of protection, and Peril even more so, without so much as a small knife. They sat in a semicircle around a cart that was enclosed on all sides by wooden partitions, each carved with the sun symbol of the lightwielders, as if it would ward off any evil intentions toward the contents.

The back was hinged to swing open, but a heavy iron lock had been put in place to keep it bolted tight.

This was the keeping place of the ancient Executor Blade. Executor Mourne's many warnings and admonitions had piqued Koristad's curiosity, and he was considerably disappointed he didn't have a chance to see the artifact up close.

The lightwielders rose to their feet as the pair approached, and it might have seemed a warm welcome, had Vincent not pushed his way to the front of the party to act as representative.

He demanded in his usual, composed manner, "What are you doing here, necromancer?"

"Don't be dense," Koristad provoked. "You know why we're here."

The statement was true enough; though all of the party could sense the necromancer's tainted blood, he was also wearing the blazing sun around his neck.

"The Executor gave us this writ!" Peril chimed in, pulling Jester around to the young paladin and handing him the sealed parchment.

Vincent didn't even glance at it; he handed it to a man with a thick moustache whose face animated with amused interest.

"This is a sacred procession," Vincent insisted. "There's no place in it for a child of darkness. The idea is laughable."

"I admit, I thought it was funny, myself," Koristad prodded him on.

"This is Executor Mourne's seal, Vincent," the man with the moustache announced. "There's no doubt these two are the last members of our party."

"I won't have it," Vincent spat, his self-control already wearing thin. "The girl is welcome among us, but you can return to your sanctuary."

He waved Koristad off dismissively.

"Don't act like you don't know who I am!" Peril said indignantly, but she was ignored in the commotion.

"I'm not going anywhere," Koristad taunted. "If that presents a quandary, maybe you should be the one to leave."

Vincent took a step toward him, as if he might grab him by the collar, but the man in the moustache put his hand on the paladin's shoulder. The gesture wasn't forceful, but Vincent halted immediately and took a deep breath, though his eyes didn't budge from his antagonist.

"Think about what you're saying, Vincent," the man tried to reason with him. "Would this duty be any less desecrated by undertaking our journey with only thirteen? He may not have the blood of Aura but, from the rumors I've heard, he's a protector of the people, just like we are."

"You think that's enough?" Vincent questioned seriously. "Gabrial shouldn't be dishonored like this."

"The papers are right here, signed and sealed by Executor Mourne," the man replied, pushing the documents into the paladin's hands. "If you don't agree with the executor's actions, then you have the right to take it up with him, *after* the Executor Blade is safely in the capital. Until that duty is done, delaying our departure with this pointless bickering is shameful."

Vincent stuffed the parchment into his surcoat and stormed away from the company, muttering something about checking on his horse.

"Thank you for sticking up for us!" Peril expressed her gratitude toward the helpful man, wearing a bright smile.

"It was nothing, little girl."

Peril frowned and turned red.

"I'm not a little girl!" she seethed.

The man let out a hearty laugh and replied, "Like it or not, you're both little and a girl. So, really, there was nothing wrong with what I said."

Peril turned an even darker shade of red and found herself completely speechless, which only made the man laugh harder.

Finally, he raised his hands at her and offered, "Please, you shouldn't take what I say too seriously...no one else here does. I have to say, though, I've never seen the captain so ill-composed. He must really dislike you, if you don't mind me saying so."

"Captain?" Koristad said, raising his eyebrows. "You mean he's..."

"That's right," the man explained, "He's the leader of our company and the only paladin among us."

"This just gets better and better," Koristad muttered acerbically. "The way you spoke to him, I thought maybe *you* were in charge."

"Me?" the man put his hand on his breastplate in an exaggerated gesture of surprise. "Please, I'm merely here to entertain the rest of you. But Vincent and I are both from the Silversword Sanctuary, and we've known each other a long time. He might want to wring my neck right now, but he would never admit to it, and he knows I'm right."

While the company awaited Vincent's return, the man with the moustache felt introductions were in order, considering the company would be traveling a long road together.

"I am a twelfth year lightwielder, practically an ancient compared to the rest of you," he said with a chuckle. "As I've already stated, I'm from Silversword. Vian Jerrica is my name."

After learning that much, Koristad quickly lost interest. In his experience the children of Aura were terrible bores, and he had no genuine interest in befriending them. Peril, however, seemed to pay close attention as each member stepped forward to speak their name and sanctuary of residence.

When they'd all finished, Peril drew herself up proudly and announced with an impetuous grin, "I'm a first year lightwielder of the Sunrise Sanctuary. My name is Peril."

When Koristad showed no interest in making his own introduction, (indeed he looked half asleep after the extended proceedings) she added with a quick gesture in his direction, "This is Koristad Altessor."

"You seem to have forgotten to share your surname, Peril," Vian said good-naturedly.

"I didn't forget!" Peril chimed merrily. "I don't have one. I grew up in an orphanage until Executor Kailas found me and took me to the Snowdove Sanctuary."

"Really?" Koristad said with a furrowed brow, proving he had, in fact, been paying some modicum of attention. "You never told me that."

He might have gone on to express how odd it seemed for a lightwielder to be orphaned, considering the overwhelming prestige afforded to the families that carried Aura's blood, but it was at that moment Vincent decided to return to the company. Such a statement, he realized, may not have been in the best taste, besides. But it did finally dawn on him why Peril had always considered the lightwielders her family.

"It's time we began our journey," Vincent announced, prancing up on his magnificent steed. "I will lead us in a prayer before we set out."

The lightwielders bowed their heads and instinctively went silent. Koristad, on the other hand, simply yawned and rubbed his eyes, having no intention of joining them. After a moment had passed and the prayer hadn't begun, he became aware of Vincent staring in his direction. There was something about the look in his eyes; it wasn't ire or loathing. It wasn't even disappointment or dissatisfaction.

It was a simple, unspoken message that he wouldn't begin until the final member of their party had bowed his head.

Koristad had never prayed to Aura. He had vague recollections of being in school when he was a boy, before the mark had appeared, and the class offering a morning prayer to the goddess. Even then he hadn't taken part, and the instructor had been content so long as he remained silent and didn't disturb the litany.

The whole premise seemed ridiculous. Even the faithful claimed Aura had departed the world, or *ascended*, as they called it, and could never return. Or perhaps he'd merely never developed an interest because it had never been a part of his family's way of life. Arach the Black Guardian had harbored little interest for theology, preferring to spend his time studying what he considered to be more pertinent knowledge.

But Vincent's dead stare refused to waver. Koristad let out a silent sigh, flexing his mind and sharpening his focus. It couldn't be so hard to pray, could it? The lightwielders always seemed to manage, and they seemed to be a depressingly simple bunch. He slowly closed his eyes and lowered his head, listening for the first time as Paladin Night began his prayer.

4

DUSK HAD FALLEN ON the city of Marketway, draping the rooftops in a heavy blanket of darkness. To all appearances, the entire populace had taken to their beds. The vendors had packed up their wares for the day, turning the streets into wide, barren corridors. The only exceptions were a handful of taverns scattered about the grounds, pouring firelight into the streets, along with the sounds of music and merriment. While these may have seemed to be the only locales of interest in the sleepy town, in truth they were quite ordinary; especially when compared to a nefarious scene unfolding in a secluded, nearby alleyway.

A hobbled man draped in a heavy cloak moved forward cautiously, looking left and right in the dim corridor, as if he were expecting someone amongst the piles of empty crates and garbage. His hood was pulled up over his face and he clasped the garment with both hands beneath his chin, as if he feared his identity might be discovered.

"Ralyn?" he chanced a harsh whisper. "Are you there?"

After a brief moment, a tall man stepped slowly from the dark shadows. He was young and powerfully built, with messy, chestnut colored hair. His presence was undeniably striking; not because he was especially handsome, which wasn't quite true, or because he was unsightly, which also wasn't the case. There was simply something in his bearing, the glint in his eye; he was commanding and menacing, inciting a desire to both approach and to flee. An odd looking bundle was strapped to his back. It was shaped like a wedge, about five feet long, and wrapped in a thick, dark fabric that concealed its true nature.

The cloaked man had no inkling as to what was concealed in the unusual package; he thought perhaps it was a musical instrument, though Ralyn had never struck him as a performer. Or, he thought, perhaps it was a weapon, though it seemed odd to keep it wrapped up like that. It would be impossible to access quickly. Moreover, Ralyn kept a long-bladed dagger at his belt, so lugging around a second weapon that couldn't be readily drawn seemed unreasonable.

"Your little brother isn't here?" the older man asked, searching for a smaller form in the shadows behind the large man.

It was impossible to see Ralyn's eyes in the dim light, but the man imagined he affixed him with his dark, intimidating stare that could speak violent threats with only a glance.

"He's asleep at the inn," Ralyn grumbled. "Kids need a lot of sleep, you know."

"Yes, I suppose that's true," the man said in a weak, shaky voice.

"You called me out here," Ralyn said shortly. "I trust you have it with you?"

"I-I do," the man stammered, "But I'll need to be paid for my services, first."

"That's only good business, I suppose," Ralyn said with a shrug, lifting a coin purse from his belt and tossing it at the old man.

It slipped through his bony fingers and hit the cobbled streets with a clang. Stooping over with a low groan, he quickly snatched it up and peered inside.

"Fifty gold crowns, as we arranged," Ralyn announced. "More than enough for you to retire, apothecary."

The man's eyes lit up, reflecting the bright gold, and an involuntary grin spread across his face. He couldn't believe it; with this sum, all of his troubles were over. He could live out the rest of his days in comfort, watching his grandchildren grow into fine young men and women. He was so absorbed by his own musings he nearly forgot about Ralyn's presence, and the big man cleared his throat impatiently.

The apothecary drew a small, wooden dish from the folds of his cloak, about as big as a fist and sealed tight with a glass lid. He didn't dare throw the package, but rather walked to his benefactor and placed it warily in his hands.

"Devil's extract," he said in a low voice, with both pride and shame for what he'd created. "A single drop is enough to kill a man in a matter of minutes. For its maximum potential, it needs to be introduced directly into the blood; if it's consumed, it might only make the victim ill."

"It's exactly what I need," Ralyn said in a throaty whisper as he unstoppered the lid and examined the contents.

It appeared to be dark, thick goo, but in the darkness it was impossible to discern any more. It emitted a bitter, sickening aroma.

"Keep in mind, this poison is very dangerous, and extremely illegal," the apothecary counseled. "If you're caught with it, you'll probably be hanged."

"If you think that concerns me," Ralyn spoke with a disgusted shake of his head, "Then you have severely misjudged the kind of person I am."

Something about the way he said it made the old man's skin crawl.

"Just what do you need this for, anyway?" he asked without thinking.

"You've been paid well enough to mind your own business," the younger man snapped.

"O-of course," he spluttered. "I apologize. I was merely curious."

"You know what they say about curiosity."

"I've been told," the man answered, taking a step back, feeling a sudden urge to get away.

A broad smile crept across Ralyn's face, but there was no humor or affability in it. Only malice was reflected in his dark eyes.

"It's for killing lightwielders."

"What!?" the old man yelped in surprise, speaking far too loudly and earning a grimace from the younger man. "You can't be serious!"

"I'm dead serious," Ralyn growled.

The apothecary wasn't sure what to do. Should he ask for the poison back and return his pay? Would Ralyn accept that? Could he part with the gold that would allow him to live out his final days in luxury?

"I-it might not even work on a lightwielder," he reasoned. "The blood of Aura gives them the power to heal mortal injuries."

"You're not trying to back out of our deal, are you?" Ralyn threatened.

"N-no, of course not."

"Good," the big man said in a condescending tone. "You had better keep your mouth shut about all of this."

"I will, sir," the apothecary replied, backing further away from the younger man.

Ralyn reached out without warning, grabbing the old man by his slender wrist and pulling him back into the shadows. The apothecary's heart was pounding with fear, as if it could burst. He suddenly regretted involving himself in this whole mess, regardless of the compensation.

"Before you go," Ralyn said in a harsh growl, "I'll need a demonstration of this concoction's lethality. For all I know, you could be trying to sell me horse fat."

"I-I don't have a test subject," the man protested, his mind racing.

At this point, he didn't ever want to see Ralyn again. But if it would assuage some of his apprehensions, he would have him visit his shop in the morning. By then he could arrange to have a stray dog or some other poor animal as an exhibition.

"That won't be necessary," Ralyn explained, his shadowed eyes reflecting the starlight like a bottomless pit lined with precious diamonds. "I have a test subject already."

The apothecary hadn't even seen the young man draw his dagger from its sheathe, but now he saw it was in his hand, and even in the dim illumination he could make out a dark streak along its edge where he'd applied the deadly toxin. The old man tried to scream to alert the town watch but, before he emitted even the slightest sound, Ralyn wrapped his big fingers around his mouth. In a panic, the cloaked man lost his grip on the pouch filled with gold crowns—his blood money—and it fell to the street, spilling the coins across the cobblestones.

The wound burned as the blade bit into the apothecary's neck, just under his ear. The laceration wasn't deep, certainly not a deathblow, but after only a matter of seconds he began to shake and convulse. When his eyes rolled back into his head, Ralyn released his grip and let him fall to the ground in a pile; his thick cloak spread out across the street like a rippling pool of blood. The shaking continued as his hands curled up into petrified claws. Dark bile and vomit began to spill from his mouth and nose. Then all movement stopped, and he was gone. Ralyn whistled, impressed.

"It kills rapidly, just like you said, old man," he announced in a bare whisper, squatting down and patting the apothecary on the back. "You do good work."

He reached over and snatched up the dropped pouch, pushing all of the spilled contents back inside. As he exited the alleyway, he hesitated for a moment. He turned and looked at the fallen corpse. With an amused smile, he reached into his pocket and flicked a coin toward his victim.

As it skipped across the ground, he said, "For your trouble, old man."

It came to a halt near the dead man's hand, spinning in a circle before it finally rattled to a stop.

It was a copper crown.

Chapter Nine

DEALING WITH DEVILS

Looking at the night sky, gazing into the vast cosmos which exist on such an incomprehensible scale, we cannot help but ponder our own insignificance. It is little wonder, then, that we humans think nothing of stepping on ants.

1

KORISTAD GROANED, "IT FEELS good to finally be away from all of those uppity lightwielders!"

"That's funny," Peril said. "When Vincent ordered you to pick up supplies for the company, you squabbled with him until you were both blue in the face."

The two of them walked down the bustling streets of Marketway, Peril leading Jester by the reigns. Stalls lined the road on either side, where vendors were advertising all sorts of wares: from pottery, to potatoes, to potions that cured baldness. Voices filled the air, the sounds of haggling and arguments, and even brawls when the first two failed. There were street performers trying to play their music over the din of the crowd, as well as dancers and jugglers plying their trade. Koristad had never seen a place quite like it; it was an undeniable sign they were drawing nearer to the capital. It was so hectic, in fact, even a man dressed in an unseasonably warm cloak and carrying an enormous halberd, while talking to a young girl about lightwielders, drew little attention.

"I wasn't arguing about having to do the work," Koristad said, "I just didn't like the way he ordered the two of us to do it because we were the lowest ranked. I should have knocked some sense into him."

"You're not going to get anywhere thinking like that, Koristad," Peril sighed, "It's just the way of the world."

"Who says I'm trying to get anywhere?" Koristad grumbled. "I'm not going to stay at the sanctuary forever."

Peril frowned.

"Maybe we should just hurry and finish up here," she said. "Vincent said they'd slow their pace so we could catch up on the other side of town, but if we take too long they'll be in the capital by the time we get through Marketway."

"Fine," Koristad conceded disagreeably. "What provisions do we need?"

"Vincent wrote out a list for me!" she said, pulling a wrinkled parchment from one of Jester's saddlebags.

Before she had a chance to look at it, Koristad stole it from her hands.

"It doesn't look like anything too exotic," he decided, looking it over. "This shouldn't take long."

Peril snatched the paper back, glaring at him.

"There certainly is a lot of it though," she said, patting Jester on the nose. "I hope he can carry it all back."

The small horse had been outfitted with a pack saddle for the occasion, though he'd done everything in his power to make it impossible for Peril to secure it to his back. It made him look even more like a mule, and Koristad was silently looking forward to piling as much weight onto the animal as he could.

The two of them went from stall to stall, picking out what they needed and paying out of a pouch Vincent had entrusted to them. They spent more time fighting through the crowds than anything else, and Koristad was disappointed to find it was taking longer than he'd expected.

As they moved about, Peril began to feel a strange sensation in the pit of her stomach. It was a stirring she'd never experienced before and, though it was faint at first, the more time that passed the more certain and undeniable it became.

Was she sensing a mage somewhere in the throng of shoppers? It was hard to know for certain, and she had no inkling as to its direction. More troubling still was she couldn't tell what kind of mage it might be. If it was some sort of tainted being she'd never encountered before, then what was it? A vampire? It seemed unlikely, with the hot sun beating down upon them.

"What's the matter?" Koristad demanded in annoyance.

He'd already walked three stalls over before he realized she'd stayed behind, staring off into space, and he'd been forced to return to get her attention.

"There's something…unusual here," she said.

"You were the one who said we had to hurry if we were going to catch up with the others," Koristad said. "Do we really have time for your daydreaming?"

"I'm not daydreaming!" Peril insisted fervently. "I think we should look around for anything out of the ordinary."

"And *I* think we should finish the job we came here to do, and then get back on the road," Koristad said, crossing his arms. "We're busy enough already, in case you've forgotten."

Peril ignored his protests and pushed Jester's reigns into his hands, a gesture that both man and horse reacted to with dismay.

"I just want to take a look," she said. "I'll be back before you're finished, I promise!"

She dodged into the crowd and Koristad yelled after her, "You're not really going to leave me to do this by myself, are you? Peril!?"

But she was gone, and given her diminutive stature it was impossible to spot her in the throng. He shook his head and looked over at Jester, who's equine eyes were filled with anxiety and loathing.

"Well, I guess it's just you and me, pal," he said, pulling the animal toward the next stall. He groaned to himself, "Why am I talking to a stupid horse?"

He began sorting through stacked loaves of hard bread, but was finding it difficult to concentrate. He had a bad feeling. But what was the worst that could happen? Then he realized he was thinking about Peril, and the worst was likely even more severe than he could imagine.

"Wraith?" for the first time, he tried to call on his spectral companion. "Are you there?"

For a moment there was no response, a fact that left him little surprised. Wraith certainly wasn't bound to him by any sort of necromancy, and therefore wasn't forcibly compelled to heed his summons. Just as Koristad had decided it wasn't going to appear, he felt the hairs on the back of his neck stand on end as the shadowy figure materialized by his side. It hung there motionless, gazing at him with its icy stare, but said nothing.

"I want you to keep an eye on Peril for me," Koristad explained to the dark spirit. "I don't want her to get into any trouble."

"I've no interest in that," Wraith replied simply.

There was no annoyance or disrespect in the ghost's disembodied voice. The words simply echoed through Koristad's head, like an epitaph rebounding off of tombstones, stating a plainly evident fact.

"You're always helping me, why is this any different?" Koristad demanded.

His continued conversation with the unseen was beginning to draw a disconcerted stare from the stall's vendor. It was an old woman with a lazy eye, and she looked like the kind of wicked battle-axe who would cause trouble if he carried on.

But Wraith remained silent opposite his question, so Koristad turned his back on the vendor and continued in a low voice, "What is it going to take to get you to do this?"

"What can the living offer the dead?" was Wraith's response, only mildly interested.

Koristad had to admit, it had a point. If only he was able to utilize the dark power in his blood, he could force the creature to obey his commands. However, things being what they were, the situation seemed hopeless.

"You'll have my gratitude," he hissed unconvincingly.

"I will do this for you only if you agree to grant me a boon," Wraith demanded in his hollow voice, so bereft of inflection that, at first, Koristad doubted what he'd heard.

"What can the living offer the dead?" he mocked suspiciously.

"When the time comes, I will give you that answer."

It was a cryptic response, and Koristad didn't like it. He felt as if he was being tempted to make a deal with a devil. But how bad was Wraith, really? It had always seemed loyal in its own sort of way. He recalled the first time he'd seen the ghost, watching silently as Executor Mourne had freed him from his bindings. At first, he thought it was his mind playing tricks on him, his psyche reeling from his interminable confinement. But it quickly became clear that Wraith was an entity unto himself, though the spirit's nature had always struck Koristad as unusual.

From the moment the mark of the necromancer appeared on his face, he'd been able to perceive the spirits of the dearly departed. Ordinarily, they were bound to the world of the living by some sort of deep regret or longing, the nature of which would quickly become clear if he dared to speak to one. Wraith, however, seemed to have no memory of his former life, or any impression of having been alive in the first place.

And there was this: the other ghosts Koristad had encountered had always looked as they had in life; in fact, when he was a boy, he'd had a hard time telling the difference between the living and the dead. Why was Wraith bound to an often shapeless, obscure spiritual body? Had it simply been dead for so long that it had lost the memory of what it had looked like, and was therefore trapped in its current form? If that were the case, shouldn't it have passed on once it forgot its clinging regrets? There didn't seem to be any manner of dark arcana binding it to the world of the living.

Of course, asking Wraith these sorts of questions was useless. Being asked for a boon was the most intimate interaction Koristad had ever had with the specter. There was no time to ponder such trivialities now; he feared if he waited any longer, Peril would be too long gone to be sniffed out in the crowd.

"Fine," Koristad growled. "You'll have your boon."

2

"OH!" PERIL EXCLAIMED EXCITEDLY. "That looks delicious!"

She'd only managed to wander a few stalls over before she'd come across one that was marketing an entire universe of cakes, pies, and assorted sweets. She knew she shouldn't let herself be distracted, but even as she told herself so, her legs and nose had pulled her forcibly toward the delightful displays.

"Would you care to purchase one, young lady?" asked the vendor, a pudgy, bald man with skin the color of fresh dough. "Perhaps this one, here?"

He waved his flour covered hands over a large, round cake with pink frosting, artistically decorated with pale marzipan. Despite herself, she bounced up and down with excitement, imagining the treat would taste every bit as delicious as it looked. The bald man smiled at her happily, but she realized Koristad was still in possession of all of the funds they'd brought. (And spending the company's assets on an enormous cake may have been something she regretted later, besides.)

Her heart sank and, noting the disappointed look in her eyes, the vendor offered, "Perhaps just a cupcake instead, while you think it over. Free of charge."

He presented her with a wrapped pastry, topped with the same frosting as the cake she'd been offered, and she accepted it delightedly. After one bite, she was so pleased she could have jumped the counter and hugged the man.

As she loitered about the stall, enjoying her gratis treat and cheerfully looking over the scrumptious merchandise, she began to feel a nagging sensation that there was something she was supposed to be doing. It was as if one of her superiors was forcing some superficial chore upon her, which made her try her hardest to put it out of her mind. Then came the slow realization it was an errand she'd deemed important herself. This made her marginally more interested. At last, her purpose sprang back to the forefront of her mind.

She could still detect the faint presence of tainted, but unfamiliar, blood. She bid the baker farewell and pushed her way back into the thick crowd, trying to sniff it out. But with so many wonderful sights and sounds assailing her from every direction, she was finding it especially difficult to concentrate.

She was gleefully clapping for a pair of fire jugglers when she spotted a timid looking young man, two or three years younger than she was, skulking into a nearby inn. He was short and thin with straight, black hair. His attire wasn't unusual, and nothing about his appearance was particularly striking. In fact, Peril might not have noted his presence at all, but the strange feeling that had been causing her such distress seemed to linger in his wake.

Though, after seeing him, she was beginning to doubt herself. She didn't think she had much talent for detection but, even with her meager skills, she'd never had such difficulty identifying a source. When she and Koristad had encountered the werewolf, she'd never detected a lycanthrope before, but she was immediately able to feel the connection between the monster and its primal blood. So what was this strange sensation the young boy was emitting? She thought maybe it really was just her imagination, after all. But she knew she wouldn't be satisfied at that, so she slipped away from the street performers and passed through the open portal behind him.

Inside was a meager tavern without a proper dining area, but merely a long, wooden bar and many patrons standing about as they ate and drank. It was clearly the kind of place a person would stay if they didn't have the money to afford decent accommodations, or if they simply didn't want to be bothered. Peril found it odd that such a small young boy would be in this kind of place by himself; the room was thick with undesirables, unwashed and desperate. Many of them were probably criminals or mercenaries, and she was instantly disconcerted by the lascivious stares some of the men were casting her way. She wanted to turn and walk out of that place immediately, but she couldn't bring herself to go back to Koristad and admit she'd simply gotten scared and given up.

She scooted across the chamber, her nostrils assailed by the aroma of heavy beer and spilled, sour ale. Broken crockery was on the floor, swept indifferently into every corner, and the ceiling was stained black with smoke. She was able to follow her senses to a stairwell on the far wall, the steps old and worn. It led her to the second level, where the inn's guests were quartered. She found herself in a long hallway with alternating doors on either wall, some of them with proper numbers, but others were simply painted or scratched into the wood. The floor was littered with dust and garbage, as if it hadn't been properly cleaned in weeks.

Peril took a deep breath and closed her eyes, trying to pinpoint which of the many entrances would lead her to her target. She slowly put one foot in front of the other, counting every pace, until she reached the number sixteen and was certain the door on her left concealed what she was looking for. When she opened her eyes, however, there was nothing but an impenetrable, blank wall. She immediately recanted her intuition and decided it was the door on her *right* that would lead her to her target, marked with the number six.

As quiet as a mouse, she crept to the door and tested the handle, finding it unlocked. She wondered if, in such poor accommodations, any of the rooms even had locks. Not daring to take a breath, she slowly inched the door open, pressing her face against the frame and attempting to peek inside.

What she saw nearly caused her to slam the door in embarrassment. The young man whom she'd seen moments before was undressing before a bathing pot set in the middle of the floor, his back to the entrance. He folded his clothes carefully and set them on the nearby table, giving no hint he was aware of Peril's presence. Then, she saw it: an intricate, geometric pattern on his right shoulder blade. Before that moment, it was a design she'd only seen in textbooks at the sanctuary. It was a mark she'd been told no longer existed.

"An artificer!" she whispered in spite of herself.

She wasn't certain what to do; the artificers had all been condemned nearly a millennia ago. Did that same death mark still apply? She knew she wasn't about to carry it out. But she thought it would be prudent to hurry to Koristad and let him know what she'd found. However, before she could take one step from the door, she felt a large hand wrap around her neck.

She gasped for air and tried to scream as she was pushed inside. The door slammed shut behind her. The pressure on her throat was intense; she could already feel her awareness slipping away as the dingy room spun wildly around her. She was only vaguely aware of the cold-blooded look on the face of the man who was choking her, as if he were merely wringing out his laundry, or the look of shock and dismay in the young boy's eyes.

"Ralyn, what are you doing!?" she heard the boy yell out, his voice like a distant echo as the revolving chamber began to grow dim. "Let her go!"

"She's seen your mark, little brother," the big man said without compassion. "We can't allow her to live."

"Let her go, Ralyn!" the boy insisted, grabbing hold of his brother's wrist. "Let her go, now!"

Ralyn scowled deeply and stooped down until he and Peril were standing at the same level.

Pulling her deep purple face close to his, he said with snarling wrath, "Make one sound, try to run away, and I'll snap your neck. You know I can."

He unkindly pushed her to the dirty floor as she coughed and gasped for air. He stood over her and glowered as his little brother knelt down to make sure she was alright, clad in only his underclothes.

Peril gasped and wheezed, lightly rubbing her tender neck. She felt lightheaded and disoriented; she'd been close to losing consciousness when Ralyn had finally let her go. The boy helped her to her feet and kindly dusted off her gown, which had been sullied by contact with the grimy floor.

"Please, forgive my brother, he…"

Before the boy could finish his sentence, he caught a glimpse of Peril's medallion, the blazing sun. He took an involuntary step back, suddenly frightened and unsure of what to do.

Ralyn spotted the ornament in the same instant, and his hand crept slowly to the dagger at his belt, the same blade he'd used to kill the elderly apothecary the night before. Quickly regaining his composure, the boy placed his hand on his brother's before the blade could be drawn.

"What are you doing?" Ralyn demanded. "A lightwielder has identified you for what you are. You know what we have to do."

Peril took a terrified step back, but there was nowhere to run. She was cornered and too frightened to scream. She glanced around frantically, somehow expecting Koristad to appear as if from nowhere to rescue her. But he was nowhere to be seen.

"Stop it!" the boy demanded. "You're scaring her!"

"She should be scared," Ralyn growled in a voice as deep as a rumbling earthquake, and Peril thought she saw the slightest smile play across his lips.

"Don't be afraid," the boy tried to assuage her apprehensions. "I won't let him do anything to you."

The words brought her little comfort; she couldn't imagine anything the small boy could do to stop his brutish older brother.

"What do you think you're doing?" Ralyn's voice was firm, but less aggressive as he addressed his brother, filled more with annoyance than violence. "If she were just an ordinary girl, maybe we could let her go. *Maybe*. We'll be out of town soon enough, and no one would believe she'd seen an artificer. But she's a child of Aura; if she reports our presence to the others, we'll be hunted to the edge of the world. We have to put an end to this immediately."

"We'll bring her with us!" the boy pleaded. "We can't just kill her!"

Ralyn sighed with frustration.

"You're a hell of a lot smarter than I am, Slayne, but you sure aren't showing it. I know you're getting to that age, but right now you need to think with your head instead of that thing between your legs. If you don't have the stomach for it, then you can wait outside."

Peril suddenly cried out, "Don't go, Slayne! I'm scared!"

Growing up in the orphanage she'd learned, if she asked the right way, she could almost always get what she wanted. She'd been an adorable little girl, after all. She'd carried those talents with her into womanhood, to the Snowdove Sanctuary. She had already grown accustomed to getting what she wanted, but she quickly found that her new benefactors were more difficult to cajole. So she'd been forced to hone her abilities, until they were so sharp she could even convince Executor Kailas to reassign her to a sanctuary of her choosing. Those skills, so delicately cultivated, had presently produced a masterpiece, and both she and Ralyn knew it. Slayne stepped between the small girl and his brother defiantly.

"Can't you see what she's doing?" Ralyn groaned in disbelief.

"I'm not going to let you hurt her," Slayne upheld doggedly.

The big man sighed in defeat.

"We're all we have left in this world, little brother," he said solemnly. "I would never do anything that would hurt you."

He turned his back on the two of them and stomped to a pile of bags under the room's only window.

Slayne turned toward Peril and asked sincerely, "Are you alright?"

Peril wanted to cry; her neck was already beginning to bruise. But that was the least of her worries.

"What's going to happen to me?" she whimpered.

Slayne drew himself up and puffed out his chest, trying to make himself look more mature and in control.

"You're going to have to come with us," he said resolutely. "For the time being, at least. We're performing an important task, and we can't risk anything going wrong."

"Don't tell her too much," Ralyn snapped, stepping between the two of them and shoving something made of cloth into Peril's hands.

She unraveled the article and saw it was an old, brown scarf.

"Put it on," he ordered.

"It doesn't match my dress," she complained dimly, "And it's too hot out for a scarf."

"We don't want anyone to see the bruises on your neck," he growled, taking a step toward her and placing himself at an intimidating proximity.

Peril immediately threw the cloth over her shoulders, then reached behind her neck and unclasped her medallion.

"What are you doing?" Ralyn demanded suspiciously.

"You're trying not to draw any attention, right?" she said smartly. "Then you won't want me wearing a badge that distinguishes me as a child of Aura."

Ralyn frowned. He didn't understand why the girl would try to be helpful in her own kidnapping, but there was sense in what she said.

"Fine," he said. "Leave it."

Peril let the medallion fall to the floor with a thud, the long chain pouring onto the ground like liquid brass.

Ralyn turned to his brother and instructed, "Get everything together so we can go."

"But I thought we weren't leaving until nightfall," Slayne said, surprised.

"We don't want to be here in case others come looking for her," he explained, gesturing at Peril, "And our target is moving ahead of schedule. We have work to do, little brother, and our task won't wait."

3

"WHERE DO YOU THINK you're going!?" a heavy-set man with a glass eye demanded. "You can't be up here unless you've paid for a room! Our guests demand their privacy!"

Koristad ignored the old innkeeper and stormed up the stairway, rushing to the door marked with a six and flinging it open. The knob slammed into the far wall as he surveyed the dirty, but empty, room.

"She's not here," he growled.

Emotionless, Wraith said, "I told you. She was taken."

"Why didn't you stop them!?" he demanded angrily.

The innkeeper was perplexed (and annoyed) at the question, thinking it directed at him.

Wraith replied, "What can I do to the living?"

"Don't give me that," Koristad spat, his face turning red with anger. "If you materialize your spiritual body, you can affect the world of the living. I know quite a bit about necromancy, if you recall."

He thought he heard the spirit make a soft hissing sound.

"You disappoint me, Koristad. Can you still not tell the difference between them and I?"

Koristad was bewildered by the question, but he didn't have a chance to probe any further. The innkeeper was backing out of the room, giving him a look as if he thought he was insane and possibly dangerous. Then again, that sort of reaction could serve him well.

He roughly grabbed the old man by the collar, demanding, "Where are this room's tenants!?"

The man nearly collapsed under the force of the necromancer's grip, but he let no anxiety creep into his eyes.

"That's none of your business, lightwielder!" he proclaimed defiantly.

He'd already seen the medallion around Koristad's neck, and knew what it meant, as did all the citizens of the empire.

"The children of Aura are supposed to be protectors of the people, but you're nothing but a bunch of thugs!"

Koristad drug the man toward him until his face was just inches away, and growled, "You're wrong, old man. I'm not a lightwielder."

"What do you mean?" he questioned anxiously, his nerves starting to get the better of him.

Koristad reached to the high collar of his cloak with his free hand, pulling it down and exposing the mark on his face. The innkeeper grew pale and tried to wriggle away, but it was pointless to try to escape.

"I'll ask you again, where are this room's tenants?" he said with a harsh rasp. "Before you answer, keep in mind I have the power to torment you in this life, as well as the next."

"Y-you're a necromancer!" he whined.

"I'm growing impatient," Koristad warned.

"They checked out, not long ago!" the old man confessed.

"Where did they go?"

"They didn't say," the innkeeper sighed in defeat, his shoulders slumping. "They kept to themselves."

Koristad glowered at him, "You'd better have more to offer me."

"I-I don't know what you want me to say!" he exclaimed, terrified by the murderous look in Koristad's fierce eyes. "There were two of them; a large man who always carried a strange package on his back, and a young boy. I think they were brothers."

"I already know all that," Koristad said, having received a disinterested report from Wraith.

"The big one, his name was Ryan...," the innkeeper corrected himself, "No, I think it was Ralyn. And the boy was Slayne. That's all I know!"

Koristad let go of the man's collar and the innkeeper stumbled backwards out the door. He quickly sprang to his feet, quite a feat for a man of his size, and fled down the hall.

Koristad turned back into the room, surveying the area for anything that might give him some sort of clue. The tenants had taken everything, aside from one small trinket he spotted on the floor. He stooped over to pick it up. It was Peril's medallion. He stared at it for a moment, wondered if she was alright, and cursed himself for letting her go. He should have been there to protect her.

He shoved the bauble into his pocket and glanced left and right, but Wraith had vanished. He knew it wouldn't be wise for him to stay any longer; unless he missed his guess, the innkeeper was on his way to inform the watch of a dangerous necromancer masquerading as a lightwielder. He let out a long, heavy sigh.

"I'm afraid I may not be able to find her on my own."

4

"KORISTAD AND PERIL STILL haven't returned with our supplies," Vian made the comment off handedly, as if he were talking only to himself, though he made certain Paladin Night was in earshot.

"Are you surprised?" Vincent said calmly. "The necromancer isn't reliable, and the girl is little better."

"Then why did you send them?" Vian questioned with a lopsided smile, though Vincent's silence informed him he wasn't amused by his wit. "Actually, I thought we should further slow our pace, to ensure they catch up by nightfall."

"Out of the question," Vincent stated bluntly. "We're already moving at a crawl. Would you have us stop?"

"Why not?" he said with a shrug. "You've been pushing this company since we set out. We wouldn't be doing any disservice by resting here."

"It would be a disservice to Executor Night," Vincent said, casting a sidelong glance at the noncompliant lightwielder. "He is awaiting the arrival of his blade."

Vian wanted to inform the paladin that his cousin hadn't been named high executor yet, but he knew his scathing wit would make any statement to the effect seem disrespectful, so he bit his tongue. After all, they both knew Gabrial was all but assured the title.

"Someone's approaching from the rear!" one of the lightwielders announced. "It looks like a man pulling a mule, but they're coming up terribly fast."

Vincent brought his proud steed around and saw the man was Koristad, and the mule was Jester. They were closing at a dead sprint, clearly pushing the horse to the point of exhaustion, and exceeding the limits of any normal human.

"We have to turn back!" Koristad panted, letting go of Jester's reigns.

The undersized horse was more than happy to put some distance between himself and the necromancer.

"Peril's been taken!"

"Taken?" Vian asked. "What do you mean?"

"Kidnapped! What else could I mean!? We have to go back and find her!"

The eyes of every member of the company turned toward Vincent expectantly.

"Absolutely not," the paladin's stern and immediate response caught everyone off guard.

Koristad wanted to give the man a furious look, but the expression of shock eclipsed all other emotions.

"What did you say?" he demanded bitterly.

"Must I repeat myself?" Vincent said, standing firm. "We will *not* be going back."

"I know you don't like me," Koristad said through gritted teeth, "But you can't make Peril pay for that. I won't let you."

"He's right, Vincent," Vian agreed. "What are you saying?"

Vincent shook his head, disgusted with both of them.

"This has nothing to do with how I feel," the paladin said. "In fact, I don't dislike you. I don't think anything of you at all. The simple fact is this: one of our party has been lost and, given the weight of our duty, we must assume it's a direct consequence of the relic we carry. It's a basic rule of warfare to divide your enemy before launching an attack. We should make our way to the capital as quickly as possible; we must stay together and present a united front to this enemy, should it choose to show itself."

"You'd just abandon her, then?" Koristad said in disbelief.

"Don't tire me with your petty attachments, necromancer," Vincent said with a disinterested sigh. "My only concern is my obligation to the order."

"You bastard!" Koristad cried in a nearly unintelligible snarl as he leapt at the paladin, fully intending to throw him from his horse and give him the beating of his life in front of his subordinates.

But he was stopped short by the point of Vincent's blade, halting his advance just in time to receive little more than a pinprick. He could feel a stream of blood run down his chest. He hadn't even seen the lightwielder reach for his weapon.

"You forget yourself," Vincent announced with an authoritative calm. "I am the commander of this company, and I won't have my orders questioned by you or anyone else. Now pull yourself together and get moving. We've lost enough time as it is."

He sheathed his sword and reared his horse around, signaling the party to continue their march.

"Fine!" Koristad proclaimed with ire. "If you won't help me, then I'll just find a way to save her myself."

Vincent brought his horse to a halt and looked over his shoulder.

"I forbid it. I already told you we must stay together in case this enemy presents itself," he explained. "That includes you. Proxy or not, you serve the order, and you will obey."

"To hell with your order!" Koristad barked and turned on his heel, marching back the way he came.

Vincent called after him, "Consider carefully, necromancer. If you abandon your post now, I will have no choice but to inform the high executor of your insubordination."

Koristad was reminded of why Executor Mourne had sent him on this mission to begin with. He was supposed to be earning Executor Night's trust and favor but, if he walked away now, he would be in an even worse position than before. But he could also imagine Peril, captured and afraid, or worse. He wondered what Gregan would have done; what the old man would have wanted him to do. But in that moment, none of it mattered. He kept walking without looking back.

"So be it," Vincent said as he directed his horse forward, no hint of disappointment in his voice. "You had no place in this procession to begin with."

The collection of lightwielders continued their journey westward toward the capital as Koristad stormed the other way, growing ever farther away from one another. He imagined the procession growing small in the distance, ultimately vanishing into the glare of the setting sun, but he refused to let himself look. He wouldn't give Vincent the satisfaction of believing he was having second thoughts. He wanted nothing more than to clobber the paladin, but the thought of it reminded him of the stinging flesh wound on his chest.

He wondered how he would go about trying to find Peril. After all, he'd only sought out the lightwielders' help because he wasn't certain how else to proceed. But all he'd accomplished was losing time; he was no better off than before, and the day was quickly coming to a close.

He heard hoof beats coming up from behind, and he wheeled around to see who it was. He was hoping it would be Vincent, coming to his senses and offering the aid of the company, but it was only Vian.

"What do you want?" Koristad grumbled at him. "If you're going to try to convince me to rejoin the party, you can forget it."

"I wasn't thinking anything of the sort," Vian said with a cock of his head. "Your mind is clearly made up, and it would be disrespectful to try and change it."

"How can you follow that man's orders?" Koristad demanded. "You know this is wrong."

"Paladin Night is only doing what he thinks is best," Vian explained earnestly, "And he's right. He's already lost one member of his company and I'm certain it pains him deeply, though he may never show it. He's only doing what's necessary to protect the remaining troupe from harm. He may be cold, but he's also wise and calm. That's why he was appointed the commander of this mission."

"He's an ass," Koristad spat, kicking a rock from his road. "Someday, he'll get what's coming to him."

"We all have our opinions," Vian offered agreeably.

"Is this why you chased after me?" Koristad demanded. "To stand up for your superior?"

"Of course not," Vian said with a shake of his head. "I don't want Peril to come to harm any more than you do. I'm not about to abandon my post, but since you already have," he let out a snort of a laugh, "I thought you might be willing to act on my behalf."

"What the hell is that supposed to mean?"

"If I were looking for Peril, the first thing I'd do is check with the guard houses at each of the roads leaving town," he explained. "Whoever took her has most likely already fled Marketway—it would be risky to keep a captured lightwielder in one place, since the rest of us would be able to sense her presence. Marketway is a trade center, and the watch try to keep a close eye on everyone coming and going. If they witnessed anything out of the ordinary, they would probably remember it."

Koristad nodded as the lightwielder spoke and grunted in thanks, then lied, "Well, I already have my own ideas on how to find her, but if they don't work out, maybe I'll give that a try."

"I wish you luck, Koristad," Vian said, turning his horse toward the caravan, now some distance off. "The next time I see you, I expect Peril to be at your side."

5

ERIL DIDN'T THINK SHE could possibly feel more awkward. After fleeing Marketway, Ralyn and Slayne had brought her to a small camp just a few miles outside of town. The location was far from empty; there must have been more than two dozen men scattered about, soldiers if one were to judge by their equipment. Ralyn ordered her to sit quietly on a log bench in the center of the crowd, where he could keep an eye on her while he conducted business with the company's leader.

Slayne plopped down next to her, offering a smile far too friendly to belong to a kidnapper. Then again, he hadn't acted like one, either. He'd been nothing but kind to her, scolding his brother when he was too gruff, talking to her as if she was his friend, and tending to her needs on the road. But, in spite of all this, and even if his smile seemed innocent and gentle, there was something about the boy that made her skin crawl.

"These men are Mountain Wolves," Slayne said.

When Peril looked at him as if she didn't understand, he elaborated, "They're a mercenary band; that's the name they've taken for themselves. They're some of the most skilled and battle hardened skirmish fighters in the whole empire. They earned a substantial reputation in the north fighting the barbarians."

"What are you and your brother doing with a group of mercenaries?" she asked.

"Well...Ralyn will probably be mad if I tell you too much," he replied, looking at the ground. "But I guess there's no harm in telling you we're hiring them. You'd know that soon enough, anyway."

"But what does an artificer want with a gang of mercenaries?" she asked stubbornly.

"I'm sorry," Slayne kicked the log with his heel, "I really can't say."

Peril sighed with disappointment and asked, "Well, is there anything you can tell me?"

"I...well, I really shouldn't talk about our mission."

Peril crossed her arms and fumed, "Hmph! You probably *can't* tell me anything! You're just tagging along with your brother, and he keeps you in the dark as much as me!"

As she spoke, Slayne's face grew dark, and he ground his teeth as he tried to keep himself under control.

"What do you know?!" he snarled at her. "Don't treat me like I'm a little kid! I'm not that much younger than you!"

Peril was genuinely startled by the heavy rage in his voice and the murderous look that flashed in his eyes. For a moment, it was as if he was a completely different person; for just a few seconds, he looked like Ralyn. His expression quickly returned to normal, as if it had never happened.

"I-I'm sorry," Peril apologized in a soft voice, "I didn't mean to..."

"My brother's an artificer, too, you know," he said quietly, as if he didn't want Ralyn to hear. "For generations, my family lived far to the west, overlooking the wastelands. It's a tough life out there, but it's a long way from the capital, and lightwielders don't go out that far. My brother and I have taken the name Lourdess, the name used by our ancestors, but back home our family was called Shepherd.

"It's a burden we've always had to bear; if the mark appeared on a child, then that child had to be disposed of, to keep the family's horrible secret hidden. Of course, nobody tells the kids about it while they're growing up. Parents don't like to think about it. But it's always a dark cloud that hangs in the back of their mind, every time a mother looks into the eyes of her children.

"Ralyn's mark appeared on the bottom of his foot, and when he asked my parents about it, they were mortified. But my mother pleaded with my father, and they decided no one would see it in such a hidden spot, so they allowed him to live. But they explained to him the consequences of his tainted blood, so he would know to always keep it hidden. I imagine my parents were relieved. One of their children had exhibited the mark, so the odds must have seemed slim that I, just a toddler at the time, would grow up to exhibit it as well.

"Of course, the mark did appear, and not in a spot as easily hidden as my brother's. I had no idea what it meant, but Ralyn did. He didn't have the heart to tell me, I suppose, and he tried to keep it hidden from our parents. But it was only a matter of time before I was found out.

"My father took me behind the house where he chopped wood. I was so oblivious, I didn't think twice about the shallow hole dug where none had been before, the perfect size for a child's grave.

"It wasn't until the last moment I realized I was going to die. I closed my eyes and cried out for help, never expecting to open them again. But Ralyn...he saved me. I guess he'd been traumatized by what had nearly happened to him, and he wouldn't allow that fate to befall his little brother. He killed my father, and together we fled our home. We didn't have a plan, or any means, we just ran as far and as fast as we could."

Slayne grew quiet and looked over at his brother solemnly.

"That's awful!" Peril said compassionately. "But are you certain being an artificer is that dangerous? I mean, the extermination order was issued centuries ago. I'm honestly not sure if an artificer would be considered a threat anymore. No more so than the other mages, at least."

Slayne shook his head and let out a derisive chuckle, "I'm not about to go to a sanctuary and ask. Not that I could set foot in one, anyway."

"But, maybe if…," Peril was suddenly distracted by a disagreement between Ralyn and the leader of the mercenaries.

"…just saying, killing lightwielders is a dangerous job. Their power aside, if even *one* of them escapes, we'll all be hunted men."

"Did he say light…," Peril began, but Slayne quickly put his hand over her mouth.

Ralyn turned his gaze in her direction, a dire warning in his eyes.

"Mind your tongue!" he hissed at her. "Or I'll cut it out!"

Peril didn't doubt for a second that he meant every word.

"I'm merely suggesting a little more pay would go a long way toward easing the minds of my men," the mercenary leader said.

He went by the name of Mason, though not even the mercenaries who served him knew if it was his first or last name. His hair was thick and brown, and patches of silver were beginning to show at his temples as he grew older. He wasn't a big man, but he was densely packed with muscle, and scars crisscrossed his body from his many battles. One in particular ran from the bridge of his nose all the way down to his jaw.

"So," Ralyn said with a disappointed shake of his head, "This is about money."

Mason shrugged and raised his eyebrows, trying to look innocent, and explained, "Well, it is what makes the world go 'round."

For a moment, it looked as if Ralyn was going to say something, but he simply shook his head again and unstrapped the mysterious package he always had at his back and let it fall to the ground.

"What are you doing?" Mason demanded, apprehensive at his silence.

But Ralyn paid him no mind and unrolled the thick, cloth bundle, revealing at its core a menacing looking axe.

Though to say it was menacing hardly commands the same presence of such an instrument; all weapons are, by their very nature, menacing. It was double-bladed, nearly five feet long, with enormous steel crescents on either side. The blades were like the silhouette of a demon's wings, with only a small point on the top and a blade like a scythe coming down. The shining steel was interlaced with ridges and grooves, though they were too perfect to be from natural wear, and too ugly to be artful ornamentation. To the untrained eye, they looked like the random scribblings of a madman.

"*Mountain Wolves*," Ralyn wrapped his lips around the name of the mercenary band as if he could taste it. "It's a funny thing about a wolf pack. If there's any doubt about who's in charge, about who the alpha male is, then it breeds chaos. Not just for those at the top, but for everyone."

"Is there a point to this rant of yours?" Mason asked in a rough voice.

"I only mean to make it clear," Ralyn announced, hefting the enormous axe over his shoulder, "That I'm exerting my dominance as the alpha of *this* pack."

Mason chuckled. Who did this man think he was? The mercenary leader had been bathed in the fire of battle and hardened beneath the cold reality of violence. He'd been fighting since Ralyn was just a boy. It seemed unfathomable that the upstart actually wanted to fight him one-on-one.

The Mountain Wolves, drawn by the commotion, had gathered around, waiting to see how their leader would react. Mason knew it wasn't an option for him to back down, though he didn't have any genuine desire to fight the young man. He was trying to think of a good way to put Ralyn in his place without injuring him too badly; if their employer was dead, they wouldn't be getting paid. At the same time, he knew he couldn't take that axe of his lightly.

Then again, it seemed likely he was carrying the rest of their wages with him and, if that were the case, they could simply take the crowns off his body. Mason had always been a mercenary, not a thief, but he supposed he could make an exception just this once.

He reached to his belt with both of his hands, drawing a long, curved sword and a small, thin bladed dagger. He held the sword in front of his body threateningly, but the dagger he folded under his wrist to keep it hidden. In the heat of battle, many enemies had been caught off guard, overlooking the off-handed weapon. It was an oversight that almost invariably proved fatal.

"Well, kid," he said in a condescending tone, "If I can, I'll try to let you live. But I won't make you any promises."

Ralyn flashed a wicked smile.

"Don't hold back. If you do, you won't live long enough to regret it."

He carefully positioned his hand just an inch over the axe's blade and called over his shoulder, "Is it here, Slayne?"

"Just a hair lower," Slayne said, "But remember, if you change your facing then..."

"I know, I know. Do you think I haven't learned anything?" Ralyn waved him off, then turned back to Mason and asked, "Are you ready?"

"Just waiting on you, kid," he replied, appearing almost disinterested. "I'll let you take the first swing."

"Oh, joy!" Ralyn cried, wheeling back his weapon and letting it fly, as if he intended to chop down an oak tree with a single swing.

Mason was caught off guard by the swiftness of the attack and was forced backward as he ducked and weaved, preoccupied only with keeping his head. There was something wrong. A weapon of that size shouldn't have been so fast.

He was having difficulty reading Ralyn's movements, as well; he was an expert at interpreting subtle changes in an enemy's stance or grip, the almost imperceptible drop of a shoulder or twitch of an eye to one side. If he wasn't, he wouldn't have lasted on the battlefield as long as he had. But it seemed as if it wasn't Ralyn swinging the weapon, but rather it was dragging the fighter's arms along behind it; as if the weapon had a murderous intent entirely of its own.

Mason was losing ground fast, and he knew one misstep would be his last mistake. He had to find a way to end this battle quickly. Any thoughts of letting Ralyn live vanished instantly. This was a fight for survival, now. Ralyn's swings were wide and wild, like the combat style of a novice, in spite of his lethal speed. Mason waited for an opening, that moment when the axe reached the end of its swing and Ralyn would have to adjust his grip to bring it around for another pass. In that instant, he lunged forward, his sword braced at his side defensively and his clever dagger aimed at Ralyn's heart.

Mason hoped the rookie fighter had forgotten about the weapon, and maybe he had. But the axe came around on its cross swing faster than Mason had anticipated; he'd committed himself too much to his offensive to dodge. He let the dagger fall to the ground and pressed his palm against the flat back of his sword, leaning all his weight in anticipation of the powerful blow. He knew it was going to be painful, the impact could even break his wrist, but he'd stopped attacks from the inhumanly powerful barbarians with the same technique. The instant the axe rebounded off his weapon, he was positioned for a killer strike to Ralyn's neck.

The moment the two weapons connected, Mason discovered he could no more hold back the razor sharp blade than he could have stopped the sun from setting. He didn't understand it. As the attack crashed against his blade, the sword was knocked wide, altering the deadly axe's course just enough to slash open his gut, rather than cleave him clean in half.

He fell to his knees as a waterfall of hot blood rushed down his legs. His vision was already going dark, and he knew in a few moments his suffering would all be over. Though his enemy was already mortally wounded, Ralyn lifted the axe high above his head for the killing strike.

"No, wait!" Peril cried as Slayne held her back, stopping her from rushing into the fray. "I can save him!"

But her words did nothing to slow the blade's descent; the gory blow ended Mason's life instantly. She was speechless at the scene; even the Mountain Wolves, most of whom had seen more combat than peace, were silent.

Ralyn wiped the blood and ichor from his axe and asked in a booming voice, "Does anyone else think the wage I've offered is unfair?!"

There were a few murmurs from the mercenaries, but none would dare oppose him directly. With their leader gone, the crowns they'd been promised would be divided more generously, besides. They quickly dispersed, resuming their preparations.

"I'm sorry you had to see that," Slayne apologized to Peril.

She was surprised to find he seemed little disturbed by the gruesome execution he'd just witnessed.

"That wasn't a fair fight," she said grudgingly, though certainly not in a voice loud enough for Ralyn to hear. "What kind of weapon is that?"

A smile flashed across Slayne's face, and he seemed to grow larger with pride.

"It's a family heirloom my brother took before we left home," he said, gazing at the weapon longingly. "If I were a little bigger, I could wield it with even more power than he does. I'm afraid my brother wouldn't be able to tell the difference between a ley line and a key line without my help."

"An heirloom?" Peril wondered just how ancient the weapon might be, and she quickly received her answer.

"It was crafted by our ancestor, one of the first artificers," he explained, "Aleister Lourdess. He named it the Edge of Abaddon. An entire city had to be sacrificed in order to produce enough raw power to create such an awesome weapon."

"A whole city?" Peril couldn't believe what she was hearing. "Then this is the weapon that..."

"That's right," Slayne said with a nod, appearing disconcertingly pleased. "It was this very weapon, and the methods used to create it, that lead to the order to exterminate all artificers, and destroy their creations."

6

(More than eight centuries before present)

"NO! LET ME GO!" a young woman screamed at two men in military uniform, bracing herself as best she could as they pulled her down a wide hallway, one clinging to each arm.

"Stop your struggling!" one of the men threatened. "By the order of the high executor, all artificers are to be brought to the capital to stand trial for crimes against the empire!"

"But I haven't done anything wrong!" the woman pleaded, struggling harder than ever against her captors. "Please, believe me!"

There was commotion everywhere as imperial guardsmen stormed the academy, seizing every artificer they could find. The site had been constructed as a place of learning, but now it seemed like an inescapable deathtrap as the arresting soldiers stood at every exit, cutting off any hope of flight.

Rumors of the sinister machinations playing across the empire had begun to spread only that morning. The artificers realized too late they should have fled. It was simply too hard for them to believe the order that had been passed down, and too difficult to comprehend that a place of such peace and solidarity could be the victim of such a brazen raid.

The rumors claimed the emperor's so called "trials" were merely for show, and every artificer they'd rounded up so far had been put to death. So the young woman couldn't even consider going with the two soldiers willingly; she would fight them until her arms came off, if that was what it took.

"Don't think you can weasel your way out of this just because you're a girl!" one of the soldiers snarled, reaching for the saber at his hip. "We know what your kind has been doing!"

"Aleister Lourdess is a monster!" she cried, her eyes going wide as the blade was drawn from its scabbard. "But I'm not like him, I swear!"

The soldiers had clearly listened to enough of her lies, and grew weary of fighting her with every step. Their orders had been quite specific: all artificers were to be brought to the capital to stand trial, and those who resisted were to be killed on the spot. As the first soldier readied his sword, the other wrenched her arm around behind her back, forcing her to cry out in pain.

"I'll give it up!" she cried, shutting her eyes tight. "I don't care about my magic; I'll never use it again! Please, I don't want to die!"

"My whole family lived in Asheridge," the soldier growled at her, the naked steel glinting in his hand. "Your kind doesn't deserve to live."

As he cocked back his arm for a final swipe, a woman's voice from behind commanded, "Put away your weapon at once."

Thinking it was likely some other artificer who'd come to the defense of her classmate, the soldier wheeled around but, when he saw the speaker, he lowered his eyes and blade respectfully.

"High Executor Laurel!" he said, surprised and confused. "Ma'am, we're… only carrying out your orders."

"Didn't you hear me?" Tricia said sternly, crossing her arms. "I told you to put your weapon away. I will *not* repeat myself again."

The sword slid into its sheathe instantly.

"Now let her go and be on your way."

"But…high executor, we have orders!" they protested fervidly. "If we fail to carry them out, we'll be reprimanded!"

Tricia didn't have to speak another word; with only a look their resolve evaporated. The girl was set free, and they retreated out of her sight as quickly as they could.

The young artificer collapsed to the floor, rubbing her shoulder in pain. She looked up fearfully at the high executor, uncertain of what was about to happen to her.

She flinched when Tricia reached out her hand, offering to help her to her feet, and asked, "They didn't hurt you too badly, did they?"

The girl shook her head slowly, too frightened to speak, as if her voice might scare away her sudden good fortune.

"My name is Tricia Laurel, and I've recently been appointed to the new position of high executor. Might I know your name?"

"Lisa," she said softly. "Lisa Atherton."

"It's a pleasure to meet you, Lisa," Tricia said in a friendly voice. "Are you going to let me help you up, or are you too hurt to stand?"

Lisa was almost too frightened to touch the woman's hand, but she didn't dare refuse such a direct request, and she allowed Tricia to help her to her feet.

"I don't understand," Lisa said in a voice so quiet it was barely audible. "I thought you were the one who ordered all the artificers arrested."

"I never gave such an order," Tricia said simply, glancing over her shoulder. "But I don't have time to discuss that now. I need your help."

"My help, high executor?"

"I'm looking for Ilaron Reede," Tricia explained. "I was told I could find him here."

"Professor Reede?" Lisa seemed surprised. "I haven't seen him at all today. He may have already been taken away by the soldiers."

"If you had to guess, where would you say he was?"

Lisa thought for only a split second before answering, "He can almost always be found in his study."

Tricia nodded at the girl and ordered, "Take me there."

Lisa wanted nothing more than to be away from the academy; somewhere far, far away, but she didn't feel she could refuse a favor from a woman who had undoubtedly saved her life.

She led Tricia to a set of stairs that descended into the academy basement. It appeared the soldiers hadn't come this way—not yet, at least. The staircase spilled into a long hall with wide, open archways on either side. The chambers beyond were mostly dark and unoccupied, but there was a single light shining brightly at the far end. Lisa announced it was Professor Reede's study.

As the two of them entered the chamber, Tricia felt the word "study" hardly seemed appropriate. It looked more like a warehouse, with piles of papers fanned out on every available surface and, when there were no more surfaces left, simply scattered across the floor. Tall bookshelves, so high that the utmost volumes could only be reached by using a ladder, lined every wall. There were crates filled with wood, steel, bone, and every other sort of material she could think of, piled so high they were like hills. And, in the middle of it all, Ilaron stood before a large desk, brooding over an unrolled parchment inked with delicate, arcane diagrams.

He'd aged since she'd last seen him, as people do. His dark brown hair, once worn so wild and long, was trimmed short. His vision had begun to fail him, so he now wore a pair of small framed spectacles. Tricia supposed she had aged, as well. The years of her youth were behind her, and the days of soldiers' awestruck expressions, discovering their commander was such a young girl, had past. Years on the battlefield had left her body adorned with scars, though (by the grace of a sturdy helmet) her face had remained unblemished.

"Ilaron!" Tricia scolded. "What are you doing!?"

He looked up at her with tired, glazed-over eyes and displayed a subtle spark of recognition.

"It's good to see you again, Tricia," he said in a pleasant but weary voice. "I've heard the lightwielders are united under a single banner for the first time in more than eleven centuries, and you're the culprit behind it. And they named you the high executor, besides. Congratulations."

Tricia seemed less than pleased with his accolade.

"I asked you what you were doing. Don't you realize there are imperial soldiers raiding the academy above?"

"Of course I do," Ilaron said with a shrug of disinterest. "It seems a sad day that a place of learning is turned into a battlefield."

"I swear, I had nothing to do with this," Tricia said in her defense.

"I never thought you did."

"Emperor Arescin made the proclamation in my name," she said bitterly. "I don't understand why."

"He's a very clever man."

"What does that mean?" she demanded.

"Many of the kingdoms under his rule were independent until a few years ago," Ilaron explained. "They fell under his sway only under the pressure presented by the ongoing war. But they still view him as a tyrant, and his hold over them is tenuous. He knew something had to be done swiftly and decisively about the atrocities perpetrated by the artificers, but if he gave the order, it would only cement the people's view of him as a ruthless dictator. But you, the first high executor, are a heroine and the voice of Aura in this world. Your command is beyond question. By giving the order in your name, he avoids being labeled as a genocidal murderer, yet he can still approve of your supposed dictum and win the respect of those who fear the artificers."

Lisa, who had been quiet thus far, spoke up, "So, you really didn't order this?"

Tricia shook her head, "The people are terrified after what happened in Asheridge. But I never would have done something this drastic."

"Then can't you make the soldiers stop?" Lisa said in a shaky, excitable voice. "They'd listen to you!"

Tricia grew silent and looked down at the floor.

"She can't, Lisa," Ilaron explained.

"But why!?" the girl seemed to be on the brink of tears. "You're the only person with the power to stop this!"

Still, Tricia gave no answer.

Ilaron said, "If the emperor and the high executor clash over this, the fragile alliances that have kept the kingdoms together will shatter. It would be civil war and, even if it didn't come to that, the empire can't afford to be divided before the enemy standing at our gates."

Lisa hung her head and whimpered, "How could Emperor Arescin do something so heartless?"

"Perhaps his actions have been heartless," Ilaron said thoughtfully, "But the actions of Aleister Lourdess are only one piece to a larger puzzle. Certainly there hasn't been anything on the same scale, but reports of artificers using human life as fuel for their magic have surfaced across the empire. How many people do you suppose died in Asheridge? Certainly many times the number of artificers who are now in peril. Perhaps this is the only way to prevent something like that from happening again."

"You can't mean that, professor!" Lisa exclaimed, astonished.

"What do you think, high executor?" Ilaron asked seriously.

Tricia spotted a stool in the corner of the study, surrounded by piles of loose papers, and she collapsed into it, feeling discouraged.

"I honestly don't know," she sighed. "Sometimes I wonder if I'm any better than those guilty artificers. I've sacrificed entire battalions, good and loyal men, to secure victories on the battlefield. So, too, did they sacrifice good people in order to create tools that could be used against the Black Legion. What makes us so different, them and I?"

Ilaron scoffed, "You always were overly sentimental. You still wear that amulet I gave you all those years ago, even though I told you back then it had no more power."

She reached to her chest and took the small, iron pyramid in her hand and gazed at it, reminiscing.

"It saved my life that day."

"Yes, you've told me. But now it's just an ugly lump of iron," Ilaron said. "A woman of your status should be clad in jewelry of gold and sapphires, not such crude ornaments."

She frowned at him.

"I wear it because it was a gift from you," she asserted. "But you're just the opposite. You're not sentimental about anything. Not even your own life, it would seem. Have you just been waiting for the soldiers to find you down here?"

"I've been researching," Ilaron said with an unconcerned shrug. "I'm on the brink of a breakthrough concerning paralateral key lines. Besides, what would you have me do? Run away?"

"You can't just give up!"

"How can you ask me to go into hiding while so many innocent mages are persecuted?" Ilaron said with a shake of his head. "I have no intention of resisting."

"I see what this is about," Tricia said with a scowl. "You think you're responsible for this."

"We both know I am," Ilaron looked her directly in the eyes as he spoke, without so much as glancing down at the papers he'd been studying since she'd arrived.

"Aleister Lourdess was only a student!" she protested, leaping from her seat. "You didn't tell him to kill all those people!"

"His actions were a direct result of knowledge he acquired under my tutelage," Ilaron said. "In fact, all of the crimes committed by the artificers were, directly or indirectly, a result of my dissertations."

Lisa made no comment on the subject, though she herself had read every treatise Professor Reede had made available, and was well aware of the works he was referencing. The notes had been far too advanced for her (indeed, for most students at the academy), and so most of it seemed incomprehensible. However, she was able to glean it was a dissertation on external power sources, most notably living energy, and how to seal that power within ley lines.

Tricia said, "You're a brilliant artificer. That doesn't mean you can control the morality of others who follow in your footsteps."

Ilaron didn't seem convinced, or even particularly interested.

"Don't give me that look. I'm not going to let you stay here."

"Why is this so important to you?" he demanded. "I haven't seen you in years. I can't imagine you're that attached to me. Do you think you're paying me back for saving you?"

"That's not it," Tricia answered, unruffled by Ilaron's insolence. "I'm not doing this for you. Or for me. I'm doing this for everyone."

Ilaron cocked his head at her, truly fascinated.

"What is *that* supposed to mean?"

"The archangels created the mages to defend us all from the Black Legion," she explained thoughtfully. "That includes the artificers. I think they knew what they were doing; I believe it was all part of a bigger plan. We need *all* the mages. Without the artificers, I don't think we can stop the archdevils."

"I was under the impression the war was almost over," Ilaron said with a deep frown. "I heard you even destroyed one of the archdevils personally."

"Is that what they're saying?" she said, looking down and touching her temple with her fingertips. "The situation is much more dire at the front. We may have managed to secure a few cities but, the fact is, our control hangs by a thread. Things are worse now than ever, and I'm afraid if something doesn't happen soon, then all will be lost."

"And the archdevil?"

"It's true I confronted one," she admitted, shifting uncomfortably, "But I was only able to wound it. No matter how ruthlessly I maimed the monster, I couldn't inflict a mortal injury. If my company hadn't pressed in when they did, I wouldn't have survived the encounter. It escaped, retreating to lick its wounds and plot its next offensive, I'm sure."

"Isn't there anything that can be done?" Lisa pleaded.

"There is always a way," Ilaron expressed absentmindedly and without hesitation, shuffling the papers on the table before him. "However, I don't think even the high executor can slay an archdevil wielding a mere weapon of steel, sanctified or not."

Tricia smiled at him cleverly, "You think you can make something better, artificer?"

"I'll need time," Ilaron said, "As well as an isolated place to research and experiment."

"I didn't come here without a plan," Tricia announced. "Give me that much credit, at least. I know of a small island in the eastern sea. It's near enough to look out across the water and see the shore, but there are rarely any visitors. The only residents are an order of priests. If I asked them, I'm certain they would shelter you there."

"What about me?" Lisa asked, afraid she was going to be left to fend for herself.

"I could use a research assistant," Ilaron said, looking hopefully at Tricia.

"Of course," she said with a sigh. "I suppose I can hide two artificers as easily as one."

Chapter Ten

REACHING OUT TO TOUCH THE UNTOUCHABLE

We are all born like rain.
We descend through the freedom of the sky toward a hard inevitability.
We coalesce to form the stream of fate, from which there can be no escape.
All we can do is say, "This is as it should be."
To fight against the current is only to give over to desperation and loss.
Fate is a cruel thing.

1

PERIL WASN'T CERTAIN WHAT the Lourdess brothers were planning but, as far as she knew, the only lightwielders in the area were those commanded by Paladin Night. Were they planning to try to steal the Executor Blade? Gregan had said only the high executor could wield the weapon; it would destroy anyone else who dared to touch it. There seemed little need to defend such a deadly relic, and she assumed that was why such a small procession was required. But that supposition had been made based on the understanding that the artificers were all gone; it was possible the brothers possessed some means to force the holy weapon to submit.

She hadn't counted how many mercenaries were traveling with them, but there was no doubt they outnumbered Vincent's troupe. Even if they were lightwielders, she wasn't confident they could stand against such overwhelming odds, especially after seeing Ralyn's axe, the Edge of Abaddon, in action. She had to escape and find some way to warn them what was coming.

That was the only thought in her mind as she lay on the hard earth, surrounded by a blanket of thick darkness. Ralyn had stuffed her into a small tent, posting one of the mercenaries outside in case she thought to run away during the night. The rest of the camp had gone silent, resting in preparation for the impending raid, while Peril lay awake.

She scooted her sleeping bag to the back of the tent, as if she thought abandoning it would somehow alert the guard outside. She ran her hands softly down the cloth partition and tried to wiggle her fingers under the fabric to the outside, gauging if there was enough room for her to slip through. But the tent had been staked down tight and she knew that, even if she could manage to wriggle through, doing so what make enough noise to draw the attention of the guard who was just a few feet away.

She groaned silently, trying to come up with a better plan. Could she dig a tunnel out to the edge of camp? No, that would take too long. Maybe she could use the power of Aura to blind the mercenary outside, giving her the element of surprise to make her escape? But that wouldn't work; a flash that bright would wake up everyone else in the camp, even if she could muster enough power to make one.

She sighed in frustration. She wondered what Koristad would have done. Knowing him, he would have tried to fight his way out, regardless of the odds. The thought wasn't exactly helpful; it was even worse than her own ideas. She couldn't believe Executor Mourne had spoken of Koristad as if he was some kind of genius—or, at least, had been as a child.

She pouted and wished Koristad would come swooping out of the darkness to save her. She wondered if he was worried; if he was looking for her. He probably didn't even care, she thought to herself. She imagined him shrugging off her disappearance and shirking his duty to gather supplies, instead spending all the money he'd been given at the bakery she'd wandered into in Marketway. Then he would take Jester and sell him to an old man with a glass eye who had dogs to feed, just so he could get enough money to buy that delicious looking cake, and eat it all himself.

"What a horrible thing to do, Koristad!" she said aloud.

She covered her mouth with her hands, suddenly realizing the whole ordeal had occurred only in her imagination. She heard a rustling outside her tent; the dim glow of a lantern shined through the fabric. She sat up as she heard the muffled discourse of two men outside. Had Koristad really come to save her?

The tent flap parted as a figure moved inside. At first, she was too blinded by the sudden influx of light to make out who it was. As her eyes adjusted, a face began to come into focus: it was Ralyn, and he fixed his eyes upon her with a glowering expression.

"So, you're still awake," he said.

Peril didn't like this; he was acting almost friendly, though there was certainly no kindness behind his eyes.

"What do you want?" she demanded.

"I couldn't sleep."

Peril frowned at him, asserting, "That doesn't answer my question."

She hoped she'd made it clear she didn't want him anywhere near, but he showed no intention of leaving. He plopped down on the ground in front of her, setting the lantern beside him, and stretched his arms over his head. She noticed he wasn't carrying the concealed Edge of Abaddon; it was the first time she'd seen him without it. She supposed he couldn't sleep with it strapped to his back.

"I've been watching you ever since we set out," he confessed, though no hint of shyness or discomfort crept into his voice or eyes. "It's hard not to. You're a very pretty girl. A man like me could fall for someone like you."

"Then why aren't you nicer to me?" she snapped at him, crossing her arms over her chest.

"Come now, I *have* been nice," Ralyn said with a menacing smile. "I've brought you on this journey with us, taken care of your needs, and I've even posted a guard to look over you while you rest. The Mountain Wolves really don't enjoy missing sleep, but I made certain they'd do it for you."

Peril glowered at him.

"That guard isn't there to keep me safe. He's there to keep me from running away. And I never wanted to go with you in the first place!"

"There's no need to be defiant," Ralyn's voice grew deeper and more threatening as he spoke. "Whether you admit it or not, I've gone out of my way for you. I think I deserve to get something in return."

He reached out with his big hand and wrapped his thick fingers around Peril's leg. His grip was strong, painful even through her sleeping bag.

"Take your hand off me!" she demanded.

She tried to sound firm, but a tremor crept into her voice.

"What are you going to do if I don't?" Ralyn growled, leaning toward her.

At such close proximity, the man's impressive size became even more intimidating. She could barely breathe. She knew there was no chance she could stop him forcibly, even if she was a lightwielder. Her mind was frantic, shrieking for her to run away, but Ralyn's grip held her tight.

"If you don't, I'll scream," was all she could think to say.

The instant the words left her lips, Ralyn's free arm flew forward with shocking speed, fixing his hand over her mouth. She struggled to get away, but he held her down and refused to budge.

"We can't have that," he hissed, murder in his voice. "We wouldn't want my little brother to hear."

"He already has."

The voice startled them both, and Ralyn looked over his shoulder to find Slayne standing in the entryway. The boy looked both mortified and enraged, as if he wasn't certain whether he should run away or pounce on his despicable older brother.

"Go to bed, Slayne," Ralyn said. His voice didn't carry the slightest hint of remorse. "You'll understand when you're older."

"I understand now!" Slayne yelled at him. "Let her go, right now!"

Peril felt it was a wonderful idea. Ralyn was monstrously strong and not minding what he was doing. She feared she might suffocate under his oppressive restraint.

"I said go back to bed," Peril had never heard Ralyn speak to his brother in such a harsh tone. "We'll talk in the morning."

"No!" Slayne stood firm. "I won't let you hurt her!"

Ralyn wheeled around, releasing his hold on Peril. She gasped for air and scurried as far away as she could, which wasn't far, since the large man was blocking the only exit.

"I see what this is about," Ralyn growled, his face just inches from the young boy's. "You want her for yourself."

"What's that supposed to mean?"

"You're getting greedy, little brother," he shook his head in disgust. "We've shared everything up until now. This should be no different."

When he said it, he gestured at Peril as if she were a mindless object. Slayne was clearly unsettled, but one had to give him credit for standing up to someone more than twice his size. For a moment he was silent, but when he spoke there was loathing in his voice.

"You make me sick," he said, barely a whisper.

Both Peril and Slayne were caught off guard when Ralyn lashed out with the back of his hand, striking his brother across the side of the face. It wasn't a half-hearted warning; Slayne toppled over backward under the force of the blow, stunned and reeling in pain. When he struggled to his feet, there was an oozing gash above his eye. He didn't need to wait until morning to know he was going to be bruised and swollen.

"I-I'm sorry, Slayne," Ralyn stammered out a sudden apology, his eyes wide at what he'd done. "I shouldn't have done that. I won't ever do it again."

Slayne didn't offer any sort of response; he just stared at his brother, trying with all his might to fight back the tears that were welling up in his eyes.

"I'm sorry, alright?" Ralyn repeated, reaching forward to muss his brother's hair, but Slayne flinched away from him.

Ralyn groaned and looked back at Peril, glaring at her as if he blamed her for the entire incident.

"Fine," he spat out. "I'm going to bed. I'll see you in the morning."

He stormed out of the tent, nearly bowling his brother over in his hasty withdrawal. Slayne didn't turn to watch him leave, nor did he look at Peril. He simply stared off into a dark corner of the tent, as if he was dreaming.

Peril was shaken up and clearly not comfortable with the boy's presence. She gathered up her sleeping bag and wrapped it tight around her body, as if it could keep her safe from harm.

Slayne sniffed, wiped his eyes, and asked, "Are you okay?"

"Go away!" Peril screamed at him, a sudden flood of tears running down her cheeks. "I hate both of you! Go away and never come back!"

She pulled the bedding over her head and curled into a ball, her back to him. The young boy lingered for only a moment longer before he picked up the lantern and exited the tent, leaving Peril in pitch darkness. She sobbed and cried, certain she would never be able to sleep.

"You have to help me, Koristad," she cried. "I don't want to do this anymore."

2

ORISTAD SPENT MOST OF the night crisscrossing Marketway, traveling from one guard house to another, searching for any information regarding his missing companion. The guards had been surprisingly agreeable with him; with the medallion around his neck, they assumed he was a lightwielder on an important errand. He had no intention of correcting them.

However, questioning one guard after another had left him empty handed. He was beginning to curse Vian's bad idea after speaking with the guards at the final outpost. Seeing his disappointment, though, they'd informed him of two more paths that lead out of town. Neither path saw much use, but they were both watched over like the rest. They were known as "small roads," though Koristad wasn't certain if it was a reference to the volume of traffic that traversed upon them, or to the weeds and grasses that had begun to invade from either side, causing them to appear uncomfortably narrow.

He'd chosen to check the western small road first, and found his first bit of luck.

"Well, I don't recall the man you're talking about," the guard, a portly man in his late thirties had said, "But I remember the girl. You don't see many as pretty as her, traveling the small roads, leastways."

He couldn't give an accurate time of when she'd left besides "sometime in the afternoon", but Koristad was grateful regardless.

In the dead of night, he set out on the road at a pace that even a mounted traveler would have been pressed to match. The route seemed eerily abandoned, without a single traveler moving in either direction. He'd been told the road didn't lead anywhere; it was only used by the rustic locals to cart goods in and out of the city, and ultimately came to an abrupt and senseless end. Thus, as the bright sun began to climb the eastern horizon, he was startled to hear swift hoof beats from behind.

He wheeled around quickly, reaching for his halberd. What he saw surprised him more than an army of bandits, and only displeased him slightly less.

"Jester!" he growled at the horse. "I thought I left you with the lightwielders!"

The horse snorted at him, stamped his hooves and shook his head.

"What, have you decided you like me now?" Koristad demanded, reaching out to pat the animal on the nose.

He quickly recoiled as the beast snapped at him, a reaction he'd been more than prepared for.

"I see," Koristad said with a sigh, "You're trying to find Peril, too."

The horse snorted again and trotted down the path, pushing the proxy lightwielder out of his way. With a heavy sigh, Koristad followed behind, though Jester quickly outpaced him.

Koristad slowed when he spotted a lone man on the road ahead. The man stood there, motionless, staring off into the scattered brush to the south, as if he was waiting for something. Jester continued on at a gallop, and Koristad yelled when he saw the horse was so intent on its course it was about to run the man down. How could the dumb beast be so blind? Jester passed half a step in front of him, neither of them giving an inch, as if they were both unaware of the other's presence.

As Koristad drew closer, the cause of the near collision became apparent. The man was horrifically wounded with a gash across his belly, as well as a gaping wound between his shoulder and neck. They were both plainly fatal wounds; the figure standing before him was a spirit of the recently departed. Jester hadn't been blind after all; to the animal, the man hadn't even been there.

"Good morning, sir," Koristad said in greeting.

As a boy he'd spoken to spirits from time to time, though at first he'd almost never recognized them for what they were. When he figured it out, it had sent a tremor of fear down his spine, and sometimes he'd even run from them and hid. But he knew if he wanted to be a powerful necromancer like his father, he would need to be as comfortable with the dead as he was with the living. He'd forced himself to overcome his apprehension and learned that most spirits didn't even realize what they were. Even when he tried to explain, they would often refuse to believe him.

So, it was unexpected when the spirit replied in a somber tone, "This is a surprise. I didn't realize lightwielders could see the dead."

Koristad wrapped his fingers around his medallion, as if he was trying to conceal it, and said, "I'm only a proxy lightwielder. In truth, I'm a child of darkness."

The spirit turned and raised his eyebrows at him, "Proxy lightwielder? That's a new one, kid."

Koristad shrugged, quickly changing the subject, "The wounds appearing on your spiritual body mean you haven't passed on because of regret over your own death. But you've clearly accepted the fact that you're no longer alive. So what is it that keeps you here?"

"What do you care?" the ghost said bitterly.

"Indulge my curiosity."

The spirit let out a deep sigh, even though it no longer had any need to breathe, and began, "The name's Mason. Until recently, I was the leader of a band of mercenaries called the Mountain Wolves. Maybe you've heard of us? No? Well, I guess it doesn't matter. I saw the company was breaking camp and departing, and I chased after them, demanding they await my orders. I didn't understand why they wouldn't respond, and I was even more confused when I found I couldn't bring myself to chase them any further than where I'm standing now.

"I returned to where our camp had been, and it was there that I found a bloody corpse lying in the grass. When I bent down to look, I was staring into my own face. It wasn't hard to figure out what was going on, and the memories of what had happened flooded into my mind. I'd died fighting a duel with a young upstart in front of my own men.

"The bastard hadn't even shown me enough respect to give me a burial. But, more than that, his actions and insolence had cost me my dignity. Maybe that's the reason I haven't been able to pass on."

Koristad crossed his arms, gazing at the spirit with pity, and said, "I'll give you some advice. In your current state, your soul can be tangibly influenced by your heart. If you let that hatred burn inside you, in time you'll be consumed by it."

"You're trying to say I'll disappear?"

"The soul is eternal," Koristad tried hard to remember his studies of necromancy, though it had been some time since he'd pondered the subject. "You will exist until you pass on to the other side. But you can lose all sense of reason; all memory of who you once were, and become a ghost who's only thought is to harm the living. We call them revenants. You might even lose your will to exist and drift mindlessly through the world as an intangible evil. We call them urges. One way or another, I suggest you let go of your grudge for your killer."

Mason looked at him with malevolence, baring his teeth, "Don't patronize me, kid. I won't allow myself to rest until that bastard Ralyn is buried."

"Ralyn?" Koristad said with surprise, recognizing the name from the old innkeeper in Marketway. "Tell me, was he traveling with a young, blonde girl?"

Now it was Mason's turn to look surprised, "You know him?"

"I've never met him," Koristad confessed. "But the girl is a companion of mine. He kidnapped her, and I've been trying to hunt them down."

A wicked smile crossed the ghost's face.

"You're going to kill him?" he asked, the thought filling him with glee.

Koristad was stunned by the blunt abruptness of the question, and he thought it was best to avoid the subject while dealing with such a begrudging spirit.

"Tell me where I can find them," Koristad demanded. "I don't have any time to waste. Are they still on this road?"

"No," Mason said, looking at the necromancer with clever eyes, "They've left the road. I could tell you where they're headed, but only if you promise to avenge my death."

"You're asking me to kill Ralyn for you?"

Mason shrugged, "It seems a small price to pay for the safe return of your little friend."

Koristad frowned at him, "Maybe for you it would be. But I have no intention of taking any life I don't have to, especially not to exact the punishment of a vengeful ghost."

"I didn't realize I was asking for such a great favor," Mason said with disappointment. "After all, he abducted one of your own; I assumed his death was a matter of course for you."

"If there is any way I can avoid it, I have no intention of killing him, regardless of what he's done," Koristad maintained. "Judges will decide his fate, not me."

Mason snorted derisively and said, "You really are just a kid."

"And *you* live up to the term 'mercenary sensibilities,'" Koristad offered in return.

Mason chuckled at the taunt and turned his back on the young man. Thinking their business was through, Koristad resumed his journey down the western small road, stepping around the disagreeable ghost.

"I told you already, they left the road," Mason called after him. "Weren't you listening?"

"What else can I do?" Koristad demanded. "I have to keep looking."

"It was my understanding that necromancers could command the dead to do their bidding," Mason said. "I didn't expect I would be allowed to hold my tongue."

Of course, Mason had no idea of what had become of Koristad's dark power.

Even without it, Koristad believed he could have called Wraith and the dark specter could have forced Mason to speak. The spirit's presence could be quite unsettling, and he imagined it would be even more so to a fellow ghost. But he didn't.

"If you truly have no intention of letting go of your grudge, then you will suffer until there's nothing left of the man you once were," Koristad explained. "I've already painted a picture of what awaits you. I couldn't bring myself to cause you more misery."

There was something about the gentle sentiment that weakened the mercenary's resolve, and the threat of suffering made him wish to settle his bitterness in any way he could.

"They left the road where we're standing now," he said with a heavy sigh. "They're heading southwest to intercept the main road." Koristad raised his eyebrows at him.

"I thought you weren't going to help me."

"Just shut up and listen, or I won't," Mason threatened. "Ralyn, along with a troupe of skilled mercenaries, will attack the lightwielders bearing the Executor Blade."

Koristad could have expressed surprise at their intention, but chose to remain silent as the spirit had requested.

"You have to catch them before then, because I can't tell you where they'll be going afterwards."

Koristad nodded in gratitude and said, "I appreciate your assistance, spirit."

Mason snorted and answered, "I suppose I'm not going to see many helpful necromancers coming down the small road. Even if you don't kill him, knowing his scheme was foiled may be all the peace I can hope for."

3

"SIR, IF WE KEEP pushing through this rough terrain, we're going to start losing horses!" a mountain wolf complained to Ralyn. "They're already in a bad temperament from all the brambles we've had to walk through. But if we're not careful, one of them is going to break its leg. You can count on that!"

Ralyn hadn't acknowledged the man's input or even bothered to look at him, and for a moment it seemed he hadn't heard the protest at all.

"Didn't you hear what our scout said?" Ralyn said, still not looking at the mercenary.

"Of course, sir," he grumbled.

Ralyn decided to re-inform the man, since it seemed he'd forgotten.

"The procession has quickened its pace for some reason," he said gruffly. "If we don't move quickly, we'll lose our chance to cut them off. It's not much farther now; the horses will hold out."

"Sir!" the mercenary barked, reining his horse away from the intimidating artificer.

Peril squirmed in the saddle uncomfortably. After the incident the night before, Ralyn was the last person she'd wanted to see but, when they set out that morning, he'd given her no other choice but to ride with him. She hadn't expected to be given her own horse, even though Mason's steed was available, but she would have rather ridden with one of the mercenaries than with him.

To make matters worse, the horse wasn't equipped for riding side saddle (especially with two riders) as she was accustomed to with Jester. She'd been forced to hike up her dress to straddle the beast, exposing her soft, pale legs. She could feel Ralyn breathing on the back of her neck; it filled her with an overwhelming feeling of vulnerability and disgust.

She turned her gaze toward Slayne, who'd taken a spot as far from her and his brother as he could. She wasn't certain which of them he was trying to avoid; probably both. She felt guilty about what she'd said to him the night before. She didn't know why, and she told herself she shouldn't. He *had* partaken in her abduction, after all, and was part of a conspiracy to attack her fellow lightwielders. But he was so young; how much of it could he be held responsible for, really? Wasn't he simply a victim of his brother's ambition, the same as she was?

He'd already proven himself to be far kinder and more honorable than Ralyn. One could say her abduction was his idea but, when the alternative was murder, she might have felt lucky for it. In his own way, he'd saved her life. Then he'd protected her from his brother's lust, and paid for it in blood. Even separated by such a great distance, she could see his face was swollen and deep purple. Ralyn certainly hadn't held back when he'd struck him.

She decided she owed him an apology. But, so long as he continued avoiding her, there was no way she could offer one.

Almost as if he was reading her thoughts, Ralyn leaned in and whispered in her ear, "It appears my brother doesn't like you very much anymore."

"I think he's just afraid of your temper," she snapped.

Ralyn chuckled and replied, "I heard what you said to him after I left. I'm certain it was more of a blow than what he got from me. I wonder if he'll still come to your rescue if I come to your tent again...but I guess we'll find out tonight."

Peril wanted to turn around and slap him, or to break down and cry, but she knew both gestures would be meaningless.

Instead, she fired back, "I wonder if he'll help *you* use that axe the next time you need it."

"What makes you think I need his help?"

"Oh, he told me all about it," she said in a snotty tone. "He's the brain, and you're nothing but dumb muscle."

Ralyn's face turned red with anger and he grabbed Peril by the arm. His fingers bit into her flesh painfully.

"Listen to me, girl," he snarled at her. "You're going to start showing me respect, or I'm going to teach you proper manners."

Peril grimaced in pain and grew silent.

"Don't worry about me and Slayne. We're brothers, and that means that no matter what happens, he'll always be there for me, and I for him."

"Sir!" one of the Mountain Wolves called out, bringing his horse in from behind.

The animal was glistening with sweat and breathing heavily from a swift run, and the mercenary had a spyglass tucked under his arm. He was one of several scouts Ralyn had dispatched, desiring a complete briefing of the terrain and any possible interlopers. All of his efforts would boil down to just a few moments, and he wanted to leave nothing to chance.

"What is it?" he demanded.

"There's someone approaching from the rear," he said. "He's armed and on foot, but covering ground at a frightening pace."

The man had clearly exerted himself trying to prod his horse along; he brushed the gray, sweat soaked hair out of his eyes.

"I returned as quickly as I could, but I'm afraid he can't be far behind."

"You're certain he's headed in this direction?"

"Absolutely certain," the gray haired mercenary replied. "Either he's tracking us, or he knows where we're headed."

Ralyn frowned and grabbed Peril by the shoulder, whipping her around so he could look her in the face.

"This is because of you, isn't it?" he growled.

"I have no more idea what you mean!" she lied.

There was only one man who could move as quickly on foot as a man on horseback. She couldn't believe he'd actually come for her. But her relief was sullied by a deeper concern; why would he come alone? What chance could he possibly stand against an entire band of mercenaries? He clearly didn't realize what he was getting himself into.

"Sir?" the mercenary said. "What are your orders?"

Ralyn drew his mouth up in a grimace as he considered his options.

Slayne pulled his horse around and answered for his brother, "Set up an ambush for him. Kill him if you can, but slowing him down or deterring him is just as good. When you're through, return to the main group to assist in the raid."

The gray haired mercenary looked from one brother to the other, uncertain if he should take anything from the young boy seriously.

"You heard him!" Ralyn barked at the man. "You two will stay behind."

He pointed to the scout and another mercenary who happened to be nearby, a younger man with a thin beard and brown hair. He didn't know their names; to him, they were merely tools to be used and then discarded.

"But, sir," the older mercenary protested, "I can handle this myself!"

"You have your orders," Ralyn snapped at him, prodding his horse forward. "Question them again and I'll bury you out here."

As the remainder of the company continued toward their objective, the two ambushers looked at each other and groaned.

4

THE MERCENARY PAIR SET up their ambush in an area spotted with tall trees; many had been choked out by rampant weeds and were in poor condition. The older mercenary, who went by the name Raynard, had observed this area with caution as they'd passed. He'd thought it was a good place for an ambush. The party wasn't expecting an attack, but he was a grizzled veteran who'd seen more combat than he cared to remember. Certain observations had simply become second nature to him.

He glanced at his companion—the younger, brown haired mercenary, who they called Jece. He was a rookie who'd only joined the Mountain Wolves two seasons ago. Raynard doubted the young man had thought anything of this area when they'd passed through, or that he would have known how to set up an ambush without the older man's expert guidance. They'd only been waiting a few minutes, and already the novice was fidgeting back and forth, pulling on his bow string and clattering his scabbard back and forth nervously.

"I thought you said he was moving fast," Jece complained. "Where is he?"

"Keep quiet, rookie," Raynard replied in a harsh whisper. "You'll give us away."

"Shove it, you old geezer," Jece snapped. "Why did we have to leave our horses behind?"

"Because horses don't know how to keep quiet and set up an ambush," Raynard explained gruffly. "Just like you. Now shut it."

The two men scowled at each other. When they heard something approaching, however, they both went deathly silent and crouched down in the brush.

From where they hid, they wouldn't be able to see the source until it was little more than thirty feet from them, but their target wouldn't be able to see them until at least that range, either. They both soundlessly notched arrows, prepared to bring down their adversary before he even knew they were there.

The tension was heavy in the air; at such short range, they knew they could only fire two or three projectiles before the man would close the gap. Both were trained archers (it was a requirement to join the Mountain Wolves), but Raynard wished Ralyn had provided them with some of the poison he'd spoken of. The noise was drawing close now, and he drew in a sharp intake of breath the instant before the source appeared, sighting down the shaft of his arrow.

What came into their sight wasn't a man; it was a small, white horse with brown splotches on its rump. It plodded past, oblivious to their presence. It appeared to be on a mission, even without a rider. Both of them groaned and lowered their bows.

"You blind old geezer," Jece growled. "Is that stupid animal what you saw?"

"I thought I told you to keep your mouth shut," Raynard said, ready to pummel the ill-mannered rookie.

"Fighting amongst yourselves?" a voice came from behind. "That's pretty disappointing."

Both men reached reflexively for the sabers at their belts, but the instant their fingers touched the pommels, the visitor's hands came down on theirs, preventing them from drawing the weapons. They struggled to push him away, but he had monstrous strength; even between the two of them they couldn't get free. Then they noticed the blazing sun medallion around his neck, and his inhuman strength suddenly made sense, or so they thought.

Koristad said, "There's no need for that. I only wanted to ask you a few questions."

"What do you want with us?" Raynard protested, thinking hard to come up with a lie. "We're just hunters! How dare you treat us like this!?"

"I suppose you were preparing to ambush a deer?" Koristad shook his head. "Please, I already know you were waiting for me."

"Damn it, Jece, this happened because you couldn't keep your mouth shut!"

"You're blaming me?" Jece growled defensively. "This happened because you're too old and soft in the head to set up a proper ambush!"

"You both give me too little credit," Koristad said arrogantly. "I knew you were here before I was close enough to see or even hear you."

Raynard frowned deeply and asked, "What do you want with us? If you wanted us dead, you were given the perfect opportunity, and you chose not to take it."

"First," Koristad said, "I want you to drop your bows and remove your hands from your swords."

Jece obliged immediately, throwing his bow to the ground and dropping both hands to his sides. For Raynard, the request wasn't so easily fulfilled. His pride begged him not to surrender without a fight. Over his years, the old mercenary had fought more foes than he could recall, and from time to time things had turned sour and his company had been forced to retreat. It was an expected facet of the profession; as a soldier for hire, sometimes his only choices were to run or die. He'd always fought for pay, and a dead man doesn't have any use for gold.

But never in his career had Raynard been completely disarmed or captured. He glanced over his shoulder to his quiver, filled with sharp arrows. He considered drawing one to slash at his captor. It wasn't much of a weapon, but at the very least it might force the man to dodge out of his reach, giving Raynard a chance to draw his sword.

"I won't ask you again," Koristad said in a deep, commanding voice, growing impatient with the delay.

With a helpless groan, Raynard allowed himself to be disarmed. Koristad drew both swords from their sheaths and took a step away from the two mercenaries. They turned to face him, able to make a clear appraisal of their interceptor for the first time.

"You're just a kid!" Raynard balked.

Koristad ignored his incredulity and turned the swords over, pinning them under his arms to make it clear he had no intention of using them.

"My second request," Koristad said, "Is for information."

Raynard frowned and spat on the ground.

"If you think we'll betray our fellow Mountain Wolves," he said with a grimace, "You've misjudged us."

"Your loyalty to your comrades is commendable," Koristad expressed a genuine respect for the man. "But there's nothing you could offer me about them, anyway. I already know where you're headed, and that you're planning to attack the procession of lightwielders transporting the Executor Blade."

"How do you know all that?!" Jece cried, provoking a painful elbow jab from Raynard.

"That makes little difference," Koristad said with a shrug. "All that matters is that I know."

"Then what is it you expect to get from us?" Raynard demanded.

"I'm searching for a lightwielder your leader has taken hostage."

"I don't know what you mean," Raynard said in bewilderment. "There was no lightwielder with us."

Koristad remembered Peril had left her medallion behind in Marketway. There would have been no clear indication of her status.

"A young, blonde girl, small in stature," he explained, holding out his hand to show Peril's height. "Not very bright and kind of annoying."

The mercenaries' faces both went white.

"So, you *do* know who I'm talking about. I want to know two things; is she still traveling with the rest of your party, and has she been hurt?"

Koristad wasn't certain if the mercenaries would take Peril to the scene of the raid or stash her somewhere out of the way until it was all over. His only concern was locating the young lightwielder. As much as he disliked Vincent, the paladin was capable, and Koristad was prepared to trust him to look after the blade on his own.

Raynard shook his head, wondering how he'd ever gotten himself into such a mess.

"Ralyn hasn't let the girl out of his sight. She hasn't been harmed, though I'm certain she's suffered some bruises from his rough handling."

Koristad frowned at the thought, letting out a deep sigh.

"Take a step back," he ordered in a harsh voice.

There was a violent look behind his fierce eyes, and the mercenaries looked at each other with concern before doing as they were told. Quick as a flash, Koristad brought both swords down in broad arcs.

Raynard and Jece cried out in fear, closing their eyes and leaping backward in fright. When they looked, they saw both of their bows, lying on the ground, had been cleaved in two.

"Now get out of my sight," Koristad snarled. "If I see the two of you again, I won't show you any further mercy."

This was one request the two men were more than happy to fulfill, turning and running from the scene. After they'd covered some ground, they looked over their shoulders; the proxy lightwielder was no longer anywhere to be seen. They slowed their pace, sweating and breathing heavily.

"We have to hurry to the horses!" Jece shouted anxiously.

"What for?" Raynard replied in a deep voice, taking a seat on the ground to catch his breath.

"We have to overtake that lightwielder and warn the others before he arrives!" Jece cried.

Raynard shook his head at the rookie.

"You go right ahead. I'll be taking my horse the other way."

"What?" Jece looked at the grizzled veteran in disbelief. "How can you just abandon the Mountain Wolves?"

In a fit of sudden rage, which had been building up in him since the very moment he'd met the younger man, Raynard grabbed him by the collar and pushed him against a nearby tree.

"The Mountain Wolves died with Mason," he growled. "A wolf without a head isn't a wolf anymore. It's just a pelt. Who do we follow now? Ralyn? If you want to report what happened here to that animal, like I said, you go right ahead. Personally, I'd like to live a little bit longer."

With a stiff shove, Raynard turned away from Jece and stomped toward the spot where they'd left their mounts. Jece rubbed his neck, briefly knocked off balance by the older man's wrathful diatribe.

"Wait!" he called, rushing after him. "Where are we going?"

"*We?*" Raynard asked, as if he'd never heard the word before. "I'm going to start looking for a new company to join. With my knowledge and experience, it shouldn't take me long. You, on the other hand," he gestured at the younger man dismissively, "I suppose you could find a job shoveling dung, somewhere."

"Don't be like that," Jece tried to sound amicable, bounding up to the man's side. "The two of us should stick together. Who knows, this could be the start of a long friendship."

"Don't make me laugh."

"C'mon, someday I might be naming one of my children after you," Jece said with a smile; "If I have any that are ugly enough."

5

"IS SOMETHING THE MATTER, commander?" Vian asked. "You've looked distracted for some time now."

"There's something odd on the wind," Vincent cautioned, his eyes scanning back and forth across the horizon.

The procession was drawing nearer to the capital, and soon the untamed wilderness would give way to orderly fields of corn and wheat, high fences and quaint cottages. Then the bustling capital of Highcrest, in all its grandeur and sprawling magnitude, would lie before them. But, for now, the road was surrounded by tall, wild brush and gnarled, old trees.

"Are you supposed to be a bloodhound, now?" Vian asked with a chuckle. "I think you're just worried about the two who are missing from our company."

Vincent grunted in protest, stating, "I pray to Aura no harm has befallen Peril, but Koristad willingly abandoned his post. It's no concern of mine what happens to him, or whether he lives or dies."

Vian whistled, "Those are harsh words, commander."

Vincent ignored him, insisting, "I'm certain I can sense the presence of tainted blood. But it's...different, somehow. As if it's something I've never felt before."

Vian looked back and forth across the horizon.

"Really? I don't sense anything."

"It's very faint," Vincent maintained. "Whatever it is may still be a long way off. However..."

Vincent seemed to be thinking deeply while staring down the long, winding road.

"What is it?" Vian asked suspiciously.

"Ready your shields," were the next words out of Vincent's mouth, though the apprehension and doubt with which he spoke them seemed to bring only confusion to his fellow lightwielders.

He called out again, this time in a booming, frantic voice, thick with urgency, "Ready your shields!"

Long, black arrows screamed through the air, raining down upon the company. Many planted themselves in the defender's bulwarks, readied at the last moment, or glanced off their heavy armor, but a few bit into the exposed flesh of the horses where they were unprotected by their barding. They whinnied in pain and lurched frantically, but the wounds weren't serious, and soon the riders were able to bring the trained beasts back under control.

The ambushers were cleverly concealed in the foliage ahead, their hands and faces painted in dark tones. It was difficult to determine how many there were, and how many remained unseen, but Vincent estimated there were a dozen of them. They drew their bowstrings for a second volley but, at their current range, the lightwielders felt they were in little danger, encased in suits of steel and with shields poised above them.

"Starshine and Snowdove with me!" Vincent ordered, referring to the four children of Aura from the named sanctuaries. "The rest of you stay with the blade! Guard it with your lives!"

The young paladin charged toward the attackers, the quartet of lightwielders close in suit.

Arrows whizzed over their heads as they closed the gap, and when they drew near the ambushers sprung to their feet in an attempt to put distance between themselves and the holy warriors. To Vincent, it seemed almost too easy; on foot, they would have no chance to avoid being ridden down, even in the thick undergrowth.

He realized too late that he'd been baited into a trap. More attackers sprung up on either side as they galloped past, loosing more arrows upon the unprepared riders. Two of the lightwielders cried out as the sharp steel punctured their flesh, though the injuries appeared superficial. The bolts had been delivered at close range and with expert accuracy, passing lithely through the weak points in their heavy plate, but had been mitigated by the mail underneath.

The lightwielders broke off in either direction, abandoning pursuit of the original ambushers for these much nearer adversaries. But the men quickly scattered into the brush, ducking out of range of deadly sword cuts and throwing themselves to the ground to avoid being struck by additional volleys from their comrades.

Vincent heard a commotion from behind. When he looked to the carriage, he saw the remaining children of Aura were being harassed by mounted archers. There seemed to be no end to these deplorable villains but, Vincent thought with a vengeful scowl, they didn't realize what they were getting themselves into. In all the years it had been tradition, the sacred procession that carried the Executor Blade had never fallen victim to such a brazen attack. Vincent wouldn't allow it to be taken now; these scoundrels had yet to face off against the might of a paladin.

Vincent felt his horse, who had suffered a grazing blow across its flank, stagger as it moved, as if it might collapse. The sudden change in momentum brought him off balance, forcing him to abandon his offensive against a nearby ambusher and try to regain control of his steed.

"Commander?!" one of the nearby lightwielders called out.

Vincent saw the man staring in bewilderment at his bloodstained gauntlet; he'd tried to cover his mouth to stop the sudden flow of warm liquid. The thick blood ran down his chin and stained his breastplate. There was an arrow lodged in his armor under his armpit.

"Poison!" Vincent cried out in disgust, scarcely believing such a despicable tactic had been used against them.

It was a tool of cowards and weaklings, without the strength or bravery to face their adversaries in fair combat.

"Use the power of Aura to fight off the venom!" he commanded, though it was clear if his subordinate had succumbed to the toxin so rapidly, it was a truly deadly concoction.

He wasn't certain how long they would be able to stave off the effects and his horse, even with its considerable size, wouldn't last long.

Out of the corner of his eye, he saw three mercenaries spring from the brush at the bloodied lightwielder, pulling him from his horse as he struggled frantically against both his attackers and the diabolical poison. Vincent rushed to the man's aid, leaning from his horse's flank and swiping in broad arcs with his sword. One of the ambushers fell to his blade, and he'd locked swords with a second when his horse suddenly collapsed, sending him crashing to the ground with a grunt.

Vincent quickly scrambled to his feet, pushing his attackers back with powerful slashes. The other lightwielder remained on the ground, shaking and spitting up blood, never to rise again.

The paladin felt a sting on his back where his arm met his shoulder. A cleverly aimed arrow had found its way through his armor, piercing his flesh. He could feel the burning hot venom pollute his blood, invading his tissue and organs. He grimaced through the pain, thrusting his sword into the guts of one of the ambushers, sending him to the ground clutching his belly and crying out in pain.

As he looked about, he could see both sides had suffered losses, but his troupe was plainly getting the worse of it. All but he and one of the others who had charged with him had already fallen. The seven who had remained with the Executor Blade had fared better, but were quickly being overrun.

Men with cruel eyes and painted, dark faces closed in from every direction. They moved like a pack of wolves circling in for the kill. They knew he'd been poisoned and believed him a weak and easy target. They'd seen the other lightwielders quickly fade away under the toxin's lethal effects.

But Vincent was more than just a lightwielder—he was a paladin, a holy warrior overflowing with the might of Aura. He had faced down ghouls, werebeasts and other monsters that would have made these honorless vagabonds soil themselves. He raised his shield and prepared for their assault.

By his life, he would not see his cousin's sword taken.

6
(Two weeks before present)

"EXECUTOR NIGHT! I'VE BEEN looking for you everywhere, sir," Gabrial flinched at Vincent's words as the paladin hastily approached and presented himself with a formal bow.

Whenever the young man addressed him so properly, it meant he had some sort of important business or grievances to discuss. More often than not, Vincent seemed filled with courtesies.

"What can I do for you, cousin?" he asked with a cocked eyebrow.

He was tall and proud, with thick shoulders and a regal air; speaking to him was akin to addressing the emperor himself. But there was something about him that seemed friendly and approachable, as well. He wore his hair long and sported a full beard, both blonde with flecks of gray. Though he and Vincent were cousins, they looked more like uncle and nephew. Gabrial was more than thirty years his senior. However, for a man of his age, the executor was remarkably lean and fit, as if he'd found a way to stave off the effects of his many years.

"I apologize for bothering you while you're taking a walk," Vincent said, bowing again and refusing to make eye contact. "I've visited your office several times, and sought out your attendants, but I haven't been able to. . ."

"It's nothing, Vincent," Gabrial brushed off his concerns. "We're old friends, aren't we? There's no need for you to worry so much."

"Of course," Vincent replied, drawing himself up and taking a deep breath. "I've been told you've selected Vian Jerrica and William Crosse to represent our sanctuary in the procession transporting the Executor Blade."

"You heard correctly."

Vincent momentarily appeared to be at a loss for what he wanted to say, but when he found the words they came out in a rush.

"I would consider it a great honor to guard the procession that delivers your sword."

Gabrial shrugged, appearing unconcerned.

"The procession is a mere tradition, as is the weapon itself. There's very little reason to guard it; no thief would possess the purity of spirit to handle such a holy relic. Your talents would be wasted on such a task."

Vincent almost scoffed at Gabrial's praise. There was no question the young man possessed more skill and power than almost any lightwielder; even more than many of his fellow paladins. He'd practiced swordplay since he was only a child. The Night family was magnificently wealthy, affording him the finest teachers money could buy. Before he'd come to the Silversword Sanctuary, he'd bested them all. Having heard rumors of the young man's talents, Executor Night had happily decided to test his cousin's abilities in a sparring match the very day he arrived.

Vincent had no intentions of winning. He would throw the match sooner

than disgrace his honorable cousin, a great man who was respected by all of the
noble families. As it happened, such niceties were unnecessary. Gabrial defeated
him with a practiced ease, as effortlessly as Vincent could have beaten a stable
boy. Even then, Gabrial had offered words of praise, claiming his young cousin
was a swordsman of consummate talent and asserting it would be his privilege to
spar with him in the future. Since that day, they'd drawn foils against each other
many times, and Vincent had never bested him.

"Be that as it may," Vincent asserted, "I request that I be assigned to the
procession."

Gabrial narrowed his eyes, appraising the paladin.

"Why is this so important to you?"

"I...I'm not sure what you mean," Vincent was caught off guard by the
question. "Like I said, it..."

"Yes, yes," Gabrial waved off the sentiment with a groan, "It would be a great
honor. But there's something more, isn't there? Don't think you can put one past
me, cousin."

Vincent lowered his eyes and explained, "It's just a feeling I have. There's
something unusual afoot...a strange presence that has no place in the empire."
The paladin sighed and ran his fingers through his hair uncomfortably and added,
"I suppose I sound like a fool."

No," Gabrial said with a shake of his head. "You've always possessed a keen
intuition. It's uncanny, really."

Vincent cocked his head at the executor suspiciously and asked, "You've
sensed the same thing, haven't you?"

Gabrial nodded slowly and cautiously, glancing quickly to the left and right,
as if he worried someone else might be watching. There was a moment of silence
as he seemed to contemplate the matter at hand. Finally, he nodded at his cousin
with a smile.

"I think you may be right," Gabrial agreed with a jovial slap on Vincent's
shoulder. "A man of your insight would be an excellent addition to the
procession."

"Thank you, executor!" Vincent answered with a deep bow. "I give you my
word, so long as I breathe, I will not allow the Executor Blade to fall into enemy
hands."

7

THE LIFELESS BODIES OF lightwielders and mercenaries alike were strewn across the western road, staining the dirt and grass red with their blood. It was a massacre, a bloodbath that made the stomach turn. Only one lightwielder yet breathed: Paladin Vincent Night. But he knew he was facing his final moments of life. He sat, slumped over, before the carriage that held the Executor Blade, refusing to the very last to allow it to be taken.

His armor was stained with the blood of his enemies. His shield was battered beyond repair and far out of reach, and even the bastard sword he gripped with all the strength left in his body had been broken in two. Three of the poisoned arrows jutted from the gaps in his armor. The damage had been diminished by the suit of mail under the steel plates, but had punctured deeply enough to pour more and more of the lethal devil's extract into his blood.

The air rang with the slow and deliberate clapping of hands. Ralyn approached the helpless lightwielder through the carnage, the Edge of Abaddon cradled over his shoulder.

He came to a halt before he drew too close, emitting a loud whistle, and announced, "That was truly impressive, Ser Lightwielder. Your enemies scattered before your blade like ashes on the wind, and you didn't let a single one escape."

Vincent wanted to curse the man, to swear vengeance upon him, *anything*. But he couldn't find the strength to speak.

Ralyn went on, "Before the battle, I was disappointed I couldn't take part. After all, if I came too close, I was certain you would sense my tainted blood and spoil our ambush. But, now that I've seen what you're capable of, I think it may have been for the best. Even now, I don't dare approach near enough to strike you down," at that he cracked a self-assured smile. "At least, not when I can simply wait for you to die on your own."

Vincent knew if Ralyn moved in to finish him, there would be nothing he could do. It would be as easy as killing a newborn. He'd used so much of his power trying to fight off the effects of the poison, and desperately fighting off the attackers, now he had nothing left at all. Still, it brought him pride to know that, in the final moments of his life, his presence would prevent this thief from seizing the blade, even if only for a short while.

"You monster!" Peril screamed at Ralyn, running at him and striking with her tiny fists.

There was no power behind the blows; she lashed out in hopeless sorrow against him as salty tears poured down her face.

"Slayne," Ralyn growled, "I thought I told you to keep her under control."

"I'm sorry, brother," Slayne apologized, wheezing and out of breath from chasing after the young girl. "She got away from me."

Peril collapsed to the ground with a terrific sob. Her knees felt wet, and when she looked at her hands she saw they'd been stained with blood by coming in contact with the ground. It was like something out of a nightmare. She wanted it to be a nightmare; she couldn't believe something so terrible had befallen her comrades.

Just a few feet away, she spotted the corpse of a man clad in heavy armor. She recognized him. It was Vian, the friendly and high-spirited lightwielder, now nothing more than a lifeless husk. She was grateful his head was turned away so she couldn't see his eyes. She didn't think she could have handled it.

His sword had fallen from his hand, and she found it was only inches from her own. Uncertain of what she intended to do, she wrapped her tiny fingers around the grip and drug it close to her body, the tip of the blade dragging across the earth. When she looked up at Ralyn, he smiled at her—that cruel smile she'd grown so familiar with.

"You have a weapon, eh?" he said in a harsh voice. "I didn't think you had it in you. But you don't have any fire in your eyes; you can't kill me. You can't do *anything.*"

She wondered if he was right. She hated this man, more than she'd ever hated anyone, and she believed he deserved to die. But she couldn't imagine herself hurting him; thrusting the blade in his guts and feeling the hot blood wash across her hand. She wasn't the type of person who could actually hurt anyone.

"If you're not going to use it, then put it down," Ralyn ordered.

"No," she whispered, barely loud enough to hear.

"Why refuse? Just to be obstinate?" Ralyn demanded with a scowl. After a moment, he believed he had an insight into her motivations. "I see it now. All your comrades are here, dead or dying. You think it would be the noble thing to join them?"

Peril refused to answer him, still grasping Vian's discarded sword.

"Very well," he barked at her, his patience at its end. "Then I'll grant you your wish."

As Ralyn lifted the axe high into the air, Slayne screamed at him, "Brother, no!"

But it was too late. Even if Ralyn had wanted to stop his swing, the axe had already begun to fall, and Peril looked up at the blade with wide eyes, unable to even move. There was no doubt her tiny body would be cleaved in two by such a massive instrument. She was going to die. Everything went dark.

The heavy clash of metal on metal reverberated through the air. Peril desperately pushed the heavy fabric from her face, trying to see what was happening. Then she saw him, standing over her with his halberd drawn, holding back Ralyn's deadly swing.

"Koristad!" she cried.

He didn't turn her way, rather keeping his eyes fixed on his enemy.

"Koristad, is it?" Ralyn said with a scowl. "Another lightwielder, I suppose?"

"I am Koristad Altessor, the son of Arach the Black Guardian," he announced, the two blades still rattling against one another. "I'm a *proxy* lightwielder."

"That's an impressive introduction," Ralyn replied with a nod. "I'm Ralyn Lourdess, and you should have killed me while my guard was down."

Peril shouted, "Be careful, Koristad, he's an artificer!"

Before the words had reached his ears, Koristad felt the Edge of Abaddon pushing down on his sanctified blade with astounding pressure. He grunted and shook under the strain, his muscles tightening to their limits. How was it possible this rogue could have so much strength?

"Get back!" Koristad yelled; as soon as Peril had stepped away he leapt backward, allowing the axe to crash into the ground.

The blade embedded itself deeply in the earth and, seeing an opening, he sprung forward with speed surpassing the restrictions placed on the human body. An ordinary adversary could have never wrested the weapon free in time; they would have been forced to either abandon it or die.

Dirt and rocks flew in every direction as Ralyn lifted the weapon in defense. It was as if a powerful steam vent had been opened for an instant, liberating the axe along with an abundance of debris. Koristad stopped his attack short, shielding his eyes and trying to spot his enemy through the cloud of dust.

He heard a grunt of exertion as Ralyn made a wide, sweeping pass through the obscurement. He braced himself to absorb the attack, but the blow nearly bowled him over. He angled his weapon to force the axe to slide away from him; he could then use his superior speed to sidestep the artificer and attack his unguarded flank. But the axe seemed to reverse its direction almost instantly, coming around for another pass, and all Koristad could do was deflect the incoming blows and try to put some distance between himself and the enemy.

Sweat was pouring down his face. It took all of his strength to stop the powerful blows from striking through to his body. The attacks were fast, as well—far too fast for a weapon of that size. He had to seal off all distractions to keep track of the flying blade, and he was caught entirely off guard when Ralyn lashed out with the butt of the weapon, hitting him in the chest.

Koristad stumbled away, letting out a wheeze as all the air was forced from his lungs. He held up his halberd defensively, but Ralyn didn't push the attack, instead pausing to catch his breath and look down on his opponent with an undeniably smug look on his face. Koristad grimaced through the pain; he thought he could taste blood in his mouth, and his hands were numb from the force of the absorbed blows. The only feeling left in them was a pulsating sting that kept rhythm with his rapid heartbeat.

He saw in the exchange he'd been pushed toward the carriage holding the Executor Blade, as well as the motionless Vincent. The paladin wasn't looking well. His eyes were barely open and seemed sightless; his skin had begun to turn an ashen gray. He'd be dead soon, if he wasn't already. Koristad had certainly never felt anything good about the arrogant lightwielder, but he was surprised that seeing the man in such dire condition didn't bring him the satisfaction he thought it would.

Koristad knew he couldn't lose. He had to survive, and Vincent had to as well, or else they'd never get the chance to fight one another again; this time, without Gregan's unwelcome interference. If they both died here, then he could never have the pleasure of giving Vincent the sound thrashing he'd always thought he deserved.

Peril was looking at him, wringing her hands, distress plain in her eyes. Had she lost her faith in him? He'd certainly taken a beating, but she should have known he'd find a way to turn things around. Somehow. He'd have to remember to tease her about it after this was all over.

But first he had to figure out a way to survive. It was hard to explain, but Ralyn seemed stronger than him. Even more unbelievable, he'd proven more than a match for his speed. How was he doing it? The artificers were supposed to be extinct, but he'd never heard stories of them having heightened physical abilities. They were crafters of magic. Was it the axe, then? What kind of power did it possess?

"It's air pressure," Ralyn announced as he hefted the Edge of Abaddon over his shoulder.

"Excuse me?" Koristad demanded, still fighting for breath.

"You were trying to understand my weapon, weren't you?" he said with a knowing smile. "The Edge of Abaddon has the ability to manipulate air pressure. For instance, by explosively compressing the air behind the blade, and decompressing the air in front of it, it can magnify the speed and force of my attacks."

"That's awfully generous of you, explaining how it all works," Koristad said. "Aren't you worried I might take advantage of that knowledge to get an edge on you? Or are you just so overconfident you don't care?"

"It's not a matter of confidence," Ralyn said, readying the blade. "There's nothing you can do. The moment you chose to draw blades against me, your fate was sealed."

"Is that right?"

"Allow me to demonstrate the true strength of this weapon." Ralyn sucked in a powerful breath of air. "When one knows how to control the flow of its ley lines, it can be used like this."

He drew the weapon far back to his side, as if he were preparing to make a powerful swing with only his right hand. Even with the weapon's long reach, Koristad was clearly out of range. The necromancer wondered if he was planning on throwing the axe and somehow using its power to retrieve it. But wouldn't its abilities be inaccessible once it left his hand? There was no time to consider; the attack was coming, and all Koristad could do was ready his halberd to absorb the impact.

When the swing came, the Edge of Abaddon didn't leave Ralyn's hand, but the earth before him was torn asunder by the pressure created by his swing. The energy streaked toward Koristad, an invisible shock wave that could only be detected by the dust and debris thrown from its path. His halberd was no defense; he took the brunt of the blow full on, knocking the weapon from his grip and flattening him like a sapling in the path of a tornado.

Behind him, the carriage was blasted to pieces by the shock, sending broken wood and splinters in every direction. Vincent tumbled across the grass, his lifeless arms and legs making no attempt to cushion his fall.

"Koristad!" Peril cried out, losing sight of her protector as a cloud of dust rose up, enveloping everything.

Ralyn dropped to one knee, looking weak and unwell. His breathing was rapid and heavy, as if he'd sprinted half a mile, though he hadn't appeared especially fatigued before unleashing the Edge of Abaddon's devastating power.

"That seemed unnecessary," Slayne said, shaking his head at his brother. "You were already winning, but you had to show off and use a technique you haven't even mastered. Now look at you."

"Shut up," Ralyn snapped at him through his panting. "It's over now, anyhow."

As if prompted by the words, the dust around the shattered carriage began to settle, and a solitary figure rose in the haze. Koristad was swaying heavily, barely able to keep his feet under him with his injuries, and he was unarmed. He wasn't sure what direction his halberd had flown after it was knocked from his hands. But, even in such a sorry condition, he remained defiant.

"Nothing's over yet, artificer," he growled.

The brothers looked at each other in surprise.

"Well, aren't you a stubborn one," Ralyn said with disdain. "You should be dead."

"From that?" Koristad retorted bitterly. "Don't think you can kill me by using a warm breeze."

He tried to laugh, but the gesture was too painful and caused him to grip his chest in agony. He knew his words were nothing but bravado. His body ached all over, but his upper body especially. He was finding it difficult to breathe, and he was almost certain his ribs had been broken by the force of the blow. On top of that, he was disoriented; his ears were filled with a high pitched ringing, and behind it all other sounds seemed vague and far away.

He removed his hand from his chest and saw it was stained scarlet with blood. The warm liquid was running down his body from numerous cuts inflicted by flying shrapnel, as well as from his nose. He could taste it in his mouth. He sniffed and wiped his face assertively, but Ralyn only glowered at him and climbed to his feet once again.

"It's certainly impressive you survived," Ralyn said as he approached the defenseless necromancer, axe in hand. "You seem very interesting. But I'm afraid my brother and I don't have any more time to deal with you. This ends now."

Koristad felt completely helpless as the artificer drew close, like a doomed criminal watching the approach of the executioner. He could barely move, and certainly wasn't in any condition to run. But fleeing was the last thing on his mind. His eyes swept his surroundings, searching for his halberd. Even if he found it, he probably wouldn't be able to put up much of a fight, but at least he could die with a little dignity.

Like a wisp of steam, Wraith materialized beside him. Or maybe it had been there the whole time, and simply hadn't let Koristad see it.

"You look desperate," it said in its deep monotone, "As if you've been unarmed."

The world around them seemed to grind to a halt, just as it had when Koristad was defeated by Azoman.

"Are you blind?" Koristad said, annoyed. "I've lost my halberd. Can you see it anywhere?"

Wraith ignored his question, and went on, "Working with these lightwielders has made you forget, I think, that you're a necromancer. An entire universe of black power is at your fingertips, and yet you cower in fear, like a helpless child. Pitiful."

"I'm not cowering," Koristad snarled. "And I think *you've* forgotten, I've crossed that threshold once before. Do you want me to turn?"

He knew even if he tried to flood his body with dark power, as he had in his battle against Azoman, facing down the Edge of Abaddon with his bare hands would be a lost cause. He could still feel the corruption from his encounter with the barbarian, as if it had stained his soul eternally. But what Wraith was suggesting, his only real chance, was to call on black magic, bringing forth the howling souls of the damned to tear his enemies apart.

"Do you really believe the executor ordered you not to use your magic for your own safety?"

For a moment, Koristad thought he could hear a tremor of stress in the spirit's voice, but he decided it was surely his imagination.

"You know your limits better than they. I'm merely trying to save your life; though, I suppose I could use the company of a ghost."

"I do know my limits," Koristad whispered. "I can feel the darkness of the abyss at my heels. It's there, always. I won't allow myself to turn into a monster."

"Even if it costs you your life? If you die, the girl will, as well."

"The curse of vampirism is a fate worse than death," Koristad stood firm in his decision. "Even if I did take that step, Peril would be one of the first victims of my bloodlust. No, I will sooner die."

"Then so you shall," the words of the spirit echoed through the empty air as it vanished into nothingness.

Furious with the spirit's temptation, Koristad scowled and shook his head in disgust.

That's when he saw it: a hilt protruding from the wrecked carriage. It had a long grip and a wide, upward sweeping cross-guard. The Executor Blade, the holy relic, had been thrown free of its resting place and now lay on the ground like an ignoble and ordinary piece of weaponry. It was only a few steps from him. He thought, perhaps, he could manage a quick stride or two.

But, even if he did reach the sword before Ralyn cut him down, wouldn't touching the relic kill him? Gregan had been very explicit on that matter. In the heat of the moment, Koristad couldn't recall exactly what had been said, but he was certain the blade was intended for the high executor alone.

Of course, he would die anyway, even if he did nothing. He saw Peril looking at him, terrified. Not only for his safety, but also for what would happen to her if she was left alone. He couldn't let that happen. He wasn't the sort of scoundrel who would give up on protecting someone when they needed him most.

He managed a clever little smile at the terrified girl the instant before he leapt toward the sword, evading Ralyn's swinging axe by a mere fraction of an inch. He wrapped his fingers around the hilt and instantly felt the weapon's energy flooding into him, like grabbing a glowing hot rail. In an instant, the world melted away, replaced by an endless expanse of featureless white.

8

(more than eight centuries before present)

THE SMALL ROWBOAT ROCKED madly amidst the waves as Tricia Laurel crossed a narrow channel, the water beneath hued white and gray. This was the crossing that separated the mainland from the island where

Ilaron Reede had taken refuge. The oarsman, a man who had made this jaunt a hundred times before, seemed unfazed by the lurching waters, but Tricia thought she was going to be sick. Adding to her discomfort was the fact that she had no idea how to swim and, even if she did, she was clad in her ceremonial plate armor. She'd heard accounts of armored knights swimming thusly adorned, but it wasn't a rumor she wanted to test.

Fortunately, the crossing wasn't wide, and they were already nearing the monastery-bearing islet. The landmass was tiny, without enough ground to cultivate, and thus support, a community of monks. They cared for a small garden on the grounds, but the majority of their food and supplies had to be shipped in from the outside. It was a domain of quiet contemplation, of prayer and solitude.

The monastery itself wasn't particularly impressive. The residents worked diligently to keep it in good condition, but they weren't a wealthy order. The structure was constantly bombarded by harsh salt sprays and an ever present gale from the open seas to the south. It looked old and weathered but, in its own humble way, it also seemed proud and dignified, like a wise and respected old man.

Dark, wispy clouds fluttered in the sky overhead, turning the sun dim and robbing the blue waters of their bright luster. Light rains had come and gone throughout the day, leaving everything draped in a moist residue, like morning dew, despite the fact that night was quickly approaching.

The oarsman guided the boat to an old, wooden dock of a proper height for just such a craft. Much like everything else on the island, it was beaten and worn, but Tricia could see several newer planks that had been replaced to prevent the landing from becoming unsafe.

"Would you like me to wait for you, ma'am?" the oarsman asked in a gruff voice.

His long, dark hair and shaggy beard obscured most of his face. He had the look (and odor) of a veteran seaman.

"Why don't you come and wait inside?" she offered. "The rain may start again at any moment."

The man snorted and spat into the water.

"I'll pass," he said. "I always get the feeling these monks don't have much of a liking for me."

Tricia nodded, agreeing with the man's assessment and chose not to pursue the matter further. She could understand the monks' sentiment; he wasn't the type of man who belonged in a holy house of Aura, though he would always be welcomed there.

She climbed onto the dock, wobbling back and forth as her legs tried to readjust to solid ground. A solitary man dressed in a long, brown robe approached. His hands were clasped in front of his body, hidden beneath the long sleeves of his garment, and his head was bowed in respect, showing nothing of his face behind his hood. A simple rope belt was wrapped around his waist, and designs of golden thread were stitched into his garment to designate him as a priest of Aura.

When he was just a few steps away, he lifted his head and pulled back his hood, revealing a round face and a receding hairline. He smiled brightly at the high executor and waited in patient stillness for her to speak.

"It's good to see you're well," Tricia expressed sincerely.

Though she'd seen the man before, she had no idea of his name. His was a silent order; they believed their voices should only be used in the service of the goddess Aura, only to pray and sing her hymns. Language was one of the first gifts bestowed by the goddess, and Tricia could understand why they regarded it as such a holy capacity. Of course, most of the faithful could understand the sentiment, though they had no intention of following their ways.

"You know why I'm here?" she asked.

The monk nodded and gestured for her to follow. Together they walked to the monastery, pushed open the heavy double doors, and stepped inside.

The large chamber was dimly lit, with only a handful of candles here and there next to monks who sat in tall chairs, leaning over small desks. They were busily inscribing the teachings of Aura, a thousand times over, so the tomes they created might be sent to the four corners of the empire. So absorbed were they in their toil that they didn't seem to notice Tricia's entrance. One might have thought the visit of the high executor warranted a grand welcome, but her elevated position was only amongst her fellow lightwielders. (And Emperor Arescin had certainly made a point that she should be respected by all the soldiers and citizens within his domain.) But, to the holy men of Aura, she was meant to be loved and respected, but only inasmuch as every child of the goddess was.

The monk led her to the back of the chamber where a narrow set of stairs descended into the monastery basement. They creaked and groaned under the weight of her armor. She found herself in a narrow corridor with many chambers opening up on either side. Only one of them was emitting any light. She was reminded of the time she'd rescued Ilaron and Lisa from the academy, all those years ago.

The monk gestured with an outstretched palm for her to go on ahead of him, silently returning to the upper level to resume his duties. Tricia proceeded down the hall alone, entering the luminous chamber.

The contents were both familiar and foreign, as if Ilaron had painstakingly attempted to recreate his study from the academy, but lost interest halfway through and let his imagination further dictate the room's function. As before, the walls were lined with tall bookshelves that nearly reached the ceiling, but many of them were sparsely filled or even completely empty. The back wall sported an anvil and a charcoal forge with a flue that rose to the ceiling, jutting into the open air above, though Tricia hadn't seen any sign of smoke during her approach.

Relative to the previous study, this one was noticeably neater. Stacks of wood, metal and bone were carefully organized and moved out of the way, leaving a central table that was almost entirely free of clutter. Even Ilaron's papers and diagrams she'd grown accustomed to seeing littered upon every available surface were mysteriously absent. The only object upon the wide table was a long and slender item, about five feet in length, wrapped in a red cloth that looked like velvet. The fabric itself seemed plain at first glance, but a closer inspection revealed it was stitched with strange and seemingly random patterns with thread of the same color.

"Miss Laurel!" Lisa exclaimed, approaching the high executor with a weak but friendly smile.

Her arms were laden with books and papers which she hurriedly poured onto the table so she might properly present herself to the esteemed visitor. Lisa was still a young woman, though not so young as she had once been. She would have been married, perhaps even had children, were it not for her incarceration in the monastery. Her hands and clothes were soiled with dust from the day's work; it appeared she'd been laboring to tidy up the study for some time. Tricia realized, to no surprise, Ilaron had had nothing to do with the overdue invasion of order and cleanliness.

"Please, I told you to call me Tricia, remember?" the lightwielder chastised.

"I-I'm sorry, I guess I forgot," Lisa offered a nervous apology. "It's good to see you again."

Tricia nodded, "It's been far too long. I'm afraid my duties don't allow me much time to attend to matters of a personal nature."

"Of course," Lisa said. "I wasn't expecting you to arrive so soon. I was hoping to have everything cleaned up by the time you arrived, but I'm afraid it's still a dreadful mess."

"Don't be silly," Tricia brushed the sentiment aside with a wave of her hand. "It's far cleaner than what Ilaron had ever maintained on his own. His letter said it was urgent that I come here; that's why I made a special trip. Where is he?"

Lisa seemed disturbed by the question, hanging her head and wringing her hands. Tricia hadn't noticed before, but there were dark rings under her eyes and her complexion was unusually pale.

"Are you feeling well, child?" Tricia asked, concern in her voice. "You look ill."

"I...haven't been sleeping well," Lisa explained. "Not for several nights, now."

"I'm sorry to hear that."

"Ilaron is...," Lisa began, but she stopped herself short as if she wasn't quite sure what to say.

Her continued silence on the matter was allowing anxiety to creep into Tricia's blood.

The young artificer turned toward the study's wide table, carefully picking up the velvet wrapped package. When she turned to the high executor, her head was bowed deeply and she offered it to Tricia silently.

"What's this?" Tricia asked softly as she took the object in her hands.

"Professor Reede put his soul into it," she explained.

Tricia carefully unwrapped the packaging, revealing the glimmering blade of a sword. It was long and broad, straight as an arrow, and with an unusually wide fuller. There were unusual designs carved into the base of the groove, though one could only see them up close and if the sword were held at the proper angle to prevent them from being lost in shadow. The work was exquisite. Tricia hadn't known Ilaron could forge a sword, but the archangels had gifted artifice upon only the most skilled craftsman of the kingdoms, so she found it a small surprise.

"It's magnificent," Tricia whispered breathlessly. "I must thank Ilaron for such a wonderful gift. Where is he?"

Lisa looked as if she was about to cry, and if Tricia had had her suspicions prior something was wrong, now there could be no doubt.

"H-he put his soul into it," Lisa repeated.

The words' true meaning suddenly set off a spark in Tricia's mind.

"I begged him not to do it. He even promised me he wouldn't. But the next morning, I found the sword laying on the table and a note he'd written. I guess he realized I would have tried to interfere if I knew what he was preparing to attempt."

Tricia's face grew pale as Lisa spoke, then burned red with anger. She threw the sword to the ground with a deafening clang and turned on her heel as if she was going to storm out of the room. But her legs refused to budge. She stood there, looking down at the rough stone floor. She felt something wet on her face. Was she crying? She couldn't understand why; she wasn't sad. She was just angry, wasn't she?

"Please, don't be like that, Miss Laurel."

"I told you to call me Tricia," she sobbed.

"Professor Reede wouldn't have wanted you to be sad," Lisa said softly, moving to her side and tenderly taking the high executor's hand in an attempt to comfort her.

"I don't care what he would have wanted," Tricia blurted out. "I can't believe he would do something like this. Was he really so miserable here he didn't want to live anymore?"

Lisa seemed surprised by the question.

"He wasn't unhappy at all," she explained. "I honestly don't think I'd ever seen the professor happier."

"Then why would he do such a thing?"

Lisa took a moment to put her thoughts in order.

In a voice she hoped was reassuring, she explained, "He realized that...his theories, on sealing external power sources within artifacts, were incomplete. His formulae led him to believe that, while some power could be garnered by sacrificing ordinary humans, as was done at Asheridge, the amount of raw energy that could be generated by an artificer was greater by an order of magnitude, and much more pure.

"I remember one of the last things he said to me. He said, 'We were wrong all along. We always assumed the archangels had created the artificers to craft weapons to fight against the demons. But, the truth is, we were always intended to *become* weapons to fight them.' Though I'm afraid I haven't the courage to follow him."

Tricia sniffed and slowly turned to face the artificer. She didn't feel much better, but her tears had begun to dry up. She looked down at the sword she'd thrown to the floor, now completely naked of its cloth wrapping.

Ilaron had clearly spent a great deal of time perfecting every detail. The cross-guard swept up toward the blade like a pair of bent, pointing talons. The grip was long and bound in soft, dark leather. But it was the pommel that most caught her eye: it was the plainest ornament of the weapon, a simple iron pyramid, identical to the one Ilaron had given her all those years ago. She touched her breastplate, thinking of the amulet that lay hidden just underneath. It brought the subtlest smile to her lips to think she'd accused him of not being sentimental.

"It's enormous," she said with a sigh. "A monster of a sword. Didn't he realize I prefer to fight with lighter, one handed blades?"

"He designed it so you might use it against an archdevil," Lisa explained. "He was worried a smaller weapon might not be able to inflict enough damage."

"He truly believed this sword bore enough power to fight their kind?"

"It does!" Lisa asserted fervently. "This weapon is the culmination of all his years of research; of all his theories. Professor Reede was a genius. If the archdevils can be harmed, this weapon *will* do it."

Tricia, more intrigued than ever at the artifact, stooped down to pick it up. But before her fingers touched the hilt, Lisa spoke a warning that froze her hand in place.

"Professor Reede wrote I should warn you," she uttered uncertainly. "The first time you touch it may be a little...unusual."

9

KORISTAD FOUND HIMSELF DRIFTING through an endless expanse of monochrome nothingness, though he wasn't certain how he'd come to be there. He tried to look at his hands, but he saw nothing, as if he was engulfed in an opaque mist, or his body wasn't there at all. Now considering his body, he realized he wasn't able to feel anything; not the cloak wrapped around his shoulders, or the shoes on his feet, or even when he tried to touch his fingers together. But it was impossible for him to know if he was actually moving his body, or if he was merely thinking it.

"This is odd," a voice filled the emptiness as if emanating from all directions. "You aren't what I expected."

It sounded distant and broken, as if someone were yelling across a canyon. Koristad couldn't even determine the gender of the speaker.

"Where am I?" he asked in confusion. "Who are you?"

He couldn't feel his lips or his tongue; it seemed as if he wasn't speaking at all. It was as if he willed the words into existence, and they sprung readily into the air.

"You mean you don't know?" the voice returned. "Who else could I be?"

Koristad found it rude to have his question answered with another question, but he was bewildered enough by his unusual predicament to disregard the impoliteness.

"Am I dead?" he asked, afraid of the answer.

"You're still alive," the voice replied. "Which is to say, you haven't died *yet*."

Urgency crept into Koristad's voice as he asserted, "Then I don't have time to be doing this! Peril is alone. . ."

"There's no need to worry. Time has no meaning in this place."

Koristad reiterated his question suspiciously, "You're sure I'm not dead?"

The voice gave no reply. The fact that the voice mentioned an absence of time made him think of something.

"Could you be Wraith?"

"I don't know who you mean," the voice returned. "You truly don't know who I am? Then perhaps it would be best if we met face to face."

"That seems like a good idea," Koristad said, "But I can't seem to move, and I don't know where you are."

"There's no need for you to move. Simply move the world around you. We're within your soul, after all; this place will respond to your desires and take any form you wish."

They were within his soul? It was a peculiar concept, but Koristad knew there was little choice but to take the voice seriously. If it wanted him to create a meeting place, he would make the attempt.

The results were almost instantaneous. The blank eternity evaporated, and Koristad found himself standing on solid ground, his body returned to its physical form. The sky was filled with dark, stormy clouds, and behind them the sky was scarlet, as if the world was locked in a perpetual sunset. But, as he scanned the horizon, Koristad saw there was no sun. The flat ground stretched endlessly in every direction. That was when he noticed the floor—human bones held together with chalky, white mortar. Here and there the end of a femur would jut out, or the eye sockets of a skull could be plainly seen.

He heard footsteps approaching from his side.

"Charming," the man said with a disgusted shake of his head, checking the bottom of his feet as if he was worried he'd stepped in something. "Really."

"I *am* a necromancer," Koristad tried to explain himself; "This must be a manifestation of my power."

"More likely it's a reflection of a morbid personality," the man replied acerbically, ensuring that Koristad was duly aware he wasn't impressed.

"I've done as you asked," Koristad complained. "Now tell me who you are."

"My name is Ilaron Reede," he said. "I was an artificer, once. Or maybe I'm only a creation of an artificer; I haven't figured that part out. As far as it concerns you, I'm the spirit that gives power to the sword that brought you here."

The man was tall and lean, with dark hair and a pair of glasses sitting on the bridge of his nose. He looked exactly as he had in life, many centuries before Koristad had even been born.

"You mean you're…"

"The polite thing to do," Ilaron said, tapping his foot impatiently, "Would be to introduce yourself."

Koristad groaned in frustration, seeing no alternative but to comply.

"My name is Koristad Altessor, son of Arach the Black Guardian."

"Black Guardian?" Ilaron seemed perplexed. "I've never heard that title before. But I suppose I may have been here for a very long time. It's very difficult for me to know, you see."

"You're the Executor Blade?" Koristad said, brushing aside Ilaron's comments in a rush to sate his own curiosity. "I'm having a conversation with the sword?"

"I suppose one could look at it that way."

"This isn't what I expected," Koristad confessed. "I was told if I touched the sword it would destroy me."

"You wanted to die, then?"

"Of course not," Koristad glowered and shook his head. "I didn't have any other choice."

"There have been many who have tried to wield me," Ilaron said in a low voice. "Most were the children of Aura, successors of Tricia Laurel to the station of high executor. Their hearts were pure and they sought to rid the world of evil, so I chose to fight with them. There have been others; their hearts were always filled with greed or rage. They suffered the ultimate penalty for their trespass."

"You're here to judge me, then?" Koristad sneered, finding the proposition distasteful. "I've already told you I'm not a lightwielder. I'm a necromancer."

"That's true," Ilaron said, "But when you touched the blade, your heart wasn't filled with dark thoughts. It was filled with a desire to protect those you care about, a feverish drive the likes of which I haven't felt in ages. If that weren't the case, you would already be dead."

"Does that mean you're going to fight with me?" Koristad asked hopefully. Ilaron shook his head.

"Though your intentions are pure, there is also a dark shadow that lingers in the periphery of your soul," he explained; "A desire for revenge. You are uncertain of your place in this world, and so, I am uncertain of you. You must be tested if I'm to know you're worthy; to know you have strength. Not just of body, but in your heart, as well."

Koristad grimaced, shaking his head and raising his hands.

"I can't pass this test," he said.

"You seem so certain, even though you have no idea what it could be," Ilaron said, disappointed.

"You want someone who's good and pure," Koristad crossed his arms over his chest and lifted his chin, "But that isn't me. I only do the work of a lightwielder to repay a debt I owe. If it weren't for that, I would never obey the commands of a bunch of stuffy, sanctimonious children of Aura. And once my debt is repaid, I'm done with it for good.

"I'm not the most honorable man out there and, more often than not, the only person I'm thinking about is myself. The fact that I don't want to let those I care about get hurt doesn't make me a saint, and it certainly doesn't define who I am."

Illaron sighed deeply and said, "Very well, then. You understand you cannot leave this place with your life unless I've accepted you as my master."

"Yes, I understand that," Koristad said, seeming little unsettled by the comment. "However, I would like to ask you for a favor."

"A favor?" Illaron seemed surprised.

"I need one minute," Koristad said. "Just to make sure Peril's safe before I go. After that, my life is yours for the taking."

Ilaron eyed the young man suspiciously. How could he claim to be such a scoundrel, but then offer up his life in order to save someone else? And how could he seem so calm while in such a dire predicament? But Koristad wasn't as composed as he seemed on the surface; Ilaron could pick up subtle hints of his apprehension. His clenched jaw, and white knuckles, even his breathing was forcibly shallow.

The necromancer understood what he was doing, and even though it terrified him, he was willing to walk that path. Ilaron cast his eyes down, thinking of the distant past, and a subtle smile crossed his lips. Yes, the young man wasn't unlike Tricia Laurel, the young woman who had swallowed her fears and taken command of the armies of the fractured kingdoms against their most dreadful adversary.

"Very well, Koristad Altessor," Ilaron nodded in agreement; "What kind of ignoble creature would I be to refuse such a humble and virtuous request? You may help your friend."

The instant the artificer spoke those words, Koristad could feel the illusory world around him begin to crumble. The clouds fled from the crimson skies and the floor of human bones plummeted beneath his feet, leaving him hanging in mid-air, once again surrounded only by that empty, endless expanse. And, as quickly as it had come, it was gone.

He stood amidst the wooden wreckage of the carriage, stooped over, his hand on the grip of the Executor Blade. He could smell blood thick in the air and feel the wind wafting across his skin. He was so dazed by his sudden change in awareness that he barely heard Ralyn grunt with the effort of swinging his mighty axe and only narrowly escaped decapitation.

Koristad tumbled out of the weapon's path and wheeled around to face his enemy, brandishing the holy sword before him. Ralyn didn't think twice. He brought the Edge of Abaddon down on his enemy in a powerful, overhead strike; he knew if he exploited the full potential of the artifact, there was no man who could stop him.

A mighty clash filled the air as the weapons met, freezing both men in place as they vied for dominance. Ralyn couldn't believe it; how could his attack have been thwarted? It wasn't possible. Dust and splinters were propelled into the air, the victims of a powerful wind that emanated from the two opposing weapons.

Ralyn was aware of what the Executor Blade was but, as to the nature of its power, he hadn't an inkling. He never would have thought it could withstand the raw power of the weapon crafted by Alleister Lourdess, born of the souls of an entire city. No other weapon had ever been created with so much raw material. So, how was it possible it could be overwhelmed? It seemed as if the axe's energy was being dispersed, pouring away in every direction and causing disturbance in the locale, like a ring of angry dust devils twirling madly about the two men.

Koristad was pushed to his limits trying to keep the mighty artifact at bay. The weapons rattled madly, poised over head, and the pressure pushing down on his body forced him to grit his teeth in pain as every wound he'd sustained was aggravated. It felt as if his ribcage would collapse, and every cut was pouring blood as his pulse raced faster and faster. As his mortal vigor began to fail, he let his dark power take over, allowing that black sin and bloodlust invade his body, giving ground inch by inch. At first, the process terrified him even more than the promise of his own death. It wasn't until the pollution began to fill him with lust and ecstasy that he realized he couldn't allow it any further. He could only hope the artificer's strength would give out before his.

The further Ralyn tried to force his power, the more quickly it seemed to drain away. He'd already nearly exhausted himself before his adversary had even acquired the Executor Blade. His strength vanished all at once, sending out one final gust of energy, kicking up a cloud of dirt that rose quickly into the air. Slayne and Peril, both standing some distance away, were knocked to the ground by the powerful blast. As strong as Ralyn was, without the power of the axe, he was no match for Koristad's preternatural might. No longer able to maintain his leverage, the axe recoiled away from its target, propelling Ralyn's arms over his head.

Koristad knew there was no time for hesitation; he had only a moment to end this and secure Peril's safety. With a single slash, he brought the edge of the Executor Blade across Ralyn's brawny chest, lacerating his heart and releasing a torrent of dark blood from the grievous wound. Both parties vanished behind the cloud of dust.

"Koristad!" Peril cried out, rushing into the debris without delay.

She could hardly breathe inside the cloud; the dust stung her eyes no matter how hard she tried to shield them. She called out his name again and again and reached out with her hands.

She felt something soft: Koristad's sackcloth cloak. He was sitting on the ground, slumped over, clearly injured and exhausted from his ordeal, but his eyes were bright and alive. Peril wrapped her arms tightly around him and began to sob.

"Oh, Koristad, I'm so happy you're safe!" she cried.

"Peril...," Koristad grunted, certain now more than ever that Ralyn's attack had broken his ribs, "...that really hurts."

Peril released her grip and took a step back, looking at the necromancer with concern. She didn't notice her dress was spotted with blood where her body had been pressed against his.

"I'm sorry!" she exclaimed, turning red. "I didn't think..."

Koristad brushed off her apology with a wave of his hand. He reached into his cloak, drawing out the blazing sun medallion Peril had left behind in Marketway.

"You must have dropped this," he offered with a lopsided smile. "I swear; you must have been daydreaming again."

She snatched the amulet from his hand, relieved to finally have it back. She fastened it around her neck, once again feeling like a proper lightwielder, rather than a helpless girl being held captive by dangerous men. The sudden sense of duty brought another thought to her mind.

"You've really gotten yourself beaten up this time," she said, feigning complaint. "But it's okay. I can heal you."

"This isn't going to kill me," Koristad protested. "Not right away, at least. But I'm not so sure about Vincent; we can only hope he hasn't fallen victim to his injuries already."

Peril quickly glanced left and right. In the excitement, she'd forgotten about the injured paladin. When she finally found him, he was lying face down in the grass, still as a stone. She rushed to his side with worry in her eyes. Koristad pulled himself to his feet with a groan and hobbled after her, holding the Executor Blade behind his back.

The Executor Blade. He could hardly believe what he'd experienced when he touched it. He couldn't even consider sharing the tale with anyone else. No one would ever believe him. The thought at the forefront of his mind, however, was a question. Why was he still alive? Wasn't Ilaron supposed to take his life after he'd made certain Peril was safe? Perhaps the spirit within the weapon had decided to accept him as its master, after all. He wasn't certain how to ask, and he preferred not to brood over the dilemma. Other matters were vying for his attention, as well.

Though he would never admit it aloud, Ralyn's murder weighed heavily upon him. He'd never killed another person before—not like that, anyway. The artificer's corpse, lying still in the grass, was unquestionably due to his actions.

The thought made his stomach churn. He tried to turn his mind away from the matter, focusing instead on Vincent and Peril.

"Is he still alive?"

He tried his best to make it clear he wasn't really concerned; merely curious. Peril rolled the paladin over with a good deal of effort, fighting against his heavy armor, and held her ear close to his mouth.

"He's hanging on by a thread," Peril said, rubbing her hands together. "But I think I can save him!"

"Good," Koristad said with a snort. "If he didn't make it, I wouldn't be able to give him the beating he *really* deserves. He won't be getting off that easy."

Koristad glanced left and right and added, "That reminds me…what happened to that boy who was with you? He may only be a child, but he still has a lot to answer for."

"You mean he's gone!?" Peril exclaimed.

She should have realized he wasn't going to stick around to turn himself in. But, with everything that had happened, she hadn't been watching him. In fact, the last moment she recalled seeing him was when the dust cloud had lifted into the air. A quick glance around confirmed he was nowhere to be seen, and also brought another chilling realization.

"Koristad!" she cried, pointing toward the fallen Ralyn. "The axe is missing, too!"

10

GABRIAL NIGHT SAT IN a high-backed wooden chair before a broad desk. His brow was furrowed with concentration as he quickly scribbled on a piece of paper, identical to the hundreds of sheets that composed two neat piles, one on his left, the other his right. His appointment to high executor had been the most expeditious ever recorded; though other names had been put forward, not a single participant would raise their voice in protest of his nomination.

His position wouldn't be official until the Executor Blade arrived. Gabrial himself felt the notion was silly, but many members of his order were infatuated with ceremony and protocol, and so he was left with no choice but to wait. That hadn't prevented him from taking residence in the high executor's office and beginning to work. Alexander Kanan had been in poor health for some time, even before he'd taken ill in Bainsreach. He'd allowed paperwork and petitions to pile up, leaving his successor with a mountain of toil.

The chamber was vast, much larger than his office in the sanctuary, and had a high, vaulted ceiling. The walls were lined with bookshelves and drawers, all finely crafted but remarkably dull, with little ornamentation to speak of. Gabrial supposed he would have his servants bring some of his effects from his chambers; he found the austere nature of his surroundings stifling.

The only piece of interest was the office's entryway, a heavy oak door gilded in bronze. Symbols were etched into the soft metal, icons that had, through the ages, represented the children of Aura. The contemporary blazing sun symbol stood bold and proud in the center while the others spiraled away, like moons orbiting a heavenly body. Many of the icons Gabrial was familiar with from his studies as a young lightwielder, but there were a few even he didn't recognize.

In addition to a pair of wide, stained glass windows behind his desk, there was a solitary opening cut into the wall high above. A shaft of clean light poured through the pane that, at a certain hour of the morning, would shine down upon the bronze door, and it would glitter like gold. But, as the morning wore on, the shaft would draw closer and closer to the high executor's desk until it vanished entirely. At present, it was shining directly upon Gabrial and, while he found the glare and heat obstinately annoying, it appeared as if he was wreathed in a halo of divine light. Perhaps that was appropriate, as he was now the chosen voice of the goddess, Aura.

There was a light tapping on the heavy door as it slowly creaked open. A thin man with sunken cheeks and a wrinkled brow poked his head into the chamber, an uncertain look in his eyes. He'd been the servant of the prior high executor and, though he now served Gabrial, he seemed uncertain of how to behave around his new master.

"I apologize for the intrusion, high executor," he said in a soft, apologetic voice, "But I'm afraid I have crucial news to report."

"Don't stand out in the hallway," Gabrial chastised, gesturing for the man to enter. He made no attempt to correct the use of his (as of yet) unattained title, nor had he with anyone else. "Share your news, but quickly. I have matters that require my attention."

The man hurried into the office, his eyes fixed on the ground, as if he'd done something wrong.

"Sir, the procession bearing the Executor Blade was ambushed," he explained in a quavering voice. "There were only three survivors."

"Three survivors?" Gabrial echoed, his eyes growing wide and his skin pale.

"I'm told Paladin Night was among them," the servant offered, hoping to assuage Gabrial's apprehension, "But he was grievously injured in the attack."

"Thank goodness. Aura must truly be watching over him," Gabrial said with a grimace, taking a deep breath as he drew himself up in his tall seat and looked up at the high ceiling. "And the other two?"

"The representatives of the Sunrise Sanctuary," the man answered. "They're waiting outside, along with Executor Mourne."

"Waiting outside?" Gabrial snapped, frowning at the man with disappointment. "Why have they been made to wait? See them in at once!"

The servant sprang into action at the demand, darting into the hall and, after a moment, holding the door open as Gregan passed through, followed by Peril and, finally, Koristad.

"You may take your leave," Gabrial instructed the servant gravely.

The man quickly disappeared, closing the door behind him.

"Good morning, high executor," Gregan nodded in greeting. "I would like you to meet Koristad Altessor and Peril, two of the survivors from the procession."

"Ah, the necromancer you've taken under your wing," Gabrial said with a nod. "My cousin was eager to inform me of your presence after he'd met you. He doesn't seem to think you're fit to perform our holy labors."

Koristad clenched his jaw tight and remained silent, staring at the new high executor and trying not to say anything he'd regret.

His tension was quickly assuaged when Gabrial continued, "But I'm not of the same opinion; any man who's willing to risk his own safety for the sake of others shares the blessing of Aura with the rest of us, even if he doesn't carry her blood."

Koristad offered a slight nod of gratitude.

Seeing that the young man had no intention of speaking up to show Gabrial the respect he was accorded, Gregan spoke for him, "That's most kind, high executor."

Still addressing Koristad, Gabrial continued, "I'm happy to have a man of such a distinguished lineage serving the order. I knew your father, though not nearly as well as Executor Mourne. He was a great man. What happened to him was a tragedy."

Koristad wasn't sure how he was expected to respond to such a sentiment, so he merely shrugged as if it didn't interest him. Still, he was silent.

"I see the boy carries the Executor Blade on his back," Gabrial said with some concern, this time directing the comment at Gregan. "That's most...unusual."

The enormous sword was holstered behind Koristad's back, alongside his sanctified halberd, which he'd managed to recover after some searching. (At the same time, they'd even found Jester lurking about the outskirts of the scene, and the horse was rewarded for its loyalty with the task of carrying the injured paladin back to civilization.) With one oversized weapon, Koristad had looked intimidating, but with two he looked absolutely menacing, bordering on comical.

"You see, sir...," Gregan began, but Koristad cut him off.

"I was disarmed while fighting those who attacked the procession," he offered up boldly, no hint of remorse in his voice. "In order to defend myself and the others, I had no choice but to use the Executor Blade."

"He really didn't!" Peril chimed in, trying to help make his case. "If Koristad hadn't done what he did, they would have killed the rest of us and stolen the sword!"

"I see," Gabrial said in a low voice, "You've handled the sword, and it didn't destroy you."

Koristad drew the weapon from its hanger in a swift motion, much to the surprise and dismay of both Peril and Gregan. Though he hadn't brandished the weapon in any threatening way, even drawing a weapon in the presence of the high executor was a dire offense. Men had been sent to the gallows for less. Gabrial, however, didn't flinch or appear distressed; he merely watched the young necromancer with interest.

Koristad took the sword by the blade, offered the handle to Gabrial, and said, "I know this doesn't belong to me. It's yours. Take it."

Gabrial put up his hands, clearly having no intention of accepting the weapon; he even appeared threatened by the prospect.

"I wouldn't dare," he said. "If the sword didn't destroy you, then that means it has accepted you as its rightful owner."

Koristad sighed and looked at the sword with appreciation; in truth, he hadn't wanted to give it up. He'd simply felt it was the right thing to do, but it took little prompting to convince him otherwise. He quickly returned the weapon to its sheathe.

"Koristad!" Peril cried in a chastising voice, frowning deeply. "You should say something!"

He looked down at the young girl with annoyance.

"What do you expect me to say?"

"You should apologize!" she cried.

Koristad looked at her as if she'd suggested he swallow molten lead.

"What should I apologize for?" he persisted obstinately. "I didn't do anything!"

With a chuckle, Gabrial brought their disagreement to a halt, stating, "It's quite alright. Though I'm certain some of my subordinates will see this as an unfortunate incident, I'm inclined to disagree. The Executor Blade is a powerful weapon, and you've proven yourself a man of both means and measure. I'm certain it will do far more good in your hands than in mine, collecting dust in the office of a boring, old bureaucrat. Yes, I believe Aura must have guided your hand in this, Koristad."

The necromancer inspected the old man uncertainly, as if he might suddenly change his mind and have him thrown in a dungeon for stealing the artifact.

"That isn't the reaction I expected," Koristad confessed. "It seems both fair and wise, something very rare in this world. I can understand how you've become a man of such great respect among your peers. I'll do my best not to disappoint you."

"I trust you will," Gabrial said with a subtle nod, turning back to Gregan. "I'm told my cousin was wounded in this attack. How severe are his injuries?"

"The physicians believe he's going to live," Gregan replied, happy to offer some good news, "Thanks in no small part to the skill and effort of Peril."

Peril smiled sheepishly and scratched the back of her head.

"I didn't do that much, really," she said humbly. "It was Vincent's strength and will to live that pulled him through, not me."

"Regardless, I am truly grateful for your aid," Gabrial said, rising to his feet and bowing his head at the young girl. "If Vincent had been killed, it would have been a terrible blow to the order. And to me, personally."

"Thank you, high executor."

"What of those who attacked you?" Gabrial asked in a harsher voice. "Who were they?"

"It was a band of mercenaries called the Mountain Wolves," Peril explained, "But they were hired by a pair of artificers!"

"Artificers?" Gabrial hardly seemed surprised. "Is that so?"

"Yes, sir," Peril said with questioning eyes. "I thought the artificers were supposed to be extinct."

Gabrial let out a deep sigh.

"Gregan, perhaps you've heard of my research into artificers a few years back?" he asked.

Executor Mourne seemed baffled.

"No, high executor, I'd heard of no such thing."

"I'd heard rumors that there were cloistered pockets of survivors here and there," Gabrial explained. "I tried to seek them out, but my efforts proved fruitless. It seemed a waste of time and resources to continue the search. The artificers, if there really were any out there, appeared content to leave well enough alone. I believed it was fair if I adopted the same principle. I suppose I may have been too lenient; but at least they're gone, now."

"Well, sir," Peril said nervously, "They aren't exactly gone..."

Koristad decided to offer up a quick explanation, rather than allowing Peril to stammer on uncertainly.

"We killed the older of the two, but the other, a young boy, managed to escape."

Gabrial looked at the two with doubt. Had the boy escaped, or had they allowed him to get away? Showing mercy to a boy was compassionate, but could prove disastrous in the future.

"I see," he said with a scowl. "Before you leave, I want you to share everything you know about this artificer with my servant, and tell him to write it all down. Don't leave out a single detail. I will not see this rogue mage escape justice."

"Is that really necessary, sir?" Peril seemed distressed at the prospect of Slayne being hunted down like an animal. She was certain he already had enough trouble, a young boy alone in the world with nothing but an axe that he was too small to even use.

"There's no need to look like that," Gabrial tried to comfort the young girl with a soft smile. "We aren't monsters. He'll be given a fair chance to explain himself, and to make amends for what he's done. But his actions show that he may be dangerous if left on his own. He must be made to answer for what he's done, and the innocent must be kept safe from what he *might* do."

"I understand, sir," Peril answered in a soft voice, though she still bore her apprehensions.

"Now, if that's everything, I'm afraid you'll have to excuse me," Gabrial announced. "I have a great deal of work to catch up on."

Gregan turned to leave, but Peril and Koristad didn't budge.

"Actually, there is one more thing," Peril said. "I think the artificers had been given information by someone within the order. They may have even been hired by a lightwielder."

Gabrial raised his eyebrows in confusion and concern.

"That's a dire accusation. What could make you think such a thing?"

"Well, they seemed to know where we were going," she explained. "Of course, anyone who knew what we had would have assumed we were headed for the capital. But they knew the exact route we would be taking, and were able to cut off the procession with that knowledge. Who could have known that?"

Gabrial sighed and said, "I understand your concern. Only the highest ranking lightwielders would have had that information, but perhaps it wasn't kept as secret as it should have been. We never expected the procession would be attacked. It's unheard of. But we will certainly need to investigate how this information was leaked."

Peril went on, "Also, hiring such a large group of mercenaries would have required a great deal of money. From what I learned of the two artificers, I don't think they could have had the means to hire the soldiers themselves. Someone else with substantial resources must have been behind the scheme."

"That's a very wise deduction," Gabrial said. "I'm impressed."

"Well, I didn't come up with any of it," Peril confessed. "When I explained everything I'd learned to Koristad, he felt something was amiss."

"Rest assured your concerns will be taken into consideration," Gabrial's words were quick and disinterested, as if he didn't place much merit in their anxieties. "Now, please excuse me."

This time all three of the representatives of the Sunrise Sanctuary turned to exit the chamber. As they opened the door and began to file out, Gabrial suddenly raised his head as if something had occurred to him.

"Executor Mourne, if I might have just one more moment of your time."

"Of course, sir," Gregan answered.

He turned toward Peril and Koristad and told them to wait for him outside. He pushed the door shut and returned to Gabrial's desk.

"That girl, Peril," Gabrial began, "You must have noticed that she has a great deal of potential. Enough to be a paladin, were she to dedicate herself adequately."

Gregan shrugged, "She does have some ability, but I'm not certain if I would go so far. She's naïve and delicate; she doesn't even know how to properly wield a sword. Even worse, she has no interest in learning how to fight. How can someone like that be a paladin?"

"Still," Gabrial insisted, "With the proper instruction, I think she would go far. Perhaps you would consider allowing her to come and work for me? I would take her under my wing and instruct her myself."

"That's very generous of you, high executor," Gregan replied. "But I'm afraid she's grown rather attached to Koristad, and I don't think even such a great opportunity would convince her to leave his side. As for Koristad...well, his service is the result of a personal debt. As such, he works only for me."

Gabrial offered up a clever smile.

"You don't want to give her up, then?" he chuckled.

Before Gregan could offer any sort of protest, he added, "I understand. I wouldn't want to let her go, either. That will be all, executor."

In the next volume. . .

Now wielding Ilaron, the Executor Blade, Koristad dutifully continues his chores as a proxy lightwielder.
However, following the coronation of a new emperor, a sinister series of events begin to unfold that will ultimately bring the young necromancer face-to-face with the infamous Vampire King.

Connect with the author at:

JRBAILEYNOVELS.COM